For Sandy Harding
Thank you.

Gone with the Witch

A WISHCRAFT MYSTERY

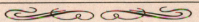

HEATHER BLAKE

AN OBSIDIAN MYSTERY

OBSIDIAN
Published by New American Library,
an imprint of Penguin Random House LLC
375 Hudson Street, New York, New York 10014

This book is an original publication of New American Library.

First Printing, May 2016

For more information about Penguin Random House, visit penguin.com.

ISBN 978-1-101-99011-7

Printed in the United States of America
10 9 8 7 6 5 4 3 2

OTHER MYSTERIES BY HEATHER BLAKE

The Wishcraft Series

Book 1: *It Takes a Witch*
Book 2: *A Witch Before Dying*
Book 3: *The Good, the Bad, and the Witchy*
Book 4: *The Goodbye Witch*
Book 5: *Some Like It Witchy*

A Magic Potion Mystery

Book 1: *A Potion to Die For*
Book 2: *One Potion in the Grave*
Book 3: *Ghost of a Potion*

Acknowledgments

A big thank-you to Jess Wade and everyone at Penguin Random House who help make Darcy's books the best they can be. And a special thank-you to Bella Pilar for her beautiful cover art.

I also want to thank Lois Rotella, Janet Cearley, Stephanie Berba-Cornock, Christy Hesseltine, and Kathleen Fortun for suggesting the name "Cookie" for the goat in this story.

As always, much gratitude goes to all the readers who've shown such wonderful support to Darcy and me throughout the years. Thank you.

Chapter One

Sunlight burst through the front windows of As You Wish, spotlighting the pink streaks in Ivy Teasdale's shoulder-length strawberry blond hair and the vehemence in her blue eyes.

"The integrity of the event is at stake, Darcy," Ivy said to me, the sound of hammering outside punctuating her words like exclamation points. "Along with its sterling reputation."

She sat ramrod straight on the velvet sofa across from me, her hands fisted, her black-tipped fingernails pressing deeply into the fleshy skin of her palms. Her perfectly sculpted right eyebrow twitched every few seconds, probably a result of too much stress or a caffeine addiction. Or both. Above average height and slightly heavyset, she was in her early forties and as tightly wound as I'd ever witnessed another human to be.

This bright and airy parlor with its soothing aquamarine and silver color palette and whimsical design usually set visitors at ease.

Not so with Ivy.

Fairly shimmering with restrained anxious energy, she said, "If she is cheating at the event, she must be caught and stopped."

The "she" in question was villager Natasha Norcliffe.

The "event" in question was the Pawsitively Enchanting Pet Extravaganza.

And Ivy was hiring me to oversee the catching and the stopping. I was used to unusual requests that came to me through my work at As You Wish, a personal concierge service that was quickly becoming known for private investigating, but this one topped the list. Ivy knew of my involvement in several criminal cases that had occurred in the village over the past year and had deemed me the perfect person to take on a cheater.

"Have you been to the Extravaganza before, Darcy?" Ivy, the Extravaganza's founder, was also the owner of the Fairytail Magic pet-grooming salon, which everyone around here simply called Fairytails. She wore a black-and-white polka-dot pencil skirt that hit just below her knees along with a turquoise blouse that set off her eyes. Angled to the right, her long toned legs were crossed tightly at the ankles. Black peep-toed heels showed off glittery silver-painted toenails.

Her stylish flair hinted at a fun-loving personality, but I wasn't seeing any trace of it right now. All I saw was a white-hot intensity that made me question why she was so high-strung.

"No, I haven't been yet. I moved to the village shortly after last year's event." Right up until Ivy had come knocking, I'd simply planned to attend the Extravaganza to soak in the fantastical hoopla of it all. "But I've heard all about it. Good things," I quickly clarified so she wouldn't glare at me with that scorching blue gaze of hers.

The Extravaganza was one of the preeminent annual events in the Enchanted Village, a themed neighborhood of Salem, Massachusetts. As a tourist destination, the village often drew large crowds to its events, which generally focused on a mystical element thanks to its location and history.

Which was entirely appropriate, considering that the village was full of witches, known as Crafters, who lived here secretly among mortals. We hid in plain sight working at businesses like the Gingerbread Shack Bakery, the Bewitching Boutique, and of course here at As You Wish, the personal concierge service that I'd always believed to be owned by my aunt Ve. In reality, the business had once belonged to my late mother, Deryn Merriweather, who'd died when I was seven. A few weeks ago I'd learned that the company had actually been bequeathed to *me*, and had been held in a trust overseen by my aunt Ve until I was ready to take over.

As You Wish was *mine*.

That news had shocking to say the least.

Since I'd found out, I had been easing myself into the daily running of As You Wish. Though Aunt Ve technically still worked for the business part-time, she was now busy doing her own thing as village council chairwoman, a position that was similar to a mayoral role in the village.

As I spoke with Ivy, discussing her suspicions of cheating at the event, I was feeling a bit overwhelmed with responsibility but tried not to show my apprehension at taking on a new client.

"You're in for such a treat," Ivy said. "It's so much fun. It's not so much a competition as a festival of sorts." Her eyes brightened with excitement.

The glimmer was a nice change from the rabid anxiety usually present in her gaze, and I suspected it reflected her true nature.

The Extravaganza was one of the few celebrations in the village that truly had nothing to do with witchcraft. It was completely pet-centric. But that didn't mean there wasn't Craft involvement. . . . I knew of at least one familiar, a witch spirit who resided in an animal form, entered in the contest, and more than a few witches, including my own sister, Harper, and my best friend, Starla Sullivan, were attending as well. Harper was entering her tabby cat, Pie, and Starla was entering Twink, her bichon frise. Aunt Ve had considered entering Tilda, her beautiful but cranky Himalayan, but only for a moment.

It was a wise decision, considering Tilda's tendency to scratch . . . and hold grudges.

Ivy added, "Which is why I must ensure that its respectability doesn't suffer. Nothing untoward must happen at this year's event."

And with those words the brightness dimmed, and the obsessive angst returned.

I wished my friend Curecrafter Cherise Goodwin was here to deliver a calming spell. If a person was ever in need of Cherise's magic, it was Ivy.

Truly, I wasn't sure whether Ivy had good reason to be worried about potential sabotage at the event or not. Cheating was entirely possible, I supposed. Even though I'd never attended the Extravaganza, which was set to kick off late tomorrow morning, I knew it wasn't just a blockbuster event for the village . . . it was also one for its participants.

People took their pet pageantry very seriously.

So seriously, in fact, that the illustrious competition now drew contestants from across New England, even as far away as northern Maine. Driving six-plus hours to enter Fido in the Pooch-Smooch category boggled my mind, but there was no denying the Extravaganza's charm. There was a wait list a mile long, which was due to space limitations at the Will-o'-the-Wisp, the reception hall that hosted the contest. Entries had been capped at two hundred forty, twenty competitors per twelve categories. It seemed as though the more difficult it was to register a pet, the more desirable the event became.

It helped, too, that the Extravaganza wasn't a prim and fussy pet competition. Nine years ago, Ivy had created it to be lighthearted and fun. All household pets were allowed to be entered, including dogs, cats, hamsters, birds, ferrets, guinea pigs, turtles, and even a Nigerian dwarf goat.

Given all that, it didn't seem so far-fetched to imagine someone going a little overboard to ensure a win for their pet. But to go so far as to *hurt* someone, as Ivy suspected? That was taking overzealousness to a whole new level.

Ivy reached into her purse and pulled out an official-looking name badge, a frilly clip that had a laminated purple-printed number (240) attached, a folder of paperwork, and a fancy pen. "Here is everything you need, Darcy. The badge is secretly marked as all-access, which grants you the ability to roam around without being questioned. The paperwork includes the rules and regulations as well as a map of the booths and the facility. The clip attaches to Missy's collar."

I took it all from her outstretched hands. The badge read DARCY MERRIWEATHER, ENCHANTED VILLAGE. On the clip, beneath the purple 240, was my dog Missy's name printed in curlicue font along with the category in which she was entered: Easy on the Eyes.

The Extravaganza boasted twelve categories ranging from Splish Splash (swimwear) to Wag It (best tail), and the winner of each would be featured in the event's highly sought after calendar. From those twelve pets a grand-prize winner would be chosen to grace the coveted spot on the calendar's cover. Landing it was quite the triumph.

For the past three years running, that cover girl had been Titania, a beautiful black ragamuffin cat with owl-like amber eyes, who belonged to Natasha Norcliffe.

And for the past two years, Natasha's top competitors had suffered an unfortunate accident or illness that had required them to withdraw their pet from the event at the last minute. The mishaps had begun the year before last when Marigold Coe, whose cat, Khan, had been rumored to be a favorite to win the grand prize, had tumbled down a crowded set of steps and broken an arm and ankle, and had needed immediate surgery to repair both.

Fortunately, Marigold had fully recovered and was returning to the competition this year, but Khan had since retired. This time around Marigold was entering her dog, Lady Catherine, a year-old fawn-colored whippet, in the Crankypuss category.

The second "accident" that had occurred took place during last year's event when villager Baz Lucas had come down with food poisoning hours before the winners were to be announced. He and his wife, Vivienne, had to withdraw their dog, Audrey Pupburn, a black-and-white long-haired Morkie (a hybrid breed of Maltese and Yorkshire terrier) from judging so Baz could seek treatment at a local hospital.

Soon after, Ivy had started to become a little suspicious that these incidents had not been accidents at all.

Which was where I had come in.

Ivy had hired As You Wish to sniff out a possible cheater.

Missy, my miniature Schnoodle, and I were going undercover.

And I was nervous about it.

Nervous enough that I found myself secretly hoping that Ivy would simply wish for what she wanted, as oftentimes clients would because of the name of the company. Though my father had been a mortal, on my mother's side I hailed from a long line of Wishcrafters, witches who had the ability to grant wishes using a spell. The ability came in handy, especially in my line of work.

The wishes of mortals were granted immediately if they abided by Wishcraft laws and regulations. However, because of previous egregious abuses of our powers, wishes from other Crafters now had to first go through the Elder, the Craft's governess, in some sort of magical judicial system. In an instant, she decided if a wish was pure of heart and could be granted immediately, or whether the wishee had to be summoned before her to plead his or her case.

As far as I knew, Ivy was a mortal, but it didn't seem that she was going to take any cues from the name of the business. Since it was against Wishcraft Law to solicit a wish, I paid close attention to everything she was telling me.

"The pen," Ivy said, her eyes wide with enthusiasm, "is a spy pen. It takes both still pictures and video." She winced as the hammering outside continued, and said loudly, "It is imperative that you document any wrongdoing you may witness by Natasha."

The hammering came from two doors down, where my new home was being renovated. The house, which was zoned as a home-based business, had been bought as a new location for the As You Wish office—and as a home of my own—by Aunt Ve, who'd been acting as a trustee on my behalf. The funds for the purchase had come from my mother's estate, an inheritance I'd known nothing about until Aunt Ve had handed me the keys to the house . . . and the news that I was now in charge of the company.

I said, "Do you really believe Natasha is cheating to win? And harming people in the process?"

Thirty-something Natasha, who managed the local playhouse, was an actress who loved the sound of her own voice.

I set the paperwork on the coffee table. "I can maybe see her cheating to win, for the attention factor alone, but not hurting anyone. She doesn't seem the malicious type."

Self-centered, yes. Malicious, no.

"Competition changes people. Trust me," Ivy said somberly. "It brings out their worst. I've witnessed it many times. As I mentioned to you the last time we met up, I'm not one hundred percent positive that Natasha was responsible for the *accidents*, but I heard through the grapevine that she was on the steps at the time Marigold fell, and that she'd been seen loitering near Baz and Vivienne's booth at lunchtime. It seems too coincidental."

It did at that.

Ivy's hands curled into fists once again. "Missy is entered in the same category as Titania, Easy on the Eyes, so Natasha will be watching you, no pun intended. Missy has lovely eyes, so she'll certainly be viewed as a threat by the competition."

I couldn't help feeling a puff of pride. Missy did have nice eyes, a rich brown color full of emotion and personality. She would definitely give Titania a run for her money. Of course, working undercover would disqualify Missy from winning, but her competition wouldn't know that, only the judges.

"Your booth will be directly across the aisle from Natasha's, affording you an unfettered view of her movements," Ivy said. "I don't want her getting suspicious that she's being watched, but do not let her out of your sight."

"At all?" I asked.

"At all. If she uses the restroom, you use the restroom. If she takes a lunch break, you take a lunch break. . . ."

Yeah, *that* wouldn't be suspicious at all.

"If Natasha *has* been sabotaging her toughest competition," Ivy said, her words clipped, "it's imperative she be stopped before word leaks out. Not only would it be a PR nightmare for the event, it would be a PR nightmare for the whole community. The Extravaganza floods the village with tourist dollars. It would be quite a loss to our fiscal influx if one rotten egg causes the downfall of such a wonderful village tradition."

Fervor had caused a red flush to creep up Ivy's neck and settle in her full cheeks. She had painted a nice picture of not wanting the village to be hurt by the Extravaganza's potential downfall, but I knew it would hurt her financially as well. Despite owning Fairytails, she seemed to live for the Extravaganza, and I had to wonder how well the grooming business was faring. On the surface it seemed successful, but I knew appearances could be deceiving. Especially in this village.

Ivy shifted her legs to the left. "Report immediately to me if you witness anything unusual at the show, so I can take action. You're all set?"

"I think so." I mentally ticked off all I needed, which wasn't much. "All I really need is Missy, right?"

"Technically, yes, but you will want to get there an hour or two early to decorate your booth," Ivy said.

"Decorate?"

"Of course." Ivy frowned as though I should already have known this. "The gaudier, the better. Bunting, balloons, sparkles. Think pizzazz!" she added in a staccato cadence, using jazz hands to accent the last word. "Go all out."

"Pizzazz. Got it." I added pizzazz-shopping to my

day's to-do list. The snazziness of it all would be item-
ized on her bill for my services, which I could already
tell was not going to be nearly enough for what I was
about to endure.

Ivy glanced at a chunky gold watch on her wrist and
abruptly stood up. "I've got to get going."

I walked her to the front door and glanced around
for Missy. She was nowhere to be seen, which was odd.
Usually, the little dog loved company, and I knew her
doggy door was closed, so she hadn't been able to escape
outside and into the village (as she had a tendency to
do). Perhaps she was upstairs with Ve.

I pulled open the front door. "We'll see you tomorrow, then. Bright and early."

Ivy unclenched a fist long enough to grip the front
door, her knuckles quickly turning white. "I know I'm
asking a lot of you, Darcy, but I wasn't sure where else
to turn. I cannot allow my event to become sullied. I
don't want to hear even a hint of a whisper that something troublesome might be going on behind the scenes."

It *was* a lot to ask, but I wouldn't say so to her. I'd
wait until she was long out of earshot and then complain
ruthlessly to Aunt Ve. "Our motto here at As You Wish
is no job too big or too small."

"Where does 'dangerous' fit in that motto?" Ivy
asked, her blue eyes narrowed in earnestness.

"What do you mean?"

As she stepped out onto the porch, a warm June
breeze ruffled her pink-tinged hair. "If Missy is viewed
as a threat, then in all likelihood you will be viewed as
one, too. If what I suspect about Natasha is true, then
you're in danger of becoming yet another *accident* victim, and who knows how far she'll go this time to assure
a win for Titania? Stay away from the stairs and don't
leave any of your food unattended. Above all else, please

don't get yourself killed. That wouldn't be a PR nightmare. It'd be a PR catastrophe."

Sheesh. I'd hate to inconvenience her with my *death*.

"Just be careful tomorrow," she said. Then sharply added, "And be aware at all times that the future of the event is in your hands."

With that, she marched down the front steps, looked both ways before she crossed the street, and rushed across the green, the parklike center of town.

Stunned, I watched her go and instantly regretted taking her on as a client. I should have said no to this job. However, there was nothing I could do about it now other than to tackle the work head-on . . . and hope and that there wouldn't be any deaths at all to contend with.

Especially mine.

Chapter Two

I was about to close the front door when someone called out, "Hold up, Darcy!"

A petite woman with long wavy black hair came hurrying toward the front walkway from the direction of my new house. "Sorry I'm a little early," Vivienne Lucas said as she rushed up the steps. She was a third-generation Korean-American, a true beauty, and one of the best Spellcrafters in the village.

At the edge of the front walkway, Vivienne's husband, Baz, slowed to a stop. He gave me a friendly wave and kept a close eye on Audrey the Morkie, who strained her leash to sniff the corner of the white picket fence that enclosed the side yard. The bow fastened to the top of her head bobbled as she explored.

"Early?" I asked loudly in an awkward attempt to be heard over the hammering.

Large brown deep-set eyes widened. "I have an appointment with Ve. She didn't tell you?"

"Nope, she didn't." The last I'd seen of Ve, she was parked at the writing desk in her bedroom reading what looked to be an encyclopedia of boredom but was actually the village officer's manual.

"No offense, Darcy," Baz called out with a mischievous smile, "but we just walked by your new place on our way here and it looks worse than it did before."

In his late thirties, mortal Baz Lucas was a hip local college history professor, and he looked every bit the role. Tall and thin, he had shoulder-length thick hair, rimmed black glasses, and intelligent eyes. He wore long gray plaid shorts, a crisp pink polo shirt, and what looked like Birkenstock sandals. A natural flirt, he was as charming as all get-out, but he also possessed just a smidge of pretentiousness that tended to grate on my nerves—though others seemed to find the trait endearing. I'd bet my last frozen peppermint patty that his classes always had a long wait list.

Returning the smile, I said, "That's saying something." The house had been in sad shape for many years, left in a state of disrepair by its former owner. "The contractor did warn me that it would look worse before getting better."

Caution crept into Vivienne's eyes. "How much worse?"

I craned my neck to try to see the house, but Terry Goodwin's place blocked my view. The Numbercrafter—and one of Ve's ex-husbands—could be seen peeking out an upstairs window. He was notoriously elusive . . . and nosy. "That bad?"

"The missing roof isn't helping my opinion," she said.

Today the roofline was being adjusted to make way for a new addition on the back of the house. Rotted shingles were also getting the old heave-ho. A new roof would be on by the end of the day.

Warily, I said, "It's probably best I can't see it."

"Definitely." She swept a thick lock of dark hair behind her ear.

When Audrey barked at a passing butterfly, Baz whistled, and the little dog trotted over to him, her tiny pink tongue lolling. Baz patted her head and said, "Good girl, protecting us from the fearsome winged beast."

He pronounced winged with two syllables. Wing-ed.

It took all I had in me not to roll my eyes. Archie, a scarlet macaw familiar who lived next door with Terry, probably loved Baz. Unlike some other forms of witchcraft in the world, Craft familiars belonged to no one but themselves; however, they often lived with witches who took on a caretaking role. For Archie, that witch was Terry, and even though I'd lived next door to them for almost a year, I had no idea how they'd become paired up. It was something to ask my feathered friend sometime.

Archie had once been a London actor back in the 1800s, and still had a flair for the dramatic, using his deep, theatrical voice and British accent to his advantage. He and Baz were probably the only two in the village who could get away with such a pompous manner of speaking.

"Come on inside," I said to Baz and Vivienne, waving them toward the door. "I'll grab Ve, and I'm sure Missy would love to play with Audrey for a while."

"Alas, I'm not staying," Baz said. "Simply seeing off my ladylove before embarking on some last-minute errands prior to tomorrow's Extravaganza."

Out of the corner of my eye, I noted that Vivienne stiffened a bit when he'd said "ladylove." She pressed her lips tightly together.

Tension suddenly plumed in the air along with the

scent of the climbing roses covering the arbor that arched over the side gate.

I was working on minding my own business these days, so I pretended not to notice. "Decorations for your booth?" I guessed, wondering what in the world I was going to do with my own booth on such short notice.

Vivienne nodded. "We're doing a *Breakfast at Tiffany's* theme to play off Audrey's name."

I tipped my head. "Wasn't Audrey Hepburn a call girl in that movie?" Exactly what kind of booth did they have in mind?

Baz frowned, then said loudly to be heard over the hammering, "Them are fighting words within Audrey fan club circles, Darcy. I prefer to believe the character of Holly Golightly had what these days we would call"— he used air quotes—"'sugar daddies.'"

I studied him. He was dead serious.

I glanced at Vivienne. She drew in a deep breath of the long-suffering.

She explained, "He's a movie and theater fanatic, and the biggest Audrey Hepburn fan around."

"I prefer the term 'aficionado,'" he said loftily.

As *My Fair Lady* was my favorite movie, I could relate to loving Audrey Hepburn's work, but he took his adoration to a whole new level.

"Yes, well," Vivienne went on, not even looking his way, "the nature of the character truly doesn't matter for our purposes. We're focusing our attention on the scene that takes place in front of Tiffany's, where Holly is looking in, eating a pastry and sipping coffee."

It was an iconic image, one I could conjure easily in my head.

"I'm headed to the Gingerbread Shack now to confirm a very large order of raspberry, lemon, and cheese Danish," Baz supplied.

Vivienne said, "Don't forget to stop at the Witch's Brew to see about the coffee, too."

I noticed his jaw jut to the left before he abruptly nodded.

"Danish *and* coffee?" I tried my best to ignore the tension between them. "Yours is going to be the most popular booth tomorrow morning."

"That's the plan," Vivienne said with a bright smile.

Baz bade us farewell—which included a deep bow— and I ushered Vivienne into the house. "Would you like something to drink?"

"No, thanks. I'm good."

I closed the door, quieting the hammering noise somewhat. As a home-based business, when the house was done, part of the downstairs would house the new As You Wish office space, and the rest of the house . . . was mine.

Vivienne headed for the sofa. "When are you moving into your new place?"

It was a good question. But I didn't know whether I was going to actually move in there or in with Village Police Chief Nick Sawyer at his place—it was all still up in the air.

Nick and I had been dating for almost a year now, and I had fallen head over heels for him . . . and also for his teenage daughter, Mimi. Sure, Nick and I had gone through some growing pains, but with a little patience and understanding, we had overcome those obstacles.

It seemed that it was time to take the next step. I was just waiting for Nick to mention moving in together, or perhaps asking me to marry him. . . . We'd been talking in circles about the possibilities for months now.

I held in a sigh. I had four months until my house was done, so there was time enough to be patient. It was just that I was a planner, and would like to know soon where I was going to be laying my head at night.

"I'm sorry, Darcy," Vivienne said. "Did I say something wrong?"

"No, no. Not at all." I gave myself a good mental shake. "Just got lost in thought for a minute. Hank, my contractor, says four months or so. As you noticed, there's a lot of work to be done."

"Truer words have never been spoken." Her gaze landed on the pile o' stuff Ivy had given me a few minutes ago, and Vivienne leaned in for a closer look.

I pointed up the stairs. "Let me see if I can find V—"

"You're entering the Pawsitively Enchanted competition, Darcy?" she asked, cutting me off.

With one hand on the banister, I said, "Well, not me. *Missy*. Ve's up—"

"Of course, Missy." Vivienne laughed and picked up Missy's clip-on tag. "Number two hundred and forty. You just squeaked in. Lucky you. The same thing happened with us last year—we were the last ones registered. This year we applied the first hour registration was open."

Would she still think I was lucky if she knew Ivy was willing to put my life on the line for her competition's reputation? I dropped my hand and gave in to the conversation. "There was a last-minute cancellation. . . ."

"Easy on the Eyes, eh? At least you're not direct competition, or I might have to put on my game face. It's fierce, trust me."

"Audrey's not entered in the eyes category again?" This was news.

"We switched Audrey over to Picture-Perfect this year."

Picture-Perfect was the group vying for most photogenic. "You did? Why?"

"It was Baz's idea. To better Audrey's chances of winning. Going against Titania is tough. Missy has her work cut out for her."

I bit back a laugh. "We're just entering the competition for the fun of it."

"You're in the minority, then," she said solemnly. "The rest of us are cutthroat as hell."

So I was learning. "Audrey is utterly photogenic, so I think she has a good chance at winning her group."

"That's nice of you to say." Vivienne plopped onto the sofa. "Let's hope the judges agree."

There were four judges in all. Godfrey Baleaux, a good friend and owner of the Bewitching Boutique; Regina "Reggie" Beeson, the soon-to-be-retiring owner of the Furry Toadstool, the village pet shop; Ivy Teasdale (who swore she was impartial); and Dorothy Hansel Dewitt, all-around royal pain in the patootie.

"I'm sure they will," I assured her.

Vivienne was about as tall as my sister Harper, which was five feet nothing, and barely took up any room on the couch at all. Dressed in skinny jeans, a Bob Ross T-shirt, and scuffed loafers, she glanced out the window and sighed. "Darcy, have you—"

Baz, I noticed, was dillydallying on the village green. When she said nothing else, I said, "Have I what?"

Waving a hand, she said, "It's just that Baz . . . Never mind. Forget I said anything."

There was little that incited my curiosity more than being told to "never mind."

"Is everything okay with you two?" I was being blatantly nosy, but she'd opened the door for me to barge on through.

Ve had told me all about how Vivienne and Baz had gone through a rough patch a year and a half ago after Vivienne was hit by a car early one morning while she was on her way to her job as a pet-sitter. A hit-and-run. She'd nearly died from blood loss, and her recovery had been slow and painful, and Baz hadn't helped the matter. Not long after the accident, Baz checked out of the relationship emotionally, distancing himself from his wife. He often left for work early, returned late, and left Vivienne to deal with her medical appointments on her own with little moral support. Depressed and lonely, Vivienne had wandered into the Furry Toadstool one afternoon, and it was Reggie Beeson who suggested a dog would help with her recovery. That was when Audrey came into the Lucases' lives.

It had been the turning point for Vivienne's health, but Baz's emotional distance had escalated to the point that they had considered divorcing. The news hadn't come as a big shock to the witches in the village. Marriages were hard enough between a Crafter and a mortal without the stress of a major illness, especially when the mortal didn't know about the Craft, which Baz didn't.

When a witch married a mortal, she was presented with two options. One was to tell the mortal of the Craft but lose all powers. The other was to keep silent and retain the powers. A marriage where the mortal was told of the Craft heritage was often a successful union, as the mortal became what we witches called a Halfcrafter— half mortal, half Crafter. That person was adopted fully by the spouse's Craft, essentially becoming a full-fledged witch, except for one little detail: no powers. It was important for that spouse to learn all the Crafts' ins and outs so children produced during the marriage could flourish, as the kids would have full powers. Case in point: Mimi was a full Wishcrafter, but Nick was a Wish-Halfcrafter. He had none of the powers his daughter possessed, couldn't have his wishes granted, and had to comply with all Wishcraft laws.

A marriage in which the witch didn't tell the spouse of the Craft was laced with deception and lies and often ended quickly. But so far Vivienne and Baz had beaten the odds. After the accident, they'd sought marriage counseling and had slowly put the pieces of their lives back together.

Up until I felt that tension on the front porch minutes ago, I'd believed that their marriage was on solid ground, but it seemed as though there might still be a few fractures under the surface.

Picking at a loose thread on the velvet sofa, she said, "We're . . . okay."

Uh-oh.

"It's just that . . ." She shrugged, then sighed. "Do you ever wish you could change the future?"

At the sound of the word "wish," my skin tingled, but Vivienne hadn't actually wished for anything, so I didn't need to cast a spell.

I tipped my head to the side. "The future hasn't happened yet, so you *do* have the ability to change it."

"You'd think so, wouldn't you?" She kept tugging at the loose threads. "It seems to me that every moment of the past dictates what becomes of the future. Every word. Every action. It can't be erased. Its imprint carries forward with you, almost like a shadow that darkens everything to come."

She'd put a lot of thought into this, and I hated hearing the ache tainting her words. I agreed with some of what she'd said but not all of it. Those who'd dealt with a painful experience in their life carried its memory within them. It changed you. Sometimes for the better. Sometimes for the worse.

"Maybe not so much a shadow as a lesson," I said softly. "You learn from the past so you can change the future. You might not have all the control, but you have some. Use it."

"I am," she said, looking thoughtful. "Or, at least, I'm trying. Thanks. Could you let Ve know I'm here?"

She didn't seem to want to talk anymore, but now I was worried.

I was a worrier by nature.

Also, a fixer. It was the mama hen in me, clucking about. I didn't like uneasiness in my coop.

"Give me a sec and I'll grab her," I said, wishing I could do more to help Vivienne. Relationship troubles were never easy to deal with. But she hadn't asked for my help. I had to keep that in mind.

"Thanks, Darcy, and thanks for listening to me yammer on."

"Anytime. If you need an ear, I'm here," I said, hoping she'd take me up on it so I had her permission to stick my nose into her business. "I'm an expert at listening to yammering. I live with Ve, after all."

Vivienne cracked a smile. "I appreciate that, but I'm fine. Everything's fine. Really."

Dismissed. I sighed. "I'll be right back."

When I hit the lower landing of the staircase, I glanced through the large oval window overlooking the side yard, hoping to see the mourning dove that had been a constant visitor at As You Wish during the time I lived here.

Well, until recently, that was.

The bird had been oddly elusive since I'd taken its photo a few weeks ago.

Or, rather, I had *tried* to take its picture.

All that had shown up on my camera's display was a white starburst, a telltale sign that I'd photographed a Wishcrafter. Bright starbursts were how we appeared on film.

I'd done my best to convince myself that I'd accidentally had a finger in front of the lens when I snapped the shot and *hadn't* photographed a familiar. In this case, a Wishcrafter familiar, as the spirits of of Crafters retained their magical traits.

If I'd had my finger over the lens, it would absolutely distort the photo.

It made sense.

It absolutely made sense. I'd done it before.

Yet . . .

There was something deep down inside me that felt otherwise—that I had in fact captured a Wishcrafter familiar in action, but the only way to prove that theory was to take another photo of the bird.

It seemed an easy enough plan, except for one small snafu.

The bird was now MIA.

Which made me even more suspicious that it wasn't your everyday average mourning dove I'd encountered.

Shoving those thoughts aside for now, I pushed on up the stairs, the runner on the wooden steps absorbing the sound of my footfalls.

At the top of the steps, I followed the wide hallway toward Ve's bedroom at the far end, near the back staircase. Her door was ajar, and I was surprised to hear voices from within the room.

"Time is running out," a woman said, a sharp whine in her voice. "Frankly, I am astonished I personally haven't run into this conundrum before now."

I'd heard the voice before, mostly after first moving here, but rarely since. It wasn't the Elder's voice, which had become quite familiar over the past year.

The woman went on. "I don't need to remind you what's at risk here if—"

"No," Ve said, cutting her off with a long sigh. "You don't need to remind me. I know. We *all* know the risks."

"I can certainly attest to them," another woman said dryly.

That was the Elder.

I knew her voice, but I didn't know who she was. There was a rule in place that the earliest a Crafter could learn of the Elder's identity was only when he or she had lived in the village for a full year.

Next week marked the anniversary of the date that Harper, Missy, and I had pulled up to the curb in front of As You Wish, our car and a small trailer packed to the gills with the odds and ends we had brought with us from our former life in Ohio.

It had been only after our father's funeral that Aunt Ve had told us that we were Wishcrafters. . . . He, a mortal, hadn't wanted us to know while he was still alive, and Aunt Ve had honored his wishes. She'd asked us to move in with her, here in the Enchanted Village, and desperately wanting change . . . and a connection to family . . . we readily accepted.

It felt like a lifetime ago.

Harper and I had arrived, wide-eyed and eager to learn about a heritage that had been kept secret from us all our lives.

Well, I'd been wide-eyed and eager.

Harper had been wide-eyed and skeptical.

Almost a year later, she still wasn't ready to embrace her witchy birthright.

The anniversary of our moving here didn't guarantee I'd be told who the Elder was, but I was optimistic.

After all, the Elder had appointed me as an official Craft investigator a while back, to review criminal cases within the village when witchcraft was involved. With that position, I'd been able to help solve a few murder cases that had occurred over the past year. I hoped the Elder knew she could trust me, because I was dying of curiosity about who she might be.

"Have mercy," Ve mumbled. "I'm getting a headache."

I wanted to eavesdrop all day, but Vivienne was waiting downstairs. I gently tapped on the door. "Ve?"

There was a flurry of activity inside the room before

Ve wedged herself in the slight opening of the doorway, holding the door close to her body. In a high-pitched unnatural voice, she said, "Darcy? I didn't hear you coming. Is something wrong?"

Raising an eyebrow, I said, "Not at all. Vivienne Lucas is downstairs. She said she has an appointment with you."

"Oh! Yes! Thank you." Thin eyebrows were nearly touching her hairline, and her golden blue eyes held my gaze without blinking. Her coppery hair was pulled back in its usual twist, which was threaded with silvery strands. She'd been so busy lately, she hadn't had time to visit the Magic Wand Salon for a touch-up dye job.

"Why's she here? Is it for As You Wish? If so, maybe I can help. . . ."

"No, no. I asked her over. Nothing you can do to help at all." She pasted on a faux smile. "I'll be right down."

"Why?" I asked.

"Why what?"

"Why did you ask her over?" I pressed. Ve was behaving so bizarrely that I was truly curious.

"Oh, you know," she said lightly. "I was in the market for a spell, and she's the best Spellcrafter around, you know."

That was a fact. "What kind of spell?"

Laughing hollowly, she said, "Well, aren't you full of questions? You'll see soon enough." She pressed the door tighter against her. "Please let Vivienne know I'll be right down."

"Is everything all right up here?" I asked as I tried to peer around her.

"What? Yes! Peachy. Why do you ask?"

"I thought I heard voices. . . ."

She pulled the door even tighter, squishing her left breast atop her right, creating one giant vertical mono-boob. It bumped against her chin.

With a nervous laugh, she exclaimed, "Nope! Just me up here talking to . . . myself. I'm quite the conversationalist, you know. Even with myself. Ha-ha-ha."

"Ha-ha," I echoed drolly, not buying it for a minute.

"Please tell Vivienne I'll be right down," she said again in a rush. "Right down. I just need a sec to . . ."

"Finish your conversation?" I suggested.

"That's right." Nodding, she slammed the door in my face.

I knew one of the voices had been the Elder's. But who was the other woman?

A familiar?

Was it Missy? I still wasn't sure where she'd gotten off to.

Or Tilda, Ve's crabby Himalayan?

More than once I'd suspected that one or both of them might be a familiar. . . . I didn't know for certain, but if either was, they weren't willing to reveal themselves to me for whatever reason.

As I headed back downstairs, I could only hope that soon I wouldn't just learn the secret regarding the Elder's identity . . . but *all* of the village's secrets as well.

Chapter Three

Pizzazz hadn't been easy to come by.

Tipping my head to the side, I squinted with one eye closed as I studied my booth early the next morning at the Will-o'-the-Wisp.

The previous afternoon, after my meeting with Ivy, I'd gone from shop to shop in hopes of finding something fitting for Missy's and my booth at the Extravaganza, but it turned out that every last sequin, sparkle, and dog-themed ribbon in the village had already been snapped up.

So I'd improvised.

"It'll have to do," I finally said to Harper. She'd finagled the booth next to mine, and her orange tabby cat, Pumpkin Pie, was lolling inside a big cage, apparently already bored with the festivities.

It was too bad there wasn't a Lazy Bones category at

the Extravaganza or Pie would win it, hands, uh, paws down.

He was in for a long day.

"Have to do?" Harper's eyes flashed with exasperation as she fastened a garland made of silky autumn leaves to a burnt-umber tablecloth. She'd opted for a Thanksgiving theme (cleverly, to go with Pumpkin Pie) for her booth. "For the love, Darcy . . ."

"What?"

Walking over to stand by my side, she said, "Are you kidding? It's the best display here."

If someone were to glance our way, I wasn't sure they'd immediately peg us as sisters. I was nearly six inches taller than she was. I worked hard at staying trim, but she was naturally thin and waiflike. My long hair was a dark brown, almost black, while Harper's short and spiky cut was a sandy brown. My eyes were golden blue, average in size, and hers were big and golden brown, intense and expressive. Also, she had the longest darkest natural lashes I'd ever seen.

Except for the eyes, she favored our mother more than our father, while I was the opposite.

Yet . . . if you looked closely, you'd spot the family resemblance. It was there in the curve of our high cheekbones, the sharp angles of our jawlines, our heart-shaped faces. We walked alike, laughed alike, but . . . didn't often think alike.

I was cautious; she was a risk-taker.

I was a pacifist; she was a fighter.

I was a mama hen; she was my wayward chick.

I'd taken her under my wing the day she was born by emergency C-section, which also happened to be the day our mother had died. Because my father had fallen apart in the aftermath of the tragic car accident that had killed my mother, he hadn't been that great at caring for

a newborn. In one fell swoop, I'd become sister, protec-
tor, caregiver, friend, mother.

I'd been seven years old.

Twenty-four years later, I loved Harper more than
myself.

"No, it's not the best display," I said, looking around.
I'd never seen so much animal print and taffeta in my
whole life.

The showroom was packed as people readied their pets
and displays. Throughout the day, I was bound to run into
familiar faces. Aside from Harper entering Pie in the
Charmed, I'm Sure category (best personality), Mimi
Sawyer had entered her Saint Bernard, Higgins, in Pooch
Smooch (best doggy kiss), and my best friend, Starla Sullivan, had put her bichon frise, Twink, in the Fancy Pants
(best outfit) group. My recluse neighbor Terry Goodwin
was entering the loquacious Archie in Let's Hear It (best
voice), and Harmony Atchison, a friend and owner of the
Pixie Cottage, along with her life partner, Angela Curtis,
had entered their new dwarf goat, Cookie, in the same
category. Many villagers were involved with the event,
either with pets as contestants or behind the scenes. It
was bound to be an entertaining day.

The room was nearly full, and energetic chatter and
barking reverberated off the high ceilings. I hadn't seen
Nick and Mimi yet, but the next aisle over, Terry Goodwin was at his booth, chatting with Aunt Ve, who was
here spreading village goodwill in her role as village
council chairwoman. Surprisingly, she and Terry were
still on speaking terms after their somewhat-contentious
breakup a couple of weeks ago. Terry, an Elvis looka-
like, had donned a disguise for today's event. The wig
of long white hair and fake beard made him look a little
like one of the wizards from the *Lord of the Rings*.

The man knew how to do disguises right.

Aunt Ve and Terry had probably remained friends,

because they had both moved on from each other fairly quickly. Terry with Cherise Goodwin and Ve with Andreus Woodshall, who was often out of town. Thank goodness. I didn't quite know what to think of him, whether he was good or bad, because he was often both. For now, he made Ve happy and that was enough.

"All these other displays are so bright and colorful," I said, my gaze skipping around the room. "Mine sticks out like a sore thumb."

To the left of Harper's table, Baz and Vivienne Lucas stood in front of their booth, which was decorated to the nines with its *Breakfast at Tiffany's* theme. They'd designed the booth to make it appear as though it was *in* the famous window, on display. Delicate glass platters were loaded with pastries, Tiffany-blue disposable coffee cups were stacked next to several coffee carafes, and there was so much sparkle that it was nearly blinding. In front of the booth, Audrey rested on a blue dog bed, a jeweled tiara somehow fastened to the top of her head instead of her usual bow.

Next to them, with a less elaborate motorcycle-themed booth, my best friends, Starla Sullivan and her twin brother, Evan, who had Twink dressed in a sequined Evel Knievel–style jumpsuit, were putting the final touches on their display.

Starla and Evan were both Cross-Crafters, or Crossers as we called them around here. Half Wishcrafter, half Bakecrafter. With Crossers, one craft was usually predominant over the other. In the twins' case, Evan was a master baker but had issues granting wishes. Starla was the opposite.

It was Evan who was in charge of the booth all day, as Starla, a photographer who owned Hocus Pocus Photography, was freelancing for the *Toil and Trouble* newspaper today, taking photos of the show for next week's edition. Everyone was busy trying to get everything *just right* before the doors opened to the public in little less than half an hour, and the judges started making rounds.

I glanced over my shoulder at the booth across from mine. A long table had been draped in several ruby-colored cloths that had coinlike tassels dangling from the edging, so Natasha Norcliffe had been here at some point. But she and the lovely Titania were currently nowhere to be seen, and I had to admit to being relieved. It was a welcome reprieve.

"That's why your booth works," Harper said, twining a piece of orange ribbon around her long fingers. "It's unusual. Unique. Like you."

I slid her a sideways glance. "Uh, thanks?"

Happiness glinted in her eyes as she laughed. "Unique is good. These are amazing paintings."

It did my heart good to see her so content. A year ago, she'd been rather lost. We both had been. This village had anchored us, giving us roots to grow.

Although Harper still wasn't all that keen on using her Craft abilities, she'd embraced this village whole-heartedly. She'd bought Spellbound almost immediately after we moved here, and the bookshop was now thriving under her care. She had also fallen in love, not that she'd say so. Her stubbornness was legendary, and she'd probably rather suffer a vicious stomach bug than admit she might have been wrong about love and marriage.

Harper hated being wrong about *anything*.

Most of her life, she'd disavowed traditional relationship parameters. She ridiculed the idea of marriage. Called it imprisonment. But now that Lawcrafter Marcus Debrowski was in her life, Harper had begun to have an attitude adjustment.

If she still believed marriage was imprisonment, then she was well on her way to inviting Marcus to share her one-bedroom, one-bath cell, with cat hair included in the deal.

It was Marcus who was manning her bookshop today, as she was here at the Extravaganza and so were her usual part-time employees, Mimi Sawyer and Angela Curtis. I was surprised Harper hadn't yet called him eight times to check on the shop.

She was a bit of a micromanager.

The fact that she hadn't called just proved to me how much she trusted him, and I hoped he never took that for granted. Harper didn't trust easily.

My sister's praise of my artwork made me smile with pride. I had to admit, I was pleased with the way my display had turned out, but if you asked me, around here at the Extravaganza *unique* was not the preferred method of decor, and I rather wished I had been able to round up a bottle of glitter glue or *something* to make my display pop just a little bit more.

Critically, I once again studied my artwork, wondering if I could add something from Harper's table to the vignette. Some garland. Ribbon. Anything. Why hadn't I barged into Bewitching Boutique yesterday to beg Godfrey and Pepe for satin and sequins?

Because Godfrey was one of the judges for this contest, that's why. I hadn't wanted any link between my booth and his shop, so no one could accuse him of playing favorites. He knew I was working undercover, but we needed to keep up pretenses that I was just another contestant.

I'd been up most of the night hand-painting quotes about eyes onto eight canvases of varying sizes. I'd taken all of them over to Nick's wood workshop earlier this morning for his help in bracketing the canvases together to form one big collage that he'd mounted on a wooden stand. It was a freestanding piece, about six feet tall and four feet across.

Among many other quotes, I had used Henry David Thoreau's "It's not what you look at that matters, it's what you see," Roald Dahl's "Above all, watch with glittering eyes the whole world around you," Gandhi's "An eye for an eye only makes the whole world blind," and "Eyes that do not cry, do not see," which was a Swedish proverb.

Each saying was written on a canvas painted with an animal's face shown in profile with the focus being on its eye. I'd used the animals in my life as inspiration. Missy, Tilda, Higgins, Pie, Archie, Pepe, Mrs. P, and Twink.

"Darcy, how lovely!" a woman's voice said from behind me. "Your paintings are darling. These should be in a gallery, or at the very least, allow me to sell them on your behalf at the shop."

I turned and found one of the Extravaganza's judges, Reggie Beeson, studying my display.

In her mid-seventies, Reggie had fair skin, blue eyes, henna-colored hair, apple cheeks, a narrow chin, and a beautiful smile, which had lost none of its luster, even though the right side of it drooped slightly, a result of the stroke she'd suffered last winter.

Although she was doing quite well with her recovery, her health was one of the reasons why she had recently decided to close up the Furry Toadstool to move to Florida to live with an elderly friend of her family who was in need of a companion. She was due to leave in a little over a week, and the village was going to sorely miss her—and also the pet shop as well. It was practically a landmark in the village, one of the oldest businesses in the square. There was a big block party happening the following weekend, a kickoff to summer planned by the village council, and it was the perfect time for all Reggie's friends to have the chance to say good-bye. I had the feeling it was going to be a bittersweet affair.

She stepped closer to my paintings, seemingly studying my brushstrokes. "Absolutely beautiful."

"Thanks," I said, unable to stop my grin.

"Told you," Harper said as she wandered back to her table.

"Would you consider selling?" Reggie asked as she balanced her weight on a pink cane decorated in zebra stripes. Wrinkles pulled at the corners of her eyes. "My customers would love them."

"Aren't you closing up shop soon?" I asked.

"One week," she said on a bit of a wistful sigh as she bent to pat Missy. "But these drawings will sell quickly, long before the doors close for good."

Reggie had kept the Furry Toadstool open longer than anyone had ever anticipated—she should have retired long ago. Aunt Ve suspected Reggie had kept the shop running as a tribute to her late husband, Samuel. Reggie had been a self-proclaimed spinster when she met Zoacrafter Samuel Beeson and fell in love at first sight. When he'd died more than a decade ago, Reggie inherited the shop. She had stepped in to fill his role, and had quickly become the heart of the store.

Missy, I noticed, perked up at Reggie's attention. The little dog wagged her stubby tail and drank in the affection that flowed naturally from Reggie—not because she was a Zoacrafter, a witch who had a magical way with animals like Samuel, but simply because she adored animals. Reggie had been a mortal when she married Samuel, but when he told her of his Craft, she'd become a Halfcrafter.

Missy's ebullience at seeing the woman might also be because Reggie always carried dog treats with her. Reggie didn't disappoint—she slipped her hand into her pocket and pulled out a treat. Missy lapped it up.

Reggie faced me. "What do you say, Darcy? Will you let me sell them? My commission will be minimal, I promise."

I looked at the paintings. "Maybe. Let me think about it."

"Just don't think too long." With a smile, Reggie glanced at her watch. "I need to check in at the judges' booth, but you know where to find me, Darcy."

Reggie limped away, and I smiled as I heard a dog bark upstairs at the front entry of the Wisp. It was a loud baritone woof that carried through the whole building.

Higgins.

I'd recognize that voice anywhere.

If the big Saint Bernard was here, that meant Mimi and Nick had finally arrived, too.

I'd bet they had glitter. . . . Mimi had gone all out for her display. In fact, she might be the one who'd depleted the village of all its sparkly notions.

"They are good enough to sell," Harper said, returning to my side. "I'll buy the one of Pie."

"I'll *give* you the one of Pie, no charge."

"How're you supposed to make money on your art if you give it away?"

"I don't create the art to make money," I said, meaning it.

"In that case, you could give the money to me." She blinked innocently.

"You're doing okay on your own." Harper's ideas often exceeded her budget, but her budget had recently expanded, thanks to that trust fund our mother had left me. I'd done everything possible to fairly share that money with Harper, who hadn't been born when the trust was created. The trust had just paid off the mortgage on Harper's bookshop, which would now hopefully start turning a nice profit without the burden of an enormous overhead.

"I can always use more," she muttered. "Who couldn't?"

Ignoring her, I walked over to Missy's pen to check on her. With her head on her front paws, she lay in her doggy bed, watching Harper and me with a look of pure disgust in her eyes. Except for her time with Reggie, she'd been mopey since we arrived. Not even Higgins' arrival had lifted her spirits, and she loved that big slobbery dog.

Poor thing.

"What has you down? Is it this pen?" I asked her. She had never been fond of being fenced in. I patted her curly-topped head. "It's only for one day. Not even. Six, seven hours . . ."

Lifting an eyebrow, she glared at me.

There were some days she was just so humanlike that I could easily imagine that she was a familiar. Maybe she was. Who knew?

The Elder, that's who.

Perhaps she'd tell me if I asked especially nicely.

Or maybe I'd inhaled too many paint fumes.

"Darcy!" a shrill voice called out, and Missy whimpered.

I almost whimpered, too.

"Six, seven hours," I repeated to Missy with a smile and scratch under her chin before I stood and found Ivy Teasdale rushing toward me, a lanyard bobbing on her chest as if it were playing a game of hopscotch, a clipboard grasped tightly in her hand. Her pink-tipped hair had been pulled back into a tight knot, and she wore neon green sneakers with her tailored black suit.

"Hi, Ivy," I said, trying to keep the weariness out of my voice. "You know my sister, Harper?"

"Yes, of course." Her gaze flicked from Harper, then back to me in a flash. "Where's the rest of your decor, Darcy?"

"There is no more," I said with a shrug. "This is it."

Confusion dripped from her words. "What do you mean, no more?"

It felt as though the temperature had dropped a good twenty degrees from Ivy's icy glare, and I was glad I'd worn a cardigan over my vintage Tweety Bird T-shirt.

"Where's the tulle? The lace? The ribbons? The animal print?" Ivy awkwardly tucked the clipboard under her armpit and made frantic jazz hands. "The pizzazz!"

Harper's eyes went wide with horror. "Oh my God, you weren't kidding about the jazz hands."

Ivy shot her an annoyed look, then faced me and dropped her voice. "You need to be the best of the best, Darcy. Nothing else will do to get on you-know-who's radar. You don't have much time before she . . ." Ivy's gaze settled on something over my shoulder, and then she pasted on a phony smile.

I glanced over my shoulder.

Not a something, after all. A *someone.*

Ivy said, "Natasha! So good to see you again!"

Natasha wore a billowy long white dress with braided halter straps, gold sandals, and about a dozen gold chains of varying lengths around her neck. Although the outfit should have swallowed her petite frame, it didn't. Instead she looked nothing but glamorous.

I was suddenly regretting my choice of jeans and T-shirt.

As Ivy brushed past me to greet the reigning Extravaganza champion, she whispered, "Do not blow it, Darcy."

Harper came to stand at my elbow. "Why'd you take this job again?"

"No job too big or too small, remember?"

"That's a stupid motto."

Missy barked as though agreeing.

I was beginning to think so, too, as I said, "Be that as it may, I—"

I broke off, too stunned at the sight before me to finish my sentence.

"What?" Harper asked, then gasped as she followed my gaze.

A bare-chested muscular man stood at the end of the aisle and began to beat a tambourine against his thick thigh. He wore nothing but a tiny swath of white cloth across his hips that barely covered all his manly bits and a black shoulder-length headdress, banded at the temples with thin gold fabric.

Harper grabbed my arm. "Holy Mr. Tambourine Man. Tell me I'm hallucinating."

"If you are, I am, too," I said.

Behind him, two other men dressed identically to the first carried a palanquin, one of those fancy bedlike conveyances that Egyptian royalty had used, down the wide aisle. People parted as though Moses himself were on board. The rectangular litter looked hand-carved and was painted a vibrant gold. It had a dome roof and thick purple velvet curtains.

Harper and I watched in awe as the men marched methodically toward Natasha's booth.

Ivy turned toward me, frowning while doing the jazz-hand thing, and turned back toward the spectacle.

Pizzazz. Right.

Natasha had pizzazz up the wazoo.

While Mr. Tambourine Man kept the beat going, the other men set the carrier on top of the table draped with silken cloths and, with a flourish, drew back the curtains to reveal Titania sitting majestically on a velvet purple cushion. The cat wore a gold headdress, and one of the men held a jeweled leash, attached to a golden collar.

And damn if that cat didn't look like a queen with her stately demeanor, sitting perfectly still, her tail curved around her body. Her amber eyes were bright and intelligent as she surveyed her kingdom.

The tambourine finished with a flourish, and all three

men retreated, one behind the table, the other two separated on each side.

The people around us—the contestants *not* entered in the same category—burst into applause.

"I *am* hallucinating." Harper rubbed her eyes.

"My theme," Natasha said loudly and dramatically, "is ancient Egypt. Today Titania will be playing the role of *Cleocatra*." She bowed in the direction of the cat.

More applause erupted, and I felt a little queasy.

Harper looked at the ribbon in her hand and tossed it over her shoulder. "Why bother? Pie doesn't stand a chance against that."

"You're not even entered in the same category," I pointed out.

"Doesn't matter."

"That's the spirit," I teased her.

"She has naked men," Harper said. "Naked. Men."

I looked at the guys, their hands clasped behind their backs. They appeared here to stay.

"Half-naked," I corrected.

"The loincloths hardly count. Did you see their chest muscles? I think one just waved at me."

"One of the guys?"

"One of the *pectorals*. Mr. Nipples, the one on the left, has quite the talent with that particular muscle."

Mr. Tambourine Man. Mr. Nipples. It was going to be a long day.

"Darcy," Natasha said, striding across the aisle once the applause died down and Ivy had fled. "I didn't know you had registered Missy in the competition. Hello, Harper." Bright blue eye shadow and long fake lashes highlighted her dark eyes as she glanced up at me.

"That was some entrance," Harper said, sending curious glances toward the muscled men.

"Well, you know. I have a reputation to uphold. Titania and I are going for a four-peat." She cut her gaze to Missy, who was also staring at the faux-Egyptian men, ears perked. "What category are you entered in?"

"Easy on the Eyes," I said as breezily as I could.

Something flickered in Natasha's gaze, and her face froze. "I see." Cracking a thin smile, she walked over to my display. Dryly, she added over her bare shoulder, "Pun intended."

"Oh." I faked a laugh. "Funny."

Harper made faces behind her back.

"Interesting," Natasha said of my art, the same way one might comment on hearing of a great-aunt's trip to the dentist. "Sometimes simplest is best."

"Are the beefcakes sticking around all day?" Harper asked abruptly. "They're making me uncomfortable. One of them won't stop winking at me."

"That's not a wink," Natasha said with a staccato laugh. "He's allergic to cats and his itchy eyes are driving him crazy."

"Oh," Harper said, redness climbing up her neck. "That makes me feel better. But if Mr. Blinky is allergic, why's he here?"

"His name is Chip. And because I asked," Natasha said with a sly smile. "They're all staying. Private security."

"Private security?" I asked, testing the waters. "For what?"

"My cat is quite valuable," Natasha said with a haughty tone. "I need to ensure that Titania's protected at all times. . . ." She glanced at Missy. "Titania is not just some common pet. She's an award-winning purebred."

Harper smiled sweetly.

Too sweetly.

She'd gone into fight mode.

I quickly linked arms with her to prevent her from *accidentally* shoving Natasha. Harper rarely got physical when angry, but Natasha was testing those limits.

"As a matter of fact," Natasha said, "Titania has an audition with an animal talent agency next week in Hollywood. She's going to be famous. Her grand-prize win today will look fabulous on her résumé."

Harper chuckled mirthlessly. "Let me guess. She's going to be a catactress." Looking at me, my sister wore a puzzled expression, despite her eyes flashing with mischief. "A cactress? A cactor?"

With pursed lips, Natasha stared at Harper for a long moment, and then she smiled. Thin. Brittle. Evil.

It chilled me to my bones.

"Yes. Well, good luck today, Darcy." Natasha spun around, her dress flaring out behind her. "You'll need it."

Competition changes people. Trust me.

Ivy had been right about that.

And I was beginning to suspect that she'd been right about Natasha sabotaging Titania's competition as well.

Chapter Four

Hours later, it was becoming clear that Lady Catherine, Marigold Coe's whippet, was stealing the show right out from under Titania's regal nose.

The dog, named after *Pride and Prejudice*'s Lady Catherine de Bourgh, had been entered in the Crankypuss group, and her name and the category were both entirely appropriate. When her big brown eyes narrowed as she looked down her long snout at passersby, she always appeared to be *most seriously displeased*, a trait shared with the literary character.

In my opinion, the Jane Austen connection to the gorgeous dog sealed her place as the favorite to win the Extravaganza. That, and the fact that she was one of the sweetest dogs in the village. The contrast between her docile demeanor and her imperious appearance had stolen the hearts of the crowd gathered around her.

She was the Grumpy Cat of the dog world.

It was hours yet before the winners would be chosen, but the judges with their matching clipboards were spending a lot of time at Lady Catherine's booth with big smiles on their faces. They weren't alone. A sizable group of spectators surrounded them. They couldn't seem to get enough of the dog's innate hauteur.

The event photographer was having a field day, darting around to take pictures from every angle. Nearby, Starla was snapping her photos for the *Toil and Trouble*. Even she seemed charmed by Lady Catherine despite the fact that her own dog was a competitor.

Marigold stood proudly by her pet, beaming at the attention the dog was receiving.

No one could have predicted such an upset.

Especially Natasha.

Across the aisle from me, there was most certainly not a smile on Natasha's lips. In fact, it appeared as though she could barely contain a scowl as she eyed Lady Catherine's growing crowd.

I made a mental note to pay close attention to Natasha's dealings with Marigold, because if anyone was now at risk for an unfortunate accident, it was Marigold. Again.

I truly hoped she stayed away from the curved staircase.

As I turned my attention back to my own display, I couldn't help feeling a surge of pride. Come to find out, I hadn't needed glittery or golden or half-naked pizzazz to attract attention. People had been swarming my booth to visit with Missy and see my paintings, and several had asked if I took commissions—they wanted portraits painted of their beloved pets.

I'd been taking phone numbers all morning.

Natasha most definitely was not happy with the crowd around my table, even though she'd also had a solid stream of visitors.

But I supposed they weren't the type of people she'd intended to attract.

I'd never seen so many giggling teenagers in all my life.

Even now, a gaggle of them sashayed past the faux Egyptians, who didn't seem to mind the attention, as underage as it might be.

One of those teenagers peeled off from the flock and headed my way, barely taking her gaze from the men keeping guard over Titania.

"Is Missy feeling any better?" Mimi asked me for at least the sixth time today as she crouched next to Missy's pen to say hello to the dog.

Mimi Sawyer had turned thirteen a few months ago, and though she was an inquisitive bookworm by nature, even she couldn't resist the lure of barely dressed attractive men.

"Still the same," I said, suppressing a smile.

"That's good," she said absently, her attention focused across the aisle.

I almost laughed at her transparent behavior. "How's Higgins doing?"

She glanced at me with her big dark brown eyes. "Not winning any votes with his drooling."

I'd been on the receiving end of his drool many times. Laughing, I asked, "Are you handing out wet wipes?"

"And hand sanitizer."

There wasn't enough sanitizer in the world for Higgins' drool, in my opinion.

Mimi stood. "Dad sent me over to ask if you wanted to go to lunch soon."

I could barely see the far corner of the showroom floor where Higgins' booth was located, and certainly couldn't spot Nick from so far away. I eyed Mimi. "He sent you over, did he?"

A blush crept up her neck. "Okay, I might have volunteered." She shrugged. "Okay, begged. Same difference."

Smiling, I resisted teasing her, and glanced at my watch. "Tell him half an hour is good with me." I'd ask Harper to watch my booth—and Natasha—while I was away. Right now I was manning Harper's booth while she was at lunch with Aunt Ve. Watching over Pie was easy, as it seemed his preferred method of dealing with the crowds was to nap.

Mimi gave me a halfhearted wave as she wandered off, and as I watched her thread through the crowd, I noticed the judges finally on the move. The crowd around Lady Catherine's booth remained.

"Danish?" someone said from nearby.

I jumped, not having heard Vivienne approach.

She held up a glass platter. "Seems Baz and I overestimated how many pastries we needed, and I really don't want to take them home."

"No, thanks," I said. "I'm headed to lunch soon."

"How about you, Natasha?" Vivienne asked. "Would you like a Danish?"

Disgust filled Natasha's eyes. "No, thanks. A moment on the lips, forever on the hips," she said, her gaze flicking downward to my thighs. She lifted a smug eyebrow.

Vivienne rolled her eyes.

I glanced down the aisle toward the Lucases' booth, wondering just how many pastries remained. There were still a dozen pink Gingerbread Shack boxes stacked behind their display. That was a lot of leftovers.

Natasha had turned her back on us and pulled a mirror from her bag to check her lipstick. I could have sworn I saw her eyeing the Danish in her reflection.

Biting back a smile, I faced Vivienne and found her frowning at the plate in her hand. "I'm not looking forward to hearing from Baz about how it was my idea to order extra."

"Is he on his lunch break?" I asked, not seeing him—or Audrey. Was he at all concerned about getting food poisoning again this year?

"Nature called. He took Audrey outside to the dog play yard."

I looked at Missy—she'd be due to go out soon as well, and I hoped the fresh air would perk her up a little before the judges made their rounds. I knew we weren't eligible to win, but I rather hoped she wouldn't look so morose when they stopped by.

A young couple with two little kids wandered over to Vivienne's booth, and she said, "Ooh, gotta go." She dashed over to foist Danish on them.

A moment later, I spotted Evan Sullivan and Twink headed this way. He walked slowly, his lips pursed as though whistling a quiet tune. As he neared, I heard the song.

"It's Raining Men."

The color was high in his freckled fair cheeks as he pulled to a stop in front of my display. He set Twink down inside the pen, and he bounced over to say hello to Missy. She eyed the little dog with what looked like pity. The Evel Knievel outfit *was* a bit over-the-top.

Evan said, "Just, uh, taking Twink out for a quick walk." He smoothed his short ginger-blond hair and picked an imaginary piece of lint off his perfectly pressed light blue button-down shirt.

"Et tu, Brute?" I said with a broad smile. "Mimi's been by half a dozen times already."

Theatrically, his body sagged and he tipped his head back and groaned. In a whisper, he said, "Come on, Darcy. Can you blame us?"

I leaned around Evan to take another look at the scantily clad men.

Chip, aka Mr. Blinky, was dabbing at his eyes with a

handkerchief, Mr. Tambourine Man was fighting a yawn, and Mr. Nipples wiggled his pectorals at me.

Have mercy, as Ve would say.

Evan whistled low. "They're gorgeous. Especially Chip, the one on the right."

"Not my type," I said, meeting Evan's sky blue eyes. "And you're in a relationship, remember?"

He'd recently started seeing FBI agent Scott Abramson.

"A casual relationship." He tossed a surreptitious glance over his shoulder. "Besides, just because I enjoy man candy doesn't mean I'm going to sample it." He raised an eyebrow. "Unless an offer presents itself. . . ."

I smacked his shoulder and he laughed.

"You don't have to worry," he said. "Chip Goldman is an actor who's hopelessly devoted to only two people. Himself and Natasha. They've been seeing each other off and on for years. It's mostly on during theater season, since they work together." He dropped his voice. "Natasha toys with him, and he happily lets her, the dimwit."

Once again, I glanced across the aisle. Chip was still dabbing his eyes. Now that I knew he and Natasha were seeing each other, it made much more sense as to why he'd put himself through the torture of guarding a cat he was allergic to.

Evan might have proclaimed the trio of men gorgeous, but I didn't see the appeal of any of the male models. Sure, they were buff and handsome, but they did nothing for me.

Then I realized why.

Nick.

He'd ruined me for all other men. In my eyes, my heart, no one could compare.

And I didn't mind one little bit.

"What's that goofy smile all about?" Evan asked, eyeing me.

"Noth—oh my God!" I quickly looked left, looked right.

"What?" Evan asked, following my frantic gaze.

I looked around again and saw the judges had dispersed, fanning out in several directions, apparently taking a quick break.

What I didn't see was any sign of Natasha.

Ivy was not going to be happy about this. I had to find Natasha. Fast.

"What's going on?" Evan asked.

"I lost Natasha."

His eyes widened—he knew that I'd been hired to keep an eye on her . . . and why. "Well, go find her!"

I rushed over to her booth and approached Mr. Nipples, figuring I had a better chance at getting answers out of him, since he'd waved at me. Kind of. "Uh, excuse me, do you know where Natasha went?"

Titania, I noticed, was still sitting on her fluffy pillow. She blinked at me, and the majestic look I'd seen earlier was gone now, replaced with what looked like embarrassment. She meowed pitifully. I didn't blame her. Tilda would throw a hissy fit if she'd been dolled up in such a manner. I reached out to pet the cat and she tried to push her face into the palm of my hand, but the headdress stopped her. Instead I scratched her chin, and she purred loudly.

And just like that she stole my vote for the grand-prize winner.

"Restroom," said Mr. Nipples, who was apparently a man of few words.

"Thanks." I gave Titania one last scratch. Hurrying back to my booth, I grabbed my spy pen and said to Evan, "Can you watch my booth for a couple of minutes?"

He grinned and leaned against the table as if settling in for a long stay. "Take as long as you want, Darcy."

I shook a finger at him, then broke into a fast jog, headed toward the bathroom that was located at the far end of the room. As I rushed along, I glanced toward Lady Catherine's booth and was dismayed to see neither she nor Marigold Coe was there.

Oh no, oh no. No, no, no.

I pushed through the restroom's door to find a line of women waiting to use the facilities. None of them were Natasha. I scooted past the queue, heading for the sink area. As I did so, I glanced under stall doors, looking for strappy gold sandals.

There were none.

Great. Fabulous.

Spinning around, I ran out, receiving curious glances as I did so.

Back in the main room, I looked around but couldn't see much because of the crowd. I headed up the stairs to get a bird's-eye view.

On the upper landing, I squinted, searching the room. No Natasha. No Marigold. I did, however, spot the colorful Archie. The scarlet macaw familiar was singing loudly, and I strained to hear the song.

"One Is the Loneliest Number."

It fit, I supposed, considering that his booth was empty except for the presence of Terry. Archie was used to entertaining a crowd.

I also saw Nick. I gave him a smile and a curt wave, then spun around and headed down a long hallway toward the dining room. At an intersecting corridor, the sound of a staccato laugh echoed. I knew that laugh. Natasha.

I stopped. Listened. I heard another laugh—softer this time. More of a giggle. The noise had definitely come from the deserted hallway.

Veering right, I kept close to the wall and tiptoed farther away from the thrum of the event. This hallway housed smaller conference rooms, each with a recessed double doorway.

As I neared the middle of the corridor, I passed a narrow recess, a single entryway. A piece of fabric that stuck out from beneath the bottom of the door marked STORAGE caught my attention. The cloth was white and filmy and looked a lot like the hem of Natasha's dress. I approached the door cautiously and pressed my ear to it.

I heard the low murmur of voices—a man and a woman—and slurpy kissing sounds.

Ew.

At first I thought it had to be Natasha and Chip, but immediately dismissed the idea. Chip was downstairs, his eyes red and swollen, as he watched Titania.

Who, exactly, was in the storage room with Natasha?

As I debated whether to knock, the door started to open.

Panicked, I quickly dashed into the meeting room across the hall, which was offset at a diagonal. Perfect for spying without being seen. I kept one of the double doors cracked open with my foot and leaned into the doorway's portal to peek out. As Natasha emerged from the storage closet, her cheeks were bright red as she fussed with the strap of her dress and continued to giggle.

As surreptitiously as I could, I aimed the spy pen her way, just in time to catch Baz Lucas stepping out behind her. His dog, Audrey, looked bewildered as she circled his feet. Baz pinched Natasha's butt, nuzzled the back of her neck, and whispered something in her ear.

My jaw dropped.

She giggled again, swatted him, and stepped into his arms for a steamy kiss that had my eyes widening, then squeezing shut, as the kissed morphed into a grope-fest with X-rated intensity.

Ew, ew, ew. Ivy was not paying me nearly enough to witness this.

Baz said, "Soon, my dear one, soon. We'll be together. All our dreams will come true."

"Promise?" Natasha asked, cuddling close to his chest.

"I promise. I love you."

"Not as much as I love you."

I was feeling a little queasy as they fell into another steamy embrace.

When they parted again, Baz said, "'Well . . . I guess we'd better get Irving's car and get out of here.'"

It took me a moment to recognize the quote from *Roman Holiday.* That's right. Baz had an Audrey Hepburn obsession. And now that I looked more closely at Natasha, I saw that she resembled the famous actress quite a bit, with her thin petite stature, her triangular face and big brown eyes.

It couldn't be a coincidence.

Natasha laughed and swatted him, promising to see him later. She fluffed her hair, and sashayed down the hallway. At its end, she turned left, back toward the showroom.

Baz watched her go, then tugged Audrey's leash. At the end of the hallway, he turned right, heading toward the dog yard.

Blinking in disbelief, I took a deep breath, tucked the spy pen back into my pocket, and was about to follow Natasha when I heard the barest puff of an exhalation.

It hadn't been mine.

The noise had come from behind me.

Close behind me.

Adrenaline shot through me, and bumps formed on my arms as I suddenly suspected I wasn't alone.

Bracing myself, I slowly turned and gasped. Sunshine

spotlighted the woman standing there, which made her look like an angel with her beautiful fair skin and long blond hair.

But I considered her to be a devil in disguise.

She let out a gusty sigh. "Why am I not surprised to see you here, Darcy Merriweather?"

Chapter Five

Setting a hand over my pounding heart, I backed up a step and leaned against the door. "I'm not sure," I said to Broomcrafter Glinda Hansel as I tried to catch my breath, "because I'm surprised as hell to see *you* here."

Her nose wrinkled, and the barest of smiles graced her sparkling pink glossy lips. "Did Ms. Goody Two-witch just say 'hell'? I don't believe my ears."

"What can I say?" I drew my shoulders back and tugged the hem of my T-shirt. "You're a bad influence."

At that she laughed. It was a beautiful melodious sound that only added to her angelic appearance. She adjusted the strap of a pink sundress and said, "I'll deny it to my last breath."

Glinda and I had our many differences, and were what some would call frenemies. Friendly enemies. We were working on being more friends than enemies, but change was hard. We'd become set in our ways over the past year. She'd once had romantic feelings for Nick, and had used her prior relationship with his former wife, Melina (they'd been best friends as teenagers), to get close to his daughter, Mimi. It had been a brilliant plan to worm her way into their lives.

Once Glinda realized how committed Nick was to me, she'd eventually moved on from him and was currently dating Liam Chadwick, a talented village artist. Even still, about six months ago, her dislike of me got the better of her, which had resulted in her leaving the village police force and driving what we all thought was a permanent wedge between herself and Nick and Mimi.

However, it turned out that her feelings for Mimi hadn't been an act, and we'd all eventually called a truce in the interest of Mimi's happiness.

Glinda's and my mutual love for Mimi was truly the only thing holding our so-called friendship together, but that lone tie was enough to firmly anchor our acquaintance.

"Aren't you supposed to be downstairs with Clarence?" I asked, wondering what she was doing up here.

Clarence was Glinda's energetic golden retriever. I had a fondness for him, despite whom he belonged to. He was entered in the Wag It category and had a good chance at winning.

"Liam's with him." She pursed her lips. "Aren't you supposed to be with Missy?"

"Evan's covering for me while . . ." I broke off, not wanting to explain why I was following Natasha, who was now out there somewhere, possibly tripping or poisoning people, namely Marigold Coe. "Actually, I need to get going."

Glinda grabbed my arm as I turned. "What are you doing up here, Darcy? Did Vivienne Lucas hire you, too?" Suspicion clouded her blue eyes. One sandaled foot tapped a furious beat against the tile floor.

It took me a moment to process what she'd said. "Vivienne? No, I'm working for Ivy."

In addition to putting her Broomcrafting talents to good use at the local art center creating beautiful wooden crafts, Glinda had recently opened a PI agency here in the village, and she hadn't lacked for clients. One of whom was apparently Vivienne Lucas.

Glinda let go of my arm, and a pale blond eyebrow shot upward. "_Ivy_ hired you to watch Baz Lucas?"

"No, not Baz," I clarified. Sunlight streamed in through tall paned windows, highlighting dust mites floating in the beams. "So, Vivienne hired you to tail Baz?"

"Yep," Glinda said. "To catch the cheating bastard in the act."

I suddenly recalled that butt pinch in the hallway and felt heat flooding my cheeks. If Vivienne had hired Glinda, then she had to have suspected Baz was stepping out.

"Do you ever wish you could change the future?"

Vivienne's words from yesterday swirled inside my head, creating a tiny storm of empathy, but now I realized what she meant by saying she was trying to take control. Good for her.

Shaking my head, I said, "I can't believe he's cheating."

"Well, believe it," Glinda said. "He's a cheating dirty dog."

It certainly seemed that way. "How long has he been seeing Natasha?"

"I'm not sure." She tucked a long blond strand of hair behind her ear. "I've been on the case for a month, but can never seem to catch them in the act. I have a couple of silhouetted pictures and some blurry video of them sneaking around in the dead of night, but nothing definitive. Baz is extremely careful when they meet. He makes sure of that. The money, you know."

"Money?" I said, not really following.

"He's loaded, remember?"

I did now that she mentioned it. He came from old money. The kind that built additions onto museums and hospitals.

"He and Vivienne have an ironclad prenup," Glinda explained. "If they divorce, she gets a pittance. Unless . . ." She tipped her head, allowing me to fill in the blank.

"He's caught cheating."

"Right. They have an infidelity clause. If he's cheating, she gets a windfall. Ten million."

"Say what?" I squeaked out. "Ten *million*?"

"Yep," Glinda said. "And if I can deliver irrefutable proof of his cheating, she's going to give me five percent of that as a bonus."

Five percent. *Five hundred thousand dollars.*

Oh. My. Gosh.

"Which is why you couldn't have come in here at a worse time. I'd have had video evidence of Baz and Natasha canoodling if you hadn't stuck your nosy head in here when you did." She held up her smartphone, which was playing the video. It showed Baz sneaking into the hall closet, then Natasha joining him a moment later.

"Did you just say the word 'canoodling'?" I couldn't help teasing.

"*You're* a bad influence, Darcy Merriweather. And no offense, but I'm just going to delete the part of this recording where you snuck in here. I see enough of you in person, thank you very much, so I don't need to hold on to this as a keepsake."

"Actually, I might be able to help your case." It was the least I could do to help Vivienne.

"How so?" Glinda asked.

I held up my pen. "It has a hidden video camera. I

had it running the whole time Natasha and Baz were in the hallway."

Her eyes widened. "I could kiss you, and that's saying something."

"Please don't." I suddenly frowned as something caught my eye.

"You don't have to make that face. I can assure you I wouldn't enjoy the kiss, either."

The video she'd taken had been playing on a loop while she was speaking, and I reached out and snatched the phone out of her hand.

"Hey!" she exclaimed.

My hand shook as I said, "How did you do this?"

"Do what?" she asked, sounding as if she were dealing with a crazy person.

Maybe she was, because I couldn't believe what I was seeing. Maybe I was losing my mind.

I held up the phone. "This! How am I on this video? Do you see me?"

"Have you gone batty, Darcy? Of course I see you. I was recording when you came in—" She abruptly stopped talking and her eyes widened as realization hit. "I—I don't know."

So I hadn't been seeing things.

My image was on this video.

Me. With my long dark hair and golden blue eyes.

It was startling to say the least.

Because I, as a Wishcrafter, should have been nothing but a bright white light on this video.

I reached for the doorknob. Forget Natasha. I had a bigger problem.

I had to find Ve.

Glinda was hot on my heels as I rushed down the grand staircases toward the showroom. We weren't the only ones in a hurry. Starla was taking the steps upward two at a time, headed toward me, her camera in hand.

I thought for certain she was going to say something about capturing a Wishcrafter image, but instead she said, "Darcy! I've been looking everywhere for you. Evan's been stalling the judges. They can't judge Missy without you there." She grabbed my hand, and her blond ponytail swished side to side as she pulled me along. "You're about to be disqualified."

At the bottom of the marble staircase, I glanced around the event hall and said, "Do you know if Ve is back from lunch? Have you seen her? I've been calling her cell phone, but she's not answering."

There must have been something in my tone that had alerted her to trouble in the air, because she stopped dead in her tracks. "She's not back yet. Why? What's wrong?" She flicked a glance at Glinda and frowned.

Glinda held up her hands in surrender. "It has nothing to do with me. This time," she added under her breath. She skirted around us and headed straight for Vivienne Lucas.

I turned my attention back to my friend. "Have you taken any pictures of Ve or Evan?"

Confusion flickered in Starla's blue eyes. "Not specifically because, well, you know, but I'm sure there are a few shots with them in the background. I haven't reviewed the photos yet, but I'll just delete those ones. Why?"

"It's the strangest thing. Take a look at the photos. I bet you'll be surprised by what you see. Glinda had this video—"

"Darcy!" Evan yelled, cutting me off as he stomped toward me. "The judges finished with Natasha five minutes ago and are waiting for you. Come on!" He grabbed my hand and tugged.

Like brother, like sister.

To Starla, I said, "Please go find Ve for me."

With a nod, she spun around and hurried off.

I stumbled along until Evan suddenly let go of my hand, stepped behind me, and pushed me forward, his hands firmly on my shoulders as though he was suspecting I'd flee at first chance.

Truth was, the thought had crossed my mind.

Right now the Pawsitively Enchanted competition was the last thing on my mind. Something big was going on in the witch world, and I needed to make sure Ve knew about it.

"Here she is," Evan said brightly as he presented me to the judges. "I told you she'd be right back." He bent and picked up Twink, gave my arm a squeeze, and blended into the crowd.

As my gaze flicked over the judges' faces, I pasted a fake smile on my face. "Hello!"

"Nice of you to join us, Darcy Merriweather," Dorothy Hansel Dewitt said, her tone dripping with condescension.

Dorothy, Glinda's mother, and I had a long history of disliking each other. She was short, busty, and crazy as a loony tune.

"Sorry," I said. "I, uh, the restroom had a line . . ." Not entirely a lie.

Next to Dorothy, Ivy Teasdale was giving me an icy glare. No wonder, as I'd obviously not been keeping an eye on Natasha as I'd been hired to do. She was clearly unhappy with me.

I peeked across the aisle to find Natasha grinning at me like the Cheshire Cat over the rim of a cardboard coffee cup. She was obviously enjoying the fact that the judges were clearly displeased with me.

Titania had fallen asleep on her velvet cushion, and the half-naked men were nowhere to be seen—probably on their lunch break.

I noticed that the coffee cup in Natasha's hand looked as though it had come from Baz and Vivienne's display—it was that telltale Tiffany blue.

Had she no shame at all?

Had *he*?

Now that I knew they were carrying on, I couldn't help replaying Natasha and Baz's every interaction today and wondered how I'd misread the obvious signs. The gooey-eyed glances. The giggly conversations. Sure, I'd witnessed them, but I had chalked them up to Baz's flirtatious personality. It made me a bit queasy as I looked his way. His attention, however, wasn't focused on Natasha right now—it had been captured by the whispered conversation going on between Vivienne and Glinda.

Vivienne's eyes had narrowed, her lips had pursed, and her face had flushed as she glared at her husband.

With her hands fisted at her sides, it was obvious she was infuriated. No doubt, Glinda had just informed her of Baz's exploits.

With a big grin, family friend Godfrey Baleaux stroked his white beard and said, "You're here now, Darcy, and that's all that matters. Let the judging begin!" His big belly jiggled, straining the buttons on his vest as he chuckled.

The event photographer busily snapped pictures of Missy in her pen as Reggie Beeson bent down and made a noise that sounded like a combination kiss and cluck. Missy trotted over to her, her tail wagging, probably expecting another dog cookie.

Missy's tail stopped wagging when she realized no snack was forthcoming.

I understood her disappointment. I could use a cookie right about now, too.

I set the spy pen on my display table and tried to focus on the judging. I scooped up Missy and held her close to my chest. Her heart beat rapidly beneath my hand, and I stroked her back to calm her down a bit. The judges stepped over, one at a time, for a closer look at Missy's eyes.

Her tiny tail wagged as Godfrey said, "Soulful eyes."

It thumped harder as Reggie leaned in and said, "Lovely. Just lovely."

Ivy shoved a pink streak strand of hair out of her eye and spent more time looking at me than Missy. She mouthed, *You're fired,* then quickly stepped backward.

My jaw dropped, but I couldn't quite defend myself to Ivy at this moment.

And after a moment of consideration, I asked myself why I would want to. I shouldn't have taken the job to begin with. I'd known it when Ivy hired me, and I knew it now.

I had to learn to say no.

Being fired was a *relief.*

After the judges departed, I'd pack up, find Aunt Ve, have lunch with Nick and Mimi, and then Missy and I would go home. She'd be thrilled.

As the event photographer snapped photos, I eyed his fancy camera and wondered what would show up on his display screen. Was he capturing a white starburst? Or was my true image showing up?

I couldn't quite ask without raising suspicions.

Dorothy moved in for her time with Missy, and the little dog bared her teeth and tried to nip her.

Missy had exceptional instincts.

"Aggressive temperament," Dorothy said, *tsk*ing as she marked something on her clipboard.

It required all I had in me not to snap that it took one to know one.

Dorothy brought out the worst in me.

I smiled tightly and tried my best to ignore her.

"Come, now, Dorothy," Godfrey said, sliding an arm

around her shoulders. "I believe a short break is in order. I know I'm in need of a cocktail."

"A great idea, Godfrey," she agreed. "One of your few."

"Don't make me close your tab at the shop, honey."

Her eyes flared with panic. "My apologies." Patting her pale blond bob, she gave me a finger wave and allowed Godfrey to lead her toward the staircase. Her stilettos clacked with each step she took.

I caught sight of Nick, Mimi, and Higgins headed this way to meet up for our lunch date, and I couldn't help sighing a little. Just looking at them did my heart good.

Nick threw me a smile as they stopped to let a couple with three young boys admire Higgins.

Perhaps Nick and Mimi could help track down Ve before we had lunch together. . . .

With her blue eyes shining, Reggie stepped up to me and said, "Don't mind Dorothy, my dear. We all know Missy has a sweet temperament. Dorothy's just . . ." She seemed to be searching for a word and finally said, "Dorothy's just Dorothy." She slipped her hand in her pocket. A second later, a treat appeared between her fingertips. Missy happily gobbled it up, and with a pat to Missy's head, Reggie was gone, hurrying along to catch up to the rest of the group.

Letting out a long sigh, I set Missy back into her pen. It was a good thing this performance had been only a ruse for the other contestants or Missy would undoubtedly have the lowest scores here, thanks to Dorothy's and Ivy's contempt for me.

I glanced again at Natasha, expecting to find her delighted with the scene she'd just witnessed. Instead her Cheshire Cat smile had vanished. A deep flush reddened the skin on her face and she had one hand pressed to her chest. The other hand was trying to set the coffee cup on the table. It slipped out of her hand and hit the floor, sending liquid streaming under her display table.

Her frightened gaze rose to meet mine, and she opened her mouth, but no words came out.

"Are you okay?" I asked, rushing over to her. "Natasha?"

Her eyes fluttered closed, and she crumpled to the floor, her white gown billowing around her like a cloud. Her body began jerking—it looked like a seizure. Dropping to my knees, I yelled for help and turned Natasha's face toward me, trying to keep it steady.

Her body stilled, but her skin was quickly turning an unhealthy shade of bright red.

Next thing I knew, Nick was at my side. "What happened?"

"I don't know," I said. "A minute ago she was fine. . . ."

He checked her pulse, then immediately started CPR. "She's not breathing."

A crowd edged in around us. A worried Baz. A stony Vivienne. Glinda, Mimi. Reggie and Ivy had returned— probably to see what the hubbub was about.

As Nick worked, it seemed to me that the room around us went deathly quiet, watching, waiting.

I scooted back, out of his way, and joined the crowd. I slid a look at Ivy Teasdale.

The color had drained from her already fair skinned face, and she had one hand clapped over her mouth as if holding in a scream.

This was exactly what she'd been trying to avoid. Another "accident."

With one twist.

The prime suspect in those incidents had just become a potential victim.

Chapter Six

"She was poisoned."

After her bold statement, Harper stuck a tortilla chip into a bowl of salsa, loaded it up, and quickly stuffed it into her mouth before even a molecule could drip from its edges onto the coffee table.

How Harper could eat at a time like this was beyond me. Even though it had been hours since Natasha collapsed at my feet, my stomach remained twisted in knots.

Painful, painful knots.

We'd stuck around at the Wisp until the police cleared everyone from the building. It had been a chaotic exodus as dogs barked, cats hissed, and Cookie, a year-old Nigerian dwarf goat, broke loose from her leash and bounded off across the village green. She was still missing.

Ve had been found, but there hadn't been time to ask her about the photographs, and though still important, the situation paled when compared to Natasha's death.

I just hoped my aunt had some insight on the whole photo situation, or I was going to have to trek into the woods to ask the Elder. I wasn't sure I'd actually receive an answer from her, but I could at least try. She was a big believer in letting me figure out Craft quirks myself.

Harper had dropped Pie off at home, and then helped Mimi and me transport our menagerie to As You Wish. We were awaiting word from Nick, but so far we hadn't heard a peep and were filling the time with speculation on what had happened to Natasha.

Staring at my sister in awe, Mimi held a chip suspended midair between the salsa bowl and where she sat on the floor next to the coffee table in Aunt Ve's family room. "You really think so? Poison?"

Higgins rested on the floor next to her, his head on his paws. His dark woebegone eyes held a silent plea that the chip would miraculously fall from Mimi's hand straight into his mouth. Enormous drool droplets hung like elastic stalactites from his lower jaw as he licked his lips in anticipation. He let out a crestfallen sigh when Mimi ate the chip in one bite.

Missy was giving me the cold shoulder, preferring to stay outside rather than in, which was fine with me as long as she remained in the yard. So far so good. The last time I'd checked, the furry little Houdini had been napping on the back step.

Aunt Ve's Himalayan, Tilda, regarded us all with thinly veiled derision from her perch at the end of the mantel. She was, as usual, content to watch us from afar.

"A fast-acting poison," Harper elaborated, simultaneously nodding while wiping her kewpie-doll lips with the back of her hand. "Someone probably slipped something into her coffee. My guess is sodium cyanide or potassium cyanide." She shrugged. "*Something* cyanide.

A capsule of it would have easily dissolved in the liquid. Bing, bang, boom . . . no one would be the wiser until she collapsed."

Long spiral curls of dark brown hair cascaded over Mimi's shoulders as she leaned back against a pillow she'd pulled down from the love seat. "Wow. Poison. Unbelievable."

"The red tint to Natasha's face is a dead giveaway that it was cyanide." Wincing, Harper added, "Bad choice of words, considering."

Natasha was dead. The paramedics who'd arrived at the Wisp hadn't even bothered to transport her to the hospital. Instead they'd called the medical examiner's office, who as far as I knew were still at the function hall.

Along with Nick, who as chief of police was heading the investigation into Natasha's untimely death.

Aunt Ve was dealing with the press. For the sake of the village's reputation, she as village council chairwoman was trying her best to downplay the incident.

Which was incredibly hard to do, seeing as how a *woman was dead*.

A PR catastrophe, Ivy had warned. Her words were proving portentous.

I wanted to argue with what Harper was saying about the cyanide, truly I did. It was such a preposterous notion that someone could be poisoned in the middle of a large crowded event.

And not just poisoned.

That someone could be *murdered*.

Because, after all, if someone had slipped Natasha cyanide, surely the intent was to kill her.

The more I thought about it, however, the more Harper's theory seemed entirely plausible.

What else could it have been but murder? Natasha had seemed perfectly healthy earlier in the day, espe-

cially when she'd been catting around with Baz Lucas.
She was young. Active. Her sudden death was highly
unusual, to say the least.

I didn't know much about cyanide at all, but I didn't
doubt Harper's knowledge of the poison. She was a forensics nut and had a steel-trap mind. If she suspected
cyanide, I had every reason to suspect it, too.

"Let's say you're right," I said to Harper as I drew my
feet up onto the sofa and tucked them beneath me. "Cyanide isn't exactly a street drug, so how would someone
even get hold of something like that?"

Distant hammering punctuated my sentence. The
construction crews were working overtime at my new
house to get the roof done before the next rainfall. As
late-afternoon sunshine filtered through the gauzy
curtains of Ve's family room, it gave the room a golden
glow. The space felt like Ve. Warm and inviting. Soft
and cozy. Fanciful and full of color and life. One could
get swallowed by the overstuffed sofa, dizzy from the
swirling patterns in the area rug, and lost for days reading all the books crammed onto built-in shelves.

"Online, of course," Harper said.

Well, of course.

"You can get anything online," she added, reaching
for another chip. "From bootleg laundry detergent to
tiny turtles, and everything in between. Including poison. The black market is a profitable one."

"Tiny turtles?" Mimi echoed, her chocolate brown
eyes narrowed with skepticism. "Really?"

"If their shell is less than four inches, they're banned
by the FDA because of salmonella risks." Sunbeams set
Harper's face aglow as she talked. "But that doesn't stop
people from selling them."

I was again impressed with Harper's steel-trap mind.
Tiny turtles. Who knew?

"Did Natasha have any enemies?" Mimi asked, turning her full attention on me.

It was times like these that I had to remind myself that Mimi was just thirteen years old. Barely a teenager. Sometimes she seemed much older and wiser than her years.

At her question, I immediately thought of Vivienne Lucas.

If I had just learned my husband had been carrying on with Natasha, I'd be mad enough to kill her. And him. But the timing was off. Glinda had confirmed to me that she told Vivienne of what we had seen in the hallway between Baz and Natasha only moments before the woman collapsed. I found it highly unlikely that Vivienne had been carrying around cyanide with her for just-in-case scenarios.

No. If Natasha had been poisoned, someone had planned it. Meticulously.

But who?

And why?

Just thinking about someone gliding around the showroom floor with poison in their pocket gave me the willies. It was so . . . menacing.

Evil.

"I'm not sure," I finally said.

Mimi shoved a spiral of hair over her shoulder, but the curl immediately sprang loose again. "Does she have family here?"

"Not that I know of," I said, pressing a throw pillow against my aching stomach. "But I didn't know her very well at all."

"Me neither," Harper chimed in. "Mrs. P and Pepe might know more about her."

"We have no business asking them about her," I said.

Mrs. P, whose real name was Eugenia Pennywhistle,

and Pepe were two of my favorites in the villages. It didn't matter a bit that they were mouse familiars—I counted them as dear friends. They were the closest the village had to town historians, which Harper knew perfectly well.

"Please?" she begged, grinning like a kid at Christmas.

She was seriously in the wrong line of work. I knew she loved the bookshop, but she ate, slept, breathed criminal justice and all its offshoots, especially forensics.

As much as I wanted to know what had happened to Natasha, too, I dashed Harper's hopes.

"No. Natasha was a mortal, so we have no business snooping around. Let Nick handle it."

If she had been a witch, as a Craft investigator I would have been obligated to check her background. It was my job to look into any criminal activities that might involve our heritage. Elder's orders. But as a mortal, I had no jurisdiction.

"Party pooper," Harper said. Then after another moment, she nodded to a fluffy black lump glued to my left side and added, "What are you going to do with her?"

Her.

I looked down.

Titania stared up at me, her amber eyes unblinking.

Earlier, I'd really had no other option than to take her home with me. The Wisp had been evacuated, and I couldn't very well leave her there.

Without her headdress and heavy jeweled collar, both of which I had removed the moment we walked through the back door, she was cuddlier than ever. I scratched her head. "I don't know. Wait until someone claims her, I guess. A distant relative, maybe. A neighbor?"

"I think she claimed you," Harper pointed out matter-of-factly.

"She does seem to like you," Mimi agreed.

It did, in fact, seem that way. Titania hadn't left my side since we left the Wisp.

If she was going to stay here for a bit, I'd need to get some supplies as soon as possible. Food, a new (lightweight) collar, a kitty litter box. The basic necessities, since I didn't think Tilda would take too kindly to sharing. I planned a visit to the Furry Toadstool as soon as it opened tomorrow morning to pick up what I needed.

I was making a mental shopping list when the sound of a rooster crowing echoed through the room, coming from the vicinity of the back door.

I knew that noise. It was Archie's version of a doorbell.

Before anyone could stand up, his muffled voice came through the door. "Darcy? Are you in there? Shake a leg! It's not safe out here for a bird like me!"

Chapter Seven

"I'll get him," Mimi said, jumping up.

"Not safe?" I looked at Harper. "What do you think he means by that?"

"I don't know, but he's definitely safer out there than in here with Higgins and Tilda," Harper said, making a good point.

Both animals tended to view Archie as a snack.

A moment later, Mimi was back. Archie flew behind her, dropping feathers as he floated along.

"I'm molting. Molting!" he exclaimed as he landed on the edge of the coffee table and began pacing.

Higgins surged to his feet. In his eyes, Archie was similar to one big chicken nugget.

"Not the drool," Archie cried in his most ardent voice as he stared at the enormous dog. "Anything but the drool. Shoo! Shoo!" He flapped his wings at Higgins.

Drool puddled on the table.

Harper snatched the chips out of the line of fire, snapped her fingers, and gave Higgins a stern "*Pzzzt. Down.*"

Obediently, he sat, his thick eyebrows twitching as he glanced between Harper and his potential dinner.

"Down," she said, dragging the word out. "All the way."

He plopped to the floor, sulking.

She was magic where he was concerned, a true dog whisperer.

As Tilda watched Archie from the mantel, he went back to pacing the table, his beady eyes frenzied, his colorful wings quivering. "Can this day get any worse? I ask you. Can it? No, no, it cannot," he said in his deep voice, answering his own question.

"What happened?" I asked. "Why do you feel unsafe?"

Archie was well-known for his theatrics, but I'd never seen him this agitated before. He was frantic.

"What happened, you ask?" He pivoted when he reached the far end of the table. "What happened, you ask? I'll—"

Harper jabbed a finger in his direction. "If you don't stop repeating yourself like that, I'm going to feed you to the dog."

He puffed out his colorful chest. His words oozing with pomposity, he said, "You would not dare."

She leaned in, her nose to his beak. "Bet me."

To prevent a fight, I said to Archie, "What's with the molting?"

He cleared his throat. "'Listen, this is embarrassing for me,'" he said in a stage whisper. "'This is hard to talk about.'"

Harper and Mimi groaned in unison. Neither enjoyed Archie's and my long-standing game of trying to stump each other with movie quotes. We, however, found it endlessly entertaining.

"The 40-Year-Old Virgin," I said, ignoring the peanut gallery. "Now spill."

"First," he said, pacing again, "I had to endure the exceeding humiliation of the Extravaganza. It wasn't enough for people passing by to touch me at every turn, to try to *pluck my feathers*," he stated emphatically while spreading his wings, which had bald spots, "but for some reason my normally effusive audience dwindled to a dribble this year. A dribble, I te—"

Harper coughed a warning.

Archie stomped a claw. "I'll tell you the reason! It's Lady Catherine's fault. An unoriginal canine pout usurping my soliloquies and a cappella melodies? It's an affront of the highest order. I'm outraged! Incensed! Aggrieved!"

Titania seemed entranced by Archie. She kept a steady watch on him, her gaze following his every move. Her interest didn't seem to be in a snack food kind of way, but simply out of curiosity. I rubbed her chin and wondered what she thought of being here with us, instead of home with Natasha where she belonged.

"Sounds to me your feathers are ruffled because you're jealous," Harper said, humor etching her tone.

"Jealous!" Archie huffed indignantly. "I beg to differ. I'm merely . . ." He trailed off.

"Jealous?" Mimi supplied, giggling.

He ignored them and said, "Never any of you mind that overhyped glowering pooch, Lady Catherine. She is but a bottom feeder in my pool of distress."

"For the love," Harper murmured.

Archie's gaze flitted between us as he waited patiently for someone—anyone—to ask for clarification of his dismay.

"Go on," I finally said, playing his game. Otherwise, I feared he'd pace the coffee table all day long.

Archie went back to pacing, and I braced myself for his forthcoming explanation. I expected to hear some sort of frivolous quibble like an insult to his plumage or some such. He'd been distraught by much less in the past.

Clearing his throat, he said, "During the anarchy of the Wisp's evacuation, someone knocked Terry down. In the ensuing confusion, a sack was thrown over my head, and the marauder scurried off with me." His voice rose to a fever pitch. "I was stolen!"

Sitting straight, Mimi said, "Is Terry okay?"

"*He's* fine," Archie assured her. "I, however, am beside myself. If not for my quick thinking, who knows where I'd be now?"

"On the back of a milk carton, no doubt," Harper quipped.

Archie threw her a withering look. He could give Lady Catherine a run for her money. "Hardy-har-har."

"What did you do?" Mimi asked. "How'd you get away?"

Archie lit up. "I mimicked a police siren. The thief dropped the bag and skedaddled quicker than you can say 'do not pass go.'"

"And you don't have any idea who it was?" I asked.

"Not a clue. Some ne'er-do-well who probably visited with me at the Extravaganza and was impressed with my charming personality." He preened. "The coward was long gone by the time I made my way out of the sack. Terry is currently at the police station filing a report."

I imagined that report wouldn't garner much attention in light of Natasha's death.

Archie said, "Now, as much as I'd love to linger and share every last detail of my escapade, I must bid you all adieu. To the woods, I go. It is imperative I inform the Elder of this disturbing episode."

It was just like Archie to drop a bombshell and take off.

"Tell her we say hi," Harper said, not meaning a word of it.

Harper wanted little to do with the Elder . . . or Wish-craft. Even though we'd been here a year, she hadn't quite accepted her role as a witch.

Mimi blanched. "Just Harper and Darcy say hi. Leave me out of it. She scares me."

Truthfully, she used to terrify me, too. But now . . .

Now I was more curious about her than fearful. Mostly. "Just Harper," I said.

Archie shook his head and mumbled under his breath. Mimi saw him out, and then dropped a handful of bright red feathers on the table when she returned. I picked one up.

A potential murder. An attempted birdnapping.

It had been a really strange day.

The front bell rang, and we all looked in that direction.

"I'll get this one," I said, standing and stretching. Usually, only clients used the front door—friends used the back door. "I can't imagine who it is; I'm not expecting anyone."

Harper stuck another chip into the salsa. "It's probably the runaway goat. She heard the news that Titania is staying here and wants some chin scratching, too. You know how fast gossip spreads through this village."

Laughing, I said, "At this point, it wouldn't surprise me."

As I walked away, Titania shadowed me, keeping close to my heels. When I was halfway down the hallway, I heard Mimi say to Harper, "Hey, Harper, is it wrong that I now kind of want a tiny turtle?"

"Yes," I heard Harper say. "Yes, it is."

I was still smiling as I pulled open the door. At the sight of my visitor, however, my humor faded. Unfortunately, it wasn't the goat.

"I need your help, Darcy."

Chapter Eight

"You fired me, remember?" I said to Ivy Teasdale.

I kept my body angled slightly in order to block the doorway. Not so Ivy couldn't see in—but so Titania wouldn't slip out. The village didn't need another lost pet to contend with.

"I know I did." Ivy's tight topknot had fallen out, and she ran a hand through her disheveled hair, the pink-tipped ends lifting in the breeze. "And I'm sorry about that. Truly I am. I lost my temper when you couldn't be found at the Extravaganza, and I let my anger get the best of me." Lifting her shoulders in a gentle shrug, she expelled a deep breath and looked me dead in the eye with a sincere expression. "I know I'm asking a lot of you, but can I have just a minute of your time?"

Just say no. Just. Say. No.

"One minute only," I said, giving in. I yelled inside to Harper and Mimi that I'd be right back, and I nudged

Titania backward with my foot before slipping outside
and closing the door behind me.

The sweet scent of roses permeated the air as I sat
on the top porch step. I had no shoes on, and the warmth
of the sun-drenched wooden planks radiated through
the sensitive skin on the soles of my bare feet.

If Ivy was insulted that I hadn't invited her into the
house, she didn't show it as she lowered herself next to
me. At some point during the day, she'd removed her
suit jacket and now wore only a sleeveless purple shell
for a top. Smoothing her black skirt, she kicked her long
legs out, resting her bright green sneakers on the lip of
the bottom step. She crossed her ankles and pressed her
knees together, ensuring that any tourists who happened
by wouldn't get a free peep show.

A steady stream of cars rolled into the village. It was
another busy June Saturday, and the death of a local
woman wasn't likely to stop the tourist trade. All of the
displaced Extravaganza contestants would also have to
stick around until the police allowed them to return to
the Wisp to collect their belongings. I could easily pick
out the displaced entrants with their stunned expres-
sions and tight grips on their pets' leashes or cages. A
makeshift staging area had been set up on the green,
and it looked as though it was turning into a lawn party
as someone started playing loud music. Dogs barked in
accompaniment.

"Was that Titania I saw in the doorway?" Ivy asked,
jerking a thumb over her shoulder.

On a few of Ivy's fingertips, her black fingernail polish was chipped along the edges as though she'd been
biting her nails. After the stress of the day, I was surprised they hadn't been bitten to the quick. With a slump
to her shoulders, she didn't seem as tightly strung as she
had been yesterday, which was most likely a result of
today's events.

It was hard to remain uptight when all hell was breaking loose around you.

"It was Titania," I confirmed.

I glanced across the street. A small search party led by Angela Curtis, Harmony's life partner, traversed the green calling Cookie's name. I hoped they found the little goat soon. Harmony and Angela had had her only a couple of months, and I knew they'd grown attached. The village was packed with tourists today, so it was entirely likely someone had seen Cookie out and about. "I couldn't just leave Titania in the evacuated building, and I don't know if Natasha has any relatives around who can take her cat. Do you know?"

"None come to mind. She was always one to keep her private life private. However, I did hear a rumor that she was dating Chip Goldman. Don't know if that's true, but if it is, you could check with him about taking Titania."

"I heard that rumor, too." Evan had seemed pretty certain of the relationship, but it wasn't my place to make an official confirmation. "Chip's allergic to cats, though, so I doubt he'll take her."

She nodded thoughtfully. "That explains his constant sniffling, watery eyes, and blinking. Why was he even there today? It's not exactly the best place for people with cat allergies."

"Apparently, Natasha is very persuasive. *Was*," I corrected absently.

"I can believe that." She picked cat hair from her skirt.

Wearing black had been an ill-advised decision. The skirt was covered in fur.

"You could check with him about Natasha's relatives," she said. "If they were close, he'd probably know. Or I can put her up for adoption through Fairytails."

Leaves rustled in a breeze that carried with it a hint of saltiness from the coast. The scent was one of my favorite things. I breathed it in, letting it soothe my rattled nerves. "Thanks, but I'll see what I can find out first."

Her eyes shimmered in the sunlight as she slid me a sideways glance. "When you talk to Chip, perhaps you can ask him if he had a reason to harm Natasha."

"What?"

Beads of sweat clung to her hairline as she twisted her body to face me. "It's why I'm here, Darcy. I want to hire you to find out what happened to Natasha."

"What?" I repeated, stunned.

I wasn't sure what I had expected to hear when I found Ivy on the doorstep, but it certainly hadn't been this.

"I know, I know. It seems crazy, especially after how horrible I was to you earlier, but I don't know where else to turn. I need to ensure that Natasha's death had absolutely nothing to do with the Extravaganza." She was wringing her hands, tears welling in her eyes. "All the TV cop shows always say that the love interest is the number-one suspect, right? A husband, a boyfriend . . . She wasn't married, so that leaves Chip."

"The number-one suspect?" I echoed. Her minute of my time was long up, but I made no move to go back inside. It sounded as though Ivy had jumped to the same conclusion that I had about Natasha's death not being from natural causes, but I wanted to hear her say it. I also wanted to know why she had made that leap. "What do you think happened to Natasha exactly?"

"I overheard the medical examiner technicians whispering about poison. Seems they suspect cyanide was used. Someone killed her, Darcy."

Harper was bound to gloat.

"And you think Chip did it?" I asked. "Do you have any reason to think that other than he might have been seeing her?"

"No. I'm just desperately grasping at reasons that don't include the Extravaganza. I heard the rumors about them dating, and how she treated him horribly. Maybe he got fed up? Maybe she dumped him, and he wasn't happy about it? I don't know. All I know is love is a powerful motivator. It can make you do crazy things. Especially when it goes bad."

"It sounds like you're talking from experience." I waved a buzzing bee away from my face. The bee by-passed the climbing roses and landed on a daisy bush, making its way to an open bloom.

"Haven't we all been there?"

I knew I had. It had been three years since my marriage went down the tubes, and it had been rough getting over it.

Ivy was right about love being a motivator, and I knew something she didn't: Natasha had also been in a relationship with Baz.

The importance of that information was twofold. It gave Chip added motivation, and it meant that Baz should be considered a suspect as well.

If Chip had somehow learned of Natasha and Baz's relationship and was crushed by the deception, he might have plotted a perfect plan for revenge. Where better to poison Natasha than to do it in front of a thousand people, before going off on his lunch break while the poison took effect? It was the perfect alibi—he hadn't been anywhere near her when she died.

It was a theory to share with Nick.

Ivy deadheaded a drooping rose bloom and began plucking browned petals. "I know I'm grasping at straws, Darcy, but I'm desperate to make Natasha's death a passion crime rather than something that hits a little closer to home."

"Like?" I questioned.

"I thought for sure that Natasha had been behind

the accidents plaguing the show, but what if she wasn't? What if someone else was behind them, and Natasha was simply the next victim on the list? What if I hired you to watch the wrong person? The event can never recover from something like that."

"That's a lot of what-ifs."

"Yes, but they're all valid. The event *still* might not recover after what happened today. I'm going to have to refund everyone's entry fees, which, thank God, I had event insurance for. But there will be no Pawsitively Enchanted calendar . . . and that's a huge moneymaker. It'll be a big loss." She crushed a petal between two fingers. "I'm not even sure I'll have enough to pay the judges their usual honorariums, never mind all the other vendors."

I again wondered about her financial situation. As there was no way to recoup those calendar funds, would her bottom line be left in the red because of the failure of the event?

The coo of a mourning dove broke through the noise of the ambient barking and my churning thoughts. It was the first time I'd heard the sound in a couple of weeks. I shaded my eyes to look for the bird in the branches that overhung the walkway and along As You Wish's many gables. I didn't see it.

Ivy craned her neck, following my gaze. "What is it?"

"Thought I heard something." I shook my head. "It's nothing."

Or was it something big?

I didn't know. Not yet at least. I had to get another picture of that bird.

"And all your points are *not* valid," I said to Ivy, trying to refocus our conversation. "You had every reason to suspect Natasha. Maybe not the first year, but most certainly after the second. It makes no sense to suspect someone else when she and Titania continued to win."

Ivy dropped the rose and started picking at her fingernails, scraping the tops, and chipping off more black polish as she did so. She wasn't a nail biter after all—but this behavior seemed just as obsessive. *Flick, flick.* The sound made me want to grab her hands to keep them still.

"It does, however, make me wonder who didn't want to see her win again this year," I added.

"That would be everyone," she speculated. "The list is enormous. Natasha made no friends with her condescending and over-the-top personality."

That was sadly true. "Did you tell anyone else about your suspicions of Natasha sabotaging the Extravaganza?"

I was thinking of Marigold Coe. And Baz. If either suspected that it had been Natasha who caused them to withdraw from previous events, would they seek to give Natasha a taste of her own medicine?

Especially Baz. After all, he'd been the one who'd had food poisoning. Had he decided to adopt his own version of an eye for an eye? One poison for another? Had he become close to Natasha just to get rid of her?

"I've told no one," Ivy said. "I didn't want word to get around that someone might be undermining the event. And I still don't want that news to get out. Which is why I need you, Darcy. You know everything that's going on. I just need to know for sure that the Extravaganza is not involved."

A cloud shifted in front of the sun, suddenly casting the village in shadow. "What if it turns out that it is?"

Despite the warmth of the day, she rubbed at goose bumps that had formed on her arms. "I don't know. I honestly don't know. I need to plan ahead for damage control, and that will be easier with you investigating the case. Will you take the job back?"

I hesitated. "I'm not sure."

Just say no.

Just. Say. No.

I ignored the internal voice as I recalled Natasha's lifeless body on the floor of the Wisp.

She hadn't been the least bit likable, but I didn't think she'd deserved to die.

"Please, Darcy. You've proven time and again since you moved here that you're good at investigating. I'll pay you double."

A loud voice split the tense air around us. Angela Curtis yelled, "Stop! Cookie! Stop right now!"

Before I could even stand up, Cookie the dwarf goat raced past As You Wish and took a hard right, headed toward the Enchanted Woods. As she passed she'd been nothing but a tiny beige-and-white blur that leaped more than ran. Angela and her search party were hot on her heels, trotting by one by one like something out of an old-fashioned cartoon.

The skin between Ivy's eyebrows wrinkled as she frowned. "What was that about?"

"Cookie got loose during the evacuation of the Wisp. You didn't know?"

"No. I was inside that whole time with the police. Everyone was long gone before I left."

"Then did you know Archie was almost birdnapped as well?"

I didn't have to specify who Archie was. Everyone in the village knew the bird.

Her face drained of color. "He was what?"

"Someone knocked down Terry Goodwin during the evacuation and tried to steal Archie. Threw a bag over his head, but he managed to get away."

"Is he okay?"

"He seems fine. Just lost some feathers. Terry's at the police station filing a report."

"A police report?" she croaked.

I nodded.

She said nothing, only pressed her eyes closed and shook her head. I thought I heard her mumble something about "nightmare."

For her, it definitely was.

It was bad enough that a woman had been killed during the Extravaganza, but if the media caught wind about a potential petnapping, the event was going to go down in flames. And police reports were public. It was only a matter of time before word leaked out.

I heard another coo and whipped around. *Aha!* The mourning dove was sitting on the arch of the gate arbor, the lighting making the pink iridescent feathers on its chest glimmer.

Searching the pockets of my jeans, I realized I'd left my smartphone inside. I faced Ivy. "Do you have a cell phone? One with a camera?"

"Yes . . . ," she said hesitantly. "Why?"

"Can I borrow it?"

She reached into her skirt pocket and pulled out a cell. With a few swipes, she had the camera ready and held it out to me. I grabbed it and aimed the phone at the bird, tapping the screen to zoom in. I made sure my fingers were out of the way and held my breath. Just as I was about to click the button, the bird took to the air with a guttural coo. I snapped the shot as it flew off.

"Darcy?" Ivy asked. "What's going on? What's with the bird?"

I quickly checked the image. It was blurry, but it clearly showed the tail feathers of a startled mourning dove.

No bright starburst.

I let out a defeated sigh. I'd been so sure . . .

I handed the phone back. "Nothing. I've just been trying to get a picture of it for a while now. To paint it," I added so she wouldn't think I was a total nut job.

"Oh," she said, looking confused.

I stood up, tugged on my T-shirt.

She stood, too. "So? The job?"

The job. Figuring out what happened to Natasha.

In my mind's eye, I kept seeing Natasha's cherry red face . . . and felt duty-bound to figure out what had happened to her. "I'll do it," I said reluctantly.

Moisture flooded Ivy's eyes. "Thank you for helping me."

I neglected to tell her that I wasn't doing this for her.

I was doing it for myself, because there was a large part of me that felt guilty about not doing my job properly. If I had been watching Natasha at all times, her death might have been prevented.

Finding her killer wouldn't change the outcome of what had happened, but it would definitely help me sleep better at night.

Ivy and I made arrangements to keep in touch, and she strode off.

As I headed back to the front door, I glanced over my shoulder as she stormed down the street, taking the long way around the village so she didn't have to cross the green. I didn't blame her for avoiding the displaced Extravaganzers for whom she had no answers.

As I watched her go, a chill came over me, raising the hair on the back of my neck. I couldn't shake the feeling that I was going to regret taking this case.

Big-time.

Chapter Nine

An hour and a half after Ivy left, I was on my way to Chip Goldman's apartment with a couple of chatty accomplices in tow. With their help, I was hoping to uncover anything and everything I could about Natasha's on-and-off-again boyfriend.

I'd just left the Bewitching Boutique, where I'd recruited the help of Pepe and Mrs. P, who resided in the shop's walls. I'd filled them in about my mission, and they were happy to help in my investigation. Their duties were clear: While I spoke with Chip under the guise of finding a home for Titania, Pepe and Mrs. P would snoop through his apartment, looking for something that might identify him as a potential killer.

A big bottle of cyanide pills in his medicine cabinet would be nice.

"Your tail, *mon amour*. It is in my face, and it keeps knocking my glasses from my nose," Pepe said to Mrs. P.

His voice easily floated upward from the depths of my purse, and I smiled at his adorable French inflection.

"*My* tail? What of yours?" Mrs. P countered in her New England accent—she'd lived in and around the Boston area all her life.

Even as a mouse she reminded me of the comedienne Phyllis Diller. Between the voice, her boisterous laugh, and her spiky hairstyle, all the similarities were still there.

She added, "It is resting in a most inappropriate place, my darling."

His throaty guilty chuckle floated upward, and Mrs. P's exclamation of "You scoundrel!" followed it. Then she laughed her high-pitched cackle before a round of kissing noises reached my ears.

I stopped walking and peeked into my purse. "Would you two rather be alone?"

Inside an empty deep plastic butter container, which helped protect them from the flotsam inside my purse, were two mice, one brown, one white. One had been a familiar for more than two hundred years, the other six months only.

The chubby brown one, Pepe, held Mrs. P in a dip and was kissing her, a scene that reminded me of the iconic V-J Day Times Square photo of a sailor kissing a nurse. I smiled—I adored seeing them so happy.

My accomplices were also still considered newly-weds . . . of a sort. There had been no official wedding, but that was just a formality neither cared to pursue. For all intents and purposes, they were together till death did them part, which was going to be a very long time. Familiars were immortal until *they* opted to pass over.

At my question, Pepe set Mrs. P on her tiny white feet and straightened his red vest, making sure the three small gold buttons were perfectly aligned. He gave me a slight bow, which caused his round gold glasses to slide down his nose. "I beg your pardon, *mon amie*."

Mrs. P fluffed the spiky tuft of fur that stuck up between her big ears and smoothed her pink velour dress. "Don't you mind us none, doll face. Are we there yet?"

"Almost," I said. "Another half block."

"Take your time," Pepe said, his throaty chuckle punctuating the sentence.

Mrs. P fanned her face and pretended to swoon. He caught her in his arms and began to nuzzle.

As much as they might want me to linger, I had to hurry. Mimi and Harper would be expecting me back soon.

Half an hour ago, I had snuck out of the house under the pretense of heading to the Crone's Cupboard to scrounge something up for supper, leaving Mimi and Harper to babysit the animals, asking them to especially keep a close eye on Titania while I was gone. She'd had a traumatic day.

If I had told Mimi and Harper where I was really going, both would undoubtedly want to come with me, which was out of the question. Harper tended toward interrogation to source her information, while I was a bit more roundabout with my queries.

And Mimi shouldn't be anywhere near a potential murder suspect, no ifs, ands, or buts about it.

Instead of heading to the local grocer as I had told them I would, I stopped by the Bewitching Boutique, and now here I was, on my way to Chip's.

"Ahem." I coughed, interrupting them. "You'll have to work quickly when we get there. We don't have much time."

Mrs. P said, "We may be old, but we're nothing if not quick, doll. In and out. Lickety-split."

"Old?" Pepe reiterated. "I think not. Age is but merely a state of mind."

"Yes, yes," she reassured him, patting his hand while rolling her eyes at me.

Pepe didn't like admitting how old he was.

Across the street on the green, a beach ball bounced from one person to another, and dogs happily chased after it. Multiple grills had appeared along with several pop-up tents. Seemed to me that the crowd had grown, and I suspected that there were more than just Extravaganzers taking part in the fun.

Chip Goldman lived on the third floor of a four-story brownstone apartment building not far from the playhouse. *Please be home,* I chanted silently as I pushed the button next to his name on the directory posted in the vestibule of the building.

A voice crackled through the intercom. "Yeah?"

"Chip?" A video surveillance system mounted near the top of the door flashed my image back at me, and for a moment I was once again startled to see myself on the screen. What in the world was happening?

"Yeah?" he repeated.

"This is Darcy Merriweather. I came to talk to you about Titania. Uh, Natasha's cat? Do you have a minute?"

Silence.

I wondered if he had dismissed me. "Chip?"

There was a briefer stretch of silence before a buzzer sounded, and the entry door clicked unlocked.

I took that as an invitation to go on up. I pulled open the heavy wooden door and went inside. The scent of sautéed garlic, onions, and peppers permeated the stairway, reminding me that I still needed to figure out what to make for dinner tonight. Mimi and Harper were expecting me to bring something home.

I decided to worry about later and focused on what I was going to say to Chip.

It was easy enough to find his apartment, as there was only one door on the third floor. A dirty mountain bike with no kickstand leaned against the banister on the landing. No lock. Apparently, Chip Goldman was the trusting sort.

I knocked on the door, and a second later he pulled it open, wearing nothing but a towel around his waist and a deep frown.

"Just out of the shower," he said by way of explanation.

As if I hadn't been able to deduce that on my own, what with the towel and the damp hair. Evan would have been beside himself, as he had a crush on the man. "So I see."

Without the Egyptian headdress, I noted that Chip's hair was flaxen blond, even now, while wet. Dry, I'd bet it was closer to a pale blond, like Starla's. And he was tall. He towered over my five feet six. Amused, I realized he looked a bit like a Ken doll.

He sat in an angular armchair and motioned me toward a futon with a threadbare mattress cushion.

Grateful the futon wasn't currently being used as a bed, I reluctantly sat and immediately felt a cushion spring pinch my thigh. I shifted to my right and set my purse on the floor. I gave it a nudge with my heel, pushing it under the futon so Pepe and Mrs. P could climb out unseen.

"I'm sorry for your loss," I said. "Natasha—"

"I appreciate it." He abruptly stood, yanking up his slipping towel. He anchored it with a new knot and headed for the kitchen. "You want a drink? I got it all, from juice to vodka."

I thought about him possibly slipping a cyanide pill into a coffee cup and said, "No, thanks."

He pulled a plastic pitcher from the stainless steel fridge. The container was filled with what looked like green goo. Pouring some into a glass, he then wiped the counter, set the pitcher back in the fridge, turning it just so, and sat back down. His movements had been precise, no energy wasted.

Short tendrils of blond hair curled around his fore-head as he sipped the green slime.

"What is that stuff?" I asked, eyeing the glass.

"Kale smoothie. A little banana, some pineapple, and protein powder. You want to taste?"

I vehemently shook my head. No way, no how.

"What's this about Titania?" he asked, sitting again, one of his legs jiggling. "Is she with you?"

"Yes, she's at my house. Well, at As You Wish."

Spreading his knees, he leaned forward and rested his elbows on their tops. The towel slipped a bit, and I averted my gaze. He was just a cough away from show-ing me all his manly goods.

He kept glancing over my shoulder toward the bed-room at the back of the apartment, and I wondered if he'd heard my accomplices at work. I didn't hear any-thing, but I was out of place here. He'd know if some-thing didn't sound normal.

"I didn't like the cat much," he said, "but I hope she finds a good home."

"You didn't like Titania?"

He shrugged. "Not a big fan of cats."

If he hadn't been crossed off my list of candidates to adopt Titania because of his allergies, he certainly was now. She needed to be with someone who wanted her. "Because you're allergic?"

"Nah. Because they look at you all judgmental-like. I get enough judgment from when I go on auditions. I don't need any more of it."

I'd been at the receiving end of my fair share of feline snobbery, so I couldn't argue about that trait. But I thought about Titania's purring and wondered if he knew that he was missing out on a lot of kitty love by not giving her a chance.

I doubted he'd care.

"Do you go on many auditions?" I asked, looking

around. To call the place Spartan was putting it mildly. Other than the living room grouping—an uncomfortable-looking chair, uncomfortable futon, and glass coffee table—there was no other furniture to be seen, especially since I didn't count the gym equipment as furniture.

The machines filled the rest of the living and dining space. A treadmill, an elliptical, some sort of weight machine that looked as if it doubled as a torture device.

Movie posters plastered the wall. Everything from the original *King Kong* to *Maleficent*. There had to be hundreds that overlapped each other, giving the look that he had decorated with eclectic motion picture wallpaper.

"Yeah," he said. "Gotta earn a living. I do plays, commercials, and an occasional local movie. Once in a while, I model on the side. Pays the bills until I get my big break and can ditch this place for Beverly Hills. Gotta dream big, right? Now that"—he frowned—"Natasha's gone, I can't wait to get out of this village. She was the only reason I was sticking around. I just need the cash. Then I'm out of here."

I thought that he wasn't shooting for the stars with his dreams but the moon itself. Beverly Hills might as well be a million miles from the village. "How well does being in commercials pay?"

He gave a laugh, but there was no humor in it. "Not enough."

"Planning to rob a bank, then?"

With a small smile, he said, "You could say that."

I couldn't tell if he was serious, so I pushed on. "Acting is where you met Natasha, right? While doing a play together here in the village?"

Darkness swept across his face before he brushed it away with a quick swipe of his hand. "Yeah."

"How long ago was that?" I asked.

"Five years."

He sipped his drink, and I cringed at the green mustache left behind.

"Were you dating all that time?" I asked.

He glanced my way, sharp intelligence radiating in his eyes. He knew what I was doing, asking all these prying questions.

I'd keep that in mind.

"Off and on. Natasha didn't like to be tied down."

I heard a loud thump from the bedroom, and panic sluiced through me. What had Pepe and Mrs. P gotten into? If I said nothing, that might look suspicious, so I said as casually as I could muster, "What was that?"

Redness climbed Chip's neck. "What?"

"The thump?"

Shrugging, he said, "I didn't hear anything."

I wondered why he wasn't curious about the noise, but his disinterest was to my benefit. It definitely wouldn't do for him to go chasing after two rogue mice.

"Were you currently on?" I asked, picking up our conversation. "You and Natasha?"

"Off, but that didn't affect our friendship. We were tight. You're dating the police guy, right? Has he said anything about what happened to her?"

"I haven't heard a thing," I said truthfully.

He took another swallow of the goo. "It just doesn't make sense. She was healthy."

"I agree. It doesn't make sense." I hoped Pepe and Mrs. P were almost done.

"You think someone killed her?" he asked. "I think maybe someone did. Poisoned her or something. I heard she was drinking coffee when she collapsed."

Another thump came from the bedroom, but he didn't so much as blink at the noise.

Well, if he was going to ignore it, so was I.

Uncomfortable, I shifted again and was poked by another mattress spring. "I'm not sure. It's possible, I guess. Did she have any enemies?"

"True enemies? Nah. But a lot of people didn't like her. Her personality wasn't the easiest to deal with."

I knew that from personal experience. "Yet you've been friends for years. . . ."

"She's . . . addicting. I couldn't walk away, and trust me—I tried."

Huh. She didn't seem all that addicting to me. "I don't suppose you know if Natasha was currently dating someone else?"

Again, he zinged me with a sharp glance.

"Or if she has family around?" I quickly added. "I need to check with them about Titania."

"She was seeing someone, yeah."

Another thump.

My palms began to sweat.

"But I don't know who," he added, his cheeks reddening. "Just that the guy was dealing with a bunch of baggage with his other woman. It was driving Natasha crazy having to sneak around."

Baz. No doubt that his prenup could be considered baggage. I played dumb about her current boyfriend being *married*. "Other woman? They had an open relationship?"

"At first. They were getting pretty serious these last few weeks. She must have really liked him, because she stayed even though she hates baggage more than strings."

There was a hint of sadness in his voice as he spoke, and I had the feeling he cared for Natasha more than he let on. "Her family?"

"A sister. Alina. Lives down the Cape. Falmouth, I think."

"I'll check with her about the cat," I said. "But just in case she doesn't want Titania, does Natasha have any friends in the village who might want her?"

"Natasha was a lone wolf," he said, shaking his head.

Lone, except when it came to men. "Well, if you think of anyone, let me know, okay?"

"Yeah. Sure."

I felt a tug on the hem of my jeans—either Pepe or Mrs. P letting me know they had concluded their search. Thank goodness. I was ready to get out of here.

"I should go, then," I said, standing. I bent and grabbed my purse. "Thanks for talking with me."

He set his cup on the glass table and walked me out. "No problem."

As I reached the landing, he said, "Hey, Darcy?"

"Yeah?"

His face was flushed as he said, "You should keep Titania. I saw you with her earlier, petting her. She liked you, and she doesn't like a lot of people."

With that, he closed the door in my face.

As I quickly ran down the steps, something was nagging at me, but I couldn't quite put my finger on it. Something Chip had said, perhaps.

Breaking into a fast jog, I ducked around the corner into an alleyway next to the building and opened my purse.

"Doll!" Mrs. P said, looking peaked. Behind her white whiskers, a green tint colored fuzzy cheeks. "I'm a little motion sick after that run. I might hoik."

Pepe took a step away from her, but reached out his hand and patted her back from his safe distance.

"Sorry, sorry," I apologized. "I wanted to hear what you found as soon as possible. What on earth was going on in that bedroom?"

Pepe pumped his fist. "Warfare!"

"We were under attack." Mrs. P blinked her long

lashes. The green color was fading. "I almost got conked on the head with a shoe."

Pepe's face turned red, and he clenched his tiny fists. "I, of course, had to avenge my love, so I snuck up behind the barbarian and bit him on his ankle."

"My hero," Mrs. P crooned, sinking into a faux swoon.

Pepe caught her and planted a kiss on her puckered lips.

"Wait, wait," I said, my head spinning. "Who was it attacking you?"

Pepe set Mrs. P upright and twirled his whiskered mustache. "Have you not been paying attention, *ma chère*? It was the man hiding in Chip's bedroom."

Chapter Ten

"Man? What man?" I glanced around to ensure no one was nearby, eavesdropping. Fortunately, it was just us and the Dumpsters.

"It was that smooth talker, *Baz Lucas*." Mrs. P said his name as though he were the devil himself. "Just wait until I get my paws on him. Throw one of those clunky Birkenstocks at me, will he?"

"What in the world was Baz doing in Chip's bedroom?" I asked, trying to make sense of it.

"Eavesdropping on your conversation, by the looks of it," Pepe answered. "Had his ear pressed to the door right up until he spotted Eugenia dart under the bed. That's when he went after her with his shoe."

Although I couldn't help smiling at the thought of a mortal seeing Pepe in his little red vest and glasses, it would be very hard to explain. "Does he need a memory cleanse? I have some at home in my dresser. . . ."

"*Non. Ma chère*, this is not our first reconnaissance mission. We left our clothing in your handbag to roam about au naturel. Arouses less suspicion that way should we encounter a mortal."

"Always thinking ahead. Thank you."

He bowed, and I couldn't help thinking about why in the world Baz would be in Chip's bedroom.

One thing was for certain. "Chip had to know Baz was in there. It's why he didn't react when he heard the thumps." I laughed. "There I was, thinking it was you two, while he was thinking it was Baz. Neither of us wanted the other to investigate. Was Baz dressed?"

"Fully clothed, head to toe. Are you thinking the two of them . . . ?" Mrs. P wiggled her eyebrows.

"I don't know what to think. I have no reason to believe either is gay, but what do I know? Chip was in a towel. . . ."

I didn't know the connection between the two, but I realized that Chip had to have known Baz had been Natasha's current boyfriend. If Chip and Natasha were still close friends, she would have told him.

Startled, I jumped as a loud noise reverberated above my head, the clanging of footsteps on the fire escape. I ducked into the shadows of the Dumpsters and crouched down.

When I heard something crunch next to me, I nearly fell backward.

Cookie the dwarf goat was chomping on a cardboard cup, looking happy as a clam. Her cream and tan coat shone in the shadows of the alley as she blinked her golden eyes with their odd rectangular pupils at me. Her short tail wagged much like the way Missy's would when she was happy.

I petted her knobby head—she didn't have horns—and whispered, "Don't put that trash in your mouth."

"*Meehhh,*" she bleated, dropping the cup.

Curiously, she eyed Pepe and Mrs. P, giving them a good sniff.

Both mice immediately ducked back into my purse, and I heard the zipper as they locked up behind themselves.

I tried to grab Cookie's braided purple collar, but she quickly turned tail and hopped away, racing down the alley.

At her noisy retreat, the footstep sounds on the fire escape had stopped, and as soon as Cookie was gone, started again.

I peeked around the edge of the Dumpster.

Baz Lucas was rushing down the steel rungs as quickly as his hands and feet could move. Ten feet from the ground, he leaped, and landed with a loud groan not three feet from where I hid.

Sweat had soaked through his shirt, and panic was etched in his features from the droop of his eyebrows and the widening of his eyes to his slightly agape mouth. He scrambled to his feet and took off running, limping slightly as he did so. He glanced back only once, upward toward the third floor.

The look on his face was as though he'd seen a ghost.

My stomach began to churn with worry. Something was wrong. Very wrong.

I heard the zipper on my purse sliding, and a moment later, Mrs. P popped her head out. "What's going on, doll?"

"Baz Lucas just tore out of here like a man running for his life." I ran around to the front of the building and rang the buzzer for Chip's apartment.

No answer.

I grabbed my cell phone from my pocket and dialed Nick's number. When there was no answer, I left a panicked message.

As I debated what to do next, I kept thinking about Chip and his strange behavior. . . . Then it suddenly hit me what had been nagging at my subconscious.

His coloring.

After sipping on his green goo, he had steadily become more flushed. I'd thought it had been from his odd reaction to the bedroom thumps, but what if his response hadn't been an emotional flush at all?

What if it had been *poison* at work?

After all, Natasha had turned red before she collapsed.

Acting purely on instinct, I quickly dialed 9-1-1, then punched every buzzer on the directory until someone let me in. I took the steps to the third floor two at a time. Breathing hard, I knocked once on Chip's door before trying the handle. Unlocked, thank goodness.

All the way up the steps, I had wished and hoped I was wrong about my poison theory, but I soon saw that I hadn't been.

Still wearing only a towel, Chip was lying facedown on his living room floor, his face—his whole body—cherry red.

I dropped my purse and bent to check for a pulse.

Mrs. P crawled out of my bag, her hand clamped over her mouth, her cheeks puffed out. She wobbled to and fro, and I realized that barreling up here probably hadn't been good for her motion sickness issues.

"Is he alive?" Pepe asked, dashing over to stand next to me.

Under my fingertips, Chip's pulse beat slow and weak. "Barely," I said. "But I don't know for how long."

An hour later, I sat on the stone steps of the playhouse, waiting for Nick. He'd been inside Chip's apartment for nearly half an hour now, long after Chip had been airlifted to a city hospital. If there was any hope for him, he needed the best medicine had to offer, and Boston had it in spades.

Pepe and Mrs. P had headed home, and Archie had swooped by twice to get the scoop. He had stopped molting for the time being, but I figured one mention of the attempted birdnapping and his feathers would start dropping again.

The village green was nearly empty now, cleared out so the medical helicopter could land. When I called Harper soon after finding Chip to tell her that I'd be a while—and why—I hadn't been prepared for her to be so blithe about the situation.

"That's fine," she'd said. "Just keep us up-to-date as much as you can."

I'd stared at the phone. "What's wrong?"

"What do you mean, what's wrong?" She tried for a laugh, but it fell short. "Nothing's wrong."

"You're not pestering me for details. Something is most definitely wrong. Is Mimi okay?"

"Darcy," she said with a huff as a horn honked in the background, "Mimi is fine. I'm fine. Nothing is wrong. Nothing at all."

The more she protested, the less I believed it. "Where are you?"

"Outside."

"Outside where?"

"Where are *you*?" she asked suddenly.

And that's when I knew for absolute certain that she was hiding something. Harper resorted to talking in circles when cornered. "Harper, what's going on?"

"Not a thing. Look, I've got to go. Call when you have news. Bye!"

Whatever was going on with her was something to figure out later on. Right now I needed to focus on Chip . . .

And why someone wanted him dead.

I'd seen Nick only briefly in the chaos surrounding the horde of emergency personnel that had swarmed Chip's apartment. I gave him the truncated version of Baz's involvement, but needed to fill in the finer points when we had a little more time.

"Darcy!"

I shaded my eyes against the late-afternoon sun to see who was calling my name.

It was Starla. Hurrying along the sidewalk, she had her camera gripped tightly in hand, a backpack slung over one shoulder, and her blond ponytail flew behind her like a golden cape. She'd changed out of the dressy capri pants and blouse that she'd worn to the Extravaganza, and into a pair of short shorts and a tank top, both of which showed off her toned body.

I hadn't seen her since the evacuation when she was running around like a loon, snapping photos of the fracas.

It seemed like days ago, not hours.

Starla sat next to me on the step, dropping her backpack between her feet and carefully setting her camera next to her. "What in the world happened? Something about Chip Goldman being poisoned? I heard you broke down his apartment door like something out of a ninja movie. *Hi-yah!*" She karate-chopped the air.

"Village tall tales," I said, amazed at how fast those tales could grow. "I merely turned the knob. The door was unlocked."

She looked crestfallen. "I liked the ninja story better." Leaning in front of me, she looked toward Chip's apartment building, where red and blue strobe lights from village police cars pulsed against the exterior. "Is Chip dead? I've heard everything from rigor mortis had set in by the time you found him to he was up and walking around and planning his next audition, which by the way was to be a spokesman for one of those infomercial blenders that whip up his protein smoothies."

I wished that last part was true. "Villagers have good imaginations."

She nodded. "And plenty of time on their hands. So what's the truth?"

"Last I saw, Chip wasn't breathing on his own. The paramedics didn't look too hopeful." I told her all I knew, from the cyanide theory right on down to Baz Lucas looking as if he'd seen a ghost.

"Whoa," she said.

"I know. It's crazy." I ran a hand through my hair, pulling it forward over my shoulder.

"Do you think Baz did them both in? Natasha *and* Chip?" she clarified.

"I really don't know. Baz looked . . . more freaked-out than guilty."

"Well, I'd be freaked beyond belief if Chip collapsed in front of me."

"Yeah," I said. I knew all about how that felt. "But why didn't Baz call the cops? Why did he run?"

"Very good questions," she said. She swatted at a mosquito. "Do you think it's possible Chip poisoned himself, unable to live with the guilt of killing Natasha this afternoon? Was today one big *Romeo and Juliet* audition gone wrong? A twisted version of it, mind you . . . but that seems to fit what I hear of their relationship."

I thought about what Starla said, and then about the lackadaisical way Chip had sipped his smoothie. "He gave me no hint that he knew there was poison in his drink."

"He is a good actor."

"Not that good."

"Okay, well, what if Natasha poisoned his smoothie mix without his knowing, then poisoned herself at the Extravaganza? It's entirely possible she committed suicide, isn't it?"

I smiled at her.

"What?" she asked, confusion crinkling the corners of her eyes.

"A year ago would you ever have dreamed that you'd be casually having a conversation with a friend, tossing around murder theories?"

"Never in a million years," she said.

The breeze sent my hair flying, and I shoved it out of my face. "A lot has changed in the twelve months since I moved here."

She nudged me with her elbow. "It definitely has."

"Some good," I said.

"Some bad," she countered, and I had the feeling she was talking about the bad business surrounding the death of her ex-husband.

A year ago I'd never dreamed I'd have two best friends in Starla and Evan, and know talking animals who were practically family.

Then there was Nick and Mimi. My heart thumped crazily.

"Mostly good," I said, giving her hand a squeeze.

"Yes," she agreed with a smile. After a long minute, she added, "Now, about my suicide theory . . ."

It was my turn to laugh. "You're as bad as Harper."

She shrugged. "There are worse things."

That there were.

"Do I think Natasha committed suicide?" I fussed with the hem of my T-shirt. "I don't think so, for one simple reason. If she knew she was going to die, she would have eaten the pastry."

Starla faced me head-on. "You lost me."

"At the Extravaganza, Vivienne Lucas offered Natasha one of the Danish from her *Breakfast at Tiffany's* display. Evan made them, so you know they were delicious, right?"

Starla nodded. "Of course. They're magical."

"Exactly. Natasha turned it down flat, making a snide comment about a moment on the lips, forever on the hips. If she knew she was going to die later on, she wouldn't have cared about her hips."

"Damn," Starla muttered. "I wish she'd eaten the Danish."

My skin tingled at the wish, but because Starla was part Wishcrafter I didn't cast a spell. Wishcrafters couldn't grant each other's wishes. "Me, too."

Across the green, I spotted a woman slowly walking a dog, her attention squarely on the apartment building.

Vivienne Lucas.

Did she have any idea that her husband was somehow involved in what happened today?

Or was she going to be blindsided when the police showed up at her door?

Neither option was particularly appealing for her.

Once again, I felt a surge of sympathy for the woman.

"By the way, your hair is *très* chic," Starla said, adopting a French accent. "I like it."

"What do you mean?" Reaching up, I patted my head. I didn't feel anything different.

"What do you mean, what do I mean? Your hair. You had it colored this afternoon, right? I mean, it's not a look I would have chosen for myself, but I have to admit, you pull it off. Then again, you'd look good with a rainbow Mohawk."

My heart started beating fast. "Seriously, what do you mean? I've barely had time to breathe today, never mind going to the salon."

Her eyes widened, and she scrounged in her backpack and came up with a mirror. "Take a look."

I angled my body to get the best light in the mirror and took a peek. "Oh. My. God."

On the left side of my head, a thin streak of brilliant silver hair framed my face, from scalp to split end.

"Wha— How?" I stammered, still staring. The silver practically glowed like neon against my dark hair.

"I don't know," Starla said. "It wasn't there when I saw you earlier, so I just assumed you went to the Magic Wand."

Well, I *hadn't* gone to the salon.

Which left only one explanation, really.

Magic.

"Do you know of any spells that would cause this?" I asked.

Shaking her head, she said, "None off the top of my head." She cringed. "No pun intended."

"What happened to the whole 'do no harm' part of the Craft?" I said, talking fast. My heart was still pounding. I wasn't a vain person by any means, but it was a little disconcerting when your dark hair developed a streak of silver in the span of a few hours.

Starla shrugged. "I mean, it's not really harmful, is it? It looks good."

"I'm thirty-one and my hair is turning silver! Right now it's a narrow streak, but who knows if my whole head will be silver tomorrow?"

"Okay, okay. We'll figure this out," she said, talking low and slow as if she were some sort of negotiator in a hostage situation. "Ve might know. And if that fails, we'll send a note to the Elder. One way or the other we'll get this reversed."

"But who cast the spell? Who did this to me? And why? Do you think it was Glinda? Dorothy?"

She let out a half chuckle, half snort. "You know I think either is capable of a lot worse than turning your hair silver. I'm surprised their antics haven't turned your whole head gray yet."

Which was truly a very good point.

Then I thought of Harper and how suspiciously she'd been behaving when I called. Could she and Mimi have

been looking through spell books while I was away? Had
I somehow become an unintended victim of a Spellcraft-
ing lesson?

I handed the mirror back to Starla—I'd seen enough.
In the grand scheme of what else had transpired today,
my hair changing color was a drop in the bucket.

First the video of me, then Natasha's death, then
Chip's poisoning . . .

Yes, definitely a drop. Maybe even a globule.

Taking a deep breath, I tried not to think about it too
hard and willed Nick to hurry up. Right now all I wanted
to do was go home. But first, I wanted to know what
clues he'd found in Chip's apartment, if any.

Thinking of Glinda reminded me of the mysterious
video, and I eyed Starla's camera sitting next to her. "Did
you look at the pictures you took today at the Extravaganza?"

"I've been through every last one of them with a
fine-tooth comb. I know you were worried about something to do with Ve and Evan on camera, but didn't see
anything questionable. What had you worried?"

"They weren't visible in the pictures?"

"Visible? Like mortals, you mean?"

I nodded.

"No. Just their usual starbursts. Why?"

I held up a wait-a-sec finger and pulled my smartphone from my jean's pocket. A few swipes later, I had
framed us in a selfie shot.

"What're you doing? You know this isn't going to
turn out," she said, sounding like a mother chiding her
child.

"Say cheese!" I said loudly.

"Crazy lady!" she murmured between clenched teeth.

I captured the shot, pulled it up on the screen, and
handed my phone to her.

The image of two wild-eyed women grinning like

hyped-up horses stared back at us. On closer reflection, the angle of the selfie hadn't been the best. Who knew we had such long faces?

With a gasp, she dropped the phone, and it clattered down three stone steps before coming to a stop.

"Oh!" Starla jumped up to retrieve it. After pushing a few buttons, she let out a deep breath. "It's okay! Don't worry." Looking again at the picture, she said, "How? Why? Who . . . ?"

I shrugged.

"But why didn't Evan and Ve . . ."

I shrugged again.

"This is . . ." She trailed off, not finishing her sentence.

As she sat back down, she looked at me and gasped again, her hand flying up to cover her mouth. Her blue eyes had rounded with wonder.

"What now?" I asked, not sure I wanted to know.

I heard her swallow hard and then she reached into her backpack and pulled out the mirror once again. Wordlessly, she handed it over.

Bracing myself, I peeked at my reflection with one eye closed. The silver streak had widened. It was still thin, but there was definitely more silver hair than before.

"It . . . looks good," Starla said in her best cheerleading voice.

I pretended not to hear the waver in her tone. Looking at her, I opened my mouth to tell her it was okay, but the words failed to come out. My eyebrows shot upward.

"What?" she asked. "Why are you looking at me that way?"

I tapped my head where my silver streak started and handed her the mirror. She held it up and let out a guttural cry.

"What is *that*?" she shrieked.

"It's *très* chic," I said, echoing her earlier comment.

She glared at me. "Don't make me push you off these steps, Darcy Merriweather."

A thin strip of jet-black hair started at her part and swooped backward, blending with the rest of her blond hair wrapped in the ponytail.

"I look like a zebra!" she cried.

"A beautiful zebra."

She pressed her eyes closed, and I swore I heard her counting to ten under her breath.

I motioned for my phone, and she slammed it into my hand. Testing a theory, I held up my phone and snapped another picture of only myself.

"What are you doing?" Starla asked, confusion lacing her tone.

"Did my streak get wider?"

She leaned in close to my head. "I think it did. Yes, it definitely did."

I tucked my phone back in my pocket. "Well, now we know."

"Know what?"

"The two are linked. The ability to be seen in pictures, and the changes in our hair." It must have been why I hadn't noticed the streak before, after the photos at the Wisp. It had probably grown and widened with each captured image. The surveillance camera outside Baz's apartment had probably made the streak so visible.

Slowly Starla nodded.

"But we still don't know *why*," I added. "Or who's behind the spell."

She grabbed my hand and tugged me to my feet. "We have to go find Ve. She's bound to be done with the press by now."

"I can't leave yet—I need to wait for Nick."

"Darcy Merriweather, he knows where to find you."

I hesitated.

"A zebra!" she cried. "And you're starting to look like Lily Munster."

My jaw dropped. "You said it looked good."

"Come on already!" She grabbed her camera and her backpack and pulled me along the sidewalk.

I glanced over my shoulder, hoping to see Nick chasing after us.

But all I saw was Vivienne Lucas.

She'd moved closer to the apartment building, and Audrey was happily sniffing bushes along the path.

Again, I wondered how much she knew.

I hoped my initial instinct that she wasn't involved in Natasha's death proved true.

But I knew from experience my instincts had been wrong before.

Chapter Eleven

Almost to As You Wish, Starla and I came across Harper, who was standing behind Terry Goodwin's picket fence, in his front yard, poking around the bushes.

"Your hair," Harper said, eyeing my head critically. "What in the world happened to it?"

"Long story." I glanced at the shrubs. "What're you doing?"

My sister slowly blinked her owlish eyes. "What do you mean, what am I doing?"

"Out here." I swept my arms out. "In the bushes."

"In the bushes?" She shrugged.

Again with the talking in circles. I narrowed my eyes. "What's going on?"

"Can you two sort this out later?" Starla cut in. "I have a date tonight with Vince, and I'd rather not show up looking like a My Little Pony gone wrong."

Starla and mortal Vincent Paxton, owner of Lotions

and Potions, had been dating since last Halloween. I still had my doubts about Vince being a good choice for her, since he was a Seeker (a mortal who sought to become a Crafter), but he was slowly wearing down my defenses. He adored Starla. But if their relationship was to progress, they were going to face some pretty big obstacles.

Harper took a moment to study Starla's hair. "It's not a very good look for either of you."

Starla said, "Don't make me come over this fence."

"Don't shoot the messenger." Harper held up her hands in surrender. "Just being honest."

"Well, don't be. Starla's a little defensive about the hair thing right now," I explained.

"Me?" Starla protested. "You were the one going on about doing no harm."

"Yeah, yeah." I faced my sister. Her deflective ploy had worked well—for a moment. "I'll tell you about the hair if you tell me what you're doing out here, searching the bushes."

Harper looked positively pained. She hated when she was left out of the loop. "I, uh . . ."

Before she could say anything more, Mimi came trotting down Terry's driveway. "She's not in the backy—"

Her words abruptly stopped when she spotted Starla and me.

"Who's not back in the backyard?" I asked.

"Cookie!" Harper said quickly. "We're helping to look for Cookie. Harmony and Angela went past a little while ago while out searching, and we thought, hey, we'll help. We're very charitable that way."

I raised an eyebrow. Charitable wasn't the word I'd been thinking.

Deceptive was more like it.

"Right. Cookie. Silly goat." Mimi smiled wide and bright as she came to stand next to me. "Dudes, your hair!"

Starla groaned.

I was too exhausted from the day to even mind the "dudes" part of Mimi's sentence. She was, after all, thirteen. Even though she often seemed much older than her age, she occasionally threw around teenage lingo as if to remind us that she was still a little girl.

Especially when she knew she was doing something wrong.

Like lying.

I glanced toward As You Wish. "Where's Missy?"

"Missy's right in the side yard. Exactly where she's been since we got back from the Extravaganza," Harper said, throwing Mimi a stern look.

A warning.

I sidestepped along the sidewalk to be able to see for myself. Missy sat at the fence, her nose sticking through a picket slat as she kept an eye on us. Higgins stood next to her, so tall that his head rose above the fence. He was drooling on the rosebushes.

Archie wasn't in his cage, or I would have asked him what was going on. He had a loose beak when it came to village gossip.

Looking for another source, I glanced at Terry's house.

A front curtain swished closed. He'd been watching, as he usually did, but apparently he was keeping out of this.

My gaze skipped to my sister. She rocked on her heels and said, "How's Chip Goldman doing? What did Nick say? Was Chip poisoned like you thought?"

Ignoring her questions, I focused on Mimi. The wind had picked up, and it blew her dark spiral curls upward, swirling them like a mini tornado.

She gave me a tight toothy smile.

"What are you and Harper doing out here?" I asked her again.

Blinking her big brown eyes, she looked everywhere but at me. "Cookie," she mumbled.

"Cyanide poisoning can be reversed if caught in time," Harper went on, talking faster and faster. "It really depends on how big a dose Chip swallowed. The good thing is the doctors know they're dealing with cyanide. He's not some random patient who just collapsed. . . . That'll save time. And possibly his life, which is really your doing, Darcy. You saved his life! You're a hero!"

Harper was shoveling for all she was worth.

Starla crossed her arms. "We don't know that. Chip could be dead as a doornail right now."

Harper blew out a breath of defeat, then perked up again. "And isn't that a strange saying? Dead as a doornail? Where'd that even come from?"

Starla threw me a your-sister-has-gone-crazy look.

It was possibly true, but I didn't think so in this instance. She was trying to fast-talk her way out of an explanation.

Looking for Cookie, my foot.

I stepped toward Mimi, close to her face, forcing her to look at me. She was the weak link between her and my sister. "Mimi . . . ," I began, drawing out her name.

Abruptly, she grabbed my hands. "We're sorry! We didn't mean for it to happen! One minute we went to check on Missy outside because you know how she likes to run away, and—"

"Mimi!" Harper interrupted. *"Pzzzt!"*

That method apparently worked better on Saint Bernards than teenagers, because Mimi rambled on undeterred.

"—and the minute the door opened, Titania slipped right past us and was over the fence before we even got off the por—"

My jaw dropped. "You lost Titania? That's what this is all about?"

Harper coughed. "Technically, we didn't lose her. Technically, she ran away."

"*Technically*," I said, trying to keep calm, "it's the same thing. She's gone."

Harper shifted on her feet. "Then, yes, I suppose we lost her."

Poor Titania. First the trauma of her owner dying, now this. She wasn't even wearing a collar, because I'd taken off the jeweled one she'd worn at the Extravaganza. If someone found her, they wouldn't know who to call. What if that person took her to the pound? Or . . . kept her.

I had to make posters as soon as possible.

Mimi nodded. Fat teardrops filled her eyes. "We're sorry. We've been looking everywhere. Aunt Ve and Archie are helping. We wanted to find her before you got back, but . . . we couldn't."

I inhaled, exhaled. Getting angry wasn't going to help this situation at all, and it wasn't as though she'd been lost on purpose. How many times had I lost track of Missy? Accidents happened.

Putting my arm around Mimi, I said, "It's okay. Where have you looked?"

"We've been around the main village loop three times." Mimi pivoted and pointed in different directions. "Archie's been looking in the outer neighborhoods. Aunt Ve is checking closer to the playhouse. We thought if you saw her you wouldn't get suspicious."

"Hold up, now," Starla said, tapping her foot. "Does this mean Ve's not home?"

Harper abandoned the search of the hedges and walked over to us. "Nope. She should be back soon. We've been rendezvousing every half hour."

"How soon until the next check-in?" Starla asked.

Harper checked the time on her cell phone. "Ten minutes. Why?"

"The hair." I pointed to my silver stripe. "We're hoping Ve has answers."

"Hey, now that you know why Mimi and I are out here," Harper said, glancing between Starla and me, "you can tell us about your hairstyles. What's with the freaky streaks? It's not a good look. On either of you."

"I like it," Mimi murmured.

Harper said to her, "I guess it's nice. If you're a skunk."

"Darcy," Starla said sweetly, bumping me with her shoulder. "Why don't you *show* Harper what the streaks are all about?"

I glanced at my friend, knowing immediately what she was asking. I thought, given the circumstances, that it was a splendid idea and tossed out some bait. "Oh, I don't know. I don't think Harper would want to know about the spell. . . . You know how she feels about the Craft in general."

"Spell?" Mimi perked up. "What spell?"

Mimi loved spells. The girl would have made an excellent Spellcrafter, truthfully. Fortunately, she could still practice spells. Her mother, Melina, had left behind a diary of spells and other Craft secrets that kept Mimi endlessly occupied.

Curiosity blazed in Harper's eyes. "Yeah, what spell?"

I knew my sister well. Although Harper wanted little to do with the Craft, she couldn't stand being denied knowledge. I reeled her in.

"That's the thing," I said, trying to sound innocent. "We know nothing of the spell, so we're hoping Ve will. All we know is that we're now visible in pictures. Let me show you how it works." I pulled out my phone, pointed it at my sister, and snapped a few photos.

Harper grabbed the phone to look at the images. Amazement accented her words. "How is this even possible? This is incredible. Think of the possibilities. Drivers' licenses. Baby albums. Weddings. This opens a whole new world for us. Pictures on the mantel," she said on a sigh. "Christmas cards!"

I didn't point out that she didn't have a mantel in her apartment and that she didn't send Christmas cards. She was too happy with the images she was creating in her mind. The way she talked about baby albums and wedding photos made me wonder if she had those things weighing on her mind these days. Her boyfriend, Marcus, would be mighty happy to hear the sappy tone of her voice right now.

Suddenly, her eyebrows dipped low, she pressed her lips together, and her jaw slid to the right.

It was an expression I knew well—as I'd witnessed it many times during her upbringing. Harper hated to cry, so she screwed up her face every which way to prevent tears from falling.

"Harper?" I asked. "You okay?"

She waved off my concern. "It's just . . . Mom."

Ah. I understood. Harper had never seen our mother and had no memories to fall back on, as she had been born the day our mother died. As Wishcrafters, we had no photographs of those we loved. If this spell had been around long before now, all that would be different. It was one thing for Aunt Ve or me to describe what our mother looked like and another for Harper to see her image with her own eyes.

I was currently drawing a family portrait that I hoped would change all that. It wasn't a photo, of course, but it was as close to one as possible. I planned to give the drawing to Harper at Christmas, my gift to her of finally being able to see our mother. It wouldn't be the same as having a photo album that highlighted our mother's life, but I hoped she loved the portrait as much as I did. Or at the very least felt the love I'd put into creating it.

"Yeah," Mimi agreed. "Pictures of my mom would be nice."

Harper nodded, still staring at the phone.

We all stood in silence for a moment, silently mourning our lack of photographic family history. It was a small price to pay for the abilities we possessed, but it was still a price.

"Uh, Harper . . . ," Mimi said, ending our reverie as she gawked at Harper's head. "Your . . ."

Harper glanced up. "What?"

Reaching in her backpack for the mirror, Starla held it out. "Welcome to the freaky streak club."

Harper snatched the mirror out of Starla's hand and let out a noise that was halfway between a scream and a cry. A silver strand of hair skimmed her face, from scalp to razor-cut end. Her streak wasn't as dramatic as mine and Starla's simply because Harper's hair was shorter, but it was still very noticeable.

"Take a picture of me," Mimi exclaimed. "I want a streak!"

Smiling, I put my arm around her again. "Let's wait until we talk to Ve. Hopefully, she knows what's going on. I just want to make sure there aren't any other consequences to our pictures being taken."

Harper was still staring at herself in the mirror. She peeked over the top of it at me. "You knew this would happen when you took the picture, didn't you?" she accused.

"Yep," I said.

"How's that for honesty?" Starla added.

Harper glowered. "It stinks."

"Exactly," Starla said succinctly. "Exactly."

"Girls!" a voice shouted from down the block. "Yoo-hoo!"

We all turned in that direction.

"I found her!" Aunt Ve said triumphantly. A wiggling

Titania was sandwiched between Ve's arms and her mighty bosom.

I nearly sagged with relief. I hated thinking of the cat out there on her own.

I'd become attached.

Which wasn't a good thing. She wasn't mine to keep.

"She was lurking around Natasha's apartment building, poor thing," Ve said as she approached. Copper tendrils of hair were stuck to Ve's red cheeks, which were flushed from exertion. Her eye makeup was smudged, and she still wore the wrap dress she'd had on at the Extravaganza.

It had been a long day for everyone.

"Oh, and I need to call Harmony and Angela. I spotted Cookie trotting down Incantation Circle, all la-di-da and having the time of her life, but I couldn't grab her because my hands were full with this one." At that, she transferred Titania over to me. The cat looked into my eyes, rolled belly-up in my arms, and started purring.

Maybe I didn't even have to mention her to Natasha's sister. . . .

Ve dusted off her hands and took a good look at us all. "Before I forget, Darcy, I ran into Glinda Hansel, who asked me to tell you that she'll stop by tomorrow for the pen. She said you'd know what she meant." Ve paused a beat. "What's she mean, dear?"

I petted Titania's head. "The spy pen. I took some video with it that she wants to copy."

"Video of Natasha?" Ve asked, knowing why I had the spy pen in the first place.

I knew where I'd inherited my nosiness. "Mostly."

"Why does Glinda want footage of Natasha?" Harper asked.

"It's a long story," I said. "Too long to go into on an empty stomach. I'm hungry and tired and need to catch a second wind."

"Well then," Ve said. "Who's ready for dinner? I'm also starv—"

Suddenly, her gaze zipped between Starla, Harper, and me.

"What did . . ." Her voice trailed off. Again, she glanced between us as though not believing her eyes. Finally, she tapped the top of her head. "What did you three do to your hair?"

"*We* didn't do anything," Starla said, her tight tone hinting at the end of her patience.

"No?" Ve asked. "Then who did?"

"We're hoping *you* can tell us," I said.

"Me?" Ve said with shock. "Why me?"

"It has to do with this." Harper handed her my phone, which still had her picture on the screen.

Ve smiled at the image. "What a great pict— Oh. Oh dear. I was afraid something like this would happen. I mean, not your hair specifically, but that there would be a side effect."

"You know about the spell, Aunt Ve?" Mimi asked.

"I'm afraid I do." Ve handed the phone back to Harper. "I commissioned it."

Chapter Twelve

"It was time," Ve said. "Past time, actually. I commissioned the spell from Vivienne Lucas months ago, when I had the idea to run for village chairwoman. Being in the public eye is difficult enough without explaining why I'm unable to appear in photographs. It took Vivienne some time to create the spell as she had to wait for a certain moon cycle. She finally brought the prototype here yesterday, knowing I wanted it in time for the Extravaganza. It's picture-palooza at that event, and I needed to be prepared."

So that was why Vivienne had met with Ve yesterday.

"It is quite the complicated spell," Ve went on, bustling about the kitchen, prepping tea as we waited for our dinner order of pizza to be delivered. "The Lunumbra. The moon ghost spell."

Harper tipped her head. "Moon ghost?"

Crafters borrowed heavily from Latin roots and

words. Luna meant moon in Latin. Umbra was ghost, among other things.

Ve nodded. "Somehow the spell uses moonlight, or the lack of it in this case, to create our images. Ghostly images, if you will."

"That's so cool," Mimi said in whispered wonderment.

Moon ghost. The name gave me the willies.

Ve reached over to where I sat at the peninsula, touched my silver stripe of hair, and said, "Vivienne was worried the spell would need adjustments. It was probably a bad decision on my part to cast it before all the kinks had been sorted out, but when I tested the spell yesterday, it seemed to work without consequence on me. Now, however, as I look more closely at my hair, I see I have extra strands of silver around my face as well." Her eyes twinkled. "Blends right in with my other hair. I must make an appointment at the Magic Wand this week for a touch-up."

As Ve spoke, I listened closely, but I was also was counting.

One, two, three, four . . .

It was probably the tenth time I'd counted the animals in the room. Missy, Higgins, Titania, Tilda. All were present and accounted for.

For now.

Titania had managed to charm the uncharmable Tilda. The two cats sat together on the top step of the back staircase, and a few times I had caught Tilda grooming Titania when she thought no one was looking.

"Is it a global spell?" Mimi asked from her spot on the hardwood floor, where Missy appeared to be snoozing in her lap.

But she wasn't. Every once in a while I caught the little dog peeking out of one eye as though also doing her own head count. She seemed to have forgiven me for the day's upheaval, as she'd happily greeted me at the gate earlier.

"Heavens no, it's not global," Ve said. "Can you imagine the chaos that would create? The Elder would be inundated with panicked Wishcrafters. Unfortunately, I do not know all the inner workings of the spell as of yet. I was in a bit of a rush when Vivienne was here."

"Cool," Mimi said again as she rubbed Missy's ears.

Ve turned to pull the tea caddy from the top of the fridge. Over her shoulder, she added, "Darcy, I was going to tell you of the spell this morning, but you were up and out of the house before I came downstairs, and then it simply slipped my mind in the pandemonium of the day. No harm, no foul. Except for the hair, of course."

She glanced at me and winked. Her cheeks were pink, and her nose twitched.

On the surface, Ve's explanation made perfect sense. However, I sensed that for some reason she wasn't telling me everything. I narrowed my eyes at her and she quickly turned away.

What was she hiding? Did it have something to do with the conversation I'd overheard between her, the Elder, and the mystery woman yesterday morning?

The mystery woman had said, *"I don't need to remind you what's at risk here if—"*

"No," Ve said, cutting her off with a long sigh. *"You don't need to remind me. I know. We all know the risks."*

Yes. There was definitely more going on here than met the eye, but Ve seemed intent on keeping secrets.

"So, what are we supposed to do about our hair?" Starla asked. "How long does the spell last? Is there a way to fix my hair ASAP?"

Ve answered as she set a teakettle onto the stove top, "We're going to have to ask Vivienne Lucas. I'll give her a call to ask her to come over straightaway."

I bristled. "That may not be a good idea right now."

"Why not?" Harper asked.

"Yeah, why not? Dinner date," Starla singsonged. "How am I going to explain my hair to Vince?"

"I suggest you wear a hat. Vivienne has bigger problems than our hair right now," I said, filling them in on the Baz situation. "If they haven't already, the police are going to be knocking on her and Baz's door any minute."

"You don't say," Ve muttered. "I've known Baz a long time, and never would have suspected him of cheating. He is an ostentatious flirt, but cheating? I'm having a hard time believing it."

"Believe it," I said. "I saw it with my own eyes. And apparently Vivienne was suspicious, because she hired Glinda to catch him in the act." I told them how I'd bumped into Glinda at the Extravaganza and what she had shared with me. "There's a clause in Baz and Vivienne's prenup that will pay her a ton of money if he's caught cheating."

"How much is a ton?" Harper asked.

"Ten million."

Starla nearly fell off her stool. "You're joking."

"Nope. And hold on to your seat, because if Glinda can prove that Baz cheated, then Vivienne has promised Glinda a percentage of the prenup money as a bonus." I paused for dramatic effect—Archie would have been proud. *"Five hundred thousand dollars."*

"Holy moly," Ve said under her breath.

"I'm in the wrong business," Starla muttered.

"No wonder Glinda wants your spy pen," Mimi said. "To her it's a half-million-dollar video!"

"Darcy, did Glinda offer you a cut for sharing the footage?" Harper demanded to know.

I shook my head. "We didn't get a chance to talk about it, because that's when I saw my image on her video . . . and took off to find Ve."

Harper jabbed a finger at me. "Don't be all softhearted

about this. Hold out for some cold hard cash, Darcy. Don't give her the pen until you get a deal in writing."

I tried not to roll my eyes. I had no intention of asking Glinda to share her profits. She would have captured the same footage I had if I hadn't walked in when I did and blocked her camera. "Right now I can't give her the pen at all."

"Why's that, dear?" Ve asked.

"I don't have it." *One, two, three, four . . .* All pets accounted for. "It's sitting on my table at the Extravaganza."

"Do you know when you'll be able to get back in?" Starla asked.

"I haven't heard," I said. "I'm guessing it might be a while if Natasha's death is ruled a homicide."

"It will be," Harper said definitively.

Starla glanced at the wall clock. "I need to get going. Will someone call me if you figure out a fix for this hair in the next hour?"

"You'd look lovely in a wig," Ve said with a smile.

Starla groaned as she headed for the back door. "On the plus side, I can finally get a picture with Vince."

Ve said, "Not—" then abruptly cut herself off. "Never mind. Have a nice evening."

Starla pulled open the back door and let out a startled scream as Archie swooped past her head, flying into the kitchen.

"Perfect timing," he intoned once he landed on the edge of the counter.

Starla opened her mouth, then closed it again, shook her head, and walked out the door, closing it behind her with more force than necessary.

"Was it something I said?" Archie asked, looking around. He let out his own yip when he caught Higgins trying to sneak up on him.

"Pzzt!" Harper said, sliding off her stool to grab Hig-

gins' collar. "You're late for the rendezvous, Archie. We could have saved you some time looking, since Ve found Titania."

"My apologies. I was waylaid by a message from the Elder," he said. "So, the fugitive feline has been found?"

I pointed to the top of the steps, where Titania was sitting.

He squinted. "Do I spy Tilda grooming her? Has the world gone mad?"

"Yes and yes," I answered.

Higgins barked at Archie and smacked his lips, sending drool droplets spraying across the kitchen.

"He's probably ready for a walk." Mimi jumped up.

"More likely he wants a tasty snack," Harper said, humor lighting her eyes.

"Curse you," Archie said, shaking his wing at her.

Mimi laughed. "He already ate, so it's a good time to take him for a walk." Missy danced around her feet. "Missy, too."

"I'll go with you," Harper said. "Just to make sure neither of them tries to sneak off to join Cookie on the lam."

The kettle whistled as the foursome trooped out the back door, and Ve grabbed a teapot and set about letting the tea steep. "I'm going to go change out of this dress. Save any village gossip for my return."

As she headed upstairs, Archie asked, "Is Starla well? She seemed a trifle vexed."

"It's been a rough day around here for all of us," I said, putting it mildly.

"Indeed," he agreed, "but I daresay my bald spots are a sight better than whatever is going on with Harper's, Starla's, and your hairstyles."

"I will bring Higgins back in here and let him lick you like a Popsicle." I took some teacups from the cabinet and set them on the counter.

He blanched. "Your hair is lovely. Just lovely."

"That's what I thought you meant," I said.

"Any word from Nick about the . . . ?" He drew the tip of his wing across his throat.

"Not yet."

"I grow weary of waiting," he said on a deep sigh.

I cleared my throat. "'You've forgotten everything I taught you about a warrior's patience.'"

"*Thor*," he answered immediately. "Oh, that Chris Hemsworth, be still, my heart."

Checking the teapot, I said, "Did Terry file his report with the police?"

"He did, but there is little to be done about it at the moment, as all police attention is currently focused on Natasha and Chip. Which"—he coughed—"brings me to why I am here."

"Oh?"

"The message I received from the Elder earlier," he began, "was about you."

Adrenaline surged through me. "Me?"

"She requests your presence."

"When?" I asked, wondering how long I could stall.

"Now."

I'd been afraid he was going to say that.

Chapter Thirteen

The sky was shifting colors as the day slipped into evening. I left Archie behind at As You Wish to explain where I'd gotten off to, and headed into the Enchanted Woods. A little ways in, I slipped on my Craft cloak and pulled its hood over my head. Although older cloaks, like Aunt Ve's, had the ability to make Crafters invisible to mortals no matter the location, recently crafted cloaks like mine made me invisible to mortals only while in these woods, a protective measure to keep the Elder's meadow from being discovered.

The cloak was proving to be a useful deterrent against mosquitos as well. Twilight was thick with the insects, buzzing about.

Shadows lengthened the deeper I ventured into the woods, moving at a good clip, as I knew this route well. I'd taken this unmarked path to the Elder's meadow at least a dozen times in the past year, and the journey still set butterflies swirling in my stomach.

I hopped over a thick exposed root and thought back to my first visit with the Elder, not long after I first arrived in the village. I'd been scared to death because I'd broken a Wishcraft Law, and she'd done little to set my mind at ease.

But over the course of the last twelve months, our relationship had taken many turns. The Elder had gone from disciplinarian to teacher to boss to . . .

I wasn't exactly sure what we were at this point. Not quite friends—I mean, I didn't even know her name— but closer than acquaintances. I'd grown quite fond of her, but if I was being completely honest, being summoned to see her still induced fear. It felt a little like a child about to be chastised by her mother.

Vivid blues and orange lit the western horizon as clouds blew across the sky in the breezy evening. A chorus of forest noise obliterated my footfalls. Heat bugs, crickets, toads, and birds were all singing their nighttime songs.

I struggled to identify the coo of the mourning dove in the woodland concerto, but I couldn't quite. Although I'd captured the back end of the bird on film, I found I kept asking myself if I was certain it had been the bird who'd been hanging about As You Wish for months. I wanted—yearned—for a different ending to that story. Because, how fantastic was it to still be uncovering the wonders of this magical world? That a simple bird could be something so much more . . .

But the reality was that sometimes a bird was just a bird.

As I rounded a bend, the sounds of the forest faded into a quiet hum. A grassy clearing in the woods came into view, at the center of which sat a majestic weeping tree, its branches heavy with silvery green leaves that brushed the ground, creating a natural shelter that felt all at once welcoming and magical. The sunset gave the area a fiery glow, but it was nothing compared to how it came alive when the Elder was holding court.

"Hello?" I called out.

There was no answer. I lowered my hood and walked over to the weeping tree, running my hand along its ridged bark. There was a hollow in the trunk where Crafters could leave notes for the Elder to find, but it was currently empty. I looked upward and marveled at the beautiful way the branches arced outward, creating a leafy canopy.

"Hello?" I yelled again.

A moment later, a noise came from the woods, from the direction of the path where I'd just emerged. I spun around, my cape swinging out. The sound had been distinctly human: a sneeze.

I saw nothing, but hair rose on my arms as I searched the shadows looking for anyone lurking in the depths of the underbrush.

The trouble was, *everything* looked out of place. Every tree trunk looked like a person, every branch like an arm.

Another sneeze came from the direction of the path, followed quickly by a grunt, as though someone had tripped.

I ducked into the leafy shelter and hid behind the wide trunk of the Elder's tree. I quickly put my hood up again. My palms were damp as I drew my cloak tighter around me, and I was beyond grateful for the knowledge that I was unable to be seen by any mortals happening by.

But suddenly I wondered if I could be *heard*. Had someone heard me calling for the Elder? Panicked, I quickly tried to recall whether I'd actually used her name, and didn't think I had. Relieved, I carefully parted the canopy to peek out.

Had someone searching for Cookie wandered this

deep into the woods? It was possible, I supposed, but then I dismissed that notion. No one was calling Cookie's name.

Squinting, I spotted someone stumbling into the clearing, swatting at bugs. He was dressed in shorts and a T-shirt and had a ball cap pulled low as he glanced around. He sneezed again and wiped his nose with the back of his hand.

I sucked in a breath.

It was Baz Lucas.

As if mesmerized by what he was seeing, he walked toward the majestic tree, and my heartbeat kicked up a notch. What was he doing here?

I held my breath as he slipped into the leafy grotto where I hid, slowly walking in a circle around the tree's trunk. As he neared where I stood, he swatted at bugs and nearly grazed my arm. I silently willed him to go away.

He sneezed again, mumbling something about pollen.

I had to bite my tongue to hold back an instinctive "Bless you."

He took a moment to glance upward into the branches of the tree, then shuffled past me. I noticed he was wearing his Birkenstocks. Not exactly good footwear for a hike through the woods . . . so why was he out here?

With one last look around, he trotted across the meadow toward the path leading back to the village. He soon disappeared from view.

I let out a relieved breath and didn't dare move. Not until I was sure he was long gone. Closing my eyes, I slowly counted to one hundred. When I opened them again, the shadows had been chased from the meadow, which was now magically illuminated as though it was noon and not nearly seven at night. The meadow's grass was gone, and in its place stood thousands of colorful wildflowers.

"You're here," I said, edging away from the tree.

"I was with you all along, Darcy." The Elder's voice came from within the weeping tree. "Sit down."

A tree stump appeared before me, and I dutifully sat. "Do you know why Baz was here?"

"He'd been following you from the moment you stepped out of As You Wish. You must be more careful," she reprimanded me.

Heat flooded my cheeks. "I didn— I'm sorry. I'll be more careful. He didn't see me put on my cloak, did he?"

"No. You're very fortunate he didn't."

I was. The Craft had very strict rules about revealing ourselves to mortals, even accidentally. A slipup like that could have cost me my powers. Although I felt like slumping in dismay, I kept my shoulders back and my chin up.

"The question remains," she said. "Why was he following you? Was his intent benign? Or malicious?"

Why indeed? "He saw me at Chip's this afternoon, but he doesn't know I am the witness who reported seeing him climbing down the fire escape." Nick had told me he would keep that information under wraps as long as possible.

"I am fully aware that he is involved in today's tragedies. To what extent remains to be seen, which is why I've summoned you."

Her stern voice had become familiar to me over the years, but I yearned to hear her softer tones. It wasn't often I heard them at all, but when I did it was as though something magical happened within me that cast me under her spell. Her laugh, especially, filled me with emotion so tender it was nearly painful.

"You want me to investigate a mortal?"

"No. I want you to investigate the poisoning of a Crafter."

A gust of wind bent the wildflowers nearly in half,

and the rustle of the leaves on the weeping tree created pleasing melody, as if each branch was a chime.

I waited until the wind died down before I spoke again. "I thought Natasha was a mortal?"

"She was. I am speaking of Chip Goldman, a Vitacrafter."

"Chip? I had no idea." A Vitacrafter could read people's energy, and I wasn't sure if that was a benefit or a detriment to an actor.

"Many don't. He is much like your sister, Harper, in eschewing his heritage. That does not mean, however, that their heritage eschews them. We take care of our own. I have already sent Cherise Goodwin to pay him a visit at the hospital."

Curecrafter Cherise was a healing witch. If the poison Chip had ingested hadn't already proved fatal, she would have him on his feet in no time.

"Do you know who poisoned him?" I asked.

"No. That is where you come in. I am aware you are investigating Natasha's death at a request from Ivy Teasdale. It would be too much a stretch of the imagination to believe the two cases are not linked. What are your theories?"

"I have only two. One is that this is a messy love triangle proven fatal. The other is that somehow the Extravaganza played a role in the deaths. Someone who did not want Natasha to win once again."

"Who are your suspects?"

"Baz, of course. Vivienne, simply because Baz was cheating on her with Natasha. But she hadn't known about the affair until moments before Natasha died, so I'm doubtful of her involvement. I'd had Chip on the list until he almost died, since he loved Natasha. Natasha had plenty of enemies at the Extravaganza, but I still need to whittle down a list to talk to."

"It is a start," she said.

The wind kicked up again, and a strand of silver hair blew across my face. I took hold of it. "I don't suppose you know how to fix this?"

"I suggest visiting a Colorcrafter at the Magic Wand for a speedy solution. Otherwise, only time and an adjustment to the spell will truly remedy the situation."

An adjustment to the spell . . . That meant getting in touch with Vivienne. It was a good reason to go see her, slip in some questions about the case. But certainly not tonight. I added it to my morning's to-do list.

"Send me updates on the case via Archie," the Elder said. "Use caution in your investigation. Do not eat or drink anything you have not prepared yourself."

A chill swept over me at the thought that someone might try to poison me as well.

Then her voice softened as she added, "We do not want anything tragic happening to you."

My heart swelled. "Thank you."

"Good night, Darcy."

I made to stand up, then sat back down. "Elder?"

She sighed. "Yes?"

"Next week . . ." I trailed off.

"Yes?" she prompted.

"Next week, are you planning to reveal your true identity to me?" There was a long stretch of silence, and I wondered if she'd heard me. "Elder?"

When she finally answered, she used that soft tone of voice again. "Darcy, you already know who I am."

It took a moment for her words to register. "No, no, I don't."

"Yes," she said. "Yes, you do."

"No, I'm not kidding. I don't."

She let out a laugh, and that tender feeling zipped through my chest, squeezing my heart for all it was worth.

Gently she insisted, "You do."

Baffled, I sat there beginning to fume. How dare she tell me what I did or didn't know? Then I suddenly recalled another time she'd taught me a lesson about my heritage. It was when I had been dealing with a tricky situation regarding Mimi and Melina's diary . . . and how to hide the journal.

I eyed the tree. "Is this another *Wizard of Oz*–ish life lesson? An I've-had-the-power-all-along kind of thing?"

"Something like th—"

In a flash, the sky went dark, and I fell with a grunt to the grassy ground. Gone was the light, the flowers, the tree stump. As the wind blew, there were no enchanting chimes coming from the weeping branches.

What in the world had happened?

Leaning up on my elbows, I said, "Hello?"

My eyes slowly adjusted to the woods around me. Fireflies danced at the edge of the trees, bright sparks in the twilight.

Suddenly, a flash of movement came from the pathway that led to the village.

Baz again?

I had no time to hide beneath the tree, so I curled into a ball, pulling my cloak over me like a blanket and drawing its hood over my whole face.

A moment later, I heard the sound of approaching, cautious footsteps, and my heart hammered in my chest.

"Mehh."

I peeked out. Cookie blinked at me.

"You naughty little goat," I said to her.

"Mehh!"

I was about to reach out to grab her when I heard the voices. A search party of three with flashlights emerged into the clearing. Angela and Colleen Curtis, and Harmony Atchison. "There she is!"

Cookie looked over her shoulder, then tried to burrow under the folds of the cloak, trying to snuggle close to me.

"No," I whispered, pushing at her. "Go away."

"Where'd she go?" Colleen asked. "Cookie?"

With a start, I realized suddenly that my cloak had made Cookie invisible, too. I quickly shoved her away.

"Mehh!"

"There!" one shouted.

Angela. I recognized the voice.

Cookie looked in her direction, then at me.

"Go!" I whispered.

She took off running, bounding with her adorable leaps across the meadow.

I curled into a ball again, but kept an opening for my eyes so I could see what was going on.

"Cookie!" Angela shouted, taking off after her.

"I'm starting to hate that goat," Colleen Curtis, Angela's college-age daughter, moaned as she passed by where I hid in the grass.

"Colleen!" Harmony admonished. Then added, "Okay, me, too."

I lay on the ground until they were gone, then sat up. That had been a close call.

"Elder?" I called out in a loud whisper.

I was hoping she would come back, but after a few minutes of silence, I realized she too had gone.

I glanced up at the sky, at the twinkling stars, and thought about what she'd said.

Darcy, you already know who I am.

When I'd sought the Elder's help about Melina's diary, she didn't give it to me. Instead her words of wisdom made me realize I had the power to safely hide the journal all along.

The power, because I was a Crafter—and I'd been trying to tackle the problem like a mortal.

Was I subconsciously doing it again? Thinking like a mortal?

Perhaps. I was going to have to look at all I did know about the Elder through the eyes of a witch.

In doing so, I had to keep in mind that things were not always as they appeared.

And how that, in the Enchanted Village, impossible things were entirely possible.

People could vanish in a blink. Animals could talk. Wishes could come true.

Because this place was magical.

My heart full, I looked at weeping tree once again and smiled.

I knew I'd figure out the Elder's identity soon . . .

Because *I* was magical.

Chapter Fourteen

I'd slept fitfully and slipped on my running shoes just after sunrise. Sunday mornings were often the most peaceful in the village, and as I jogged around the green, it seemed that the trees were yawning in the breeze, waking up as well.

The flowers around the square—the ones that hadn't been decimated by Cookie—sparkled with dew.

It was obvious Harmony and Angela had not caught up with the tiny goat, and that she had been very busy during the night. It was easy to see where she'd visited, as there was a trail of chewed vegetation left behind. She'd even hit the roses and daisies in front of As You Wish, eating every bloom within her reach.

Normally, on such a beautiful morning I'd jog along the Enchanted Trail, a pathway that looped around the village and darted in and out of the Enchanted Woods. However, there were some isolated stretches along that route I wanted to avoid until I knew why Baz Lucas had followed me to the Elder's meadow the night before.

At six in the morning all the shops along the green were closed up tight, and villagers were scarce. I'd come across more than a few unfamiliar faces out walking their dogs, and I assumed they were Extravaganza exiles waiting for the okay to gather their belongings from the Wisp.

With any luck that news would come today. People had to get back to their homes, their lives, their jobs. In the wake of another possible delay, I feared any compassion and humanity for what had happened to Natasha would go out the window and hostilities would rise.

The windows in the apartment above the bookshop were still dark, and I hoped Harper had slept better than I had, though I doubted it. When I returned last night to As You Wish after my trip to see the Elder, Harper had become obsessed with the idea that we knew the Elder's identity already. She had started a list of every female witch we knew right then and there.

The scent of vanilla hung heavily in the air, and I glanced over at the Gingerbread Shack. A dim light glowed from the back of the shop, and I easily imagined Evan working his magic on his miniature confections.

I debated whether to pop in to say hi, but decided against it. The whole point of this early run was to get out here to clear my thoughts. I'd tossed and turned thinking about Natasha, Chip, and the Elder.

My ponytail thumped against my shoulders as I jogged. The stripe hadn't changed at all overnight, and when I'd taken another picture of myself to see if the spell had worn off, I only added more silver to my hair. The spell was still very much in effect.

"Darcy! Grab him!"

A shout startled me out of my reverie, and as I turned

toward the sound of the voice, I let out a shriek. A big bundle of golden fur barreled toward me at what seemed like warp speed.

Clarence.

There was absolutely no need for me to grab him, because once he'd spotted me, he altered his course for a direct collision. With his gangly long legs, he leaped at me, and I caught him but tumbled backward, landing on the soft grass. He commenced to lick my face, and I couldn't help laughing at his exuberance.

Glinda finally caught up to us and clipped a leash onto his collar.

He kept slurping, bathing my ear, and I laughed so hard that I could barely breathe.

By the time Glinda pulled him away and got him to sit, she was laughing, too.

"Sorry about that," she said, offering me a hand up.

Glancing at her hand, I wondered if she was planning to yank it away from me at the last minute, à la Lucy and Charlie and that football in the Peanuts cartoon.

Taking a deep breath, I decided that trust had to start somewhere.

Internally bracing myself, I slipped my hand in hers, and she pulled me up.

If she had any clue of the corner we'd just turned in our relationship, she didn't show it.

"I opened the front door to get the Sunday paper, and Clarence was out like a shot," she said, patting his head.

Her story explained her outfit. A short terry cloth robe and sneakers. Her blond hair was pulled back in a messy bun, and she wore no makeup, which revealed pale blond lashes and dark circles beneath her eyes.

Another person who hadn't slept well. "Sorry he jumped at you that way," she added. "He starts obedience classes next week."

Clarence's bushy tail thumped the ground as if he was proud of his brief blast of freedom. He was just shy of a year old.

"It's okay." I noticed Clarence's nails had left scratch marks on my arms. They stung a bit, but not too bad. "I'm used to it with Higgins. And heaven help me, I think I'm becoming desensitized to dog saliva, too," I added, wiping my damp forearm on my shirt.

"Well, you'd have to adapt or go insane with all his drool. I'm surprised you don't tie a bib on him."

"Or on me."

She smiled again, and it made her eyes sparkle.

We'd come a long, long way in our relationship.

"Did Ve tell you I ran into her last night?" she asked.

"She did, but we have a problem with the pen."

Her eyebrows snapped downward, and the sparkle burst into flames. "What problem?"

"The pen is inside the Wisp, left behind in the evacuation. I don't know when we'll be able to get it, since the police have the place on lockdown."

She tipped her head back and groaned. "Nick hasn't given any hint of when the Wisp will reopen?"

"I haven't had the chance to ask him."

In fact, I hadn't seen him at all except for those brief few minutes outside Chip Goldman's apartment yesterday. He'd called last night to tell me that he was about to bring Baz in for questioning and asked if Mimi and Higgins could spend the night with me.

He'd been radio silent since.

"He's been a little busy," I added unnecessarily.

She tightened the sash on her robe. "I heard about Chip Goldman. Is he going to be okay?"

"Last I heard he was in a coma, but I know Cherise paid him a visit."

We both knew what that meant. He'd be either dead soon or completely cured. If he was too far gone, nothing

Cherise could do would bring him back. However, if he was still fighting, she was the perfect tag-team partner.

"Time will tell, I guess," Glinda said.

"How much do you know about Baz?" I asked, reaching out to rub Clarence's silky-soft ears.

"More than I want to know since I started working for Vivienne. Why?"

"Ivy hired me to prove Natasha's death had nothing to do with the Extravaganza. If you take out Natasha's ties to the event, she ran in a very small circle. We saw with our own eyes that she was close to Baz. Do you think he was capable of murder?"

Her right eyebrow went up. "You're thinking he . . ."

I shrugged. "Why not?"

"Why?"

"Love gone wrong? Love can make you do crazy things," I said, paraphrasing Ivy's comments to me yesterday. "Revenge?"

Clarence sniffed my sneakers. "Revenge for what?"

"There's a chance that Natasha might have been behind Baz getting food poisoning last year at the Extravaganza. If he found out . . ."

"There's a chance? Or she did it?"

"Right now? Leaning toward she did it."

"Whoa. Wait . . . was Marigold Coe's accident the year before that truly an accident?"

Glinda was many things, but dumb wasn't one of them. "Ivy said she heard Natasha was on the steps at the same time as Marigold's fall."

"Wow. That's why Ivy hired you this year, isn't it? To keep an eye on Natasha."

"Lot of good it did her. Ivy, not Natasha," I clarified. And before she could say something snarky about my job skills, I added, "Speaking with Marigold is on my to-do list. But until then, Baz seems a likelier suspect, considering his relationship with Natasha."

She nodded thoughtfully. "But it seems a stretch, doesn't it? That Baz would bide his time for eleven months, then woo Natasha just to kill her as payback for something that happened a year ago?"

"Well, when you put it that way . . ."

"Baz just isn't that patient," Glinda said. "Whoever killed Natasha had to have a long-term plan. Her death was calculated to the last detail. That's not Baz. He can barely match his clothes."

I recalled his outfits. It was true. "Then who? Vivienne? She is the scorned wife, after all."

"Not Vivienne," she said adamantly. "Don't even waste your time looking at her."

Which, of course, made me want to run a full background check as soon as I returned to As You Wish. "I'm not sure where that leaves me."

"It leaves you right where Ivy doesn't want you."

"At the Extravaganza," I supplied.

"Ivy's going to pop a vein if her event is somehow involved."

"Yeah," I said, because it was true.

Glinda hooked a thumb over her shoulder. "Look, I should get going before Liam wakes up and wonders where we are. You'll let me know about the pen?"

"I'll call."

She eyed me as though debating whether to believe me. After a moment, she nodded.

Apparently, I wasn't the only one with trust issues.

"Before I go, just one more thing," she said.

"What's that?"

"What happened to your hair?"

I groaned. "Spell gone wrong."

She laughed. "Been there, done that."

"Can I ask you something?" I asked.

"Sure, I guess."

"Do you know who the Elder is?"

Her eyes flared in surprise, but she shook her head. "No. Do you?"

"Not yet. Do you know anything about the Eldership? How the Elder is chosen? That kind of thing?"

Wrinkling her nose, she appeared as though debating what to tell me. Finally she said, "Not much. One thing I know for certain is that the Elder can embody all the Crafts and can change from one to another at will. She's Wishcrafter, Broomcrafter, Curecrafter, et cetera, at whim. She knows every Craft inside and out."

I tried to recall if I knew that, as it sounded familiar. If I had learned it in the past year, it had crawled off to a dusty corner of my brain. "Do you think she lives among us? That we see and speak to her regularly and just don't know her secret identity?"

"Why don't you ask her? She likes you."

"She won't tell me."

Glinda laughed. "Then that's all you should need to know. See ya, Darcy. Come on, Clarence."

Yes, it should have been all I needed to know, but it wasn't. There was something deep inside me telling me not to let this go. That her identity was important to me on a level I didn't quite understand. Whether I was acting on instincts or out of stupidity, I wasn't sure, but I was going to keep questioning until I had answers.

I watched Clarence and Glinda walk away, then decided it was time to head home to get a jump start on the day. As I pivoted and jogged across the green, I noticed a shadowy figure of a man sitting on a bench, openly staring at me, and I wondered how long he'd been there without me noticing.

Some detective I was turning out to be.

I picked up my pace, headed his way.

As I neared, he smiled and said, "I thought Glinda would never leave."

Chapter Fifteen

"How long have you been sitting here?" I asked.

"Just a couple of minutes." Nick stood up and pulled me into his arms in one smooth move.

I pushed back. "Save yourself. I'm sweaty and covered in Clarence's dog slobber."

"You're still you."

When he gently tugged me close to his chest once again, I nestled my head in the curve of his neck above the collar of his work shirt. He was in his uniform, khakis and a Polo shirt. His gun was in a holster at his hip along with his badge.

He pressed a tender kiss to my temple. "And I've missed you."

Even though it hadn't even been a full day since I'd last seen him, it had been too long. I'd missed our lively banter over dinner, sharing the colorful vignettes that made up our everyday lives. Missed feeling his heart beat under my cheek as we snuggled together to watch a movie. Missed our good-night kiss.

Missed him. "Same here."

I wrapped my arms around him and held on tight, enjoying the feel of his body next to mine. Enjoying simply being near him.

"Mimi doing okay?" he asked.

Noisy birdsong filled the air. Robins, blue jays, crows. No mourning doves.

"She's great. Last time I saw her, she and Higgins were sound asleep. I'm pretty sure both of them were drooling on the pillows."

He laughed. "Thanks for keeping her."

"You don't have to thank me. She's . . ." I struggled to find a word that adequately explained how I felt about her. Finally, I settled on " . . . family."

He caught my gaze and held it, and the loving look in his dark brown eyes nearly did me in.

"Did you get any sleep?" I asked, noting how blood-shot those eyes were.

"A few minutes at my desk."

We started walking toward As You Wish. "Any word from the medical examiner about Natasha?"

"A preliminary test indicated she died from cyanide poisoning, but it'll take two days to get results with full concentration levels. It'll be weeks before the official report will be ready."

Crossing the street, we were directly in front of my new place. I paused at the fence. "I imagine those concentrations had to be high to kill her so quickly."

The bungalow was a disaster area. A once-enormous load of lumber that had taken up most of the driveway was now only knee-high as the two-story addition off the back of the house had been framed last week. I glanced up and smiled at the way the roof replacement had come out. It had once looked like faded patchwork, but it was now solidly covered with brand-spanking-new Shaker-style shingles. I almost danced a little jig at the thought of no more leaks.

I'd been lucky with my renovation. The construction company owned by Cherise Goodwin's nephew, Hank Leduc, had a job that canceled at the last minute, so Hank and was able to start my reno right away. Commissions for structural plans had been fast-tracked and approved quickly by the county because Aunt Ve pulled a few strings for me.

It was as though the stars had aligned to make this renovation happen, or perhaps a little magic had been used.

Either way, I couldn't be happier with how fast construction was moving along. At this rate, I'd be able to move in much sooner than the estimated four months.

"Yeah, it was potent stuff. Her coffee cup tested positive for cyanide as well." Nick nodded to the house. "This place is really flying along."

"If you can afford it, it's handy to hire a magical construction company." Hank was a Crosser: half Manicrafter, half Numbercrafter. His fees, for which he earned every penny, were astronomical, but thanks to that trust fund left to me by my mother, the expenses were covered. "Cuts way back on typical delays."

"I'd say so." Nick fought a yawn. "If this was a mortal job site, you'd still be in the planning phase."

It was true. Sometimes being a witch had its benefits.

All right. Most of the time.

Except, perhaps, when one's hair turned silver.

"You want to go inside?" Nick asked.

"Maybe later. The key's at As You Wish." The weekend construction crew would be arriving soon, and I made a mental note to have some pastries and coffee sent over, which made me refocus on my conversation with Nick.

"Did Natasha's coffee cup, the one that had the poison in it, come from Baz and Vivienne's booth? It looked like one of theirs."

"It did."

"Did either one admit to giving the coffee to her?" It would have been so easy to tamper with the liquid at that point.

"No. Baz wasn't even there when Natasha picked up the coffee. Vivienne was, and though I haven't talked with her yet to verify, I ran into Evan, who had the booth next to the Lucases'. Evan saw Natasha fill the cup herself when she returned from her trip to the restroom, a destination that we know from you she never visited. It was only a ruse to meet up with Baz. She was making small talk with Vivienne the whole time, about the Extravaganza being such a wonderful place to spend time with old friends. Kind of tells you what kind of person Natasha was, doesn't it? That she'd go straight to Baz's wife, silently flaunting what she'd done."

I agreed. "It tells you everything."

"When we tested the carafe from the Lucases' table, it showed no signs of cyanide."

So the cyanide had made its way into Natasha's cup between the time she poured the coffee to when she drank it while watching Missy being judged. It was a small time frame. Perhaps fifteen minutes. "Could Vivienne have slipped something into the cup before Natasha left the booth?"

"Evan said no. Vivienne had kept her distance the whole time."

Couldn't say I blamed her.

Nick added, "There is the chance that she could have somehow slipped it in after that, however. According to Ivy, while the judges looked at Titania, Natasha's cup was left unattended for a few minutes while she held the cat."

"Does the Wisp have video surveillance?" It would make it so much easier to see who'd been near Natasha's booth during that time frame.

"Not inside the venue. Only outside."

A dead end.

We passed in front of Terry's house. The shades on all the windows were still pulled. Archie's cage was empty. He rarely slept outside, but after his near bird-napping, he was probably being extra careful by staying inside.

"Did you learn anything from your interview with Baz?" I asked, opening the side gate.

Nick paused in the front yard. "What happened to the flowers?"

"I'm assuming it was Cookie."

"Cookie?"

"Harmony and Angela's goat? She's on the lam and loving every minute of it."

"I feel so out of the loop." He closed the gate behind him and followed me to the porch swing.

"Did you hear about what happened to Archie?" I asked.

"That, I know about. How's he doing?"

"No harm done and he has a new dramatic story to tell, which probably makes his ordeal worth it. Any leads?"

"Nothing so far. It's odd that no one saw anything."

Nick was right. It was strange—the area had been jam-packed with Extravaganzers.

"What's wrong?" he asked.

"No one saw anything."

"I know . . . Oh."

"It has to be considered that witchcraft was involved. Magic." I bit my lip. If it were true, why would a Crafter try to steal Archie?

"Or," he said, "people are just unobservant."

That could be it, too.

"I'll have an officer get copies of the surveillance videos outside the Wisp, but I have to admit Archie's case hasn't been a top priority."

No. That belonged to Natasha, then Chip.

"Did Baz admit to you to having an affair with Natasha?" I asked, giving the swing a push with my toe.

"He said only that they had a close friendship."

I lifted an eyebrow. "Slimeball."

"He sure comes across that way." Nick dragged a hand down his face.

"How was he involved with Chip? Why was he hiding in Chip's bedroom?"

"According to Baz, while at the Extravaganza after Natasha collapsed, Chip asked Baz to stop by his apartment later that day to talk about something important."

"Baz arrived at the apartment just after Chip got out of the shower. Then you apparently showed up, and Chip asked Baz to hide in the 'mouse-infested' bedroom while you were there. One of the mice bit him and he's convinced he needs rabies shots. He's rather melodramatic."

Pepe and Mrs. P were bound to enjoy the shoe-tossing Baz undergoing rabies shots because of them. "He's big into movies and theater."

"He mentioned that's how he met Natasha. At some Audrey Hepburn movie marathon at the playhouse."

Poor Vivienne. "What did Chip want with Baz?"

"He wanted to blackmail him."

"What?"

"After you left the apartment, Chip told Baz that he was going to reveal Baz's affair with Natasha to the world and intimate to the press that Baz had something to do with her death if he didn't pay up."

I recalled the conversation Chip and I had.

I had asked, *"How well does being in commercials*

pay?" He'd given a laugh but there was no humor in it. *"Not enough."*

"Planning to rob a bank, then?"

With a small smile, he'd said, *"You could say that."*

"The bank in question had to have been Baz," I said to Nick after telling him about the exchange.

"Baz told me he was willing to write a check then and there. He just wanted to be done with it all, but Chip suddenly took ill. Started having trouble breathing, then had a seizure."

"Just like Natasha."

"Exactly."

"Why didn't Baz call for help?"

"He says he panicked and hightailed it down the fire escape because he didn't want to be tied to the situation. He didn't think Chip stood a chance for surviving and Baz didn't want his name linked with Natasha's, even in death."

"Well, of course not," I said. "Because of the prenup."

"The what?"

I quickly explained that situation, including Glinda's involvement. "However, Vivienne already knows about the affair. Glinda told her yesterday at the Extravaganza."

Nick closed his eyes and mumbled under his breath. "I wish *I'd* known. I'd have brought Vivienne in for questioning as well."

I ignored the wish. As a Wish-Halfcrafter, he couldn't be granted any wishes. "There's always today."

"Yeah." He glanced at his watch, frowned.

"It's interesting to me that Baz doesn't know Vivienne knows."

Nick nodded. "Maybe she's toying with him, letting him think he's off scot-free."

"Or she's waiting for the hard evidence, which is

locked inside the Wisp. Any chance the Wisp will re-open today?"

"What evidence?"

I told him about the spy pen.

His face brightened. "I need a copy of that footage. How about this? I'll call you when I have a free minute today, and you can meet me at the Wisp. Bring your laptop. You can burn a disk for Glinda, then give the pen to me for evidence."

"Sounds like a plan. So, what about Baz? Do you believe his story?"

"Not yet." He glanced at his watch. "I'm waiting for approval of the search warrant of his property, which should come in any minute now. Had to wait until the fingerprint report came back and confirmed Baz had been in Chip's apartment."

"Did Baz happen to mention why he was following me last night?"

Nick's face hardened, his eyes going cold, his jaw clenching. "He did what?"

I told him about my trip to see the Elder—and how Baz had followed me into the woods.

"No, he didn't mention that. Looks like I need to have another chat with him. So Chip is a Crafter? That explains why he took a sudden turn for the better after a visit in the ICU from his 'grandmother' in the middle of the night."

"Cherise," I said, smiling at her conning the hospital staff.

"He's doing well enough that his breathing tube has been removed. The doctors said he'll probably be discharged early. Maybe even today."

"Cherise *can* work miracles."

"I'm a believer." He stretched his legs.

"I plan to explore the Extravaganza side of the case

today," I told him. "Try to see if Marigold Coe is willing to talk to me. If she was a victim of Natasha's, she might have sought revenge."

"That's true, but what would Marigold have against Chip? Why was he poisoned?"

"I haven't quite figured that part out yet." I faced him. "Oh, at some point, do you think you can get me Natasha's sister's phone number? I need to talk to her about Titania."

"The cat? Why?"

"Because she's currently upstairs curled on my bed with Missy. I took custody of her at the Extravaganza yesterday, and I need to find her a new home. Chip couldn't take her, because he's allergic. And as far as I've learned, Natasha's sister is her only close relative, so she's next on my list to ask."

Nick studied my face. "I see," he said, humor in his undertones.

"You see what? Is it my hair?" I touched my head. "Silly stripe."

"No, it's not the hair, though I'll come back to that in a minute. You want to keep her. Titania."

I didn't even bother to deny it. Not with Nick. "Am I that obvious?"

"Probably only with someone who knows you as well as I do."

He did know me well. "Despite what I want, I have to do what's right. Titania doesn't belong to me. She belongs to whoever is Natasha's beneficiary."

As much as I might not like it.

"I'll get you the number," he said. "I'm sure it's in one of my files."

I slid him a smile. "Feel free to take your time."

"I'll be slower than molasses." He motioned to my hair. "So, new hairstyle?"

"Kind of. It's from a spell that makes Wishcrafters

visible in photographs. Ve commissioned the spell and there are some kinks to work out still. I'm surprised you're not striped, considering that the press hasn't left the Wisp."

"I dodged them, going in and out the rear doors."

"Smart, otherwise you'd look like Pepe Le Pew."

Shaking his head, he smiled and said, "You had quite the day yesterday."

I hadn't even told him about the bombshell the Elder had dropped. I didn't want to get into another guessing match right now. I'd had enough of that with Mimi and Harper last night. "Just another day in this crazy life of mine. Today's shaping up to be another doozy."

He studied me with those dark eyes of his. "I don't like missing any part of your days. I don't like not kissing you good night or good morning, either, for that matter."

I knew the feeling. "And I'm not fond of missing yours."

Were we *finally* going to talk about moving in together? It should have been such an easy conversation, because I *wanted* to live with him. Truly.

My only hesitation was that I wasn't sure I wanted to do it at *his* house, which he didn't want to leave.

The problem was I'd fallen head over heels for my new house, as dilapidated as it might be at the moment. Yes, renovations had only started two weeks ago, but with every change made it felt more and more like home. And the funny thing was, those changes felt that way because Nick and Mimi were helping me make the decisions. They were leaving their stamp on that house as much as I was. It felt like home because they had made it feel that way.

They were my home.

It was such a huge realization that I almost gasped.

The simple truth was I'd rather live with Nick and

Mimi in his house than without them in mine. I'd use my house as the As You Wish offices, and that was that.

Decision made.

Except for one small detail: Nick hadn't actually asked me to move in with him.

Smiling at my innate ability to solve a problem that I had created only in my own mind, I gave the swing another push and hoped he'd finally bring up the topic.

"We should do something about that. About missing each other," he said.

Suddenly nervous, I wiped damp palms on my shorts and ventured, "We should."

"It would be easier to do that if—"

His phone buzzed, cutting him off. He pulled his cell from a clip on his belt and looked at the message that had just come in. "The warrant is ready. I need to go. You're sure it's okay for Mimi to stay here for a while?"

"I told you—"

He gave me a long, lingering kiss. "Right. Family." In two steps, he was off the porch. "We'll pick up this conversation later?"

"All right."

Maybe then he'd ask me . . .

And I knew exactly what I was going to say.

Chapter Sixteen

The village was slowly coming to life at just past nine as I hustled along the sidewalk, headed to the pet shop to pick up a few things for Titania. I'd showered, eaten, walked the dogs, and fed all the pets without seeing hide nor hair of Ve, which was unusual, as she was an early bird like me.

Her bedroom door had remained closed all morning, but about an hour ago I'd heard her speaking to someone behind the closed door. I didn't know whether she was on the phone, or if she was with the Elder, or was with the mysterious woman again. I'd shamelessly tried to eavesdrop, but she had been talking quietly, and I hadn't heard any other voices.

Thinking of the Elder made my stomach ache. As of right now, I was still clueless as to her identity, and I didn't like the knowledge that I *should* know who she was. It was entirely frustrating, so for now I pushed it out of my thoughts and focused on the day ahead.

Mimi had been still snoozing when I left, even when both dogs had jumped on the bed with her and settled in for a morning nap. I couldn't help admiring her sleeping skills. I wished I had them.

Before I left, I had stuck a sticky note to the kitchen countertop letting both Mimi and Ve know where I was going, laced up my sneakers, and headed out, trying to ignore the baleful look Titania was giving me as I closed the back door. I hated leaving her behind, but I certainly couldn't take her with me to run errands.

I crossed a side street and weaved around a couple of displaced Extravaganzers walking their dogs around the village square. I said hello as I passed but didn't stop to make small talk. I wanted to pick up the things I needed for Titania, then get on with my day.

Located a block away from As You Wish, the Furry Toadstool was the center shop of three connected storefronts on the bottom floor of a three-story weathered brick building with ivory trim, arched windows, and elaborate cornices. Along with the shops, the structure offered office space on the second floor and apartments on the third. Purple and pink flowers spilled from window boxes set beneath every window, and charm oozed from the rafters.

Beautifully designed store shingles attached to wrought-iron brackets hung above each shop. And although the storefronts had similar architecture— two bowed display windows separated by a recessed entry door—they distinguished themselves with different colored awnings in jewel tones. To the left of the Furry Toadstool, the Snuggery, which sold furniture and home decor, had an aquamarine awning, and All That Glitters, a jewelry shop to its right, had an amethyst covering.

I stepped onto the sidewalk in front of the shops and skirted a large urn that yesterday had been overflowing with colorful annuals and dripping with ivy, but now had only half-eaten blossoms and chewed stems.

Cookie had obviously been by here, too, the sneaky little goat.

The pet shop had an emerald canopy, and as I stepped up to the store's left window to watch two puppies play, sunlight filtered through the fabric above my head and cast a green hue on the glass. The dogs rolled and tumbled in a bed of thick shavings, and I couldn't help enjoying their antics. Tension seeped out of me as I fought the urge to bring both puppies home.

A big stainless steel bowl of water sat below the opposite window, which displayed a variety of leashes, dishes, and clothes that the shop sold. But it was the two signs taped to the glass that captured my full attention. One was a discreet FOR LEASE sign that reminded me that Reggie would be gone soon, heading off to Florida.

My stomach dropped as I read the second sign, a notice for a lost dog. BIG REWARD was written in all caps at the bottom of the page.

Lady Catherine.

Her dour-looking image stared at me from the poster, and I couldn't believe my eyes. I'd seen her only yesterday. I quickly glanced around, hoping the beautiful whippet would suddenly appear. No such luck.

Peering into the store, I saw Marigold Coe inside at the counter, talking with Harmony Atchison, and an image of Lady Catherine hanging out with Cookie somewhere in the Enchanted Woods made me smile until I realized that possibility was highly unlikely. Reggie Beeson was nowhere to be seen.

I went inside, and the mixed scent of wood shavings, kibble, and sweet puppies filled my lungs. There was something so welcoming about this shop, an air that made it seem as though all you needed was a pet in your life to be happy.

I wasn't sure if that vibe was given off by Samuel Beeson's lingering magic, or if it was simply true.

I knew my life was better with Missy in it, and even Tilda.

As I approached the counter, I noticed Marigold's green eyes were red rimmed, and Harmony rested a consoling hand on her shoulder as she held a box of tissues. A stack of Lady Catherine's Lost posters were sitting on the countertop.

"I just saw the sign," I said. "What happened?"

Marigold plucked a tissue from the box and dabbed her eyes with it. She blinked as she looked at me, then tipped her head to the side. "New hairdo, Darcy?"

Harmony crinkled her face, and I tried not to take it personally.

For heaven's sake. Wishing I'd worn a hat, I said, "I'm just experimenting. It's not staying. What happened with Lady Catherine?"

"I don't know," Marigold said, dabbing her eyes again.

At fifty or so, Marigold was short and squat. She carried her weight mostly in her midsection, and she almost always smelled of apples and cinnamon, which probably explained why I always thought of apple fritters whenever I ran into her. This morning, her normally beautiful short auburn hair stuck out every which way on her head, and she wore not a trace of her usually heavy-handed makeup.

"I let Lady outside just after six," she explained, "and when I went to let her back in ten minutes later, she was gone. I've been searching for hours, and no one I've talked to has seen her at all."

I knew where Marigold lived, and could easily picture

her big house with its fenced-in yard. The puppies in the window yipped as I asked, "Was the gate open?"

Tears filled her eyes, and she nodded. "I could have sworn it was closed when I went to bed. I check it every night, when I lock the doors and shut off the lights. Maybe . . . I forgot to look last night. It had been quite the day, and I was tired."

Reggie's cane thumped against the floor as she came bustling out of the back of the shop, carrying a foam cup that had a tea string dangling down the side. "Here, my dear. Drink this," she said, handing the drink over to Marigold.

I caught the scent of chamomile and thought it was a good choice to try to calm her down.

"We'll do everything we can to help find her, won't we, ladies?" Reggie said to us.

"Absolutely," Harmony agreed. "Anything. Losing a pet is like . . . losing your heart."

We all nodded solemnly.

Harmony kept patting Marigold's shoulder. "She'll turn up. Everyone who lives here knows who she is. She's practically a local celebrity. It's just a matter of time."

Harmony also looked as if she hadn't slept well, with the discolored circles under her eyes more prominent than ever. In her early forties, she seemed more flower child than businesswoman. She wore a peasant blouse with a pair of baggy capris and sandals that looked as though they'd come from Baz's closet. Her long frizzy strawberry blond hair was pulled back in a loose braid that hung down her back nearly to her waist.

Marigold swiped at another tear and looked at her with a hopeful expression. "Did you find Cookie yet?"

"Not yet." Harmony shook her head. "But I know she's around here somewhere, as I saw the evidence on the walk over here."

Reggie said, "The flowers will regrow, dear. Don't you worry about that. Did you set out fresh water like I suggested?" She tossed me a glance. "Goats are very particular about their water. It has to be clean and fresh or they won't drink it."

"Six bowls," Harmony said as she set the tissue box on the counter. "And thank you for setting one out front as well."

"I have one out back as well. She'll be fine," Reggie said. "Goats are resilient animals."

Reggie sat on a stool behind the counter and leaned her cane on the wall behind her. Even though she seemed to have energy to spare, I could only imagine the daily toll of running the shop took on her with her current health issues. I looked around. The shelves were sparse, most of the inventory marked with Sale stickers. The shop would close for good soon, and I was glad she wouldn't have to endure another harsh New England winter.

"Keep an eye on the green today. Goats are herd animals," Reggie told us. "She'll be looking for friends to play with, and the green will be bustling with animals because everyone will be waiting there until they can get into the Wisp for their belongings. And perhaps," Reggie added in a firm yet tender voice, "when you find her, you'll consider another goat as a companion for her. Or perhaps a dog. Even a miniature donkey, but you will have to run that past the village council."

Marigold sniffed. "Donkeys come in miniature?"

"Yes." Reggie placed her hands over her heart. "And they are just the cutest things."

"Aw," Marigold said, looking at Harmony. "Think of your guests. You could have your own little petting zoo."

Harmony cracked a small smile. "No. No donkeys, and don't any of you dare mention it to Angela, or she'll be online looking for one by nightfall." She glanced around. "Her heart is way bigger than our yard."

I thought about what Harper had said yesterday, about anything being available online. I was beginning to believe it was true. From cyanide to donkeys.

"But it won't take up much space if it's *miniature*," I said, thinking a miniature donkey friend was exactly what Cookie needed in her life.

"And you have all that space behind the Pixie Cottage," Marigold added. Her tears had dried and she seemed more in control. The tea had worked its magic.

Harmony shook a finger at us. "You all are as bad as Angela. I'm not getting a miniature donkey," she insisted. "I can't even keep track of a tiny goat. If only I hadn't entered her in that competition, none of this would have happened . . ." Her voice trailed off, and an embarrassed flush colored her cheeks. "I'm sorry. Losing my goat is nothing compared to what happened to Natasha. I sound completely insensitive, don't I?"

Marigold set her cup down. "If you were insensitive, Harmony, then I'm going to be wholly callous, because I didn't care for Natasha at all. I'm sorry she died, but I won't miss her."

I was about to follow that up with some direct questions about why she felt that way when Reggie spoke up.

"She had her faults, but she seemed to love her cat. That's a mark of genuine character that cannot be ignored."

I held back a scoff at the mention of Natasha's character. I'd seen it on full display in that hallway at the Extravaganza yesterday.

"Did she love her cat?" Marigold asked with a lifted eyebrow. "Or did she only use her cat to garner more attention for herself?"

No one answered, which I thought spoke volumes.

I recalled the way Titania had snuggled against me and wondered if she'd been affection-starved, because try as I might, I couldn't remember a single time yesterday when Natasha had made a loving gesture toward her pet. It made me feel slightly ill.

"Where *is* Titania?" Reggie suddenly asked.

"I have her until I can track down someone in Natasha's family who may want her," I said. I glanced around the shop, my gaze landing on a turquoise collar that would be perfect for her. "It's actually why I'm here. She needs a few things."

Reggie laughed. "I'd been hoping this whole time that you'd come to tell me you were willing to sell your paintings here."

"You're selling your paintings?" Harmony asked, perking up. "I'd love one for the Pixie Cottage. The lovely little white mouse you painted for your display at the Extravaganza just calls out to me."

I couldn't help smiling. Mrs. P had once owned the bed-and-breakfast that now belonged to Harmony, and the two had formed a close bond. "I haven't decided to sell yet, but if I do, I'll keep your offer in mind. I'm just here to get a bowl, a collar, maybe a few toys, food, and a new litter box."

"Dear, Titania's more than welcome to come here," Reggie offered. "I don't mind at all and already have all the supplies. I know how Tilda can be."

"Thanks, but Tilda actually enjoys her company, which is a slight miracle in itself." I wrinkled my nose. "I don't want to displace Titania again at this point. Not until she leaves for good."

"Well, the offer stands," she said. "Just call if you need me." She grabbed her cane and came around the counter. "I'll help you pick out what you need. I have some stock still remaining in my storage barn. If you want something you don't see here, just ask."

Harmony bumped me with her shoulder. "Looks like Angela's not the only one with a big heart. Maybe *you* should get the mini donkey."

"At this point," Marigold cut in, picking up her stack of flyers, "*I'm* thinking of getting a miniature donkey. But first, I need to find my Lady."

"Do you want me to hand some of those out?" I asked her, pointing to the stack of paper in her hands.

"Oh! Yes, please," she said.

"I'll take some as well." Harmony held out her hand. "I'll be out and about looking for Cookie, so it's no trouble at all."

Reggie reached out. "I'll take some, too."

I glanced at the sheet again. "How much is the reward, exactly? In case anyone asks. You know how people are."

"And they will definitely ask," Harmony said, "especially since it says it's big."

"Five thousand," Marigold answered without batting an eyelash.

My jaw dropped.

Harmony squeaked something intelligible.

Reggie gasped.

"I know it's a lot," said Marigold, "but I want her back. She's worth every cent."

We were still standing there, stunned, as Marigold thanked us all and waved as she went out the front door.

As soon as the door closed, Harmony read the Lost flyer again. "It's probably wrong that I want to find Lady Catherine more than Cookie right at this moment, isn't it?"

Reggie chuckled. "I'm thinking of closing the shop for the day, grabbing my scooter, and scouring the village. Five thousand dollars. Wow."

"Once word gets out about this reward," I said, watching Marigold cross the green, handing out flyers as she went, "the village will be overrun with people looking for her."

"Not if I find Lady Catherine first," Harmony said with a sly smile as she headed for the door.

It wasn't until I paid for Titania's supplies that I remembered I hadn't asked Marigold any questions at all about her accident at the Wisp two years ago.

It was clear she hadn't like Natasha—she'd said so herself—but had she *killed* the woman?

Chapter Seventeen

The overstuffed paper bag of goodies I'd bought for Titania banged against my leg as I headed across the green toward the Gingerbread Shack. I'd ended up buying much more for the cat than I intended, including a comfy new bed.

I was a goner where Titania was concerned.

"Darcy! Wait for me!"

I turned at the sound of my name, and found Ivy fast-walking toward me. I recognized her only because of her voice. She wore a wig of long blond hair, a baseball cap, sunglasses, and a short black shift dress with red flats.

When she reached me, I said, "What's with the disguise?"

"Desperate times. I couldn't even sleep at home last night. I had to sneak in through the back of Fairytails to sleep in my office. I have Extravaganzers camped on my lawn, roasting marshmallows over an improvised fire pit made from rocks taken from my garden. I closed the shop today so people can't keep coming in to ask when the Wisp will reopen. I've been trying to reach Nick about it, but he's not available," she added, using air quotes around the last three words. "Can you get ahold of him?"

"I probably wouldn't get an answer, either. He's busy."

Ivy dropped her head back and moaned. "Where is he? What's he doing? I'm a taxpayer, too. I need these people to get their things and go home. My life has been upturned, overthrown. I'm going to have to keep Fairy-tails closed until they're gone from the village. I'm losing money left and right." She let out a heavy sigh and set her hands on her hips.

Never mind *their* lives. Just *hers* was affected.

Fighting an eye roll, I said, "Nick is at Baz Lucas' serving a search warrant."

"What? Why?"

"Something about Natasha's death," was all I said, unsure whether Baz's affair was public knowledge yet.

"Why do the police think Baz is involved?"

"Nick doesn't share that kind of information with me," I said, lying through my teeth.

She paled. "So . . . Natasha's death *is* connected to the Extravaganza?"

"We don't know that yet."

"But Baz was poisoned last year, and she was poisoned this year. . . ." She pushed a hand against her stomach. "Oh God. I think I'm going to be ill."

"Don't jump to conclusions," I cautioned. "We don't know anything yet. He's just gathering facts right now."

After a moment of processing that news, she cupped her face with her hands and said, "Maybe I should go over there. . . . I just need an idea from Nick about the Wisp, a general time frame to tell people."

"Not a good idea."

"Well, what do you suggest I do?"

I didn't really have a good answer to that other than to tell her to chill the heck out, which wasn't likely to go over well.

"Try to be patient." I handed her some of the flyers that Marigold had given me. "You can hand out some of these while you're waiting for word about the Wisp."

She lifted her sunglasses, balancing them atop her hat. "Lady Catherine is lost?"

"Slipped out an open gate this morning. Marigold is offering a five-thousand-dollar reward."

"Five *thousand* dollars?"

"She really wants her back."

"I don't blame her, but wow. That's a lot of money. And what is going on around here?" she asked. "First Archie's almost birdnapped, then Cookie broke loose, now Lady Catherine is missing?" She looked upward. "Is it a full moon?"

"I don't think so."

She said, "It sure feels like it. Listen, if you hear anything from Nick about the Wisp, please have him call me. Until then, I'll be hiding at Fairytails." She held up the flyers. "I'll pass these out on my way over there."

I heard her mumbling under her breath as she stormed off, tossing flyers at people she rushed past.

Shaking my head at her antics, I crossed the street. The bell on the Gingerbread Shack's door rang out as I pulled it open. The shop was packed. Every table was full, and a line stretched almost to the door. Three people were working behind the counter, none of whom were Evan. Seeing the employees made me smile. Not so long ago, he'd been avoiding hiring more help, but he'd come around.

I scooted past the people waiting in line and headed for the kitchen. Evan was the only one in there, and he was flushed with exertion as he hand-mixed something chocolaty in a large bowl.

"It's crazy out there," I said.

"The longer the Wisp stays closed, the better it is for me," he said with a broad smile. Flour smudged his cheek. He set the bowl down and wiped his hands on an apron hanging from his slim hips. "Did you need something? Besides a hairdresser, that is? Starla's at the Magic Wand right now. I bet if you hurry, they could squeeze you in, too."

"Don't make me take *your* picture."

He laughed. "Did you need something?"

"Two things. One, I need an order sent over to the construction crew at my house. And two, can I hang this in your front window?" I held up the Lost flyer.

He took the paper out of my hand. "Lady Catherine, too?"

Tipping my head, I said, "Too?"

"You didn't see the other signs on your way in?"

I shook my head.

"Two dogs and a cat. All went missing sometime during the night. The cat was a village cat who tends to wander off from time to time, so it's questionable whether he's even lost, but the dogs were from the Extravaganza. Their owners had camped on Ivy's front lawn last night, and when they woke up, the dogs were gone. They're frantic, of course, and claiming someone stole them."

"Did they see someone take them?"

"Not at all. But the dogs had been tied up, and the knots had been undone."

Goose bumps rose on my skin. "Were the police called?"

"Yeah, but the officer who came out said they couldn't do much but keep an eye out. The shop's been buzzing all morning with talk of a petnapper on the loose."

I thanked the Fates that Ivy hadn't yet heard that gossip. If she had, she might have to be committed.

He held up the paper. "Do you think it's possible Lady Catherine was snatched, too?"

"I don't know," I said. Marigold *had* mentioned that she thought she'd closed the gate. "I don't know what's going on."

But it was becoming obvious that something big was happening with the pets, and it had started with Archie.

I needed to talk to that bird.

On my way back to As You Wish, I stopped at Spell-bound.

Marcus Debrowski was behind the checkout counter, while Harper lay curled on her side in a corner of one of the two deep couches she had set up at the front of the shop. A book was practically glued to her nose as Pie cleaned his paws from a spot near her feet. Harper was so intent on her reading that she hadn't noticed me come in.

Marcus caught my questioning eye and said, "She's been like that all morning."

I set my bag on the floor, nudged Pie out of the way, and sat next to my sister's feet.

She didn't budge.

The shop was busy, and I was happy to see that it was an equal mix of villagers and tourists. Harper needed local support to keep the store going. Ever since she bought the place, she'd thrown her heart into it. From changing the decor to a *Starry Night* theme, adding community events that including everything from book clubs to toddler hours, to providing a coffee and snack bar, she'd made it known that she was willing to do whatever it took to make her shop thrive. People had responded in a big way, not only to the changes, but to Harper. They recognized that she put her heart in all she did, and in turn, they were willing to open their hearts—and wallets—to her. She was quickly becoming a village favorite.

The man sitting on the sofa across from me stood up and said, "She's really into that book."

As he headed to the counter, I tipped my head to the side to see the spine of the vintage book Harper held. *Witches: A Crafted History.* It was yellowed with age.

There was a whole stack of books on the floor next to the couch, each and every one the same color yellow, and all were about witchcraft.

Harper turned a page, and I peered over the top of the book. "Boo!"

She jumped, sending the book flying. It landed with a thump near Pie, and he let out a loud meow and hopped onto a nearby bookshelf.

Harper clutched her heart. "A hello would have sufficed."

"I think not," I said, retrieving the book. "You were in another world."

"I was *reading*," Harper said. "That's what books do. They take you somewhere else."

I flipped through the pages. It seemed to be a history of the village. "Where did you get this?" It definitely wasn't a book she sold here in the shop.

"Basement," she said. "There are hundreds of books down there about witchcraft. One of them is bound to mention something about the Elder."

So that was what this was all about. I wasn't the least bit surprised. I motioned to the pile on the floor. "Did any of these mention her?"

"Well, no, but I'm optimistic."

That made one of us.

"That book," she said quietly, motioning to the book in my hands, "is different. I think it was written by a Crafter."

"Who?"

"There's no author listed, which is unusual in itself, and"—she dropped her voice even lower—"it lists some magical abilities in here. Witches who can disappear, witches who can heal. No Craft is mentioned by exact name, but the person who wrote this definitely knew what he was talking about."

That was very interesting. "But no mention of the Elder."

"Not yet." She lifted an eyebrow at me. "I was only halfway through before I was so rudely interrupted."

Marcus came up behind the couch and put his arm on Harper's shoulder. She glanced up at him, and smiled a smile I rarely saw from her. Pure joy.

Oh yes, I definitely thought Harper had weddings on her mind.

"Coffee, Darcy?" Marcus asked, adjusting his eyeglasses as happiness radiated from his light green eyes.

"No, thanks," I said. "I'm not staying. I was just dropping off one of these flyers."

Harper took one out of my hands. "Another victim of the supposed petnapper?"

"You heard about that?" I asked.

"Everyone's been talking about it," Marcus said.

"I don't believe for a second that there's a petnapper on the loose," Harper said.

"Why not?" I straightened the rest of the papers. "Seems logical to me."

"Not a single person's tried to take Pie," she said, matter-of-factly.

I looked at the cat. He was still on top of one of the bookcases. Folded like a pretzel, he had one leg in the air as he cleaned his underside. "Yes, well, maybe he's just too . . ."

Harper narrowed her eyes at me.

"Protected," I finished.

Marcus laughed and headed back to the counter to help a customer.

"He's hardly ever alone," I added quickly.

"That must be it," Harper said, nodding. "Any news on Natasha?"

"Not really. Nick's searching Baz's house right now."

The bell jangled, and we looked up to see Starla walking in, Twink under one arm. Starla's hair was full and fluffy—and all one color. A sunny blond.

"I feel so much better." She plopped down next to me and set Twink on the floor. He bounded over to the bookcase to see if Pie would come down to play with him.

Pie continued his bath.

"Now I just need that stripe never to come back. I hate lying to Vince," Starla said. "I don't know what I'm going to do if . . ." She trailed off, then sent a bashful look at Harper and me. "Well, you know."

I nodded. A marriage between a mortal and Crafter was a tenuous endeavor.

"No," Harper said, a sneaky smile on her face. "What?"

Starla knew Harper was only teasing, so she shook her head and blushed more deeply. "Just be glad you're not in my shoes, Harper. You're lucky Marcus is one of us."

"I'm lucky to have Marcus," she agreed, looking over her shoulder at him, "but if he wasn't . . . one of us . . . I'd give up my powers to tell him the truth."

Starla said in hushed tones, "That's because you don't even *want* your powers. I do. But I don't want to live a lie, either. I'm not good at lying. Case in point, you should have seen me trying to explain my hair. I spun this elaborate tale about trying to color my roots. . . . I don't think he bought a word of it. And if my hair explanation wasn't enough to arouse suspicions"—she leaned forward—"the picture sure did."

"Picture?" Harper asked.

"I suggested we have our picture taken, since my hair was already messed up, and it was a lovely shot of Vince and a bright starburst. Then he insisted on taking it over and over, and"—she took a deep breath—"I might have to memory-cleanse him."

"This was last night?" I asked, my mind whirling.

"Yeah. Why?" she asked.

We all spoke quietly so as to not be overheard by mortals. "Because I took a picture of myself this morning to see if the spell still worked. It did."

Starla glanced at Harper. "How about you? Did you try a picture?"

She nodded. "Starburst city."

They both looked at me, but I had no answers. "I don't understand."

"I do," Harper said. "*You're* still under the spell, Darcy."

"Why me and not both o— Wait a sec."

"What?" Starla asked.

I looked at her. "Yesterday, I asked you to check your camera for anything unusual about Evan or Ve at the Extravaganza. . . ."

"Right," Starla said. "And I found nothing odd. Just their usual starbursts. Oh."

"What am I missing?" Harper asked.

Starla said in a whisper, "If Ve had cast the Lunumbra spell on herself so she could be photographed at the Extravaganza, her image should have been on my camera. Yet it wasn't."

I thought of all the photos taken that showed visible Wishcrafters, and there was one constant.

Me.

I took out my phone and waved Marcus over. "Will you please take a shot of us?"

Starla went to stand up, and I grabbed her arm.

She said, "Darcy, I just had my hair—"

Marcus took the picture.

"—done," Starla finished, sitting back down. She let out a sigh. "It has a stripe again, doesn't it?"

Harper nodded.

Starla slumped back, let out a whimper.

I looked at the camera. Harper had her tongue stuck out, I was in profile as I reached for Starla, and she was only photographed from waist down.

But all three of us were clearly visible.

"Harper," I said, "do me a favor and go stand over by Pie."

Without even a peep of protest, she crossed the room and scooped up Pie. I snapped the picture and looked at it. Harper was there, but her image was washed out, white around its edges.

"Now by the kids' area," I instructed. The kids' section was a good twenty feet away.

She trotted over. I snapped the picture and showed Starla.

"A starburst," she said in awe.

"There must be a radius on the witch who's under the spell. The spell affects all the Wishcrafters within that radius. I'm that witch."

Harper sat back down and looked at the pictures. "Aunt Ve cast the spell only on you," she said. "Why?"

Starla said, "I don't understand."

"Me neither," I said, glancing again at the pictures.

I was sure there was a simple explanation, but for the life of me, I couldn't come up with one.

Chapter Eighteen

Missy wagged her stubby tail as I walked through the side gate at As You Wish, and I set my bag down on the grass to give her a proper hello.

From his cage, Archie was regaling a group of tourist with the "I'll never go hungry again" monologue from *Gone with the Wind*. In Scarlett's voice, of course.

"'... they're not going to lick me! I'm going to live through this, and when it's all over, I'll never be hungry again ...'"

He paused for dramatic effect, then finished the rest of the scene. When he was done, the tourists clapped and whistled. "Bravo, bravo! Encore!"

In Rhett's voice, he said, "'No, I'm through with everything here. I want peace. I want to see if somewhere there isn't something left in life of charm and grace.'"

With that, he took a bow, and the tourists applauded

a moment more before wandering off. I carried Missy over to the fence that separated the yards and kept my back to the village green so no one could see me carrying on a conversation with Archie. "Do you ever think it crosses the tourists' minds that you're not an average bird?"

He scooted along his perch, closer to me. "I'd be highly insulted if not considered an above average bird at the very least. Which is why, after all, someone tried to steal me, lest you forget."

Out here in the sunlight, I noticed some of Missy's fur was darkening with age on the top of her head, creating brunette half-moons that curved around her ears. It only added to her adorability. "How could I when you remind me every time I see you?"

He blinked. "I choose believe that is a rhetorical question."

"So, you think it was a *tourist* who tried to steal you?"

He craned his neck and peered at me. "Do you know something I do not?"

"Not necessarily. It simply seems odd that no one saw what happened to you. There's not been a single witness to step forward."

"Perhaps that is because my abduction is not receiving the investigation it deserves," he said snidely.

"Or perhaps it is because magic was involved."

"No," he said. "I think not."

"Yes," I countered. "It's possible."

"Noooo."

"Yessss."

"No Crafter would be foolish enough to make such an attempt," he said crisply. "All know who I am. Who I represent."

The Elder. Yes, everyone knew that, and going against the Elder was grounds for being banned from the Craft, but still . . .

"There are certain lines Crafters do not cross," he continued. "I am one of them."

He sounded so certain, yet no one had witnessed anyone snatching him. No one at all. "Where is the bag that you were stuffed into? Do the police have it?"

Fanning his face with his wing, he said, "Do not remind me of that claustrophobic mothball-scented pillowcase."

"It was a pillowcase?"

"I do not know," he squawked. "I did not linger to examine the precise textile into which I had been forcefully propelled. It merely seems the class of conveyance into which a mortal would stuff a precious commodity such as myself. Like I was a piece of stale Halloween candy! For shame! *Shaaaaame*."

He started mumbling about Necco Wafers and Tootsie Rolls. I needed to cut him off before he started on a full-blown tangent about what he considered to be decent candy. "What kind of material was the bag made of?"

Feathers flew. "The torture! Have you no mercy, Darcy Merriweather? I'm *molting* again! I'll be as bald as Demi Moore in *G.I. Jane* by suppertime, mark my words."

"But still just as pretty as she was in the movie."

He tipped his head side to side, as if considering. "This is true. Prettier, even. Bald wasn't her best look. Speaking of hair—"

I held up a finger. "Hold that thought. Let me just check if Higgins is around and wants a snack."

His beak snapped closed. "Never mind."

"Listen," I said. "I was just asking about the bag because there's a chance fingerprints could be found on the offensive *textile*, thus leading the police straight to your birdnapper."

"Thus?" he repeated, blinking.

"I threw that in for you. Thought you'd like it."

"I approve. I also approve of the notion of the thief who captured me being stuffed inside a jail cell, as I was stuffed—"

I coughed loudly.

He fluffed his feathers for a moment before he said, "Yes. Well. I have no idea where the accursed pillowcase is at the moment, but the last I saw of it was in the woods behind the Wisp, near the pond."

I knew the spot. "I'll ask Nick if one of his officers picked it up after taking Terry's report, and I'll keep you informed."

Haughtily, he said, "'Frankly, my dear, I don't give a damn.'"

I narrowed my eyes.

"Perhaps I give a small damn," he amended. "Minuscule." He paused. "Inform me the moment you know." With that, he flew out of his cage and into Terry's house through a special Archie-sized door flap.

As I headed into As You Wish, I thought of what Archie said about a Crafter not being so foolish as to try to steal him.

I agreed.

Which told me one thing for certain. *If* it turned out that a Crafter was involved, that person wasn't the least bit foolish.

No.

That witch was desperate.

"Darcy, is that you?" Ve called out as soon as I stepped into the mudroom. "We've been waiting for you."

A small dog came running toward me, and it took me a moment to realize it was Audrey Pupburn.

I set the bag from the Furry Toadstool on a bench and set Missy on the floor. The two dogs started sniffing each other in the way of hellos. "It's me. Who's we?" *Please not Baz, please not Baz.*

"Vivienne's here about that spell. We're in the family room."

The spell. The one that had been cast only upon me.

Tilda and Titania eyed me from the stop of the back stairway as I passed through the kitchen, and the two dogs followed me down the hall toward the family room. I found Ve sitting on one sofa, Vivienne on the other. A plate of scones sat on the coffee table as well as a coffee tray.

"Oh my," Vivienne said when she saw my hair.

"The streak is certainly more pronounced in Darcy's hair, the silver against the black," Ve said, sipping from mug that had "There's a chance this is vodka" written on its side. "It's hardly noticeable in mine."

I sat in a wingback chair and decided to wait to see if Ve would explain why I seemed to be the only one under the spell before I outright accused her of anything.

Out of the corner of my eye, I noticed Titania creeping down the hallway. I lowered my hand next to my chair and rubbed my fingers together. She ran over to them, giving them a sniff. In a blink, she hopped onto my lap.

"She's taken a liking to you," Vivienne said.

I ran a hand down Titania's back. "The feeling's mutual." As Titania head-butted my chin and started purring, I noticed Vivienne was yet another who looked as though she hadn't slept well. In fact, I was pretty sure she was wearing the same clothes she'd had on yesterday at the Extravaganza. Which made me wonder if she'd slept at *all*. "Thanks for coming over so soon."

"When Ve explained what was happening, I came immediately. It's an easy fix."

"It is?" I asked.

Standing, she came over to the chair. "I just need a strand of your hair." She plucked.

I yelped. "Hey!"

"Sorry," she said. "It's easier not to warn people. Do you have a candle I can borrow, Ve?"

Ve set her mug on the table. "Certainly."

A few minutes later, my strand of hair had gone up in flames, and the hair on my head was back to its natural color.

"I'll need to re-create the spell to fix its flaw," Vivienne said, "but I have to wait until a black moon."

"Black moon?" I asked.

"There are several definitions, the most common being when there are two new moons within a calendar month," Vivienne said as Ve topped off her coffee. "I need ample darkness in a lunar month to counterbalance your starburst."

Mimi was going to love hearing all this.

Vivienne said, "The spell is all about dark versus light. Opposites. Which is probably why your hair turned silver, and Starla's had a brunette streak. Light and dark," she reiterated.

Magic would never, ever, cease to amaze me.

"Unfortunately, the black moon I need to permanently correct the spell won't happen again for a couple of months."

"Months?" Ve said, eyes wide.

Vivienne blew on her coffee, then took a sip. "As I said, that black moon is rare. Until then, the spell will need to be cast while burning a strand of hair from the witch who's using the spell. It will prevent the streak from occurring."

"How long does this current spell last from the time it is cast?" I asked, fact-gathering.

Ve fidgeted on the couch, fussing with the buttons on her tunic top.

"Twelve hours," Vivienne said.

Titania had flopped down next to me on the chair and

stretched out to nap. Missy and Audrey were playing tug-of-war with a chew toy. And my mind was spinning.

Twelve hours. That meant that Ve had probably only cast the spell on herself once—to test it—and on me at least three times now.

She caught me looking at her, and she reached for a scone and took a big bite. "Delicious," she murmured around falling crumbs. "That Evan sure can bake."

I turned my attention back to Vivienne. "And the spell affects all Wishcrafters within a certain radius of the witch who the spell has been cast upon?" I asked.

Vivienne nodded. "Twelve feet, as Ve requested."

"I see," I said, looking at my aunt.

And there must have been something in my tone that hinted at my displeasure, because Titania glanced up at me.

The dogs dropped the toy, and Missy came to stand near my feet.

Ve brushed crumbs from her lap and said brightly, "Would anyone like a refill?"

"Did I say something wrong?" Vivienne asked, glancing between us.

"No," I said to her. "You just cleared up something for me. Thanks."

She looked confused, but I didn't want to question Ve about the spell in front of a guest, so I let it go. For now. "Is Mimi up yet?" I asked instead. "She's love to hear all this."

"Up and out. She took Higgins home before heading to Spellbound to work her afternoon shift," Ve said, looking visibly relieved that I'd changed the subject.

Mimi worked for Harper a few times a week and loved every second of it.

"Did you get everything you needed at the Furry Toadstool?"

"More than I needed," I said. "I was a pushover when it came to the cat toys."

"Reggie has a way of getting you to buy things you don't need," Vivienne said. "Audrey has more hair accessories than I do, but Baz insists on her wearing only the bows. Just like Audrey Hepburn's dog, Mr. Famous." At the sound of her name, Audrey jumped up next to Vivienne and settled in next to her owner, dropping her head on Vivienne's leg. It was clear the two adored each other.

Ve said, "Mr. Famous? Was that really his name?"

"Oh yes," Vivienne said. "And you should have heard the argument Baz and I had when he wanted to name Audrey 'Ms. Famous.' He finally relented about that, as long as I agreed Audrey would always be styled just like the other dog. Hair bow and all. Baz works with Ivy Teasdale at Fairytails to get the look just right. I'm convinced Ivy thinks we're both crazy." She took a weary breath. "Which we probably are, so that's okay."

Vivienne was acting rather relaxed for someone whose husband had been brought in for questioning by the police last night. And whose house was now being searched inside and out. Then I glanced at her clothes again and made a leap. "When's the last time you saw Baz?"

Vivienne paled.

Ve shot me a look that clearly asked where I was going with this conversation.

Vivienne said, "We had a big fight after we got home from the Extravaganza. I told him I wanted a divorce and packed as much of my stuff as I could shove into my car. I made it clear to him that I was done and wasn't coming back. I haven't seen him since. I spent the night at the Pixie Cottage—Harmony and Angela were kind enough to let me and Audrey sleep in their personal guest quarters, since all the other rooms were full."

"Oh dear," Ve murmured.

"Was your fight about Natasha?" I asked.

"Yes. He tried to deny he'd had an affair with her, but Glinda told me what she'd seen at the Extravaganza. I'm waiting for the photos that prove it without a doubt, and I can finally be free from him."

I guessed Glinda hadn't told her that those photos were coming from me.

"I'll find another place here in the village—I belong here more than he does," she said.

Because she was a Crafter, and he was a mortal.

"It's not the first time he's cheated," she said sadly. "He's been having affairs for a while now. They started right after my accident. But I could never catch him at it. He's so smart, so smooth. Somehow he'd always convince me that I was crazy, that he loved me and only me. And I'd believe him. Over and over and over again. But this last time was different."

"How so?" Ve asked.

"*He* was different. I think . . . I think he loved her. I had the feeling he was going to leave me." She bit her bottom lip to keep it from trembling. Audrey looked up at her with such concern that it nearly broke my heart. "I didn't know who he was cheating with, so I hired Glinda. I needed to catch him cheating if I was going to get anything out of this marriage besides a broken heart. If he divorced me . . . I got a small settlement, just fifty thousand dollars. But if I caught him cheating . . ."

"Ten million," I supplied. "Glinda told me."

"Yes. I deserve that money after what he put me through."

"Hmmph," Ve said. "I think you're going easy on him. If he cheated on me like that, I'd slice off his—"

My cell phone rang, cutting off Ve, thank goodness. I pulled it from my pocket. "It's Nick."

I took the call in the kitchen, and Titania followed me.

"I'm wrapping up here at the Lucases'," he said, "and just had a call from Natasha's sister, Alina Norcliffe. She's in the village, staying at Natasha's for a few days. She asked about Titania."

The cat twined around my legs. "She did?"

"I had to tell her where she was. I'm sorry."

"No, it's fine." I vigorously rubbed a spot on the kitchen counter. "It's probably best I go talk to her, get this over with."

"I thought you'd say that, so I set up a time for you to meet her. Two, this afternoon, at Natasha's."

My heart sank. "Oh. So soon."

"If that doesn't work, you can reschedule. . . ."

"It works, it's just . . ."

"Darcy?" The tenderness in his voice was like a hug. "Are you okay?"

"Sure," I said, lying.

"Darcy."

"I'll be okay."

"All right," he relented. "I'll be done here soon. Do you want to meet at the Wisp in an hour?"

"Definitely. How are things there?"

"Not finding much at all. The neighbors say Baz has been in and out, acting strange by sneaking around the house, like he was hiding from someone."

"Hiding from who?" I asked. "You?"

"I don't see why. He was willing to talk with us last night. I have a call into his lawyer to set up another meeting."

"Maybe hiding from Vivienne?" I whispered so she wouldn't overhear me.

But no, that didn't make sense, as she had moved out and made it clear she wasn't going back.

"No clue," Nick said. "I'll ask when I see him. I've got to go. See you soon."

As I headed back to the family room, I could think of only one other reason why Baz would be acting the way he was.

If he was scared.

Not of Vivienne.

But of becoming the next victim.

Chapter Nineteen

Once I confessed to Vivienne that Nick was executing a search warrant on her house because of Baz's relationship with Natasha, she had grabbed Audrey and hightailed it out of here faster than I could say boo. There had been no explanation to Ve or me where she was going.

I was curious whether she was on the hunt for Baz—to kill him for dragging her into this situation—or was she headed to the police? Did she have information that would potentially help Nick's case?

Time would tell.

Ve had quickly exited the house as well, feeding me an excuse about a pressing village matter she had to tend to.

I recognized avoidance when I saw it.

She didn't want to talk to me about the Lunumbra spell and why she'd been casting it only on me.

Fine. I was a patient witch. I could wait.

I'd called Glinda to let her know I'd be getting the spy pen soon, and since I had time to kill, I headed up to my bedroom, passing Tilda at the top of the staircase. I took a moment to give her some love, and she mustered up a faint purr for me, for which I was grateful. It could just as easily have been a bite.

She and I had a complicated relationship.

She joined Titania and Missy as we trooped into my bedroom like some kind of ragtag conga line.

Recognizing that I was a little on edge, I turned to the one thing that usually settled me down quickly.

My art.

I'd been working on that family portrait for Harper for a long while now, and I hadn't yet finished the piece. An hour wasn't much time, but it would be enough to make a decent dent.

I carefully withdrew the gray sheet of paper from the large zippered portfolio I stored under the bed. I'd taken liberties with the drawing, carefully crafting the images of my mother and father and Harper and me in the present day. We all sat on a bench in front of a weeping willow tree, my father smiling as he watched my mother laughing, Harper looking at her with her heart in her eyes, and me grinning ear to ear. If my parents were still alive, I imagined this was exactly how we'd be behaving.

As always, my gaze had immediately gone to my mother's face first. It was finished except for her eyes, a task I'd been putting off for weeks now, for a reason I couldn't quite define. It wasn't like me to procrastinate.

Sighing, I set the paper on my draft table and fastened it down. I set out my colored pencils, a sharpener, and a highlight stick. Made myself reach for the light blue to fill in my mother's iris. After that was done, I flecked the blue with gold.

Deryn Octavia Devaney Merriweather had been a

beautiful woman. For a long time I had trouble remembering the exact details of my mom's face, but thanks to Mimi and a spell she'd found in Melina's diary, I'd could see my mom as clearly as I had when I was seven years old.

I reached for another color, a vibrant blue to line her eyes—the color had been her favorite eyeliner—and then quickly picked up a silver metallic pencil to imitate the glitter in the eyeliner. After a few swipes and smudging with my fingertip to blend, I leaned back. There. Done.

I studied the result. The image I'd drawn looked so much like my mother that my breath caught. Grief made my chest ache, and I forced myself to think of the happy times we'd had. The dancing in the rain, baking cookies, reading stories. All the dress-up playdates, the way she'd sing to me, the way she'd hold my head against her chest to soothe me, the way she'd loved me.

The pain eased from my chest but a lingering melancholy remained. I left the portrait where it was and quickly stood up. I went into the bathroom to wash my hands, and was glad to see in the mirror that my hair was still one solid color.

Above the sound of the water, I heard a distinct *arr-ooo*, the hound-dog howl that was the ring tone I used for Harper.

I wiped my hands on my shorts and grabbed my phone from where I'd thrown it on my bed.

"Darcy, why did Ve just walk in here and pluck a hair straight out of my head and walk out again without saying a word? Has she gone crazy?"

I said, "Entirely possibly, but in all likelihood, she's just fixing your hair color." I explained the temporary fix for the Lunumbra spell. "I'm guessing she didn't say anything because she didn't want to explain what was going on and potentially have to answer questions she didn't want to answer."

"But," Harper said, with a pout in her voice, "I kind of liked the streak. Once, you know, I got used to it."

I glanced at the portrait on my draft table, and my gaze went immediately to my mother's eyes again. There was something about them. . . . "I'm sure the Magic Wand Salon can re-create it."

Sounding put out, she said, "And why was Ve only casting the spell on *you*? Did she say?"

"No, and she left before I could quiz her about it." I walked over to the drafting table and packed up my supplies.

"I live in bizzarro world. One with freaky streaks and crazy witches. Speaking of, you wouldn't believe the things I'm reading in this Craft book. Apparently, we witches are big on fires. Elf fires, balefires, need fires. Bonfires here, bonfires there. We're a bunch of pyros, that's what we are."

Pyromaniacs. "I'm not sure I'd go that far, unless you're talking about Dorothy Hansel Dewitt." Dorothy was infamous around the village for being a fire-starter when she lost her temper.

"True story," Harper said, humor in the words.

In the Craft world, fire was an important element for transformation, recharging energy, and even as a remedy to fix spells, as Vivienne had used it for.

Dorothy had apparently misunderstood that memo.

I heard a shout from outside, and went to the window. The displaced Extravaganzers were back in force, but the party atmosphere had dissipated. Now, most looked solemn or angry, and I wondered if that had more to do with the gossip about a petnapper rather than being unable to get back into the Wisp.

I glanced at my own assorted critters and felt my stomach knot at the thought of one of them being stolen. It was a horrible feeling I wouldn't wish on my worst enemy.

"And there's nothing in this book about the Elder specifically," Harper went on. "Except . . ."

I perked up. "What?"

"There's this section in the book called the Renewal, which is a ritual that takes place every twenty-five years on Midsummer's Eve. I think it has to do with the Elder, which is more instinct on my part than anything."

Midsummer, the summer solstice, was a big deal with Crafters, a celebration of life. In the village, the euphoric atmosphere was marked by a weeklong observance that included a festival and a dance that was the biggest event of the year. "What kind of ritual?"

"A renewal," Harper said with a "duh" tone to her voice.

I frowned at my phone.

"The paragraph talks in circles about the gathering of a coven of seven to—and I quote—'facilitate matriarchal renewal or renaissance.' There is, of course, a fire involved. The cunning fire."

"What's that?" I asked.

"I had to look it up. It's essentially a special bonfire that's used to give omniscient powers to a chosen witch. From what I've researched, this fire can be used for either good or evil, depending on the group using it, but for Craft purposes, it's used for good. That witch becomes a high priestess, the governess of her community." She took a breath. "Sounds like the role of the Elder to me."

It definitely did.

"And didn't Ve tell us once that the Craft was a matriarchal society?" she asked.

She had. "Yes."

"Then the Renewal ritual *has* to involve renewing the Elder's powers. Right?"

"It sure sounds like it." Harper had excellent instincts, so I didn't doubt for a moment that she was right.

But one thing about what she'd read was bothering me. "Does it explain what the renaissance represents? Because to me renaissance is something entirely new, a rebirth, a change. Which doesn't fit with a renewal of old powers."

"No, but maybe it's more semantic than anything and just means that the renaissance is the beginning of another twenty-five years as governess. You know how witches can double-talk."

We certainly could. "But you said renewal *or* renaissance. It doesn't add up."

"I don't know what to tell you, Darcy. There's no clarification in this book. Maybe you should ask the Elder about it."

I lifted Titania onto my lap and adjusted her new collar. She looked at me with those big amber eyes of hers, completely trusting me.

In that moment, I knew I somehow had to convince Alina Norcliffe to let me keep the cat. Exactly how, I didn't know yet, but I had a couple of hours to figure it out.

"When have you ever known the Elder to spill any Craft secrets?" I asked.

"Never," she said. "But I've never been called to see the Elder, unlike some people I know. Cough, cough."

"That's because you refuse to have anything to do with the Craft."

"For good reason, you bunch of pyros." She laughed. "I've got to go. I left Marcus downstairs in the shop, and we're swamped."

"Hey," I said before she hung up.

"What?"

"You seem awfully interested in the Elder, Harper Merriweather, for someone who doesn't care about the Craft."

She blew a raspberry and hung up.

Smiling, I dropped the phone on the bed. Harper would eventually come around to accepting her heritage.

I hoped.

Tilda hopped up next to me and inched her way onto my lap, snuggling in next to Titania. I scratched her chin.

"Tilda and Titania. The tongue-twisting double *T*'s. That's going to get a little confusing, isn't it?" I asked them.

Tilda flicked her tail in my face while Titania flopped in my arms, stretching out.

I took that as agreement on both their parts.

Titania's name was from *A Midsummer Night's Dream* by Shakespeare. The character of Titania was a fairy queen, headstrong but perhaps a little too trusting of her husband, who'd used a magic potion to make her look like a fool.

Headstrong would be the last thing I'd call the cat in my arms. The same went with foolish. She was neither. She was . . . a marshmallow, really.

Fluffy and sweet.

"How about a nickname?" I said to Titania. Then I glanced at Missy, who was watching us intently from the floor. "I've become one of those women, haven't I? One who talks to her pets and expects an answer."

She barked, and I swore I saw her nod her head.

"I blame it on living in this village," I explained to myself under my breath. "Where animals actually do talk."

Missy dropped to the floor and yawned.

I turned my attention back to Titania. There was no way I was nicknaming her Marshmallow. Or Marsh. Or Mallow. They just didn't fit.

"Titania. Hmm. T? Tita? Tannie?" I tested. "Annie?"

At the last suggestion, her head lifted and she blinked sleepily at me.

"Annie?" I said again.

She closed her eyes and purred.

"Annie it is," I said. I scooted backward and flopped against my pillows. Titania—Annie—was still nestled in my arms, and Tilda had settled at my hip. Missy hopped onto the bed, yawned, and turned in a circle three times before finding the perfect resting spot between my knees.

Right here, right now, with the pets and under my mother's watchful gaze, was the most at peace I'd felt in weeks. . . .

Right up until I woke up thirty minutes later to the sound of a booming cheer going up outside.

Panic set in as I hazily blinked at the clock and realized I'd fallen asleep. I had ten minutes to make it to the Wisp to meet Nick.

I jumped up, and both cats meowed protests and leaped off the bed.

"Sorry!" I said.

Throwing a glance outside, I didn't see anything that would cause celebration and wondered if they'd possibly received news that the Wisp had reopened.

I sent Nick a text that I was running a few minutes late and quickly set about making my bed, a task I normally undertook every morning like clockwork, but for some reason had skipped today. My OCD insisted I make it before I left again, and as I drew the rumpled comforter toward the head of the bed, I was confused for a moment when I found my Craft cloak beneath the covers . . . until I recalled that I had tossed it on the bed last night after returning from the Elder's meadow.

I hurriedly carried the cloak from my bed to my closet. Halfway across the room something fell from the hood, which had turned partly inside out in my rushing about. Both cats immediately pounced upon the object, batting it to and fro.

I bent to see what it was and found a feather. It was

pure white along the bottom its quill, slowly blending to a grayish brown near its tip. The barbs of the feather followed the same color pattern. Fuzzy white at the bottom, narrowing to a grayish brown at the top.

I recognized it immediately.

A mourning dove feather.

Glancing at my cape, I wondered how on earth the feather had become tangled up in it.

Unless . . .

Unless it had somehow fallen into my hood while I was standing under the Elder's weeping tree last night. Had the bird been there and I just hadn't seen it?

If so, why had the bird been there? In *that* tree?

Did the bird have something to do with the Elder?

Suddenly dizzy, I sat on the edge of the bed, my mind swirling. I had suspected for a while now that the mourning dove I kept seeing around As You Wish was more than it appeared. Was it possible the bird was associated with the Elder somehow, as Archie was? A secretary of some sort? A spy, even?

Maybe so, but as I stared at the feather, the sound of the Elder's voice kept going round and round inside my head, making me even more dizzy.

"I was with you all along, Darcy."

"I was with you all along, Darcy."

"I was with you all along, Darcy."

I looked at the pets, who were all staring up at me as though sensing something was wrong.

I stood up, sat down, stood up again.

"I was with you all along, Darcy."

I thought of all the times I'd seen that bird around the village, and all the times I'd heard the Elder's voice here in this house. Had I never seen her coming or going, because she had *flown* in through Ve's bedroom window?

"Is the mourning dove the *Elder* in disguise?" I said aloud, my heart rate kicking up at the possibility.

None of the pets, however, answered me.

I sat down, stood up, sat down again. I didn't know what to do, where to go, who to ask.

Sensing my agitation, Missy barked. I patted her head. "Is it possible?"

She barked again, but I didn't know if it was a yes or a no.

My head started to ache with how hard my brain was working, trying to connect the pieces of this puzzle.

I twirled the feather between my fingers. "But if the Elder's going around as a bird, how is she doing that?"

Then I recalled something Glinda had said this morning.

"One thing I know for certain is that the Elder can embody all the Crafts and can change from one to another at will. She's Wishcrafter, Broomcrafter, Curecrafter, et cetera, at whim. She knows every Craft inside and out."

I stood up, sat down, stood up again.

Missy started to whimper. The cats darted under the bed.

Was there a variety of Craft that could morph into an animal? I'd never heard of one, but that meant little. There were so many secrets still to uncover in this village, but I had the feeling I was on the right track with this one.

As soon as possible, I had to find out if there was such a Crafter . . . or if the feather being in the Elder's meadow was just one big coincidence.

And I knew just the mice to ask.

Chapter Twenty

As much as I hated to do it, I had to postpone my trip to see Pepe and Mrs. P, but I planned to go see them immediately after meeting Nick at the Wisp.

I packed my laptop into a backpack along with the cord I needed to transfer the data from the spy pen to my hard drive. I grabbed some blank disks and a thumb drive and headed out. I was careful to lock the door behind me as I left As You Wish, just in case the rumors of a petnapper weren't just rumors.

On a normal day, driving to the Wisp, which was two blocks back from the main square, would be faster, but the village green was packed, and a steady stream of cars flowed into the village from the main entrance toward designated parking lots at the far end of the square. If I were to drive, I'd have to sit in that traffic for a while.

I set off on foot, my mind still reeling with the possibility that the mourning dove was the Elder in disguise.

As I walked, I searched branches and lampposts, bench tops and flower urns, for any sign of the bird. Although there was a steady thrum of voices out here on the green, I strained to hear that telltale coo I'd come to recognize so well.

I wasn't altogether sure what I planned to do if I actually spotted the bird—interrogate it?—but I wanted to see it again. Wanted to see if there was something subtly magical about the bird that I'd somehow missed before.

What I needed was a better picture of the bird.

Perhaps the bird had an unusual eye color or there was a magic marking . . .

"Whoa, Darcy!"

A set of hands grabbed my shoulders, and I jumped. It took me a second to realize that I'd almost knocked over Harmony, who'd been headed in the opposite direction.

"Everything okay?" she asked. "You look a little out of it, if you don't mind my saying."

I needed to push the thoughts of the Elder out of my head for a while. It was the only way to keep my wits about me.

I gave my head a small shake. "I'm just . . . in a rush and wasn't paying attention. Sorry. Any word on Cookie?"

"Nothing. No sightings of her at all today, which is strange. I'm hoping she didn't leave village limits." Harmony looked toward the woods. "She has a collar on, but she's a hornless breed, and doesn't have the defenses horns would have provided her against predators."

"I'm sure she's around here somewhere," I tried to reassure her, but it was strange that there had been no sightings of Cookie today.

"Maybe," Harmony said. "I'm a little worried about the petnapper gossip. I know Cookie got loose on her own, but what if the petnapper happened to come across her and took advantage? You hear all the time about these so-called pet flippers. Maybe that trade includes goats."

"Pet flippers?" I hadn't ever heard the term.

"It's a person who steals a pet, or sometimes even gets it for free—think of all the times you've seen free kitten signs—then puts the animal up for sale online. The flippers don't care where the pet goes as long as they get their money. Could be to a nice family, but it could be to a dog-fighting ring or to a pet-testing laboratory. It's fast cash."

I felt a little queasy. "That's . . . vile."

"Yeah." Her gaze scanned the green. "But maybe I'm jumping to conclusions. After all, Lady Catherine was found this morning, so anything's possible."

"She was found? Was that the loud cheer I heard a little while ago?"

"It was. Ivy Teasdale found her near the back door of Fairytails. She took her to Marigold straight off. I'm mourning that reward money. I've been looking for Lady Catherine all morning—don't tell Angela."

I smiled. "My lips are sealed."

"Do you know what I could do with that money?"

"Buy a miniature donkey?"

She laughed. "No. Just no."

"Never say never."

"You're a bad influence, Darcy."

My phone buzzed. "Sorry. I've got to check that."

"Actually, I've got to go, but if you could keep an eye out for Cookie, I'd appreciate it."

"I will," I promised.

As she walked away, I felt slightly guilty for not keeping hold of Cookie in the meadow last night, but I just couldn't risk anything about the Craft being uncovered.

Sighing, I pulled my phone out of my backpack and

checked the message that had come in. It was from Nick saying he was running late, too.

I let out a relieved breath and pressed on, worrying about pet flippers and the two dogs and cat that were still missing. If I was in the business of stealing pets, the Extravaganza would be the perfect place to scope out potential victims.

It was a disturbing thought that I couldn't shake as I started up the road that led to the Wisp. Had the pets that were missing been stolen? I wished I knew for certain. If for no other reason than that I could start searching online to find them listed in for-sale ads.

I was almost to the Wisp when someone stepped up next to me. "Hi."

I gasped and nearly fell off the sidewalk into the gutter. My arms looked like windmills until Glinda grabbed one of them and held on until I regained my balance.

"You're awfully jumpy," she said, laughing at my reaction.

I had to face it—I shouldn't be wandering around the village on my own today. "I didn't hear you come up."

"I'm stealthy that way. It's one of the things that makes me a good PI."

"Well, I'd appreciate it if you didn't *stealth* with me. I think I lost ten years off my life."

Her blue eyes narrowed. "Why so on edge?"

"Baz Lucas." I quickly told her about how he'd been at Chip's, then later followed me to the Elder's meadow last night.

"That's all very strange. Where's he now? In police custody?"

"Not that I know of. Nick hasn't found anything that implicates him in any crime."

"I don't like it," she said as we kept walking. "He doesn't seem the dangerous type, but people do dangerous things when they feel cornered."

That didn't make me feel better. "Why would he even think *I* was cornering him? I've barely had any contact with him."

"You said he saw you at Chip Goldman's, right? Maybe you overheard something he wants you to forget."

That sent a shiver down my spine. I tried to recall everything Chip and I had talked about, but it was all rather fuzzy at this point. "Nothing comes to mind."

"Keep thinking on it. It could be something that seems trivial to you, but is monumental to him."

There was very little traffic at all in the back neighborhoods, only a passing car or two as we walked along. Clouds dotted the sky, and it was beginning to look as though it might rain.

"What are you doing here, by the way?" I asked.

"Walking?"

I sighed. "I told you I'd get you a copy of that footage."

"It's not that I don't trust you," she began, then paused. "No, that's exactly why. I don't trust you. Five hundred thousand dollars is a lot of motivation for you to take that footage to Vivienne yourself."

My chest ached at her words, and I realized I was hurt by them. Which was all kinds of stupid on my part. She was Glinda. I should have known better than to let my guard down around her. "Oh."

She stopped walking, looked at me. "Oh? That's it? No snappy rebuttal?"

Shaking my head, I surged forward. "It is what it is. What it always is. What it will always be."

She caught up to me. "What's that mean?"

I drew up and told her the flat-out truth. "I'd allowed myself to think that we had been forming some sort of strange friendship."

"Aren't we?" she asked, her eyes full of confusion.

"Obviously not. Friends don't think friends will backstab them and steal their money." I started forward again.

"I—"

Heat surged into my face as my temper flared. I stopped and glared at her. "I don't need your money. I don't want your money. I *never* wanted your money. And if you were my friend, you'd already know that." I took off walking again, my anger making me walk faster than usual.

Glinda jogged to catch up. "I—"

I kept walking as I said, "I told you I'd give you the footage, and I will. That's it, end of story. As soon as Nick gets here, you'll have it, and then you can be on your way."

She grabbed my arm. "Darcy, stop!"

"What?" I huffed.

"If you'd let me get a word in edgewise, you'd know." I tapped my foot.

"I didn't mean to hurt your feelings." She looked upward and took a deep breath.

When she looked back at me, there was moisture in her eyes, and my anger evaporated. Glinda didn't wear her emotions on her sleeve.

"I don't trust easily, that's all," she said. "Too many people have betrayed my trust. I—I'm sorry. Truce?"

It was the first time I'd ever heard Glinda issue an apology for her bad behavior. "All right," I said reluctantly. "You're just lucky I believe in second chances."

She gave a smile, and it lit her whole face, making it look as if she were glowing from the inside out. "I must be on my fifth or sixth chance with you by now."

"True enough. Then you're just lucky I'm a big sap." She said, "You really are."

I laughed. "We all have our crosses to bear."

"It's not a cross," she said softly. "It's a badg—"

She was cut off by the ring of her cell phone. She gave

me a wait-a-sec finger and glanced at her screen and frowned. "Hello?"

I could hear a male voice, but not what he was saying.

By the stricken look on Glinda's face, it wasn't good news.

"What? When? Where?" She peppered him with questions. "I'll be right there." She hung up and looked at me. "I have to go."

"What's wrong?"

"Someone just tried to steal Clarence."

"Tried? Or did?"

"Tried."

Thank goodness. "Did Liam see who it was?"

"I don't know. I have to go. Liam's freaked out."

"The pen . . ."

"Bring me the footage when you get the chance." She paused a beat. "I trust you with it."

I rubbed my hands together. "And here I was just wondering what I could do with the five hundred grand. Another addition on the house . . . A new car . . . A bunch of miniature donkeys . . ."

"Donkeys?"

"Long story," I said, laughing.

Glinda shook her head and waved over her shoulder as she took off running down the street, her blond hair flying out behind her.

I was still laughing as I turned back toward the Wisp.

Laughter that died on my lips when I saw Baz Lucas step out from behind a large oak tree.

Chapter Twenty-one

Baz took a step toward me, and I held out my arm. "That's close enough."

In that instant, I heard a sound so soothing I immediately relaxed a bit. It was the coo of a mourning dove, and it was somewhere nearby. I wasn't alone.

The Elder was with me.

I could feel deep down that it was true—that she was using the bird as a method to travel in and around the village. Why had I never noticed the immense comfort the bird's call had brought to me before now?

Confusion slashed across Baz's features. "What? Why?"

Bolstered with the knowledge that I had the governess of the Craft as potential protection against Baz, I took a moment to study him. The past twenty-four hours hadn't been kind to him. He, like Vivienne, was still wearing the clothes he'd had on at the Wisp yesterday.

His shirt was untucked, and his long coral-colored cargo shorts were filthy. Thick stubble covered his cheeks and chin, and his hair was flat on one side, standing on end on the other. Cuts and scratches covered his arms, his legs, including one nasty-looking wound near his ankle that I was sure had come from Pepe.

And what I saw of him didn't paint the picture of a cold-blooded killer, but rather a man who'd lost control of his life.

"Why were you following me last night?" I asked.

"How did you—" He ran a hand down his face. "I refuse to deny it. Yes, I followed you into the woods, but quickly lost you in the growing darkness. I sought your help, nothing more. I didn't know where else to turn, and Vivienne always spoke so highly of you and your sleuthing skills at your job through As You Wish."

He'd thrown me for a loop. "Help? With what?"

"I am fearful. Fearful the police are going to look no farther than my doorstep for Natasha's killer. Fearful I am being used as a scapegoat." His voice rose louder and louder. "Fearful my good name will be forever besmirched because of the company I chose to keep, and for simply being in the wrong place at the wrong time. Fearful that perhaps I will be the next victim." Taking a shuddering breath, he dropped his chin to his chest, and his eyelids fluttered closed.

Once again, he reminded me of Archie, with his theatrical litanies. But if Baz was looking for an encore, he was not going to get it from me.

"Did you kill Natasha?" I asked.

He wasn't wearing his glasses, and he squinted as if trying to read my facial features to determine if I was kidding. "No! Why would I?"

I wasn't sure I believed him. His dramatics hinted that he was an actor, and he'd probably picked up a lot of tips being the movie buff that he was. "That remains to be seen. One theory is that you wanted revenge because Natasha might have been responsible for your food poisoning at last year's Extravaganza."

"What? That's nonsense. Why would she do such a thing?"

"Why? So you'd have to withdraw Audrey from the competition, and Titania could win."

"You're joking."

I shook my head. "Like I said, it's a theory."

"It's a ridiculous one."

"Why do you think so?"

"Natasha wouldn't have stooped to such a level. Yes, she liked to win, but not by cheating. She had self-respect, which was why . . ."

"Why what?"

"Nothing. It does not matter now. Natasha did not slip anything into my food or drink. How would she have even known Audrey would be popular? It was only Audrey's first year in the event, and I had to pull strings with Ivy to even get a booth. Unless you're suggesting Natasha intended to poison any person whose pet she deemed competition? If so, you must believe her to be a sociopath, in which case I would start to question *your* sanity."

It wouldn't be the first time.

"She was kindhearted and misunderstood, not a sociopath."

Kindhearted? For a moment, I wondered if we were speaking of the same person.

He had, however, made a good point about Natasha and the food poisoning. Had she intended to poison *whoever* was the top competition?

There were too many variables in that situation. The timing alone would have been a nightmare with determining front-runners, what time their owners were scheduled to eat, and how to even tamper with their lunch, especially if they'd brought it from home and not bought it at the event.

It seemed a stretch, as Glinda would say.

Suddenly, I questioned if Ivy had been wrong about Natasha altogether. Had the accidents she'd been so worried about simply been accidents? Not sabotage at all? I almost groaned thinking about it. All the time I'd spent on this case, all the snooping . . . I could have enjoyed the Extravaganza as a guest instead of a competitor. I certainly wouldn't be standing here with Baz wondering if he was a killer.

I shouldn't have taken the case.

The thought flitted through my head, and I shoved it aside, hating hindsight with all my heart.

When was I ever going to learn to say no?

"To be honest," Baz said glumly, "I have always suspected Vivienne had something to do with my illness that day."

"Vivienne?" I adjusted my backpack, shifting the weight from one shoulder to the other. "Why would she?"

"We'd had a huge row the night before after she accused me of cheating on her."

"Were you cheating?"

"Irrelevant."

"Totally relevant."

He looked at his hands, stretched at his fingers, and frowned at their ragged condition. "No, it is not."

I was growing weary of him. "I'm going to ascertain from your nonanswer that you were."

"That is your prerogative. On the matter, you will not hear otherwise from me."

"Because of the prenup?" I asked.

His dirty fingers curled into fists. "I curse the day I signed that paper."

I was sure Vivienne was cursing the day she married him, so I considered it a wash between them.

I recalled how two days ago, Vivienne had sat in the front parlor of As You Wish and told me how desperately she wanted Audrey to win the Extravaganza. "Would she really have sacrificed the chance for Audrey to win the grand prize to seek revenge on you?"

He ran a hand through his hair. "Have you ever seen Vivienne angry?"

"No."

"The term she-devil comes to mind. If her desire that day was to punish me, she would have had tunnel vision. The competition would not exist next to my suffering."

With that, I crossed off any notion of a reconciliation between the two of them. There was no love lost on Baz's part, and my empathy increased for Vivienne that she'd been living with his apathy for so long.

At this point, *I* wanted to give him food poisoning.

"She denies tampering with my food, but what else would she say?"

"So, you were cheating on her, you suspect she gave you food poisoning, and you've compared her to a she-devil. Why did you stay married?"

"Divorces are costly."

My head was starting to ache. "I suppose that leads me to the second theory as to why you might kill Natasha: You wanted to be rid of Natasha before Vivienne found out that you were cheating. Again, that prenup was in play."

Drawing his shoulders back, he puffed his chest in self-righteous indignation. "Natasha was merely a friend. An acquaintance, rather."

"Yes," I said dryly. "I saw how friendly you were with her in the hallway of the Wisp yesterday afternoon when the two of you stepped out from the storage closet together. I seem to recall you declaring your love and promising that you two would be together forever very soon. That's a level of acquaintance I could do without from you, by the way, so don't get any ideas."

A vein pulsed in his forehead and sweat popped up on his brow. "You were spying on me?"

"No," I corrected. "I was spying on *Natasha*. Glinda, however, was spying on you, if that makes you feel better."

"Glinda?"

"She's a PI now, did you know?"

Swallowing hard, he nodded. "Did Vivienne hire her? I've seen them together quite a bit lately."

"It's not for me to say." Two could play his game of nonanswering.

With a heavy sigh, he sat on the curb. He set his elbows on his knees and his head in his hands. "I don't know what is happening."

I sat next to him. "Did you love her?"

"Natasha?"

"Yes, Natasha."

Fat tears filled his eyes and he blinked them away. "More than anything. It was a whirlwind relationship. We'd only been seeing each other for a month. I fell so fast for her. So hard and fast. She wasn't like the others."

The others . . . the other women. I clenched my teeth.

"Natasha was . . . special," he said. "I don't know what I'm going to do without her."

On one hand, I felt bad for him, for losing someone he clearly loved. On the other hand, he was a lying, cheating slime. It was that hand that wanted to reach out and smack him upside his head.

He could have divorced Vivienne long ago and dated Natasha on the up-and-up, yet he had chosen money over happiness.

And look where it had gotten him.

"At Natasha's urging, I decided it was finally time to leave Vivienne. My lawyer has been working on drawing up the papers. Natasha and I were planning to get married and move out of the village. . . . The divorce has been a long time coming," he said, sliding me a wounded-puppy-dog look. "I tried to make it work, time and again, but Vivienne wasn't the same after her accident."

"Baz?" I said, talking through my clenched teeth.

"Yes?"

"Let me give you a tip, okay?"

"Sure," he said reluctantly.

My jaw started to ache. I made myself relax. "If you want me to feel even an ounce of sympathy for your current predicament, do not, and I repeat, *do not* in any way, shape, or form tell me that you broke your wedding vows—time and time again from what I hear—because of something your *wife* has done. Understand?"

His Adam's apple bobbed as he nodded.

"Do you know anyone who'd want to hurt Natasha?" I asked.

"Enough to kill her? No."

"Did anyone else know of your affair?"

"Chip Goldman apparently did. He was going to blackmail me, and I'd have paid him, too, to keep him quiet, but he collapsed. . . . I think the cops are trying to pin his death on me."

"You did leave him for dead."

" 'Twas only because I thought he was *already* dead! I should not be held responsible. I did not place the cyanide in that repulsive green liquid he was consuming." He patted his pocket, where I saw the outline of a phone. "My lawyer's been calling all morning, telling me that the police want to interview me again. I have a bad feeling about all of this. A very bad feeling. I will not be railroaded. I'll find who killed Natasha myself and make them pay! I'll cast locust upon their house! Vengeance will be mi—" His eyes went wide.

Nick's black-and-yellow police car had turned the corner and pulled up to the curb next to us. He hadn't even stepped out of the car when Baz jumped to his feet and took off running down the middle of the street.

In a flash, Nick's door flew open. He'd just jumped out when a white car roared to life from where it had been parked at the end of the street. The motor revved as the driver gunned the engine, leaving skid marks behind along with the scent of burning rubber.

"Nick!" I screamed.

He glanced back over his shoulder and dove out of the way just as the car zoomed past. He landed with a grunt on the asphalt and rolled toward the curb.

"Baz!" I yelled. "Look out!"

Baz turned around, but it was too late. The car clipped him, sending him flying into the front lawn of a house nearby. The car kept on going, skidding around the corner and out of sight.

I was dialing for help as I ran first to Nick's side. "Are you okay?" I asked him, not wanting to touch him in case he was seriously hurt, yet at the same time wanting to grab him and hold him tight.

"Fine," he huffed, clearly winded. He tried to sit up, couldn't. "Go. Baz."

I didn't want to leave his side, but I knew I had to see if Baz was okay. I gave Nick my phone to talk to the emergency dispatcher and sprinted down the street. Baz was flat on his back, moaning in pain. I took one glance at the bone sticking out of his upper leg and nearly passed out.

Blood and I didn't get along.

Dizzy, I focused on Baz's face, where—thank the heavens above—there was no blood to be seen.

"Baz?"

He groaned.

"Help's coming."

"Car," he said through chattering teeth. "Hit."

"I know. I saw."

"Vivie—," he mumbled.

"Vivienne?" I repeated. "Was she the one driving?"

He nodded, his eyelids fluttering, then closing.

Vivienne was the one who'd hit him? I hadn't been able to see anyone in the driver's seat. The car had gone by too quickly. But now that I thought about it, Vivienne did drive a white car. . . .

I glanced at Baz and saw how pale he had become and wished with all my might for help to arrive soon, because I knew that broken bone in his leg had been his femur, and all that blood suggested that he might have severed an artery as well. It was a deadly injury. Until help came, there was only me. I was definitely not the right witch for this job, but I would do my best to keep him alive.

I slipped off my backpack and pulled off my T-shirt, grateful to be wearing a tank top beneath it. I didn't know how to make a tourniquet—had only seen them applied in movies—but I knew Baz needed one or he'd die from blood loss. Finding the side seam of the shirt, I yanked for all I was worth and the material split, creating one long cloth strip.

Summoning all the inner strength I possessed, I slipped a length of that cloth under Baz's leg.

Woozy, I swayed as blood oozed over my hands. Tears streamed from my eyes, making everything blurry.

I heard the coo of the mourning dove above my head, but it brought me no solace at this moment.

I thought I might be sick.

Fighting nausea, I sucked in some air and had just grabbed hold of both ends of the shirt material when I felt someone drop down next to me.

"I'll do it."

Nick's strong hands nudged mine aside and took hold of the cloth. He quickly fashioned the material into a tourniquet, slipping a nearby stick into the knot he'd made. Then he twisted the stick. It was the last thing I remembered before I passed out.

Chapter Twenty-two

An hour and a half later, I sat on a bench outside the front entrance of the Wisp, soaking in air heavily scented with pending rain. I hadn't budged from this spot in nearly twenty minutes, mostly because I was afraid to move in fear the nausea would return.

The time between the accident and now had passed in a blur. Baz had been taken to the hospital, but Nick had declined any treatment. He was banged and bruised and stubborn but okay. He was currently searching the village for any sign of Vivienne Lucas.

Voices rose and fell all around me as a steady stream of people trooped in and out of the Wisp. It had re-opened an hour ago, which was why Nick had been running late for our meeting in the first place. He'd been taking one last look at the reports before giving the okay for Extravaganzers to return to collect their belongings.

"It's chaos in there," Harper said, sliding onto the

bench next to me. She handed me the spy pen and a bottle of water. "Here."

"Thanks."

"You should see Ivy. She's rushing around like a crazy woman, alternately apologizing about the delay and barking at people to clean up after themselves. Her head might pop clean off by the end of the day."

"Honestly, I'm surprised it hasn't already."

"We should start a betting pool on when it will happen." Her golden brown eyes flared with humor, then softened as she asked, "Are you feeling any better?"

"Some."

"You're not green anymore. That was disturbing, I'm not even going to lie."

Our upper arms were touching, as she sat a little closer to me than usual. It appeared my little sister had a bit of a mother hen in her as well.

Her gaze swept over my face. "I've never seen someone actually turn green before."

"The whole incident was disturbing." I took a quick look at my fingers and battled a terrible case of the heebie-jeebies before I cracked the seal on the water.

The paramedics had thoroughly cleansed the blood from my hands, but I wanted nothing more than to go home to soak them in hot soapy water. I wondered if I could possibly douse them with bleach without burning the skin straight off my fingers.

I doubted it. Harsh chemicals tended to have that effect on skin.

"Has Nick found Vivienne yet?" she asked.

The cool water soothed my parched throat. "Not that I know of. Last I heard, she wasn't at the Pixie Cottage, where she'd been staying with Harmony and Angela, or at home. No sign of her car, either. She could be in Maine right now for all we know."

I capped the bottle, set it next to me, and rolled the

spy pen between two fingers. At this point Vivienne was going to need a good criminal defense lawyer, rather than a divorce attorney.

The good news for her was that it appeared Baz would survive his injuries.

The bad news was that she was now the lead suspect in Natasha's death.

Perhaps the footage on this pen would help her case. Proving temporary insanity or some such.

Unfortunately, I had the feeling it would do more harm than good. This little pen provided an undeniable motive.

"I'm on Vivienne's side in all this," Harper said. "I might have buttons made up. Team Vivienne. Baz had it coming. If Marcus had cheated on me with anything that walks and talks, then I might have run him over, too. I'd have finished the job, though, and not just left him with a broken leg. Bye-bye. See ya later. *Adios*."

My sister had a vigilante streak a mile wide. "I'm glad you don't own a car."

Harper hadn't yet realized that Vivienne was now a suspect in Natasha's death, and I didn't inform her, for one simple reason: I didn't want to talk about it. Didn't even want to think that somehow Vivienne had fooled me so completely. I'd felt so sorry for her.

I supposed I still did. In a way.

"Come on," Harper said. "Like you never wanted to run over Troy?"

My ex-husband. "Maybe so, but there's a big difference between thinking about hurting someone versus actually *running them down*."

"Yeah, courage." Harper waved away a fly buzzing near her face. "The guts to actually go through with it."

I seriously hoped she *never* bought a car.

"No," I countered. "*Self-control*. If I'd run over Troy,

I'd be in jail. I wouldn't be sitting here with you. I wouldn't have Nick. I wouldn't have Mimi. I wouldn't have . . . this life I love so much. As much as Troy broke my heart at the time, I had enough control over emotions not to let that situation destroy my life. Not to let a white-hot moment of hurt and anger rob me of my future. It took time, but I picked up the pieces of that broken marriage, and now I can see that he actually did me a favor."

"I suppose if you put it that way," she grumbled as she snaked her arm around my elbow and reached down to entwine her fingers with mine. "You're such a sap. The sappiest."

"I know." Smiling, I leaned my head against hers.

"You're going to marry Nick," she said.

I laughed. "Are you asking me or telling me?"

"Telling."

"I think he should ask me first, don't you?"

"He will."

For some reason tears filled my eyes. "You think?"

"No, Darcy. I *know*."

I didn't know. But I hoped with all my heart.

She squeezed my fingers, then let go of my hand. "I'd better get back inside to finish packing up our booths."

"Thanks for doing all that. I've got to drag myself off this bench to go see Natasha's sister."

"Right. About Titania."

"Annie," I corrected. "It's her new nickname."

"Cute. It fits her," Harper said as she stood up. She started to walk away, then looked back at me. "Hey."

"Yeah?"

"Remind me to send Troy a thank-you card one of these days, okay? We probably never would have come to this village if not for him. Seems to me, he did me a big favor, too."

I met her warm gaze. "And you call me the sappy one?"

"Shut up." She came back, kissed my cheek, then strode away.

I was willing myself to stand up and go when I heard the flutter of wings. The mourning dove had landed on a lower branch of a Rose of Sharon tree not five feet from the bench. Its shimmery neck bobbed as it paced back and forth along the branch before it slowed to a stop and tipped its head, looking my way.

For a moment, I simply watched it, trying to determine if the bird had any unusual features I could identify, but it was too far away to make out any detail.

Then I recalled the spy pen in my hand. If I could get a couple of pictures of the bird, I could enlarge them on the computer for a better look. . . .

As surreptitiously as I could, I aimed the lens of the spy pen toward the tree and snapped at least four photos before someone sat next to me. I turned, expecting it to be Harper again. Instead I found Ivy fanning her face with an Extravaganza program book.

Perspiration beaded along her hairline. "I just needed some fresh air. It's stifling in there."

She'd ditched the wig and sunglasses but still wore the shift dress she'd had on earlier. I supposed she no longer needed a disguise, seeing as she wasn't hiding from the Extravaganzers anymore.

With a loud burble, the bird flew into an upper branch of the tree, hidden by glossy green leaves. I tucked the spy pen into my backpack.

"Do you need anything?" she asked. "You look a little rough around the edges."

"It was a tough morning." It seemed everyone already knew what had happened, so I didn't feel the need to explain.

"Is Baz going to be okay?"

"The doctors think so."

"Is Vivienne still on the run?"

"As far as I know."

"It's been a bad weekend all around. I'm going to need a vacation after all this is said and done," she said. "I'm not sure how relaxing it will be, since I can afford approximately one night at a campground after the financial hits I took this weekend. And camping has never been my idea of fun. The bugs alone . . ." She shuddered.

I had to agree with her about that. "But I heard you came into a bit of a windfall today, so why not go somewhere nice?"

Her eyebrows dipped in confusion.

"You found Lady Catherine?" I prompted. "Didn't you collect the reward?"

Fanning faster, she said, "Oh, that. I wouldn't say found so much as came across her. Dumb luck, really."

"Came across her at Fairytails?"

"Word sure gets around fast, doesn't it?"

"Small village," I said with a shrug.

"Yes. At Fairytails. I came around the corner and there she was, sitting by the back door as though waiting for a grooming appointment."

"That is lucky."

"Don't I know it? That reward money couldn't have come at a better time."

"Especially if you want to upgrade your vacation."

She set the program down on her lap. "I would, but I need to use that money to pay the judges' honorariums. Dorothy's been harping on me about how she doesn't work for free. I'll be more than happy to pay her off. Thankfully, Reggie's been as patient as a saint, and Godfrey's been great, too. He's a good guy."

"The best," I said.

"So, the reward money will go to good use. I suppose the only good news is that I heard whispers among everyone inside about what's going on with the Lucases and Baz's affair with Natasha."

So the news of the affair had leaked. It had been only a matter of time. "How's that good news?"

She began picking at her fingernails. *Flick, flick.* "Because, Darcy, no one is connecting Natasha's death to the Extravaganza any longer. It's such a relief. Now if I could only convince them all that there is no petnapper on the loose . . . I might be able to salvage this event. I'm already daydreaming ways to make it bigger and better next year. Lots of pizzazz!" she said, complete with the use of jazz hands.

"You don't think there's a petnapper? Or, as Harmony thinks, a pet flipper?"

"It's unlikely," she said quickly. "Especially here in the village. This is one nosy town. I mean, you already knew I found Lady Catherine—and where I found her—and that was only a few hours ago. Pets get loose all the time—I should know. My clients are always asking me to hang Lost flyers in the window of Fairytails."

Now that she said it, I recalled seeing one the last time I'd been in there with Missy. Just how many pets had gone missing in the village lately?

And how many, exactly, had been clients of Ivy's?

I started to wonder just how much dumb luck was involved in her finding Lady Catherine. Or . . . perhaps . . . how much planning had gone into it. After all, it was just a couple of hours ago that I had thought the Extravaganza was the perfect place to scout targets if I were a petnapper.

But what if the petnapping had been an inside job all along?

*   *   *

I was still wondering if Ivy was the mastermind behind a petnapping ring as I walked around the back of the Wisp five minutes later.

I hadn't let on about my suspicions to her, but I had a lousy poker face, so I assumed she had known what I was thinking. Which was probably why she'd quickly proclaimed that she had to get inside and had hotfooted it back into the building.

I was still feeling a bit weak in the knees as I headed for the rear of the property, to the spot where Archie had told me he'd freed himself after his attempted bird-napping.

It was easy to see where his struggle to get out of the sack had taken place, as the grass was matted, some of it uprooted.

However, there was no sign of a bag at all.

I quickly sent a text to Nick, asking if one of his officers had retrieved the bag Archie had escaped from. Then I sent another that said there was no rush to answer—that I knew he was busy but I didn't want to forget to ask him. Then I sent a third text that said there might be somewhat of a rush as I suspected Ivy might be a petnapper. I sent a fourth asking about the surveillance videos at the Wisp. A fifth to tell him that I loved him.

I hoped the last would soften the irritation caused by the first four.

Carefully walking around the area, I looked for any clue that it had been Ivy who might have taken Archie. She'd told me she'd been inside the building with the police when it happened, but she could have been lying about that. It was an easy enough alibi to check now that I had reason to.

How much would a beautiful, talkative, somewhat pretentious macaw get on the black market?

I wasn't sure, but it had to be a lot for someone to try to steal him in broad daylight.

I'd been so sure a Crafter had been involved because there had been no witnesses and that made it seem that witchcraft might have been involved, yet Archie had been certain it was a mortal simply because of the consequences otherwise.

If it turned out that Ivy, who was very much a mortal, was in fact the one who had tried to abduct him, I was never—ever—going to hear the end of it.

Chapter Twenty-three

Natasha Norcliffe had lived in a studio apartment not far from Chip Goldman's building. I was due to meet with her sister, Alina, there in twenty minutes, so I figured I had time enough to make a quick stop at the Bewitching Boutique on my way over.

I needed to ask Pepe and Mrs. P about the possibility of a Craft I didn't know about, but I also wanted to ask a favor of Godfrey.

A crystal bell on the door chimed as I went inside, and Godfrey looked over at me. His jaw dropped, his eyes widened, and he quickly said something to the woman he'd been assisting, then rushed over to me.

"My darling, Miss Darcy, come with me. Come, come." He took my hand and pulled me to the back room of the shop, one of my favorite places in the village. I glanced around at the hundreds of bolts of colorful fabrics, the shiny notions, and the tiny door carved into the baseboard with a miniature bell hanging next to it. There was no doubt about it. The sewing room in the Bewitching Boutique was pure magic.

One chubby hand stroked his white beard, the other was set firmly on his hip as Godfrey looked me over. "I heard about your involvement with Baz Lucas' accident, but I thought certainly you would have hurried home to change by now."

"No time," I said. "Well, there *was* time, but I wasn't entirely mobile, what with the nausea and the dizziness."

Godfrey rarely looked as if he hadn't just stepped out of a fancy men's magazine, and today was no different. He wore an impeccably tailored suit, designer shirt, silk tie. A pocket square poked out from the pocket of his suit coat, and his shoes shone so brightly that I almost needed to put on my sunglasses to look at them.

His white hair was thin in spots, but he worked with what he had, combing it into a modern-day pompadour. Rosy full cheeks, a big smile, and a trimmed beard almost fully distracted from his bulbous nose. His sympathetic gaze swept over me, still assessing.

"Nausea and dizziness from seeing blood?" he guessed.

"How'd you know?"

"For one, I know it's a weakness of yours. Secondly, the blood all over your clothes. It's enough to make *me* nauseated and dizzy."

I glanced down and wished I hadn't. Rusty-looking bloodstains splattered my tank top, my shorts, my bare legs. I swayed. No wonder people had given me a wide berth at the Wisp.

Godfrey grabbed me by my shoulders and sat me on a rolling stool. "You're a mess. A disaster. I'll be right back. I need to close the shop for this."

"For what? I don't have time—"

"Make time. This is an emergency."

He zipped out of the room, and I wanted to put my head between my knees to quell the wooziness, but I didn't know if there was dried blood lurking there, too, so I closed my eyes instead.

"Doll! Holy walking crime scene. You look like you've been to war."

I popped open an eye to find Mrs. P standing on the sewing table next to me. Pepe was just coming out of the door in the baseboard when he caught sight of me as well.

"*Ma chère*! Are you injured? Shall I call for Cherise?" With lightning speed, he climbed the leg of the table to stand next to Mrs. P.

"No, I'm fine," I said, swiveling to face them head-on. "Nick's a little banged up, but he'll be okay. Baz is in surgery, but the doctor thinks he'll make a full recovery."

"I still hold a grudge about the shoe incident," Mrs. P said, "but I did not wish the man dead. I am glad he is going to be okay."

"What of Vivienne?" Pepe asked. "Any word?"

"None."

I heard the jingle of the crystal bell, and a second later, Godfrey burst through the velvet curtains that divided this area from the retail shop. "Now, now. I've turned the sign on the door to closed, so we have all the time we need. Where was I?" He clapped his hands twice and a glittery leather journal appeared in his palms. He flipped through the pages. "No, no, no. Ah yes. Here we go."

"No, here *I* go. I'm meeting Natasha Norcliffe's sister about Annie in"—I glanced at the clock—"fifteen minutes. I can't stay. I just wanted to ask—"

"Fifteen minutes is plenty of time," Godfrey cut in.

"Annie?" Pepe asked.

"Titania's new nickname," I said to him, and couldn't help smiling.

"You're keeping her, doll?" Mrs. P asked.

"I hope to. I have to get Alina to sign off on it."

"Do you have your checkbook on you?" Godfrey asked.

"What? No. It's at home," I said. "Why?"

"In that case . . ." He clapped his hands twice and a checkbook appeared. He set it on the table, grabbed a pen from a cup holder, and signed his name with a flourish on a check. He tore it off and handed it to me. "You'll need this."

I really needed to use that hand-clapping technique more. "A blank check?"

"I know you're good for it. Pay me back when you can. Alina is not the warm and fuzzy type in the least, so I doubt she wants the cat—the cat hair alone would probably make her homicidal—but she'll undoubtedly charge you up the wazoo for the honor of taking *Annie* off her hands. Perhaps one thousand? Two?" He glanced at Pepe for confirmation.

Pepe said, "Perhaps higher if you reveal your desperation, *ma chère*. Do not under any circumstances mention the nickname."

"Heavens no!" Godfrey agreed. "She'll know she has you on the ropes if you do."

I looked between them. "I don't understand. . . ."

Mrs. P sat on the edge of the table, her tail curved behind her, her tiny white feet dangling. "Alina is . . . How do I put this?"

"She's a con artist," Godfrey supplied. "I recall once Alina tried to swindle me out of a designer dress by staining it in the dressing room herself and claiming it had already been damaged. She wanted a steep discount. I banned her from the store."

"Alina used to live in the village?" I asked.

"*Oui,*" Pepe said. "She and Natasha moved here some years ago, and Alina made no secret of her aspirations to snag herself a rich tourist."

"She succeeded, too." Godfrey pushed another stool next to mine and sat down. "He's ancient, but he's rich. Filthy rich. He moved her down to the Cape, and they live in a big mansion on Buzzard's Bay. She's just waiting for him to kick the bucket to collect her payment for marrying a geezer."

"If she's so rich, why would she charge me an arm and a leg to adopt Annie?"

Mrs. P said, "Because, doll, she can. She'd rob her own sister and probably has. I don't believe anyone was more relieved than Natasha when Alina moved away."

"Alas, not for the reason you might think," Godfrey said. "Keep in mind they were both rotten apples from the same tree. Natasha was relieved only because she no longer had competition to snag herself a rich tourist as well."

"Instead she seemed to have landed herself a rich villager in Baz," I said. "Do you think she loved him at all?"

Godfrey once again stroked his beard. "The romantic in me wants to believe so, but I doubt it. Natasha loved one person, and one person only. Natasha."

Pepe and Mrs. P nodded.

If that was true, and Natasha had been killed because of her relationship with Baz, she'd certainly paid a high price in her quest for wealth. The highest.

I looked at the clock. "I have to get going, but I had a couple of questions for all of you."

"No, no," Godfrey protested. "You cannot leave looking like you do. You are much too lovely to be roaming the village looking like an extra from the *Walking Dead.*"

Mrs. P stood up and rubbed her hands together. "Something ultrafeminine. She's always wearing jeans and T-shirts."

Pepe snapped his fingers. "The vintage yellow Chanel." He motioned to his neck. "The one with the bow."

I jumped off the stool. "No, no. No Chanel, and definitely no bows. No nothing, actually. I'm fine. Perfect, in fact. I'll just run home and—"

"Calm, Darcy, calm," Godfrey said, smiling. "I know just the thing. Trust me."

He recited a spell under his breath and twirled his index finger in a tornado motion. I slammed my eyes closed, not entirely sure what was about to happen to me, but I did know one thing: I trusted him.

Brightness, like a flash of lightning, filtered through my closed eyelids, and I popped open an eye and squinted at Godfrey.

He was patting himself on the back. "Who's the best fairy godfather in all the land? I am, that's who."

"I may be ill," Pepe intoned.

Mrs. P smiled wide. "You look gorgeous, doll. Just gorgeous."

I looked down at myself, then hurried to a mirror. Gone were my blood-splattered clothes, replaced with skinny white jeans and a short-sleeve teal-green top that had fancy embroidery at the neckline. Gone were my sneakers, replaced with airy brown leather sandals that had straps crisscrossing the top of my feet. My hair was pulled back in a loose knot, and my makeup looked fresh and natural.

My skin glowed, and for the first time since the accident, I felt clean. Truly clean. No heebie-jeebie feeling to be found.

I gave Godfrey a hug. "Thank you."

He cupped my chin. "Anytime. Now, what was it you wanted to ask of us?"

"I was wondering if you still have a surveillance system that monitors the back alley?" With Fairytails a few doors down, his footage would show whether Ivy had been telling the truth about where she found Lady Catherine.

"Of course," Godfrey said. "Why?"

I explained my suspicions.

Mrs. P said, "That's low. Lower than low. To steal a pet and sell it off."

"I cannot comprehend such an action," Godfrey said. Then he chuckled. "Yes, I may have looked into selling a pudgy brown mouse a time or two, but I never followed through. Yet."

"Do not make me bite you," Pepe warned.

"Don't make me step on you," Godfrey returned.

Mrs. P and I ignored them. Sometimes it was the best tactic to take with the two of them.

"I thought Ivy's shop was doing well?" Mrs. P said. "She always has a steady stream of business, and I've never heard anyone speak badly of her."

"I don't know." I sat back on the stool. "All I know is that she seems desperate for money."

"Sadly, I've seen this time and again." Pepe stood and paced the table. "The village has had its fair share of business turnover through the years. Rent is astronomical on leased shops—there are employees to pay, inventory to update. Ivy probably earns enough to stay afloat, but little more. It takes time to become financially sound, and that is only if one has a good financial adviser and much luck."

"My guess would be that Ivy used some of the Extravaganza funds to offset the costs of the shop," Godfrey added. "Without them . . ."

No wonder Ivy had been so freaked-out about the success of the Extravaganza. Her whole livelihood depended on it.

"Even still." Mrs. P sniffed. "Stealing a pet, then selling it? Abhorrent. She must be stopped."

"Let's look at the footage first," I said, "before we go running her out of the village."

"I'll check as soon as possible and will let you know," Godfrey promised. "Now, you should go, before you're late." He handed me the blank check. "Do not forget this. You will need it."

I *was* running late, but I couldn't leave without asking one last question. I bit my lip, unsure what I should reveal about my Elder theory. "Just one more thing . . ."

"What is it, doll?" Mrs. P asked.

"There's been this bird, a mourning dove . . . ," I began.

I saw Mrs. P slide Pepe a look, and I knew I was onto something.

"A lovely breed of bird," Godfrey said, his voice high. "Lovely."

I glanced at him.

He wiped his brow with his pocket square.

I was *definitely* onto something.

"It's a long story, but I'm starting to think the bird is a Crafter, and I'm curious about one thing."

All stared at me blankly, and I could only imagine what was running through their minds if the bird was truly the Elder in disguise. Because none of them would be able to tell me the truth if I asked point-blank.

"Oh?" Mrs. P finally said as she wrung her hands. "What's that?"

"Is there a form of the Craft where the witch takes on an animal form?" I asked. "Animal morphing? Or some kind of shape-shifting?"

Godfrey continued to mop his forehead. "Animal morphing?"

I nodded. "Like, say, a woman becomes a mourning

dove and then turns back to a woman. Or, I should say, the Elder becomes a mourning dove, then turns back into the Elder, who is some woman in this village, identity unknown."

Pepe used his tail to mop *his* brow. *"Non."*

I'd clearly made them nervous. I scooted the rolling stool right up to the table and stuck my face close to his and gave him a raised eyebrow. "You wouldn't be lying to me, would you?"

"Ma chère." He pressed his hand to his chest. "On my honor, there is no such Craft that transforms a witch from human form to animal and back again. It does not exist. I do not know why it does not exist, because it would be a marvelous addition to the Craft, but *non.* I am sorry."

I glanced at Mrs. P.

The hair between her ears had drooped. "He's right. There is no such Craft."

Godfrey was my last chance. "Do you concur with Pepe as well?"

"Absolutely," he said quickly. "The old mouse knows of what he speaks. He is, after all, the expert in all things Craft, which is one of the benefits of his great age."

"That is it!" Pepe exclaimed, raising his fists. "Prepare to defend yourself, pork chop."

Mrs. P sat with a heavy sigh and put her head in her hands.

I rolled my eyes. "I'm going to head out before I witness any more bloodshed. Thanks for everything." I kissed Godfrey's cheek and the tops of Mrs. P's and Pepe's heads.

It had started to sprinkle by the time I walked out of the store, the rain spitting from the sky in random bursts. I glanced over my shoulder at the shop.

I had been so certain there had to be a Craft that

could animal morph, but if Pepe swore on his honor that there wasn't, then I believed him. He held his honor in the highest regard.

What was more curious to me at this point was why none of them had debunked my notion that the Elder had been the bird.

It was very curious indeed.

Chapter Twenty-four

Alina Norcliffe looked very much like her sister. The same long dark hair, the same triangular face. Thin and petite, she roamed around Natasha's living room, adding items to three piles she had created on the floor.

Sell. Keep. Donate.

The sell pile was overflowing.

The donate pile was laughably small.

The keep pile was mournfully minuscule.

Apparently, Alina wasn't much for sentimentality. Or respectful mourning periods.

The studio apartment was tiny but cluttered. One quick glance was all it took to see the whole place. Kitchen, bedroom, dining space. A tiny bathroom was behind me, and clothes spilled out of a closet near the bed.

"Don't you have to wait for probate before selling Natasha's things?" I asked, wincing as she tossed books into the sell pile.

She wore a long flowing halter-style maxi dress and too much perfume. The scent was making my eyes water. When I knocked, she'd given me a long once-over, and I was relieved that Godfrey had worked his magic on me. Although I wore simple jeans and a blouse, they must have been designer quality, because she had nodded in approval. I could only imagine what her look would have been if I'd showed up in what I had been wearing.

Gold bracelets clinked on her arm as she made a sweeping motion with her hand. "It's all mine. My books, my furniture, my everything. I pay the rent, the utilities. Natasha made scraps at the playhouse. What she earned barely covered her food and makeup costs."

The makeup, I imagined, had cost more than the food by far.

Alina picked up a toy mouse and tossed the faux critter at me. "I suppose we should get to the reason why you're here. Titania. She's a very valuable cat. I paid for her, so I should know."

"She's *your* cat?"

"She was a gift to my sister. Natasha didn't particularly care for cats, but she believed Titania would help her break into the acting business. Titania has an audition with a talent agent next week in Hollywood, you know."

The mouse was the only cat toy I could see. Not scratching tree, no feather-on-a-stick, no bed. I recalled how Annie craved my attention, and I grew angry on her behalf.

Do not show my hand, do not show my hand. "You'll be taking over her career, then? Wonderful. I can't wait to see her on TV."

"I actually haven't decided yet. . . ." She eyed me.

I suddenly realized Godfrey had been right. Alina didn't want Titania. At all. She was feeling me out to see how interested I was in adopting the cat—and how much money she could charge me to do it. I almost did a little jig right there on the sofa.

I decided it was time someone turned the tables on the con artist.

That someone was me.

"Well, she's a beautiful cat—that's for sure. She doesn't really like to be touched all that much by strangers, but that shouldn't be too much of an issue if you're there with her to calm her down. I'm sure show business people are used to being scratched."

"Scratched?"

I showed her the marks on my arm that Clarence's nails had left behind, and she recoiled.

"I would have brought her with me," I went on, spinning a web, "but the less jostling for her right now, the better. Her stomach has been unsettled since leaving the Wisp, and—lesson learned—I've been keeping her confined to the bathroom for easier cleanups." I wrinkled my nose as I lied through my teeth. "I'm sure the stains will come out of the rugs with a little elbow grease. Or at least I hope so. The smell, though . . . that'll take time. You can pick her up when you're ready to head back home."

Horror flashed in her eyes.

I kept tight hold of the mouse toy as I said, "I've been holding off on calling a vet, because I think maybe the stomach upset is just from the distress of being moved around so much. Do you know if she gets like that every time she travels?"

"I—I don't know. Natasha never mentioned anything."

I tipped my head. "You might want to be certain before taking her on a plane."

She sat on the arm of a chair, and her shoulders slumped.

"Or perhaps it's her new diet. She might have a particular kind of food she likes better than the type I had on hand." I silently apologized to Annie for making up all these lies. "And you'll probably want to buy some absorbent pads at the Furry Toadstool to line the cat carrier for the ride down to the Cape. Just keep the windows down, and I'm sure you'll be fine."

Thin penciled eyebrows dipped down in dismay and panic. "I don't think Titania would like my house. We have dogs. Big dogs. Guard dogs."

Somehow I doubted she had dogs at all.

"Does the Furry Toadstool have an adoption service?" she asked.

I bit back a smile as she flopped around in the web I'd woven. "No, they don't. If you don't want her, I'm sure the local shelter would take her in. It's a no-kill shelter, so that's a plus. They charge a small intake fee, but it's pennies, really."

"A fee to drop off a cat?"

"It's a nonprofit organization, and it costs to house and feed an animal. It's not that much, really. Twenty dollars, I think." She'd probably paid that much for only one of her fake eyelashes.

"Yeah," she murmured, looking as if she'd knock Tiny Tim's crutch out from beneath his hand if she passed him on a street corner.

"You could always sell her online," I said, hating the words I was speaking. "But that'll take some time to get the ad together, interview potential adopters, that kind of thing. And of course, you'd have to disclose any of her foibles, like the scratching, or risk being sued."

I had no idea if she could actually be sued for such a thing, but knew the thought alone would hurt her where it counted most. Her pocketbook.

"There are *no* other options?" she asked, the hint of a cry in her voice.

"Does Natasha have a friend here in the village who'd take her? It would probably be the easiest transaction of all."

She sighed. "Not really. Just Chip the cheapskate, and he's allergic."

"Cheapskate?"

The bracelets clinked again as she waved her hand. "Just Natasha's nickname for him. They dated for a while, but he was a penny pincher."

"And Natasha wasn't a penny-pinching type of girl."

"Not at all. There was chemistry between them, but they were never going to last as a couple if he wasn't going to spend a little money on her."

I stared at the toy mouse. "Perhaps you can ask Baz if he'd take Titania. Seems he was close to Natasha."

"He hates cats. He was trying to get Natasha to get rid of Titania before they married." Alina smiled. "He stood no chance in that argument."

"Why? If Natasha didn't like cats all that much, either?"

"Because if things turned bad with Baz, she still had Titania to fall back on."

I squeezed that tiny mouse so tight I thought its head might pop off.

"She needn't have worried," Alina said breezily. "Baz stood no chance in *any* argument. He was so smitten . . . it was almost embarrassing. I warned Natasha not to get involved with him, despite his money, but she wouldn't listen. All she saw was her ticket out of here. And now she's dead, so it seems I was right. She rarely listened to me."

It seemed to me that Alina was more upset at the fact her sister never listened to her than at the fact she was dead.

I'd never been so grateful for my relationship with Harper in all my life.

"Why the warning in the first place?" I asked.

"He had too much baggage," she said. "Too many women. Serial cheaters do not make good spouses, especially when he was chattering about prenup agreements. She might have dumped him, too, if the threats hadn't started."

"He threatened her?"

"Not him. I assume it was his wife. Natasha's car had been keyed, her house broken into and notes warning her to stay away from Baz found on her bed, and she felt as though she was being followed."

"When was all this?" Glinda had been following her for a while, so that could be explained. But not the other incidents.

"Right after she started dating him," she said. "A month or so ago."

"Did she go to the police?"

Alina laughed. "Hell no. She accepted the challenge! There's nothing she enjoyed more than competition."

I'd seen that myself at the Wisp.

"Natasha stepped up her pursuit of Baz. First, she withheld sex until he agreed to ditch his other women for just her, then reeled him in. He didn't stand a chance once she turned on her full charms. Last time I talked to her, she thought she had won the battle because Baz wanted to get married and the threats had stopped, but she underestimated the anger and jealousy of a woman scorned, and ended up losing everything."

"Seems to me that everyone lost in this situation."

She picked cat hair from her dress, frowned at it. "Yes, I guess so."

"Did she love him at all? Baz?"

"Love is for fools," she said, sounding as if she believed it. "And Natasha was no fool."

At that, I said, "I should probably get going. Let me

give you my phone number. Just call when you're ready to pick up Titania."

She jumped up. "I really can't take her back with me. I don't suppose you'd . . ." She lifted hopeful eyebrows.

I played dumb. "Me . . . what?"

"That you'd keep her?" she suggested. "She's already accustomed to your house, so I'm sure the stomach problems will stop soon."

I was dancing inside, positively twirling. On the outside, I was trying my best to look as if I thought her suggestion was the worst idea in the whole world. "I don't know . . . the rugs . . ."

She grabbed her purse and pulled a hundred dollars from her wallet. "Here, take this. Let me pay for the rug cleaning. It's the least I can do."

Pretending to weigh the decision, I tipped my head left and right. "I mean, I'd rather keep her than see her be sold online to just anyone. Okay, I'll take her, but I won't take your money."

I got what I came for, and that was more than enough.

Looking relieved, she quickly tucked the money back into her purse and rushed me to the door, apparently worried I would change my mind. "Thanks. You're doing me a big favor."

If she only knew.

I waved as I walked down the walkway, and as soon as I was out of sight, I realized I was still holding the toy mouse.

As I passed by a trash can at the street corner, I tossed the mouse in.

I didn't want to bring back any reminder to Annie of where she had come from.

Today marked a new start, a new life, for her.

One filled with nothing but the love she deserved.

Chapter Twenty-five

"What did Godfrey say when you gave him back his blank check?" Starla asked as we walked around the village green later that night.

Twink and Missy walked side by side ahead of us, straining their leashes to sniff every blade of wet grass they came across.

It was a little past eight, and the rain had stopped, but heavy cloud cover remained behind. Darkness would come early tonight.

"He dropped to his knees and kowtowed, like I was the Queen of Sheba or something."

She laughed. "He did not."

"He did so. But then he couldn't get up again, so Pepe started taunting him. . . . It turned ugly fast."

"No!" she cried, laughing so hard tears leaked from her eyes.

"I had to call Harper for help. Marcus came, too, and

he pulled a back muscle lifting Godfrey up. Then we had to call Cherise, who came and fixed up Marcus and told Godfrey he needed to go on a diet. And when Pepe started to tease about that, Cherise told him he needed a diet, too. There was a lot of outrage and cursing in both English and French, and slamming of doors, though Pepe's door doesn't quite have the same impact as Godfrey's. It was more a squeak than a slam."

Starla stopped walking and wiped tears from her eyes. "You're killing me."

"It's been quite the day." An understatement.

"I'd say so."

Her hair was back to normal, as Ve had tracked her down earlier and plucked a hair from her head, too. *I* hadn't seen my aunt since this morning. She was an expert at evasion. Earlier, I'd come home to a note from Ve that she had picked up Mimi after her bookstore shift, and they were out running errands. She didn't know when they'd be back and told me not to worry.

"Still no sign of Vivienne?" Starla asked.

"None."

Her car had been found abandoned two blocks from where Baz had been hit, behind the middle school. It had been full of her belongings, and a search had revealed a baggie of unidentified capsules hidden beneath one of the floor mats.

Preliminary tests had revealed those capsules to be cyanide.

That was the last update I'd received from Nick, hours ago. Now there was an all-out manhunt going on.

Womanhunt.

Witchhunt.

I hated thinking of Vivienne on the run. Hated thinking she'd tried to kill Baz. That she'd killed Natasha. . . .

Baz hadn't been worth it.

No one was worth it.

Missy tugged hard on her leash, veering to the right. Looking that way, I saw it was Lady Catherine who'd captured her attention.

"Good evening!" Marigold called out, all smiles, as she approached us.

Lady Catherine trotted over to sniff Missy and Twink, her long thin tail wagging happily.

"Looks like she's none the worse for wear after her adventure," I said, patting Lady Catherine's head.

"Not worse at all." Marigold loosened her grip on the dog's leash. "I think we're both ecstatic she's back home. I'm so thrilled that Ivy found her at Fairytails. Lady Catherine loves that place, so I wasn't surprised to hear it."

I hadn't heard from Godfrey yet about the surveillance footage I'd asked him to view. With his current snit, I wondered if he'd even remember to check it. If I didn't hear from him tonight, I'd check in with him tomorrow.

Before any more pets went missing.

"I love a happy ending." Starla knelt down, and Lady Catherine licked her face. "It's too bad there won't be a Pawsitively Enchanted calendar this year. I would have loved to see Lady Catherine on the cover. She had such a good chance at winning."

"You never know in those situations," Marigold said, obviously trying to be modest, "but I also thought she had a good shot. Ivy suggested that perhaps I seek representation for Lady. To do commercials and the like. She said she'd help because she thinks Lady's a star."

She'd help, all right. For a fee, I'd bet.

Thinking of Marigold and Ivy, I recalled what Baz had said about Natasha not having had anything to do with his food poisoning. "Hey, Marigold, kind of a strange question, but I'm wondering about your accident a couple of years ago at the Extravaganza. How did it happen?"

Starla glanced up at me, a question in her eyes.

"That is a strange question," Marigold said. "Why do you ask?"

I skirted the truth. "After what happened to Natasha at the Extravaganza, there have been rumors going around the village that your accident might not have been an accident, that you might have been pushed. You know how people talk. I just wanted to set the record straight. . . ."

Marigold called Lady Catherine to her side. "Please put your mind at rest, Darcy. My accident was just that. An accident. It was my own fault. I'd been drinking a bottle of water, and spilled some as I was walking down the steps." She gave me a wry smile. "I don't think there's a more slippery surface on earth than wet marble."

I *knew* I shouldn't have taken this case. It had been nothing but a wild-goose chase, all because Ivy was paranoid about her precious Extravaganza, which was rather ironic considering I was now suspicious that she was petnapping the entrants. Talk about a backfire. "That's good to know," I said.

"Well, if I'm going to get Lady home before dark, I should get going," Marigold said, eyeing the sky. "You two girls have a good night."

We waved as she and Lady Catherine wandered off and continued our walk.

Crickets were chirping loudly as Starla looked at me. "Are you still thinking Ivy had something to do with stealing Lady Catherine in the first place?"

"I hate thinking it, but I do."

"But why would Ivy bring her back to Marigold?"

"The reward money was probably a lot more than Lady Catherine could be sold for online. And now that talk about helping to get Lady Catherine into commercials? I'm sure she'll charge a commission. Lady Catherine might just be the gift that keeps on giving for the cash-strapped Ivy. I just need a little evidence before I confront her about it."

"Ivy's smart. You think she left any evidence?"

"I can only hope."

Suddenly, Starla groaned. "Ugh, look who's coming."

Looking ahead, I saw Clarence pulling Glinda our way.

"I'm out of here. I'll see you later, okay? Text me if you get any news on Vivienne," Starla said, turning away.

"I will," I promised.

In a flash, she scooped up Twink and walked off in the other direction.

Starla didn't offer forgiveness as easily as I did, and I couldn't blame her. Glinda had treated her badly. Horribly. Much worse than she'd ever treated me. And Starla had never received an apology, not that I thought it would help.

Clarence didn't give me a second look once he spotted Missy. He danced all around her, his tail wagging furiously.

Glinda was watching Starla's retreat. "She's going to hate me forever, isn't she?"

"Probably."

She sighed. "I deserve it."

"I know."

Sending me a sharp look, she said, "You didn't have to agree with me."

I shrugged. "Sorry. I'm glad to see Clarence is okay. Did Liam happen to get a look at the petnapper? I have this theo—"

"No," she said, cutting me off. "Not at all."

I studied her. She wouldn't look me in the eye. "Not even a glimpse?"

"Nothing."

"Why do I feel like you're keeping something from me?"

"Not sure. Clarence, don't eat the grass!" She sighed

at the dog's antics. "Liam isn't even sure now if someone did try to steal Clarence, or if Clarence simply escaped again. You know how he is."

"Liam or Clarence?"

She sent me a withering look. "Clarence."

She was acting odd, but I had no idea why.

"I was hoping to run into you," she said.

"The pen is at As You Wish. I haven't had time to put the footage on disk yet."

"That's fine. I'll come by tomorrow morning for it. No rush now that Vivienne's wanted for murder. That puts divorce proceedings on the back burner. Which is why I wanted to talk to you."

"About divorce? You and Liam aren't even married yet."

She sighed heavily. "About Vivienne. She didn't do this to Baz. She wouldn't do this. You need to talk to Nick, get him to listen to reason."

"The evidence is pretty overwhelming. Baz even saw her driving."

"He didn't even have his glasses on from what I heard. He wouldn't have been able to identify her if she'd been standing ten feet in front of him."

Word spread fast in this village, but she did have a point about the glasses. He'd been squinting to see me, and I'd been right in front of him. "Cyanide pills were found in her car."

"Someone's framing her, Darcy. She didn't do this. Someone must've stolen the car from the Pixie Cottage."

"It wasn't reported stolen."

She flushed. "I know, but that's what happened."

"How do you know? Have you talked to Vivienne?"

"It doesn't matter how. Listen, it makes no sense that Vivienne would run Baz over or poison Natasha. She wanted out of that marriage. We have the evidence she needs for a big payday, so why would she try to kill him?"

"If he's dead, she probably gets a lot more money than a divorce would bring, even with the cheating evidence. He's worth a gazillion dollars, isn't he? She's probably his main beneficiary."

Glinda snapped her mouth closed, frowned, then said, "Maybe so, but she certainly wouldn't have used her own car to run him down in broad daylight. That's just plain stupid."

It was my turn to frown. She made a good point. "Then maybe she's just a woman who's been pushed over the edge. There's the whole anger and revenge angle to consider," I went on. "Alina Norcliffe said Vivienne had threatened Natasha. Scratched her car up, broke in to her house, warned her off dating Baz."

Glinda shook her head. "That makes zero sense. Vivienne didn't even know it was Natasha who Baz was seeing until yesterday at the Extravaganza. Not until I told her after we saw them in the hallway."

Yesterday. It seemed forever ago. "Do you know that for certain?"

"Know what?"

"That Vivienne didn't know about Natasha? She could have hired you just so you'd tell people she hadn't known. You'd be part of her alibi."

"It wasn't Vivienne," Glinda said stubbornly. "I refuse to believe it."

"Well, okay, then. Let's say you're right. Who else is there?"

She glared at me in dismay, then took a deep breath. "I don't know. The only other person I can think of is . . ."

"Chip," we both said at the same time.

"He definitely has motive if he loved Natasha," Glinda said, latching on to the idea.

"But he's in the hospital. He couldn't have run over Baz."

"Is he still there? I heard he was getting released today."

Nick had mentioned Chip could be let out early. . . . Had that happened? And if so, what time?

"All I know," Glinda said, "is that Vivienne is innocent, and I refuse to let her take the fall."

"Do you know where Vivienne is?" I asked point-blank.

"I, uh—" She looked over my shoulder and snapped her mouth closed. "I have to go. I'll be by tomorrow morning for that video."

I turned to see what had scared her off and found Nick walking my way.

Missy happily circled his feet, barking until he paid her some attention. He flopped her ears and scratched her back, and she happily rolled in the grass.

Nick gave me a long kiss and said, "Why'd Glinda rush off when she saw me?"

"She thinks Vivienne is innocent, and probably doesn't want to hear any evidence you have against her." I explained Glinda's reasoning for thinking Vivienne was innocent, including Baz's nearsightedness and supposedly not knowing Natasha was his mistress until yesterday.

As we walked across the green, Nick said, "I don't know what to think. I don't exactly have suspects coming out of the woodwork, and Vivienne's not talking because no one can find her."

I was going to say she would turn up, that people didn't just vanish, but around this village, they did. "Disappearing isn't exactly innocent behavior, is it?"

"No." Nick shook his head.

Even so, I felt duty-bound to follow up on Chip. "I don't suppose Chip was released from the hospital earlier today, was he? Before Baz's accident?"

"Why?"

Missy walked ahead of us, and I retracted her leash a bit as we neared the road. I explained to Nick what Glinda and I had talked about. "He's the only other person who has motive for killing Natasha. If he killed her, maybe he was just as angry at Baz?"

"But that would mean Chip poisoned *himself.* You said yourself that he didn't look like he knew his smoothie had cyanide in it."

I fidgeted. "Maybe he's a better actor than I gave him credit for? Maybe he drank only enough so he'd get sick but wouldn't die. So we wouldn't suspect him."

Nick rubbed at his five o'clock shadow. "That's a lot of maybes."

It definitely was.

"I'll call the hospital, just so we can cross him off the suspect list once and for all. Oh, and I got all five of your messages about Archie's abduction."

I smiled. "Yeah, sorry about that. Do you know if the sack was found?"

"Waiting on a call back from the officer who took the original call," he said, yawning. "There was nothing in the evidence locker."

"You must be ready to drop," I said, noting the weariness etched around his eyes. "Are you off work now? How're you feeling?"

"I'm on call if anything happens with the case, but technically I'm off for the next twelve hours. And I'm fine. Really. Just had the wind knocked out of me earlier, is all. It probably won't be the last time."

I prayed it was the last time. I never wanted to see him hurting ever again.

"Have you had dinner yet?" he asked.

"Not yet. I was waiting for Ve and Mimi, but they haven't gotten home yet."

"They ate," he said.

"How do you know that?"

"Mimi texted me."

"Where are they?" I asked, thinking it would have been nice to get a text, too.

"Now? At the movies. Ve's going to drop Mimi off at my place afterward. It's a school night, or I'm sure Mimi would have talked her into a double feature."

Summer break was just around the corner, and Mimi was champing at the bit for staying up late and sleeping in.

"If you're hungry, come with me," Nick said, taking my hand.

"Where to?"

"If you'll just follow me . . ."

I smiled at him and cleared my throat. "'To the ends of the earth.'"

A half smile twitched at the corners of his lips. "I'm not Archie."

"I know, but you set me up perfectly. You used a line from—"

"*Seven Brides for Seven Brothers*."

I playfully punched his arm. "You sly devil. So you weren't sleeping all those times I made you watch that movie."

"Not *all* the times. Just *most* of the times," he conceded with a smirk. "Even when I'm sleeping, the movie seems to sneak into my subconscious. Sometimes I catch myself whistling 'Bless Her Beautiful Hide' at work, and you should see the looks I get."

I gazed up at him. "I think I just fell in love with you a little bit more, Nick Sawyer."

He nudged my chin. "It's that easy? A *Seven Brides* reference?"

"I'm kind of a pushover when it comes to you."

"Ditto, Darcy Merriweather. Ditto. Now come on." He kept hold of my hand and led me across the street to the construction zone that was my new house.

"Why are we *here*?" I asked, looking around.

"Watch your step," Nick said, guiding me around a wheelbarrow on the front walkway.

I stopped and picked up Missy. The area was littered with the remnants of the old shingles, and I worried there were roofing nails hidden in the grass. "What's going on?"

"Dinner, remember?" Nick headed up the front steps, across the rotting porch, and swung opened the front door.

"Tell me that wasn't unlocked." There was thousands of dollars' worth of material being stored inside the house.

"It wasn't. Elves came by earlier to set things up and left it open for us."

"Elves?" I walked through the front door and immediately felt a sense of peace, which was entirely unjustified considering the state of the living room. The interior walls had been gutted to replace ancient wiring, install new insulation, and update the heating and cooling system. It seemed *everything* inside the house needed to be brought up to building and fire codes, which made sense, since the previous owner hadn't allowed anyone in the house for decades.

No doubt about it: The place was an absolute mess.

But yet it still felt like home.

"Mimi and Ve helped me out," he confessed.

Ah. So this had been part of the errands they were running. As far as my aunt's avoidance tactics went, I had to approve of this one.

The scent of freshly cut lumber filled the air, and a fine coat of dust covered everything in sight. I couldn't help running down a mental checklist of everything that still needed to be done from floor refinishing to refacing the fireplace to picking out paint colors.

He led me to the back of the house, and I stood in

awe. Not at the sight of the addition and all the space it had added, but at the plaid blanket spread across the filthy subfloor where my kitchen would one day be located. The space was currently a gutted shell made up of wooden studs, copper pipes, and an electrical-wire maze, but the walls could have been made of solid gold and I wouldn't have noticed. My attention was fixated on one thing only.

The picnic basket sitting on the blanket. Two candles in tall hurricane lamps flickered in the dim light.

"Dinner," he said simply. "I didn't want another day to go by without us spending a little quality time together."

I couldn't have stopped the goofy smile on my face if I tried. I set Missy on the floor and she took off to sniff around.

Nick held my hand, helping me lower myself to the blanket. He opened the hamper. "Ve and Mimi went to the North End today and picked up some dishes from your favorite Italian restaurant. Stuffed mushroom appetizer, pasta al pomodoro, garlic bread, tiramisu."

"Special occasion?" I asked, eyebrows raised.

"Is it too cheesy to say every dinner with you is a special occasion?"

I laughed. "Yes, yes, it is."

"Then let's just say I missed you."

"I've missed you, too." I dished out a couple of plates of food and gave a meatball to Missy. I'd just have to be more patient about the moving-in thing. I could do it. I was nothing if not patient.

Nick poured two glasses of wine and then glanced around. "Actually," he said, "I've been wanting to ask you something important for a while now. . . ."

"Oh?" I noticed my hand holding the wineglass was shaking a bit, so I carefully set the glass down.

Nick glanced at me, held my gaze. What he said in

that look was more than I'd ever dreamed. It wasn't often he let his guard fully down, but he was letting it down now, allowing me to see the love he had for me.

He cleared his throat. "We've been talking in circles about moving in together for months now. . . . How are you feeling about that?"

"About talking in circles? Because honestly, that was getting a little annoying."

Smiling, he said, "The moving in, Darcy. The moving in. Do you think you'd want to . . . you know . . . live with me? With Mimi? With Higgins?"

Swallowing hard, I said, "Do I think I'd want to? I'd *love* to. Do you think you'd want to live with me? With Missy? With Annie?"

His voice thick with emotion, he said, "*I'd* love to."

Candlelight flickered on his face, and I tried with all my might to memorize every detail of this moment, from the sights, the scents, the sounds. But it was so hard to concentrate with the way my chest ached with all the love I was feeling.

We stared at each other for a moment before he said, "Then it's settled? We're moving in together?"

I could barely breathe as I nodded. "It's settled."

He casually as he glanced around. "You know, with the renovations this house is plenty big for all of us. . . . We'll have to make sure the wooden floors have extra protection against Higgins' drool, but that's not too big a deal."

My eyes widened. "What are you saying?"

"What do you think about us all living here?"

"Here? But your hou—"

"You love it here," he said, knowing where I was going. "And I love you. The decision of where to live when we get married is simple. You know. Someday. When we do that." He coughed, looking as if he had just revealed much too much.

I nearly fell over. "Live here? You'd really live here? You don't even like this place."

"This place has changed quite a bit since the first time I saw it. It's grown on me. And Mimi loves it as much as you do. You want to, right?" he asked with a smile. "Live here? Someday? With Mimi and me and Higgins." He frowned. "Don't let Higgins influence your decision too much."

"I mean, yes, but your house makes much more sense. Your workshop . . ."

He waved a hand. "I'm sure I can get Hank to work his magic on that old shed out back."

My heart pounded. "You're serious?"

"Mimi's already picked out a room upstairs. The one—"

"The one at the end of the hall that looks over the square."

"How'd you know?"

"It screams *Mimi* with all its nooks and that big window seat. . . . You're *really* serious?"

"If you'll have us. . . . I don't want to be too presumptuous, taking over your space. . . ."

Tears streamed down my face as I launched myself at him, knocking him backward with my hug. "Of course I'll have you!" I laughed, unable to keep the joy inside.

"Then it's settled. When the time comes, we'll move in here," he said, laughing with me, holding me close. He brushed a piece of my hair back behind my ear, and thumbed away a teardrop. "Why the tears?"

"I'm just happy," I said.

He held me just a little bit tighter. "Me, too, Darcy. Me, too."

Two hours later, I was back at As You Wish. Nick and I had eaten and talked and talked some more. As the candles flickered in the growing darkness, I told him all about the mourning dove adventures and Harper's fascination with the situation. I told him of Alina and Godfrey and Pepe, my suspicions about the petnapper, and everything else I could think of.

He told me about his day, too, which consisted mostly in asking questions that had no answers. And we had talked of our future, of how we wanted to furnish the house, and what color to paint our bedroom.

It had been . . . magical.

When the time comes.

When we got married.

Trying not to stress about when *that* might happen, I made myself simply enjoy the night I'd had.

I was still floating as I readied for bed. I didn't plan to go to sleep, however, until after Ve returned home and I had the chance to speak with her about that spell.

I flipped on the TV that sat on top of my dresser and surfed through cable channels until I settled on an old episode of *The Golden Girls*.

Missy hopped up onto the bed, turned three times, then settled into a ball to watch the show. Tilda, who'd been on the opposite side of the bed, oh so casually crossed the short distance between them, swatted Missy's stubby tail, then lay down next to her and pretended she'd done no such thing.

She was one odd cat.

Sitting in front of my pillows was Annie, with all the toys I had bought her at the Furry Toadstool spread out around her. I pushed them aside and scooped her up as I propped myself against the pillows.

Settled against my chest, she looked up at me, blinked those amazing eyes of hers, then reached up with her paw and tapped my glasses.

I laughed and took them off. "See? Still me under here."

I supposed cats didn't understand the whole concept

of contact lenses—taking them out was part of my normal bedtime routine. She'd get used to seeing me in glasses soon enough.

Her tail swished as I scratched her chin and said, "I hope it's okay with you that you'll be living here with me now. I think you'll be a lot happier. And eventually we're going to move in with Nick and Mimi. You'll have to get used to Higgins' drool, which is more about dodging and evading than anything. I think you can handle it." After living with Natasha, I was pretty sure she could handle anything.

I was telling her about the new house when I laughed again, this time at myself for having a full-on conversation with the cat. But I just couldn't help myself.

She reached up a paw and curved it around my hand that was patting her, pulling my palm toward her. Pressing her face against the tender skin, she closed her eyes and purred.

The gesture and sound brought moisture to my eyes, and I blinked it away. Giving her a hug, I said, "I know *I'm* a lot happier knowing you're here."

At some point, I must have drifted off, because I woke with a start, not sure what had stirred me.

The TV was still on, but instead of a sitcom, an infomercial was playing. I noticed that both Missy and Tilda were gone. Annie was still in my arms. It was just past midnight.

I kept hold of Annie as I sleepily headed for the hallway, checking to see if Ve had come back yet. Her bedroom was empty, but lights blazed downstairs. I was just about to start down the steps when I heard the mystery woman's voice.

". . . I thought I could, but I can't. I just can't. It would be too much in such close quarters. I have feelings, you know."

"What are you going to do?" Ve asked.

"I don't know. I thought I was ready to leave, but I'm not. I have to make a decision soon, obviously. I'll talk to the Elder."

"Pooh," Ve said. "Don't even say her name to me. The position she's put me with Darcy and that spell is unbearable. It's never been so hard to keep a secret."

Well, that explained Ve's hesitation to discuss the spell with me. If she was under orders to keep quiet from the Elder, she couldn't tell me about the spell without severe consequence.

But that left me wondering why the Elder was involved with the spell at all.

"Never?" the woman said, a hint of humor in her voice. "The Elder's identity . . ."

Ve chuckled. "Almost never."

"Tell me about it," the mystery woman said. "Secrets suck."

Ve said, "We're a pair, aren't we?"

As I listened, I debated about creeping down the steps a little bit farther, to see if I could finally catch a glimpse of the mystery woman.

But even though just days ago I had believed I wanted all the village secrets revealed to me, for some reason something deep down told me not to take a peek. That it was better not to know.

Trusting my instincts, I turned around and went back to my room.

Some village secrets, I reasoned, were simply meant to be kept.

Chapter Twenty-six

The next morning, I stared at the coffeemaker, thinking there wasn't enough caffeine in the world to get me going today. I'd slept poorly again the night before. Oh, I'd fall asleep okay but then would be rudely awakened by either Annie deciding the best place to snooze was on top of my head or repeated nightmares about my mother's car accident.

The nightmares were haunting me even now that I was fully awake, showered, and dressed. It wasn't unusual for me to dream about that day, but this time had been different. . . .

The crash had happened during a thunderstorm, and in my dream I was seven years old again, watching the paramedics trying to free my mother from the mangled car, watching them trying desperately to save her unborn baby. Then something above the wreckage would catch my eye. A mourning dove circling, dipping and rising, struggling to fly in the pouring rain. With its wings waterlogged, it appeared to be drowning in the downpour as it looked over at me.

"I'll always be with you," the bird said, dropping lower and lower.

Then I'd wake up, not knowing if the bird survived.

And each time I woke up, I was crying.

I was exhausted as I poured coffee to the rim of the mug, so full that I had to bend and slurp some out before lifting the cup.

"You should just put a straw in the pot and save some time," Aunt Ve said, coming down the back stairs into the kitchen.

Annie crept along the kitchen countertop, and I scooped her up, nuzzled her face for a second, and then set her on the floor. "If I wasn't afraid of the plastic melting, I would."

It was a little before eight, and I'd skipped my morning jog to spend more time in bed, trying to get an hour or two of solid sleep.

It hadn't happened.

Thanks to those nightmares.

Mother Nature didn't even have the decency to send a little sunshine to perk me up. It was a dull and dreary day.

"Are you all right, Darcy dear?" Ve asked, stepping up next to me and pressing a hand to my forehead. "You look unwell."

I had tried and tried to decipher what the nightmares meant but couldn't quite pull together a clear explanation.

"I'm fine," I said warily. "I just didn't sleep well."

Ve's coppery hair was pulled back in its usual twist, the silver streaks quite noticeable in the overhead light. She was dressed for work in a pretty navy blue A-line dress and heels. "Not because of that spell, is it? I know you want an explanation, but I can't give you one."

I lifted my mug, being careful not to slosh any of the precious caffeine over the rim. "I figured as much. Elder's orders, I presume. I've been down this road a time or two since moving to the village."

She reached for the coffeepot and wiggled her eyebrows. "I cannot confirm or deny. So you understand?"

"I understand. I don't like it, but I understand."

She patted my cheek lovingly. "That's understandable."

I cracked a smile.

"That's better." She filled a travel mug with coffee. "I didn't see you last night. . . . How was your night with Nick?" she asked in a singsong voice.

My smile widened, and I knew she could easily see how happy he made me.

She laughed. "You two make a lovely couple. I knew from the moment I saw you together that you were meant to be."

From her spot in her dog bed near the stairs, Missy started coughing, almost as if she had swallowed a bug or something. When we looked her way, she stopped just as suddenly as she had started. She licked her lips.

"You need some water?" I asked her. Her full water dish sat right next to her dog bed.

She licked her lips again, then set her head on top of her paws. I took that as a no.

As if nothing odd had just happened, Ve said, "Love is a wonderful thing."

I thought about what Alina had said about love being foolish and felt sorry for her. If she had known love, real love, whether from a parent herself or someone with whom she was in a relationship with, she wouldn't have said such a thing. Which made me feel even worse for her.

"I've been thinking about when you move out," Ve said. "Perhaps you could leave Missy with me. I could use a guard dog, and you'll have Higgins. Missy likes it here, and I'm sure she would love to stay, wouldn't you, girl?"

Missy's stubby tail started wagging.

Ve's request had caught me off guard. I couldn't possibly leave Missy here . . . could I?

No.

Definitely not.

"I . . . I know she loves it here," I said. "So do I. But I couldn't leave her behind. She's . . . family."

Missy's tail stopped wagging, then started up again.

"It was worth a shot," Ve murmured as she sipped her coffee.

"Maybe you should think about adopting a dog," I suggested. "Or the Furry Toadstool has puppies that need to find homes before this weekend. Reggie uses a reputable breeder."

"Perhaps I'll talk Andreus into moving in with me," Ve said, clearly thinking out loud. "He'd be better than any guard dog out there."

I shuddered. "That's because he's the scariest thing on the planet."

She laughed. "He is not. He's just a little . . ."

I waited.

She tapped her chin. "He's . . . unique!"

Laughing, I refilled my coffee cup.

"I'll figure it out," Ve said, tucking a loose strand of hair behind her ear. "New normals. New adventures!"

New normals. I had a lot of those in my future.

"Do you have plans for the day, dear?" Ve asked.

"Some loose ends to tie up," I said, watching Annie oh so casually sashay over to Missy's dog bed. Tilda was once again sitting at the top of the staircase, eyeing us all with disdain.

My job for Ivy was pretty much done. It didn't look as though Natasha's death had anything whatsoever to do with the Extravaganza, but I couldn't quite cut ties with Ivy yet. Not until I figured out if she was the pet-napper. I owed it to all the pets in the village to see that mystery through.

My job for the Elder was still ongoing as well, as I didn't quite know how Chip factored into Natasha's death. Was he a killer? Or a victim as well? I wouldn't know for certain until Natasha's case was solved. I made a mental note to track him down, ask him some additional questions. I also had to look at the As You Wish calendar to see what I had scheduled for the week so I could plan ahead.

I already wanted to go back to bed. For a week or so.

Annie had climbed into the dog bed with Missy and was licking the top of Missy's head. Missy sent me a pleading look, her brown eyes imploring a quick intervention.

After setting my mug on the counter, I opened the cupboard beneath the sink and pulled out a folded paper grocery bag and opened it up, making sure to give it a good rattle.

Annie immediately ceased licking and dipped low, her head nearly touching her front paws, but her backside was wagging in the air. Pounce mode.

I set the bag on its side on the floor, and within a second, Annie was inside the sack, rolling around. Out of the corner of my eye, I spotted Tilda creeping down the steps and smiled.

No cat could resist the lure of a paper bag.

Ve watched the cats with amusement and said, "I need to head out. I have a few things to do at the village office this morning, and then T-I-L-D-A has a V-E-T appointment."

"I'll pray for you."

Laughing, she headed into the mudroom. "I'd appreciate that. Call if you need anything, dear."

"I will," I promised, following her out the back door
onto the side porch.

She hurried out the side gate, and I settled on the
porch swing with my coffee. I tucked one leg beneath
me and closed my eyes, to enjoy the quiet of the morning, the chattering birds, and the scent of the flowers
that Cookie hadn't been able to reach.

I hadn't heard any news that the goat had been found,
and I wondered where she had gotten off to. It seemed
she should have been found by now, especially since
according to Reggie, goats were social animals—she
would be naturally drawn to the village's hustle and
bustle.

I heard a creak and opened my eyes, wondering if it
was Archie ready to take his post for the day, but his
elaborate iron cage remained empty. Instead I found
Nick coming through the side gate, a smile spreading
when he spotted me.

Sometimes, like right now, I worried about how much
I loved him. Worried that something would ruin it. That
something would happen to him. Or me.

I blamed this morning's bout of anxiety on those
nightmares, and forced myself to smile as he came up
the steps, carrying a duffel bag.

Stopping feet from me, he narrowed his gaze, and
said, "What's wrong?"

He knew me too well to try to outright lie. "I'm okay.
Just had nightmares last night," I said, deflecting the
truth only slightly.

Giving me a kiss, he sat next to me. "About Natasha?"
he asked.

"No. My mother . . . and the Elder." I explained the
dream to him. "All I could come up with for a link was
that I liken the Elder to a mother figure, and now that I
suspect she is flying around the village as a mourning
dove, it is only logical that my mind would use the bird

to represent her. . . . But I don't know why the bird was at the crash scene at all. Or why it was struggling."

"Do you feel like Elder is in trouble?" he asked. "Maybe that's the connection."

"Not at all. That's why it's strange."

"Maybe it could be that you're afraid on some level that you're going to lose the Elder. That something is going to happen to her."

His interpretation hit close to home, especially considering the thoughts I'd just been having about him.

"Maybe," I conceded. "But the dream just seemed so . . . real."

"Well," he said, "I have something to take your mind off it, though I'm going to guess you'll be just as agitated by it."

I leaned away from him. Apprehension was written all over his face, and it made me nervous. Really nervous. "Uh-oh."

"This morning I heard from the patrol officer who'd taken the report of Archie's abduction. He's all but given up on the case after viewing the surveillance footage."

"Why?"

"Because according to him, Archie was there one second and gone the next. My guy thinks there was a glitch in the video feed, but I know better."

Magic. I'd *known* it. Goose bumps swept up my arms. "What about the bag by the pond?"

"There was no bag, but he when he checked out the area, he did find this, which he threw in his trunk just in case it had something to do with the case." He unzipped the duffel bag, and as he pulled a swath of material out of the bag. I knew immediately what it was.

A Crafter cloak.

An old one, by the looks of it.

"As soon as I heard that it was a cloak of some sort, I knew I had to get it to you. It's a blurred line we're walking in this case, between the mortal and Craft world, but I know for certain this cloak doesn't belong in my evidence locker."

I took the cloak from him and immediately caught the scent of mothballs. Archie had been right about that at least. "Whoever took Archie must have thrown this over him—he would have disappeared immediately." Just as Cookie had disappeared under my cloak in the Elder's meadow. But . . . was the witch wearing it at the time? It would seem that was a detail Archie would have mentioned.

"Do you know whose it is?" Nick asked.

"No, but Godfrey might."

I recalled what I'd thought the day before, that if it had been a Crafter who'd taken Archie, then that person had to be desperate. Really desperate.

But no doubt about it, the abductor had to be a *witch*. I glanced at Nick. "I think I owe Ivy an apology."

This cloak cleared her of trying to steal Archie. As a mortal, she wouldn't own a Craft cloak.

Cloaks were for witches and witches only and disintegrated into ashes within three days of falling into mortal ownership.

It was a good thing Nick had taken possession of this cloak when he had. He laughed and pulled me in for a hug. "No, you don't. She had no idea you suspected her."

"Okay, a silent apology." When I sent her my bill for my work on the Extravaganza job, I'd cut my fee in half. Then I could at least keep a somewhat clear conscience.

"That's not all," he said.

"What else?"

"The two dogs that were missing showed up in the village late last night. They're back with their owners."

"And the cat?" I asked.

"He showed up just in time for breakfast this morning."

"Cookie?"

He shook his head. "I checked with Angela and Harmony, and still nothing."

"It's such a big coincidence, isn't it? That all the lost pets, except Cookie, would suddenly reappear within twelve hours of each other?"

"It definitely is. Makes you wonder where they've been, doesn't it?"

I glanced at the Craft cloak. I was more curious about who'd they had been *with*. "Are you going to pursue the case now that the pets are back with their owners?" I asked.

"Not actively, but if I discover who it is, I'm honor-bound to arrest that person, witch or not. It'll be up to the victims and/or the district attorney to press charges."

That made sense, especially since some of the families affected were mortal. There was no dealing with this solely at the Elder's discretion.

"I also called the hospital to check about Chip's whereabouts yesterday morning," Nick added. "He was released midmorning yesterday. His *grandmother* drove him back to the village."

Cherise.

"What time? Did he have time to get back, steal Vivienne's car, and run down Baz in front of the Wisp?"

"There was time," Nick said, "but only barely. Red lights or any traffic would throw off the timeline."

There had been a lot of traffic in the village yesterday. "It would be just about impossible for him to be the one who'd driven that car that hit Baz."

"Yes, but you of all people should know, Darcy, that the impossible is always possible in this village."

True. Very true.

He set us to swaying again. "Right now he's my best lead."

That was surprising. "What about Vivienne?"

"The driver's seat of the car was pushed back. Vivienne wouldn't have been able to reach the pedals if she'd been the one driving the car. And, yes, Vivienne could have pushed the seat back on purpose to avert suspicion, but why would she? If she was trying to avoid suspicion she wouldn't have used her own car and certainly wouldn't have left cyanide pills behind."

All very good points.

Nick went on. "Chip's tall—he would have had to move the seat to get behind the wheel."

I recalled how Chip had towered over me. He never would have been able to drive that car without moving the seat backward, and he'd probably been in too much of a rush to move it back when he abandoned the vehicle.

"Chip's coming into the station later today with his lawyer, and hopefully we'll get some definitive answers."

"But what about Vivienne?"

"By not coming forward, she's only adding to my suspicion that she has something to hide, but I don't think she did run Baz over."

"I'm growing worried about her. Now that we know she wasn't behind that wheel . . . where is she?"

"You think something happened to her?"

"I just don't know."

"Me neither. Hopefully, I'll know more after I talk to Chip."

"You'll let me know right away?"

"You're on speed dial," he said with a smile.

I heard the gate squeak again, and looked up to find a beautiful blond woman walking toward us.

"Sorry to interrupt," Glinda said. She held a small leather portfolio in her hands. "I thought I could take a look at that spy pen footage if you have time." She glanced at Nick. "Do you want me to come back later?"

I presumed she was asking because like Starla, Nick wasn't too keen on Glinda, either, though his dislike didn't run nearly as deep. Mostly because he knew how much his daughter loved Glinda.

Nick gave me one last squeeze and stood up. "Stay," he said to her. "I've got to get to work."

Glinda opened her mouth, then snapped it closed again, and I wondered what she had been planning to say. Whether it had something to do with the fact that she used to work with Nick . . . or something to do with Vivienne's case. Finally she said, "Okay."

Nick looked at me. "I cleared my text messages from my phone, so feel free to fill them up again. Let me know about that," he said, motioning to the cloak on my lap.

I stood. "I will."

Glinda and I watched him go, and I made a mental note to oil the gate hinges as soon as possible. As soon as he was out of sight, she turned to me and said, "You two are sickeningly cute together."

"I know," I said with a smile. "You should hear Harper mock us."

She shifted from foot to foot. "I—I'm happy for you both. You and Nick."

"That hurt, didn't it?"

She bent at the waist as she laughed. "You have no idea."

"Well, thanks. We are happy."

"What's that you have there?" she asked, eyeing the cloak.

"A Crafting cloak, but I'm not sure whose it is. It was used to abduct Archie, and I'm guessing all the other village pets that are missing as well. It's an older cloak, so mortals wouldn't be able to see the person, and Crafters wouldn't think twice about seeing a witch walking around in one of these."

Her eyes widened. "I—I don't even know what to say about that."

Which was odd, because there was something in her expression that hinted she had a lot to say about it. Opening the back door, I motioned her inside ahead of me. "I just need a minute to get the spy pen footage onto a disk and then you can get on with your day." I'd quiz her about the petnapper while I was downloading the file.

"Actually . . . ," she began as she scooted past me.

I noticed Missy stood in the doorway of the mudroom, her head cocked as though she was wondering why in the world Glinda was here and what she was up to.

I knew that feeling well.

Glinda held up the portfolio. "This is all the material I've gathered during my investigation of Baz. I was hoping you'd take a look at it with me. The spy pen video, too."

"Me? Why?"

"I'd really like an extra set of eyes to help me look it all over. I feel like I'm missing something, and I trust you and your eyes. I can pay you . . . I mean, I can become a client, if you want to write this off as a job for As You Wish."

I held her gaze for a moment, looking for any hint that she was somehow using me. I didn't find one.

"I'll brew another pot of coffee." I walked into the kitchen, set the cloak on the back of the counter stool, and said, "And just so we're clear: Today you're not a client. You're a friend."

Chapter Twenty-seven

Glinda had collected a hodgepodge of evidence against Baz, none of it the nail in his proverbial coffin.

Lots of photographs of him going into Natasha's place, and of her going into his, but none of them together except for some steamy backlit silhouettes on his bedroom window shade. She had some receipts from local hotels, but Baz had always checked in under an assumed name, and he and Natasha had never arrived together.

"Now I see why you desperately wanted that footage from the hallway of the Extravaganza." I tapped the photo of the silhouettes locked in an embrace that sat on the coffee table in Ve's family room. I kept coming back to that photo time and again, and I couldn't quite pinpoint why. "I can't believe he had an affair under his own roof. He has such nerve. Where was Vivienne?"

"At work. And she thought he was, too."

Right here, right now, I despised Baz Lucas with a passion.

My computer was open to the video I'd taken of him and Natasha. Other than some minor sound issues, peripheral clicking noises in the background, the footage was all Vivienne would need to prove a case of adultery against Baz. It was all there in full sound and color.

I couldn't help watching Natasha with a sense of regret. That I should have been able to stop what had happened somehow. She'd been so . . . alive on the film. And even though her sister had implied that Natasha didn't love Baz, she had certainly played the part well. Which made me wonder if she had in fact loved him.

We would never know.

Glinda and I sat on the sofa and worked quietly, sifting through material. Glinda bumped my shoulder and motioned across the room. "Why does she keep staring at me that way?"

Missy glared at Glinda from her spot on the armchair across the table from us.

"I don't know. Maybe she's wondering where Clarence is."

Glinda frowned and went back to watching the tape. It was her third time through.

I stretched my arms over my head and nearly knocked Annie and Tilda off the back of the couch. They were nestled together like a semicolon, and I thought that maybe instead of a dog, Aunt Ve should consider getting another cat.

"What am I seeing?" Glinda asked, eyeing the video.

"Five hundred thousand dollars?"

She smiled. "No, there's something . . . off. It's like it floats into my brain but is gone before I can grab hold of it."

"I don't know. I don't see anything. Maybe you can

tell *me* what's with this picture?" I asked, tapping the silhouettes again. "I keep coming back to it."

"Forget that," she said. "What's with all the pictures of this bird?"

She clicked off the video and opened a new window on the laptop that showed the shots of the mourning dove I'd taken with the spy pen in front of the Wisp. I'd forgotten I'd even taken them.

"Have you taken up bird-watching in your spare time?" she asked, a pale eyebrow raised.

"Something like that," I said.

The four images of the bird were on the screen side by side, and in a blink they were gone as Glinda toggled back to the video, set her elbows on her knees, and leaned in close to the screen.

I went back to sorting through the photographs of Baz.

"There!" Glinda cried. "Right there."

She paused the video.

It was a freeze frame of a swirl of colors. "How can you see anything? It's blurry."

She was staring at the screen. "That's because your arm was in motion as you pulled it back into the room after Baz and Natasha walked away." She unpaused the footage, rewound it, and played it again. "Right here. Keep an eye on that spot." She rewound again. "See it?"

My eyes were starting to cross. "I don't—wait." I looked at her. "Is that . . ."

"I think so."

It was just a flash of motion, a hand perhaps. "Someone else was there in that hallway."

"Yes."

So we hadn't been the only ones who'd been spying on Baz and Natasha. Someone had been hiding in the recessed doorway of the room next to ours.

"There's no way to tell who it is," I said.

"No," she agreed, clicking off the video. "But it's one more piece of the puzzle."

With the video closed, the images of the mourning dove popped up again, and this time, something jumped right out at me. I slid off the couch onto the floor and pulled the screen close.

"Are you okay?" Glinda asked.

"Do you see this?" I asked, pointing to a line on the bird's back.

"Yeah. It's probably from the pen. Cheap quality. . . ."

"It's not the pen," I whispered.

I glanced from the first picture to the fourth and back again. After the first shot, a thin stripe appeared, running from the top of the bird's head to its tail. With each subsequent shot, the stripe thickened.

"What is it?" Glinda asked.

It was a Wishcrafter, that's what it was. One under the Lunumbra spell. "I think—"

The doorbell rang.

Missy leaped off the armchair and skidded around the corner on her way to the front door, barking the whole way. I reluctantly stood up. Annie hopped down and followed me to see who had rung the bell, and Tilda stole Annie's spot.

"I'll be right back," I said to Glinda.

I peeked out the sidelight and was surprised to see Angela Curtis standing on the porch. I picked up Annie so she wouldn't run outside and opened the door. Missy's tail wagged as she crossed the threshold to greet our visitor.

"Hi, Darcy," Angela said, reaching down to rub Missy's head. "Sorry for dropping in unannounced."

"No, no, it's fine. Come on in. Want some coffee?"

"No, thanks. I can't stay." She followed me into the family room and looked surprised to see Glinda. "Oh, you two are working. I'll come back. . . ."

Missy took the long way around Glinda as I set Annie down next to Tilda and said, "It's fine. We needed a break anyway."

"You're sure you don't want coffee?" Glinda asked.

Angela smiled. "No, thanks. I've got to get back to work at the bookshop. I'm on break."

Forty-something Angela had started working for Harper part-time late last year, and it had been a match made in heaven. Angela loved books almost as much as my sister did. Even more, perhaps, not that I'd ever say so in front of Harper.

With her auburn hair pulled back in a low ponytail, and wearing jeans and a heather gray T-shirt that read "Last night I dreamt I went to Manderley again," she didn't look her age, or that she could possibly have a daughter in college.

"Is something wrong?" I asked. "Is Harper okay?"

"Oh! She's fine. Everything's fine. I didn't mean to worry you." She wrung her hands. "I've actually come by to ask a huge favor of you."

"Name it," I said.

"This morning when I went into work, I saw your paintings in the bookshop. The ones from the Extravaganza? Harper was getting them ready to return to you, but I was hoping . . ."

I'd forgotten that Harper had collected them from the Wisp for me. It had been a crazy few days.

"You see, Harmony's birthday is later this week, and I've been searching high and low for the perfect gift. She's never been easy to buy for. You should see what I go through at Christmas. It's a nightmare."

The two had been together for almost a decade now, so that was a lot of presents.

Angela's face lit as she said, "But she really, *really*, adores your painting of the white mouse. I'd love to be able to give her something so special for her birthday, seeing as I've run her through the wringer with this Cookie situation."

"Has Cookie been found?" I couldn't help asking.

"Not yet." Sighing, she shook her head. "We've had to get back to work, so we can't search as much as we'd like. And we don't have the deep pockets Marigold has to offer a huge reward." She shrugged. "We can only hope for the best."

Glinda suddenly busied herself with straightening photos. "I'm sure she'll show up soon."

"That's what we keep telling ourselves, anyway," Angela said. She glanced at her watch. "I have to get going. . . . Darcy, is it possible I can buy that painting? It'd mean the world to Harmony, which means it would mean the world to me."

"It's yours. Free of charge," I said.

She jumped up. "I can't let you just give it to me."

"You can and you will." I stood up, too. "I insist. You both have helped me out a time or two. It's my way of saying thanks."

She gave me a hug. "Thank you so much. I can't wait to see Harmony's face when I give it to her. All right, I need to get back. My boss . . . you know how she is."

I laughed. "Oh, I know."

Angela gave me another hug. "You don't have to see me out. Thanks again! Bye, Glinda!"

Glinda waved.

"I'll keep looking for Cookie," I promised as Angela walked down the hall.

"Well, I wish you'd find her, because we're not having any luck on our own. See you later!"

As the front door closed behind her, my skin tingled, and I whispered the simple spell to grant her wish under my breath. *Wish I might, wish I may, grant this wish without delay.* I winked my left eye twice, and the spell was cast. Because Angela was a mortal and the wish had followed all Wishcraft laws, the wish was granted immediately.

In my mind's eye, I saw where Cookie was, inside a large garage filled with woodworking tools and projects in various stages of completion. She was prancing around, looking perfectly content.

I knew the space; I'd been there before.

Almost as important as seeing where she was, I saw who she was with.

Slowly, I turned to face Glinda. "Something you want to tell me?"

She dropped her forehead against the table and turned her face a bit to peek at me out of one eye. "I can explain everything."

Chapter Twenty-eight

"We've already returned the dogs and the cat," Glinda said as we stepped off the pathway at the opposite end of the village green.

Dark clouds hung low in the sky as we crossed the street and turned a corner onto a beautiful cobblestone lane. The tree-lined street was as familiar to me as my own.

It was Nick's street.

And Glinda's as well.

It was her garage I'd seen in my vision.

As we walked, I was still trying to digest everything Glinda had told me about how she'd become entangled with the petnapper . . . and why she was harboring a murder suspect at her house.

It was Vivienne Lucas I'd seen with Cookie when I granted Angela's wish.

I slid a look at Glinda, who wore a determined expression as we hotfooted it along. For someone who, in the past, had been fervent about justice being served in all cases, Glinda was doing a lot of colluding lately.

Before we left As You Wish, Glinda had contacted the petnapper with a request to meet with us. I wanted to hear what the woman—and Vivienne as well—had to say for herself before calling Nick.

Birds chirped from high branches as we strode up Glinda's driveway. "We were waiting until tonight to take Cookie home, so as not to arouse extra suspicion. I'm kicking myself that I didn't do it the opposite way." Giving me a pointed glare, she added, "You wouldn't be here if Cookie had turned up last night."

We. Glinda had apparently become Team Petnapper after hearing some sort of sob story as to why the crimes had been committed.

"And what if I didn't find out?" I asked. "She would have gotten off scot-free."

Glinda opened the tall wooden gate leading into the fenced backyard, and I followed her through the opening. "That was the plan, yes. She's truly remorseful and promises to never do it again."

"Remorseful or not, you don't think she needs to be punished? She tried to steal Clarence, after all."

I'd never been in Glinda's backyard and was pleasantly surprised to see how nice it was, with its numerous flower beds, koi pond, and outdoor fireplace. A large oak tree in the corner of the lot provided a leafy canopy for most of the space. As I glanced around, I noticed that some of the flowers had been eaten, which confirmed what I already knew: Cookie had been here. The high fence would have hidden her from any nosy neighbors.

Glinda shrugged. "What she did was wrong—on a lot of levels—but all the pets but Cookie are back with their owners, and she will be soon, too. I figured no harm, no foul."

I stared. "Lots of harm. Lots of foul! Pets are family.

It's not so much petnapping as kidnapping. Plus, she broke a lot of people's trust."

"I know. You're right. . . . Maybe I'm just getting soft, but I feel for her." Glinda slid a key into the lock of the garage's side door, and high-pitched barking started on the other side.

Usually, I was the one with the soft side, the tender heart. But taking pets crossed a line I wasn't sure I could so easily forgive and forget.

The scent of freshly cut wood, undercut by pet odors, filled the air as I followed Glinda into the garage. She quickly closed the door behind us as Clarence dashed over to me, his tail wagging. I took a moment to pet his head and tell him what a handsome boy he was, and he agreed by slobbering on my hand.

At a folding table in the center of the garage sat two women, neither of whom seemed as happy as Clarence to see me.

I didn't blame them. The police had been looking for both of them.

A small dog charged toward me, skidding on the sawdust-covered floor. As I bent to rub Audrey Pupburn's silky ears, my thigh was head-butted by an ornery little goat. "Hey, Cookie. Long time, no see," I said to her.

"Mehh!" She head-butted me again.

"Did you miss me?" I asked the goat.

"You two know each other well, then?" Glinda asked.

I rubbed Cookie's knobby head. "We've run into each other a few times lately."

Even though the garage was spacious, it was feeling a bit claustrophobic, with all the people and animals.

A portable air conditioner buzzed from a small window, keeping the room cool. Above the unit, dim sunlight filtered in through a dusty windowpane, and overhead fixtures provided plenty of light.

The older woman who sat at the table said, "You've

a way with animals, Darcy. Are you certain there are no Zoacrafters in your bloodlines, dear?"

As Reggie Beeson studied me with those clear blue eyes of hers, as if trying to determine the possibility, I walked over to the table. Cookie followed behind me. "Fairly sure, Reggie."

"It's a shame there's no easy way to switch Crafts," she said. "You're a natural."

"I'm happy with my Craft," I said as I sat in a chair Glinda had dragged over. "By the way, I think I have something of yours at As You Wish, Reggie. A cloak?"

She pressed an age-spotted hand to her chest. "You've found it? Thank heavens. It was Samuel's, and I hated the thought that I had lost it."

"Actually, the police found it," I said. "At the pond behind the Wisp, where you dropped it when you tried to steal Archie. Nick gave it to me for safekeeping."

Reggie Beeson was the petnapper, and I was still having trouble understanding what had led her to do something so despicable.

"Oh," she said dejectedly.

That about summed it up.

I glanced at the other woman at the table. "Hello, Vivienne."

"Hi, Darcy," she said, looking embarrassed, and then she glanced at Glinda with a question in her dark eyes.

Glinda carried over another chair and dropped into it. "Angela Curtis wished to know where Cookie was, and Darcy saw you here when she granted the wish. I had to tell her everything. About you, about Cookie. About Reggie."

Everything, it turned out, had been quite the tale.

I looked at Reggie. The fiery color in her cheeks matched the red in her hair. "I'm so ashamed," she said in a whisper.

It turned out that Liam had in fact seen the

petnapper—Reggie—after she tried to steal Clarence.
He'd chased her down and taken her home with him to
deal with when Glinda arrived. Shortly afterward, Vivienne had shown up on Glinda's doorstep as well, seeking
help after hearing about Baz's accident and suspecting
she was being framed.

Glinda had had her hands full in the past twenty-four
hours.

"Why Archie?" I asked Reggie. "It was such a risk."

She nervously tapped her fingers against the table. "I
know it was, but it had been a calculated risk. I took
every precaution. I used Samuel's Crafter cape so mortals couldn't see anything going on. I tripped Terry from
behind with my cane so he didn't see anything . . . I had
it all planned, but when I heard the police sirens, I lost
my balance and dropped Archie. Panicked, I rushed as
fast as I could home that afternoon, and had to lie down
for an hour before my heart rate returned to normal.
Then I realized I didn't have Samuel's cape, that I'd lost
it somewhere along the way."

"But why Archie?" I persisted, not telling her those
sirens had come from Archie himself. "If he knew who
had taken him, you would be banned from the Craft. . . ."

"For a Halfcrafter, the risk was worth the penalty."

It was, I realized, sadly true. She wouldn't lose
powers, because she had none. . . .

"But why risk it at all?" I asked, not sure what propelled such shocking behavior.

"He's extremely valuable, and I needed money," she
said simply. "Money I need because I love my freedom
more than being any kind of witch."

"Your freedom?" I asked. "I don't understand."
Cookie put her head on my leg, and I realized she was
trying to eat my jeans. As I looked around, I noticed
that Glinda had moved all of her wood-working crafts
out of the goat's reach. Smart.

Reggie entwined her fingers. "I was the caretaker for both my parents, which was why I didn't marry until so late in life. I put their needs before my own. Then when I married, I put Samuel's needs before my own. Then when he died, I put the shop's needs before my own." She drew in a deep breath. "Don't get me wrong. I'm grateful for the life I've lived. I truly am. Very few people are loved the way I was . . . and am. I don't regret the choices I've made. I'd do them again."

The emotional strain in her voice was making my heart ache. Clarence must have sensed her distress as well, because he loped around the table to nudge Reggie with his nose.

She smiled at him and rubbed his head, then looked around the table. "But I am ready, for once in my life, to put *my* wants, *my* needs, first, and neither include moving south to be a companion for a woman I don't even know. Life is short. I knew that before my stroke, but it just served as another reminder to me of what I want to do. I'm seventy-six years old. It's time I focus on me. I want to travel. I want to dance in Spain. I want to see Kilimanjaro. I want to feel the spray of Victoria Falls on my face. I want to soak up the sun on an Australian beach. . . ." Her voice trailed off wistfully. "But to do those things I need money. In plain terms, I'm broke."

Stunned, I blinked at her. "No money? No retirement funds?"

"Retirement funds?" She laughed. "Hardly. There has been barely enough money to keep the shop open, never mind any kind of retirement account."

Suddenly, I heard Pepe's voice echoing in my head, about how some village shops barely made enough for their proprietors to get by.

"My house was mortgaged to the hilt and fortunately, when it sold, there was enough to pay off the note in full, but there was nothing extra. Any money I've scrimped and saved over the years went to paying off medical bills after my stroke. I probably would have continued running the shop until my last breath, except I didn't have enough money to renew my lease. I told myself it was the universe's way of telling me it was time to move on. On paper, becoming a companion was the answer to my problems. It would provide a roof over my head, food to eat . . . but in my heart, I know it's not the answer for me. But as the time grew closer for me to leave, I knew I simply could not do it and I panicked."

"So you took the animals?" I asked, feeling a mix of sympathy and horror.

With a guilty flush, she said, "When taking Archie failed, I was desperate enough to steal the other animals. I hid them in the storage barn behind my house, planning to sell them online as soon as possible."

"Did you take Lady Catherine, too?" I asked.

She nodded. "However, she escaped from me on the way back to the storage barn. She was just too energetic for me to handle with my cane and all."

So it *had* been dumb luck that Ivy had found the dog. I sent her another silent apology. Maybe I'd cut my bill by three-quarters. "How did you get Cookie?"

"She came by the shop for a drink of water, and I grabbed her, thinking I could sell her, too. She's terribly cute, and I was desperate. If only I'd found Lady Catherine after she broke free, all this would have been averted. I'd have been the one to receive Marigold's generous reward."

Cookie was still trying to eat my jeans. It was a very good thing I was used to drool. "Was money your motivation for wanting to sell my paintings at the shop?"

"Sorry," she said with a wince. "Though I wasn't lying when I said the paintings were beautiful. They are."

My head was starting to hurt.

Reggie said, "I thought . . . I thought if I could just get enough to start the first leg of my journey, then fate would supply the rest . . . and if it didn't, I'd come back with my tail between my legs and try not to think too hard about my hopes and dreams."

I rubbed my temples, trying to ease the growing ache. "So what changed? Why were the animals returned?"

Tear suddenly filled her eyes. "I realized the error of my ways, thank goodness. I just couldn't sell those animals. I was doing something that went against everything I've ever believed, everything I ever represented. Pets are family, and I couldn't bear knowing I was responsible for taking them away from those who loved them. It's contemptible. I decided I had to return the animals, no matter what the cost my future. Frankly, I deserve to rot for what I put those pet owners through." She sighed, clearly disgusted with herself. "I was returning Clarence when Liam caught me and got Glinda involved."

"Wait," I said, confused as I thought about the phone call Glinda had received. "He caught you *taking* Clarence, didn't he?"

"No," Reggie said. "He caught me bringing Clarence *back*. I'd already taken him an hour before, and Liam just hadn't noticed yet."

Glinda let out a sigh. "When I returned home, Reggie was telling Liam the whole sordid tale."

"That's about the time I showed up on Glinda's doorstep," Vivienne said, picking up the story. "It was my idea to help Reggie return the rest of the animals and sweep the whole matter under the rug. After my accident, it was Reggie's suggestion that a dog would help my recovery. I'm not sure what I would've done without Audrey. I owe Reggie for that, so I'm more than willing to forgive her for what she did."

"Thank you, dear," Reggie said, patting Vivienne's hand. "If only I can forgive myself. As first I believed returning the pets would be enough, but I know I've stolen my friends' trust as well as their pets, and I need to fix that, too. As soon as we're done here, I'll be heading to the police station to turn myself in. It's time to take responsibility for my actions and face my fate, whatever it may be."

"But—," Vivienne began, her eyes glistening with moisture.

"No, no." Reggie cut her off. "I have to do it. No arguments."

Vivienne faced Glinda. "Talk to her."

Glinda sighed. "If Reggie wants villagers to forgive her, she needs to go to the police. It's the only way. While I doubt any villagers whose pets were taken will press charges against Reggie, the Extravaganza outsiders whose pets were stolen might." She glanced at the older woman. "You'll need a good lawyer."

I heard Reggie gulp, and I told myself not to feel too sorry for her.

It was easier said than done.

"I'll call Marcus Debrowski right away," Vivienne said. "He's my attorney. The best in the village. He's actually at the police station right now, speaking to Nick on my behalf."

"He is?" I asked, shifting to face her.

"I certainly can't hide out here forever. I didn't run Baz over, Darcy. Though I'd like to thank the person who did. Well, except that person seems intent on framing me for the deed. Ridiculous. Nick's not buying that, is he? Tell me he's not buying that."

My temples pulsed. "I think he just has a lot of questions for you that need answers. He's been looking for you. The whole police force has. If you're innocent why have you been hiding out at all?"

"It's not safe for me out there right now," Vivienne

explained. "Not until the police figure out who killed Natasha."

Something she had said earlier nagged at me. The mention of her car accident. She'd also been struck by a car, a hit-and-run. Was that just a coincidence?

Or a clue?

"Is there anyone to vouch for your whereabouts when Baz was hit by your car?" I asked Vivienne.

"Evan Sullivan," she said. "I was at the Gingerbread Shack settling my bill with him for the Danish I'd ordered for the Extravaganza. I was there long before the ambulances went by. Darcy, I need Baz alive and well. He's worth much more to me alive than dead, especially now that you provided that footage of him and Natasha together."

"What do you mean?" I asked.

"If Baz dies, I get only a million dollars. The rest goes to a trust fund set up for the arts. He's leaving the bulk of his money to charity."

Her words rang true, and they were easy enough to confirm. "Did you ever stalk Natasha? Key her car? Break into her house?"

"Never. She could have Baz for all I cared. I stayed too long in that marriage as it was. She was doing me a favor, cheating with him. And honestly, if she had lived and they had gotten married, she would have learned soon enough the mistake she'd made. Once a cheater, always a cheater. I wouldn't be surprised if he'd been cheating on her the whole time they were together. Baz finds his validation in women, and that's not likely to change. If you ask me, the investigation should be focusing on the other possible women in Baz's life. There's always a cute little coed at his beck and call. Marcus is explaining all this to Nick, too."

I understood why Vivienne had gone into hiding, but

she had wasted nearly a day of Nick's time and energy.
While he and his investigators had been searching for
her, they could have been looking at other angles to this
case.

I stood up. "I should go." I wanted to call Nick to give
him a heads-up about Reggie, and I also wanted to stop
by to see Harper. Beyond wanting to talk over all these
new developments, she always had aspirin handy.

"Darcy, what are you . . ." Reggie wrung her hands.
"With Archie, I mean."

With Archie. Because she was a Halfcrafter, and in
the witch world, it was an entirely different set of laws
she had broken.

Part of me wanted to forget the whole incident, but
as an investigator for the Elder, I had an obligation to
the Craft. "I'll have to share what you did with the Elder.
It's my job."

"We take care of our own," the Elder had said to me
the other day.

"But I'm sure the Elder will be lenient with you," I
said, "considering you're facing mortal charges as well.
You'll probably be called before her, so you'd best prepare for that meeting."

Reggie took my hands and held them tight. "Thank
you, Darcy. I'll swing by later on for Samuel's cloak,
okay?"

"That's fine."

"One more thing?" she added.

"What's that?"

Her blue eyes sparkled with a hint of mischief. "I
really wish Cookie had a miniature donkey friend so
she won't be lonely."

I dropped my head back and sighed. After a moment,
I cast the spell. Silently, we all waited for the Elder to
either approve or deny the wish.

A moment later, a small charcoal gray donkey appeared at my feet. *"Eee-aww, eee eee eee!"*

"He's gorgeous!" Reggie exclaimed as she rubbed the spot between the donkey's ears.

"Mehh!" Cookie bleated.

Not to be outdone, Audrey barked.

I looked at Glinda. "You're explaining this one to Harmony."

Chapter Twenty-nine

"Darcy! Hey, wait up!"

I had just left Spellbound and was dashing across the village green, heading for As You Wish, when I heard my name. I had stopped by the bookshop to tell Harper all I'd found out—about the mourning dove, Reggie, and Vivienne—and to get that aspirin, only to be told that Harper had gone to As You Wish to drop off my paintings.

Turning, I found a tall blond-haired man loping toward me, but behind him—at the north end of the square—I spotted Glinda tugging twin ropes attached to Cookie and the new mini donkey. The furry pair was strongly resisting a return to the Pixie Cottage. I almost laughed out loud, imagining what Glinda would possibly tell Harmony.

As I refocused on the man as he neared, I wished Nick were here with me.

"Thanks for waiting," Chip said. "You were moving at a good clip there."

"No problem." I kept my distance, not sure of his intent in tracking me down.

As far as I knew, he was now the lead suspect in Natasha's death. I was grateful we were standing in the middle of the village at noon. In broad daylight. Still, I was nervous.

"I almost didn't recognize you with clothes on." Dressed in khaki pants and a button-down shirt, he looked even more like a Ken doll than I had previously thought.

Laughing, he said, "Yeah, well, I'm catching a flight later, and the airlines frown upon nakedness. Go figure."

He was leaving town? "Flight?"

"To Hollywood. An old director friend of mine is interested in my poisoning story. He's thinking it'd be great for a made-for-TV movie, but I'm aiming for the big screen. He's flying me out there to get things rolling."

I recalled what Alina had said about Chip being cheap and wasn't surprised he hadn't bought his own ticket. "So soon?"

"We'd been talking about collaborating on a project for a while now but were waiting for the right time. You can't get more dramatic than what happened to me."

The timing was all kinds of suspicious. Had this been his goal all along? "That's turning lemons to lemonade if I ever heard it."

"Lots of lemonade," he agreed. "Which is good, because I might never drink a smoothie again."

Uncomfortable, I shifted from foot to foot. "Did you already meet with Nick?"

"Yeah, just came from there."

"And he okayed you leaving the village?" I asked hesitantly.

Shoving his hands in his pocket, he rocked on his

heels. "I get it. You're not sure if I killed Natasha or not. I didn't. I'm not that kind of guy." He cracked a smile. "I might not be above a little attempted blackmail, but I draw the line at violence."

"It's good to know your ethical boundaries."

The breeze ruffled his hair. "Nick cleared me to travel once Cherise Goodwin confirmed I had been with her from the moment I left the hospital yesterday morning until late afternoon. It's a good thing for me she refused to leave my side until she was sure I was settled in with a fridge full of food we knew wasn't contaminated, or I might be in jail right now."

"Cherise is a force."

"She even threw away my toothpaste. Just in case."

We stepped to the side, off the path, as a woman walked by with a baby in a stroller. "That is thorough."

Looking thoughtful, he said, "I owe her my life. And you, too. It's why I stopped you. I wanted to say thanks before I left town. If you hadn't come back to check on me . . ."

"You're welcome," I said, meaning it. "I'm glad I trusted my instincts."

"If only I'd trusted mine. I knew better than to get involved with Natasha, but she was like a drug, one I couldn't quit cold turkey. Off, on, off, on. It was almost a relief when she talked Baz into seeing her exclusively and she cut me off for good. I could finally let go."

"Alina, Natasha's sister, told me someone didn't like Natasha seeing Baz. Keyed her car, broke in to her house . . ."

"The keyed car didn't bother Natasha so much. It was the break-in that freaked her out and pushed her to talk Baz into leave the village."

"You know about the stalking?"

"Yeah, Natasha told me all about it. Even though we weren't sleeping together, we were still friends. Like I said, the incidents didn't bother her too much at first. Natasha is used to her share of jealous women and she likes competition. But the break-in worried her."

Alina had said it was a woman scorned.

But *what* woman? Chip had told me the other day that Baz had been dealing with a bunch of baggage with his other woman. I'd assumed it was Vivienne. But what if it wasn't?

"Do you know who did it? Do you think it was Vivienne?"

"I don't think Vivienne even knew they were dating. I felt really bad for her, actually. I think it was someone else Baz had been seeing, which could be any number of people."

Baz's words came back to me. *"It was a whirlwind relationship. We'd only been seeing each other for a month. I fell so fast for her. So hard and fast. She wasn't like the others."*

The others . . .

"Do you have any names?" I asked.

"No, but I'm guessing whoever did it is the person who killed Natasha and poisoned me."

"Why poison you, though? How do you fit in?"

"I don't know. I can only guess it was because of my relationship with Natasha. We'll probably never know," Chip said, looking at a large watch on his wrist. "I need to get going and finish packing."

"Will you be coming back to the village? Or will you be staying in California?"

"I haven't decided yet. I was offered Natasha's job at the playhouse, but . . ." He shook his head. "It's time for a change. There are too many memories here. Bad ones. I've been wanting to leave for a long time, and now seems like the perfect opportunity to let go."

I spotted Starla with her camera walking along the green, snapping pictures of tourists. Life was slowly getting back to normal. For some, at least. "I can't say I blame you."

He looked around. "I'll miss this place."

"Well, you can always come back."

"I have some dreams to make come true first. Thanks for everything, Darcy." He flashed me a movie-star smile and strode off.

I was about to start toward As You Wish again when I heard a "*Yodel-heh*, Darcy!"

I knew that voice. Smiling, I turned to find Godfrey ambling toward me. When he reached my side, he bent and drew in a deep breath.

"Perhaps a diet," he muttered, "is not such a heinous idea—do not dare tell Cherise I spoke those words."

"I wouldn't dare."

Straightening, he reached for his pocket square, and eyed me like a germ viewed under a microscope. "What is that you are wearing? And are those flip-flops? My heart . . . it is not strong enough to withstand your insistence upon wearing footwear that flaps!"

I glanced downward. My jeans were damp, thanks to Cookie, and I rather liked my plain white T-shirt. "The shoes are comfy."

"*Argh!* Those words are the bane of my existence! If we were not in the middle of the green, I'd dress you properly. Could I possibly persuade you to return with me to the shop?"

"No way." I didn't want one of my favorite pairs of jeans to vanish in a swirl of his magic. "Did you run out here just to reprimand me?"

"No, but that alone was worth the perspiration. I know you were quite concerned about Ivy's possible connection to the petnapper. Therefore when I spied you out here speaking with Chip, I waddled on out. I finally had a chance to view the footage last night."

The surveillance footage behind Fairytails . . .

I should have called him and told him it wasn't necessary after Nick handed me that cloak this morning, but it had slipped my mind. "Thanks for looking, but—"

He dabbed his upper lip. "There was no sign of Lady Catherine at all."

I tipped my head, suddenly very interested in what he had to say. "No?"

"Not so much as a tail wag."

I was certain Ivy had said she found the dog at the back door of Fairytails. If not there, where had she come across her? "What about Ivy? Did you see her at all?"

"Oh, I saw her. I'm not sure what she was thinking with that wig. And black? Not her best color."

"The wig was rather atrocious, wasn't it?" I agreed. "But I liked the black dress. Sleek and simple. She looked good in it."

"Dress? There was no dress. Ivy was wearing gray yoga pants when I saw her, and do not even get me started on that particular fashion faux pas. I was referring to the wig."

"Wait. I'm confused. A black wig?"

"Yes. Why?"

"This was yesterday?"

He nodded. "Around ten thirty or so, I believe."

This was getting stranger and stranger. "I saw Ivy yesterday morning, but the wig I saw was blond."

"A much better color choice," he said, sounding relieved. "However, when I saw her, Ivy was wearing a midnight black wig, like something Elvira would wear." He coughed. "Not that I've put much thought into the wardrobe of the woman. Elvira, that is. Not Ivy. Oh my." He fanned himself with the pocket square. "Is it terribly warm today?"

A long black wig . . .

A driver's seat pushed back to accommodate long legs.

The clicking noises in the background of the spy pen video.

The silhouettes on the photo Glinda had taken . . .

I now knew why that photo been bothering me. The heights. Natasha would have been a lot shorter than Baz, but the woman in the photo with him had been almost as tall as him.

The woman had been Ivy. I was sure of it.

She had known Baz for a while—she was Audrey's groomer. What had Vivienne said yesterday morning when talking about Audrey's styling?

"Baz works with Ivy Teasdale at Fairytails to get the look just right."

Audrey was a year and a half old. Had Baz and Ivy been seeing each other that long? And Baz had mentioned that he pulled some strings with Ivy to get Audrey entered in the Extravaganza last year.

Knowing what I knew now, I could easily imagine what types of strings those had been.

If so, she might be really upset if she knew Baz was growing close to Natasha.

Another conversation came back to me.

Ivy had said, *"All I know is love is a powerful motivator. It can make you do crazy things. Especially when it goes bad."*

"It sounds like you're talking from experience."

"Haven't we all been there?"

A woman scorned, was right.

And that woman had been hiding right under my nose the whole time.

I kissed Godfrey's cheek. "I have to go. I need to call Nick."

"All is well, Miss Darcy?"

"Not yet," I said. "But it will be."

Chapter Thirty

I sprinted across the green, shoved open the side gate at As You Wish, and hurried toward the back door.

Archie squawked in his cage as I ran past. "'Russell! If you don't hurry up, the tigers will eat you.'"

"Up!" I yelled over my shoulder.

"Damn it," he cried.

I kicked off my flip-flops in the mudroom and nearly tripped over Missy and Annie as they greeted me. I bent to scratch their ears. "Harper? Are you still here?"

"In the family room!" she yelled. "We're just admiring your paintings."

I grabbed the cordless phone to call Nick. "You'll never guess— Wait. We?" Aunt Ve and Tilda were supposed to be at the vet's office right about now. I walked into the family room and found Harper and Ivy standing in front of the fireplace, where my paintings leaned against the stone hearth.

"Ivy was on her way over here when she saw me on the green and helped me carry over the paintings."

"I was wrong about the pizzazz, Darcy," Ivy said, looking back at me. "These are spectacular up close. You're very talented."

"I, uh—thanks." I tucked the phone under my arm and wiped suddenly damp palms on my jeans. I told myself to stay calm. To not let on what I suspected about Ivy. I needed a plan.

Harper eyed me. "Why are you all sweaty?"

So much for not letting on. "I, uh, ran over here from the bookshop when Angela told me where you were."

"You could have walked."

I forced a laugh. "I didn't get my jog in this morning. Thought I'd work in a little cardio. . . ."

"In jeans?"

I shot her a "drop it" look.

Ivy's gaze narrowed.

"I was in a rush to tell you that Cookie's been found," I said, wiping my forehead with the back of my hand.

"Really?" Ivy said. "That's fantastic news. All the missing pets are now accounted for. Now maybe those ridiculous petnapper rumors will die."

I swallowed hard as she said the word "die."

"Are you calling for some lunch delivery?" Harper asked, motioning to the phone. "Because I'm starved."

I stared at the phone. "Yes! I was. I was thinking Chinese food. Would you like to stay for lunch, Ivy?"

"Thanks, but I can't. I'm due back at Fairytails. I just stopped by to pay you." She sat in the armchair and reached in her tote bag. She pulled out her checkbook.

I hooked a thumb over my shoulder. "Then I'll hold off on calling, but let me get some water." I smacked my lips. "Dry mouth. Either of you want anything?" I asked. "We have coffee, tea, water . . ."

"I'm good," Harper said, eyeing me as if I were a crazy woman.

"Me, too," Ivy added.

I turned and nearly tripped over Missy and Annie again. They followed me into the kitchen, where I grabbed a glass and filled it with water. I rattled some ice cubes as I quickly punched in 9-1-1, then left the handset on the counter.

My hand was shaking so badly when I went back into the living room that I spilled some water on the wooden floor. I left it. I didn't want to explain why I was so sloppy.

Ivy had her pen poised, and Harper was on the sofa, sifting through the photos Glinda and I had left on the table. She must have bumped my laptop, bringing the computer out of sleep mode, because the screen was bright with the images of the mourning dove.

"What is all this?" Harper asked.

I sat next to her. "Oh, nothing really. Glinda and I were trying to find some leads in Natasha's death, but we didn't find anything," I lied. "Glinda was hoping to clear Vivienne's name, but it's looking more and more like she's guilty."

Harper nodded as she held up the photo of telltale silhouettes. I noticed the time stamp. Four days ago. So Baz *hadn't* kept his promise of exclusivity to Natasha. In my head, Vivienne's voice echoed.

"Once a cheater, always a cheater."

"I heard they found cyanide in her car," Harper said as she kept staring at the photo.

"Yeah," I said, willing her to drop the picture. "That's what Nick said."

Ivy motioned to the computer. "Looks like you finally got a good picture of that bird."

A change of subject I was grateful for, even though I knew why she was doing it.

"I did at that." I bumped Harper with my elbow. "I thought you might like some copies of the bird photos as well, being the nature lover you are."

I wanted her to make the connection that I had made . . . that the mourning dove was a Wishcrafter. If Harper did, she'd drop the photo and start running through every female Wishcrafter in the village to determine which one might be the Elder. "Isn't it a pretty bird? Look at that blue around its eye. . . ."

As I said the words, I suddenly realized that the Elder was the reason the Lunumbra spell had been created. It was because I kept trying to take her picture, which would reveal she was a Wishcrafter. No wonder Ve cast the spell only on me—I was the reason the spell was needed in the first place. But the question still remained as to why the bird always seemed to be watching over me.

Harper glanced up at me as though not really listening, then back at the photo in her hand. She didn't even look at the computer screen. "This isn't Natasha," she said, pointing at the woman in the picture.

"Oh, I know." I grabbed the photo and tucked it into a pile on the table. "Baz apparently had lots of girl-friends. A regular Romeo."

"Nick should look into that," Harper said. "It opens a whole new door as to who might have killed Natasha and run him over. Maybe Vivienne's innocent after all. She really doesn't strike me as the murderous type."

"How much do I owe you, Darcy?" Ivy asked, her voice tight.

I waved my hand. "You know what? Nothing. I truly didn't do much, and ha! I even at one point thought you might have been the petnapper. So let's just call it even."

I couldn't believe how she'd fooled me and I wondered now if she purposely planted clues that led me to believe she'd taken the animals . . . so I wouldn't become suspicious about what she'd really done.

Harper riffled through the pictures on the table. "That silhouette looked familiar," she said. "I might be able to tell who it is if I look at it a little more closely."

Curse Harper and her love of forensics.

Ivy tucked her pen away. "The petnapper? That's funny. I could never steal a pet." She pulled out a plastic container of cookies and set them on the coffee table. "I brought you some cookies. As a thank-you. Double chocolate chunk."

That got Harper's attention. She reached for the container. "I've died and gone to heaven. You're a life-saver. I'm *starving.*" Lifting the lid, she pulled out a beautiful-looking cookie.

I slapped it out of her hands.

"Darcy!" she cried.

"You don't want to eat that. Does she, Ivy?"

Ivy lifted an eyebrow. "So you *have* figured it out. The cookies are perfectly fine, by the way. I just wanted to see how you'd react to them, since you've been rambling uncomfortably since laying eyes on me."

Missy hopped down from the couch and started pacing as though sensing the danger in the air.

I just needed to keep Ivy talking until the police arrived. I strained to hear any sirens, but heard none. I did hear the coo of the mourning dove, however, and looked over to see the bird bobbing along the windowsill.

"I was with you all along, Darcy.

"I'll always be with you."

With a little more confidence, I turned back to Ivy. "I didn't know until a witness came forward today and said he saw you with a black wig on going into the back of Fairytails. *After* Baz had been hit by the car."

"It's *your* silhouette!" Harper said suddenly.

I sighed.

"Yes," Ivy confirmed. "It looks to me that the picture was taken minutes before Baz told me he was marrying Natasha and leaving the village for good. I couldn't let that happen. I had too much invested in our relationship."

"Competition changes people. Trust me."

I realized Ivy had been talking about herself, not Natasha.

Ivy glanced at me. "I thought you had figured it out yesterday, Darcy, but I see now your pointed questions were about the petnapping. My mistake."

"Why'd you run him over if you wanted a relationship with him?" Harper asked.

It was a good question.

"I got scared when Darcy suggested that the police were looking to arrest Baz for Natasha's murder. I needed someone else to take the blame. Vivienne was my next obvious choice, since framing Chip didn't work out as planned. Thanks to you," she said drolly.

"But you poisoned Chip," I said. "How was that framing him?"

"After he was found *dead*, I was going to mail a typed suicide note to the police that confessed he killed Natasha and couldn't live with himself. Darcy botched that plan by getting him medical help."

She sounded thoroughly disgusted with me, but I didn't think this was a good time to point out that she was the one who'd asked me to go to Chip's apartment in the first place.

"How'd you even get into his apartment?" Harper asked.

"During one of my break-ins at Natasha's, I stole her keys and had copies made. One of those keys belonged to Chip's apartment. I used it to sneak in there the morning of the Extravaganza to poison his smoothie mix and bide my time. When that didn't work out, I needed another scapegoat. Vivienne was the only one left. I was going to plant the cyanide at her house, but the police were there that morning. Then I saw her car at the Pixie Cottage and made a plan. By the way, *that's* where I found Lady Catherine. At the Pixie Cottage. She was there getting a drink in the garden. For some reason, there were six bowls of water set out. I took Lady Catherine back to Marigold, and went home and got the wig and the car keys and set out to find Baz, which wasn't hard, thanks to the GPS app I put on his phone a year ago."

"You could have killed him," I pointed out.

"If I wanted him dead, he'd be dead by now," Ivy said succinctly. "I only clipped him."

She was delusional. He absolutely could have died from his wound.

"Were you the one who hit Vivienne, too?" I asked. "A year and a half ago?"

Ivy smiled, cool, calm, and collected. Gone was her anxiety, her high energy. I suddenly preferred the latter. Because a calm Ivy was terrifying.

"You're good," she said. "I knew you were, but not many people would have put that together. I meant to kill her, but I wasn't as skilled then as I am now. You're not so smart, however, to have figured out that it was I who was behind the food poisoning incident last year. The salad Baz ate was meant for Vivienne. With her weakened immune system because of the accident, it would have killed her. But it didn't matter much anyway. Baz kept coming back to me."

Harper frowned. "Why'd you even hire Darcy in the first place?"

"An alibi, of course," she said. "No one would think I'd hire someone to watch the woman I was about to get rid of. The second time I hired Darcy was purely to get information on the case that the police weren't releasing to the general public, and her relationship to the chief of police paid off handsomely for me."

I didn't want to think about how I'd been used. How easily I'd fallen for her lies because I wanted to *help*.

No, I couldn't think about that right now. I had to keep her talking until the police showed up. "How'd you and Baz meet? I thought it was because of Audrey, but it had to have been earlier than that if you ran over Vivienne."

"A movie. We'd both gone to see a showing of *Charade* at the playhouse and struck up a conversation."

He'd probably been there to see Audrey Hepburn, and she'd probably gone to get tips on being a psychopath.

"It was love at first sight," she said. "On my part, at least. He made promises to me, and I intend to make him keep them."

"How?" Harper asked. "He's going to know what you did."

"How?"

"We'll tell him," she said.

Ivy lifted up a small gun. She must have pulled it out of her tote when she took out the cookies. "No, you won't. You and your sister are going to have an argument, and one of you is going to kill the other, then turn the gun on herself. Now, which one of you is that going to be?" She waved the gun between us.

Missy started whining and raced past us, through the mudroom, and out her dog door. I was glad she'd be safe at least.

Annie hopped down from the back of the couch, onto my lap.

Harper took my hand.

I prayed for sirens.

"No volunteers?" Ivy said. "Fine. Harper first. Just

because that'll hurt Darcy more, and this is all her fault for figuring out the truth."

Just as she aimed the gun, something slammed into the window—the mourning dove. Ivy turned and fired. Glass shattered. Annie dove off my lap, and I pulled Harper to her feet. "Run!"

Ivy jumped up. "No!"

We'd almost made it to the kitchen when she fired the second bullet. It hit the doorframe of the laundry room.

I glanced back and saw Ivy take aim again as she started after us. Annie darted in front of her, tripping her. Another bullet hit the ceiling. Harper screamed as I pushed her forward. I was right behind her until I slipped on the puddle of water I'd spilled earlier and went down hard. My breath wooshed out of me, and I was momentarily stunned as I fought for air.

Harper dropped next to me. "Darcy!"

"Go!" I managed to say, shoving her.

"No! Not without you."

Ivy scrambled to her feet, laughing.

I managed to get to my knees, and as I slowly caught my breath, I looked for some sort of weapon, and saw nothing. Just the counter stools and dust bunnies. But . . . no. I was wrong. There was something. . . .

Samuel Beeson's cloak. It was right where I'd left it earlier—draped over the back of the stool.

"Grab the cape," I told Harper as Ivy took her time coming down the hallway.

Harper looked as though she wanted to argue, but grabbed the cape. I quickly opened it and pulled it over Harper's and my heads, as if we were two little kids hiding in a fort we'd made out of bedsheets. I kept the seam of the cape gripped tightly. Here, within this mothball-scented fabric igloo, Ivy couldn't see us.

Ivy's footsteps stopped. "What the hell? Where'd you go?"

Harper looked at me, her eyes wide; then she smiled.

"Think like a Crafter," I whispered, then added, "Now creep around in front of the counter." We duck-walked that way.

Through the seam of the cape, I could see Ivy turning in a circle, looking every which way, the color draining from her face. She pressed on the floor where I'd been lying just moments ago as though testing for a trapdoor.

Sirens rose in the distance, and I wished Ivy would just leave. But she seemed intent on finding us as she walked back and forth, swinging the gun wildly.

Annie ran past her, keeping close to the wall, and ran straight toward Harper and me, meowing pitifully.

I'd forgotten that animals could see us, even with the cape.

Ivy focused on Annie. She aimed the gun at her. "I'll kill the cat!" she yelled. "You have three seconds! One!"

I loosened the seam of the cape and said to Harper, "Grab Annie!"

She nodded, and in a flash, Annie was tight against Harper's chest.

With a cry of alarm, Ivy's mouth dropped open. For a split second it looked as though she didn't know what to do—she was frozen, her eyes wide with fear. Then suddenly she bolted for the back door. I reached my hand out, grabbing her ankle as she passed, and she fell hard, hitting her head on the floor.

As she moaned and writhed, I hopped out of the cape and grabbed Missy's leash from a hook in the mudroom. I quickly went to work trussing Ivy up like a Christmas roast and said to Harper, "Quick! We need to memory-cleanse her before the police get here. It's up in my bedroom. Top drawer of my dresser."

Harper darted up the steps two at a time.

She was back in seconds, the memory cleanse in one

hand, the family portrait I'd been working on in the other. She tossed me the small bag of memory cleanse. I blew the powder into Ivy's face and she went still, passing out cold in a cloud of glitter that would soon dissolve.

I sat back and took a deep breath of relief. Which didn't last long. Harper sat on the bottom step of the back staircase, staring at the drawing. Her lower jaw was trembling as she turned the drawing toward me and pointed. "Is this Mom?"

As always, my gaze went straight to my mother's face. This time, however, I zeroed in on my mother's eye, at the vibrant blue eyeliner.

Eyeliner that suddenly reminded me so much of the blue that rimmed the mourning dove's eye.

I sucked in a breath as the truth hit me hard and fast like a sucker punch.

"I'll always be with you."

In that moment, I immediately knew that the nightmare I'd had last night hadn't been a nightmare at all.

It had been a *memory*.

That day at the scene of the crash, as paramedics kept her earthly body alive with chest compressions in an attempt to save her unborn baby, my mother's spirit had already been released. Above the wreckage of twisted metal, she had become a familiar, taking the form of a mourning dove. She'd flown over to me, to try to comfort me even then.

"I'll always be with you."

I hadn't put it together before, because I hadn't been thinking like a Crafter. I hadn't been thinking the impossible was possible. I had never even considered that the Elder might be a dead woman. A spirit. A familiar.

I jumped up, ran upstairs and grabbed my cape from my closet, then dashed back down the steps, going around Harper, who was still staring at the drawing. I quickly jotted a note and left it on the counter. I took the drawing from Harper and dropped it to the floor.

"Hey!" she protested. "What're you doing? Have you lost your mind?"

I grabbed Harper's hand and Samuel's cloak from the floor. "Come on!"

"What? Darcy! We can't just leave—"

I pulled her out the door. "We have to go right now!"

"Where?" she demanded.

"To see our mother."

Chapter Thirty-one

Harper gripped my hand so tightly my fingers were going numb as we jogged down a wooded path that led to a place I'd been many times, but Harper had never seen at all.

"Why did she never say anything?" Harper said, her voice thick. She wore Samuel's cloak.

"She couldn't say anything. Craft law, remember? Witches have to live in the village a year before knowing the Elder's true identity."

"Family should trump Craft law."

I personally agreed, because, well, she was our *mother*. "But that's what makes her a good Elder, no? That she is safeguarding our heritage, even at the cost of her own personal happiness."

Stubbornly, Harper said, "This is no time to get philosophical with me, Darcy. How much farther is it?"

"Not far," I said.

"Do you think Aunt Ve knows?"

"She knows. It's probably been killing her to keep the secret. A lot of our friends probably know. Like Archie and Godfrey and Pepe and Mrs. P. All were sworn to secrecy."

"Craft law stinks."

"Without it, our world would be chaos. It's a small sacrifice to make for the greater good. You're all about the greater good, remember?"

"Yeah, yeah," she grumbled.

We walked in silence for a moment, before Harper said, "Do you think she'll like me?"

I slowed to a stop and faced my sister, our hands still linking us together. My heart nearly broke in two at the tears shining in her eyes. "Like you? Yes, she'll like you. She *loves* you."

"How do you know?"

"I just do."

"How?"

"Harper." I jiggled our connected hands. "Please, just this once, don't look for the explanation, the answers. Just *feel*, okay?"

"Aren't you angry?" she asked, a cry of injustice in her voice. "She's been gone all these years."

"I'll always be with you."

Shaking my head, I said, "She hasn't been gone. She's been with us. We just didn't know it. Not consciously, anyway." I was beginning to suspect that there were going to be plenty of times I'd look back on my life and realize she'd been there all along.

"Same thing."

"No, it's not."

Harper huffed. "It *feels* like the same thing."

"It wasn't her fault that she had to leave."

Harper's jaw worked side to side. "I know. I *know*. It's just that . . . I missed her."

I pulled her into a hug, and she squeezed me the way she used to do when she was scared of strange noises in the night. "Me, too."

Her voice was muffled against my shoulder. "Do you think she's mad because I don't want to be a Crafter? I mean, she's the Elder, for the love!"

"No, I don't think she'll be mad."

"Are you sure?"

I pulled back and looked at her face. "Positive."

"I'm choosing to trust you," she said, her cheeks flushed.

"Have I ever lied to you? Well, about anything really important?"

Her bottom lip pushed out as she thought about it. "I seem to recall something about the Easter bunny. . . ."

I tugged her hand. "Come on."

"Is she even going to be there? She might still be at the house. She . . . she saved our lives."

She had. If she hadn't banged that window . . . Emotion clogged my throat. "I'm sure she will be. She probably knows we're on our way because she was watching us."

"Do you think she watched us when we were little too? In Ohio?"

"Yes," I said without hesitation.

I didn't begrudge Harper's endless questions. She was scared to death. A part of me was, too. What if I was wrong? What if the Elder was just . . . the Elder?

I shoved the what-ifs out of my head and took my own advice to *feel*.

The Elder was my mother. Tears built in my eyes, blurring the path. I recalled all the times I thought she'd sounded familiar. All the times her laugh turned my heart to mush. All the times I'd screwed up and felt as if I'd been disciplined by a parent. Even her name, Deryn, meant "bird" in Welsh. Then there was that tell-tale blue eyeliner.

I should have figured this out sooner.

But I wouldn't dwell on that now. Or ever. I was too happy to know the truth.

I couldn't possibly be angry that I hadn't known she had been with us all these long years.

I knew it now. That was the important thing.

It was a gift. A miracle, really.

"Oh my good gosh, is this the longest path ever created?" Harper moaned.

"We're almost there. See that rock?"

"The one that looks like a piece of cake?"

I nodded. "It's just past that."

"Then come on," she said, yanking my hand as she sprinted ahead of me, Samuel's mothball-scented cloak flapping in my face. "Come on, Darcy!"

I held tight to her hand and couldn't help laughing.

She glanced back at me and started laughing, too, as we raced along, jumping over roots and rocks and anything standing in our way.

At the cake rock, we slowed as the grassy meadow came into view.

"This is it?" Harper whispered, sounding let down.

"Just wait." I kept hold of her hand as we walked into the field.

"Seriously, this is disapp—"

Harper's words died on her lips as the weeping tree in the middle of the meadow lifted its branches. Sunlight burst through the clouds, blasting golden beams onto green stems that spiraled upward out of the ground, and unfolded to reveal dazzling wildflowers.

It seemed to me that the colorful blooms were even brighter and more abundant than usual. From the top of the tree, a mourning dove lifted up and took flight, circling and swooping, and I thought my heart might stop from how hard my chest was being squeezed with raw emotion.

The bird landed ten feet from us, flexed its wings,

then disappeared in a cloud of sparkle and smoke. When the smoke cleared, I gasped.

In the bird's place was our mother, barefoot and dressed in a white gauzy dress that billowed around her in the breeze along with her long brown hair.

It didn't even seem the least bit odd that her bare feet didn't touch the ground.

She was floating.

Literally floating.

With fine lines around her eyes and silver sparkling in her hair, she looked simply like an older version of the woman I loved so much. And even though I had known Harper took after her, the resemblance in person stole my breath. Her petite stature, the shape of her eyes, the wide forehead and narrow chin.

Then she smiled . . . and in that instant I saw myself in her, too.

"Hi," she said tentatively.

"Hi . . . ," I said, pushing the word out of my dry throat. " . . . Mother? Mom? Mum? Mummy? Elder? Birdie?" I rambled, not sure what to call her.

She smiled. "I rather like Birdie, but here in the meadow, just call me Mom. Like you always did. I've missed the sound of it so much. Outside of here, always refer to me as the Elder unless we're certain we are with those who know my identity."

As she spoke, I realized she'd been disguising her true voice from me nearly a year now. This voice, the one she was using here and now, was as I'd always remembered. It must have been incredibly difficult for her to keep her identity a secret from me.

"Mom," I said, testing it out. It felt strange to say it aloud after all these years. Strange, but not wrong.

I glanced at Harper. Tears streamed down her face. I squeezed her hand.

"I thought this day would never come," our mother

said. "It just about killed me. Well, you know. If I weren't already . . ." She laughed.

At the sound, I almost fell to my knees from the reaction it caused within me. To hear it straight from her lips, to see it, caused my chest to hurt as if I were having a heart attack. My throat tightened, my legs went weak.

She added, "I'm truly not one for patience. Just ask your aunt Ve. I'm working on that. It's an endless endeavor." She held out her arms, inviting us to her. "Come here, my darling girls."

I let go of Harper's hand and gave her a nudge. She stumbled forward, then stopped. Forward. Stop. Then my mother floated forward, toward Harper, and the hood of the cloak fell backward off Harper's head as she rushed to meet her halfway. Harper threw her arms around our mother's waist and squeezed her as tightly as she had done to me just a few minutes ago.

My vision blurred as I saw my mother cheek to cheek with Harper, running her hand over the back of Harper's head as she cooed and soothed. I wanted them to have this moment. I'd had seven years with my mother, whereas Harper had had none. They had a lot of time to make up for.

We all did.

Above Harper's head, my mother's gaze met mine. She waved me over, holding out an arm to invite me into the hug.

I tried to stay cool and calm as I took one step, then another. Before I knew it, I was running. As graceful as an out-of-control bowling ball, I fell into them both, knocking us all to the ground. Mom laughed. Then I did. But Harper just kept clinging to her for all she was worth.

I didn't know how we were doing it, holding on to this . . . spirit, but I wasn't going to question it. I was certain there was still a lot more we had to learn about this new development in the months to come. But we'd figure it out. In time.

Together.

Our mother being back in our lives was more than a gift.

More than a miracle.

It was magic.

The following weekend the village green was packed with people attending the first of the summer community block parties planned by the village council.

I had figured the event would be bittersweet, though my reasoning as to why had changed.

Originally, I thought that tonight we'd all be sad as we said good-bye to Reggie Beeson before she moved away. . . .

Instead the party was bittersweet because she wasn't here at all.

Even though she had been arrested on theft charges and was currently out of jail, released on bond, she had opted not to stop by. By all rights, she should be here tonight, but she was too embarrassed to attend.

I didn't blame her, but I felt for her nonetheless.

Archie had griped and grumped when he found out that Reggie had been behind his attempted abduction, but surprisingly he had opted not to press charges, which Terry complied with. Surprising because Archie was normally a vengeful kind of bird.

If he'd found it in his heart to fully forgive her, then I hoped one day I could, too.

I had time to work on it. For the foreseeable future, Reggie wasn't going anywhere. Glinda had been right about the villagers not pressing charges—but the other victims of Reggie's little crime spree had. She was to stay put until her legal matters were settled, which might take a while. Until then, she vowed to win the villagers' trust once again, and Vivienne Lucas had promised to help every step of the way.

The first of those steps being that she was the person who'd paid Reggie's bond.

The second was that Vivienne had decided to take over the Furry Toadstool.

She had signed a new lease and purchased from Reggie the shop's Web site content, its excess inventory, and its mailing list. Vivienne claimed she been wanting to expand her dog-walking business, and taking over the Furry Toadstool was the perfect segue.

The amount she was willing to pay for all those things hadn't been disclosed, but I had the feeling it was enough for Reggie to travel comfortably once she was out of legal trouble.

Not that Vivienne would miss the money. Her divorce was on a fast track, and Baz wasn't contesting it—or the prenup—at all.

Vivienne would be free of him soon . . . and a lot richer for it, in more meanings than one.

I'd heard through the grapevine that Baz had already left the village and was currently shacked up with a nurse he'd met at the hospital. To say he moved fast was putting it mildly. When asked why he hadn't told Natasha that it was probably Ivy who'd been stalking her, he simply said he hadn't wanted Ivy to get into trouble. That he cared for her too deeply.

There were some in the village who commented that he had gotten what he deserved.

I wasn't sure. I had begun to think he should have gotten worse.

I didn't like that much about myself, so I didn't think about it too much.

The moon was high in the clear sky, and stars twinkled as music floated through the air, mingling with a gentle sea breeze.

"Darcy!"

The shout nearly knocked me over, and I grabbed on to a folding table for balance.

"Sorry!" Harmony said, sidling up to me. "Didn't mean to startle you. I just wanted to say thank you for the painting. I love it so much."

"It was all Angela's doing, not mine."

"Thank you," she said again with a smile.

I smiled, too. "You're welcome."

She glanced around. "Not quite the party we had all planned for, is it?"

"Not quite." I watched Nick spin Mimi around the dance floor. Mimi had plans to spend the night at a friend's house, and Nick and I had some late-night plans of our own.

"Aside from the Midsummer Ball," Harmony said, "I bet the next big shindig will be your wedding."

I glanced at her. "I'm not even engaged!"

"I'd bet a dwarf goat and mini donkey you will be soon."

Eyeing her suspiciously, I said, "You're not just trying to pawn them off on me, are you?"

She laughed. "No. Don't tell Angela, but I've become rather attached to them. It's kind of amazing that Glinda found the two wandering around together, and that no one's claimed Scal as their own."

"Scal?"

"Scalawag, the donkey."

I smiled. "Definitely amazing. Like it was meant to be."

"Some things are. Speaking of . . ." She elbowed me, waggled her eyebrows, then slipped away.

Nick walked my way, his hand held out. "Care to dance, Darcy Merriweather?"

"Love to," I said, slipping my hand into his.

He pulled me closed, and I looped an arm around his back. "What was that about? With Harmony."

"Things that are meant to be."

"Like Higgins and drool?"

"Exactly."

Laughing, he spun me around the dance floor. As he led us along, I spotted Harper and Marcus near the buffet. Her face glowed as she laughed at something Marcus had said.

She was happy, which made me happy.

She'd been spending a lot of time at the Elder's meadow.

Our mother's meadow.

The differential was going to take some getting used to.

It seemed as though the past week had passed in a flash. Between dealing with the fallout of Ivy's arrest and learning the Elder was my mother, I'd had some late nights and early mornings.

My mother had graciously allowed me to let Nick and Mimi, Starla and Evan in on the secret of her identity, and we all swore (literally—on a Wishcraft law book) to take the secret to our graves.

Harper and I had learned a little bit about the Eldership, about how the Elder had always been a spirit. Harper had dubbed the whole process the Dead Witch Society. Our mother, unlike other familiars, could morph into human form at will—a perk of being Elder. She had many ways to travel in and around the village but mostly preferred using her mourning dove form.

Mimi had been full of questions at the revelations, but had primarily wondered if it was possible her mother, too, was a familiar that was watching over her.

I told her the one thing I knew for certain: that anything in this village was possible.

Because it was.

"Is there any particular reason Dorothy Dewitt is giving us the evil eye?" Nick asked.

I glanced over at her. She was, in fact, giving us a death stare. I recalled something Reggie had said. "Probably not. Dorothy is just being . . . Dorothy."

He laughed. "Well, I'd be glad if she did it elsewhere."

I smiled against his shoulder as he twirled me around. I caught sight of Starla and Vince, dancing close by. Starla waved when she spotted me.

I wasn't sure what was going to happen between the two, but was glad she was happy right now, in this moment. She'd been through so much but had worked hard at overcoming her personal losses.

If only Ivy had worked half as hard at letting go of the man she loved . . .

She had no memory of what had happened at As You Wish, which was blamed on her head injury when she fell. That was perfectly fine with Harper and me, as we'd told identical stories of what had happened inside the house, leaving out only the magical elements.

It had taken some digging by the police, but an online purchase order of cyanide had been traced back to Ivy via a fake name and post office box. When confronted with the evidence, she confessed she'd ordered the poison a month ago, planning ahead to kill Natasha at the Extravaganza—right in front of Baz. When the judges were at Natasha's booth, looking at Annie, Ivy had slipped the capsule into Natasha's coffee cup.

She had been counting on me not to be watching her closely in that moment, which hadn't been an issue, as I hadn't been there at all.

I woke up at night wondering, if I had been there, if I'd have been able to stop all this.

Maybe so.

Maybe not.

I'd never know.

For my peace of mind, I had to let it go.

I didn't want to dwell on the fact that I'd been bamboozled by Ivy. She'd used me, plain and simple. Now that As You Wish was mine, I was going to have to make some changes. Be more selective with my clientele. Trust my instincts more.

"What're you thinking about?" Nick asked as he played with the ends of my hair, twining the strands around his long fingers.

"Instincts and trusting them."

"What do your instincts say about me?" he asked.

"They say you're going to take me back to your place early tonight."

"I like the sound of that."

"Me, too."

"You know what I can't wait for?" he said, pulling back so he could see my face.

"What's that?"

"For the day there's no my place or your place. Just *our* place."

"When do you think that will be?" I asked as innocently as I could.

He kissed me. "I wish it were today."

I admired the way he had expertly avoided the question. "You know I can't grant that wish, as much as I want to."

"A guy can try, especially when his mother-in-law is you-know-who."

I snuggled in close to him and smiled. I didn't point out his slip of the tongue: that she wasn't his mother-in-law.

Not yet at least.

When the time comes.

I'd wait for that marriage proposal for as long as it took, because I finally agreed with Harper and Harmony and everyone else, it seemed.

It was going to happen.

It was just a matter of when.

Until then, I'd wait.

I was a patient witch that way.

Across the street from the party, a small gray-and-white dog and an iridescent gray bird with blue rims around its eyes sat on the porch swing at As You Wish.

"It's good that at least one of us is happy," Melina Sawyer, the dog, said to Deryn Merriweather, the bird. "I suppose of the two of us, it should be you, considering you're the Elder, *blah, blah, blah*."

"Mostly happy," the Elder said in that calm melodious voice of hers.

"You're worried about Dorothy and the Renewal, aren't you?" Melina puffed a breath upward, displacing the fur hanging low on her eyes. She was in desperate need of grooming, but with Ivy headed to prison—where she rightfully belonged—a haircut was probably a long time coming. Melina wished she'd been more of a help with the Ivy situation, but when she'd run for help, Archie wasn't in his cage, and she'd found no one else she could talk to. By the time she returned to the house, Harper and Darcy had been in the woods.

"The apprehension is warranted, Melina."

She knew. Dorothy was nothing if not conniving. "Harper will come around."

"And if she doesn't?"

"She will. Give her time."

"Something that is quickly running out."

"Patience," Melina advised. "We have a year."

The Elder laughed. "You know I'm not very good with that particular trait."

"To take your mind off the matter, you can get me out of the mess I'm in. I cannot live with Darcy and Nick and Mimi as though we're all one big happy family. I'm happy for them—truly I am—but I cannot witness that love day in and day out and not start to feel some sort of resentment. I'm only human. Well. You know what I mean."

"Then you've decided to move on?" the Elder asked.

Move on. It had been her intention all along, and she and the Elder had had this conversation before. It had always been Melina's intention to stay in Missy's form only long enough to restore family order to Mimi, then leave her be and pass over. Darcy was wonderful with her, and Nick had never been happier. It was all she could have ever hoped for. Except . . . "I don't want to leave Mimi."

"No," the Elder said. "I didn't think you would once you spent a significant amount of time with her. Have you considered revealing yourself to her?"

"Every day. But no. I can't do it. She misses me, yes, but she's perfectly happy the way things are, and I'm happy enough to watch her grow from afar. What are my options for staying?" Melina asked.

"They're limited. Perhaps we can somehow convince Darcy to let Missy live with Ve after all, or maybe Harper?"

"Both would be acceptable, except that would mean limited time with Mimi."

"Perhaps a new form? Mimi is desiring a mini turtle."

"And be stuck in an aquarium all day? No, thanks."

"Well, there's Cookie or the new donkey."

"No and no."

"Annie?"

"Then I am back to my original dilemma, no?"

"A bird, a fly, a dust mite."

Melina sighed. "They just don't feel right. Missy feels right."

The Elder sighed. "Then I am at a loss."

"You know what I need?"

"What?" she asked, a hint of humor in her voice.

"I need to have that animal morphing ability that

Pepe told you Darcy had asked about. Or maybe animal hopping? The ability to enter the bodies of more than one animal, one after the other? Or perhaps simply the ability for my spirit to come and go from Missy at will."

"A near impossibility."

"But not entirely impossible?" Melina asked.

"Nothing is impossible within this village. It would, however, mean creating a new Craft."

"You are the Elder, aren't you? You could create a new Craft if you wanted." Melina blew her bangs out of her eyes again, and wished a new groomer would be found soon. She very much hoped Darcy wouldn't take on the task herself. The woman was a whiz with pencils and paintbrushes but a menace with scissors. Melina remembered quite well the mess Darcy had made of her own bangs. Plus, she might notice that the dark hair around Missy's ears was missing, thanks to Ve reversing the Lunumbra spell. A spell that was going to come in quite handy in years to come. . . .

"I could," the Elder said, "but switching Crafts, especially as a familiar, is highly risky. The danger that you'll be lost forever is very real."

The thought was terrifying, but she had no other options than to leave of her own will, which had the exact same end result, or to become an insect of some sort. No, thanks. "I'll take the risk, because I certainly cannot stay as I am. I do not want to resent what I helped create."

"I'd need approval from the coven of seven."

"The next meeting is at the solstice. . . . You can broach the subject then."

"You're serious?" the Elder asked.

Melina nodded.

"Then I will see what I can do," the Elder said. "It may take a while, however, so *you* must be patient."

"I can wait."

It would be months and months, maybe even a year or two before Darcy and Nick would move in together, not until after they were married.

Yes, Melina had plenty of time to be patient. During which time she'd keep an extra close eye on Glinda. Her growing friendship with Darcy was alarming, especially considering the coming Renewal.

During that time, Melina would also do anything she could to help Harper Merriweather change her mind about accepting her role as a witch. . . .

The future of the Craft depended on it.

Read on for a sneak preview of

The Witch and the Dead

by Heather Blake.
Available in October 2016.

It was one of those crisp New England autumn days
that begged for hot chocolate piled high with whipped
cream, a good book, and a cozy spot in front of the fireplace.

But beg as the day might, this witch didn't have time
to indulge. I glanced around at all the plastic bins and
cardboard boxes that needed to be relocated from this
space to my new home and pushed up my sleeves—my
dream of curling up in front of a fire tonight was never
going to happen if I kept dragging my feet.

Try as I might, I just couldn't seem to get going. I
flitted from one side of my aunt Ve's garage to the other,
accomplishing little as early-October sunlight filtered
through grimy windows, spotlighting every dust particle
in sight.

As well as my hesitance.

I wasn't known for procrastinating, but today as I

transferred all the belongings I'd been storing in this space to my new house two doors down the street, I was taking my sweet time.

My puttering had little to do with actually moving the twenty or so boxes and assorted bits of my previous life and everything to do with leaving behind Aunt Ve and the house I'd lived in since arriving in this village a little more than a year ago.

I'd eventually have to deal with the emotions, but for right now I fortunately had help with the move: My younger sister, Harper, and my aunt Ve had both volunteered to assist with the move.

"It should all go!" Ve said, tossing her hands in the air. "All of it."

She wasn't referencing my things, though I suspected the ghostly outlines of where my boxes had once stood were what triggered her desire to eradicate everything else in the garage.

"A yard sale! Tomorrow, just in time for the weekend crowd." Spinning around, Ve faced me, her golden blue eyes alight with a spark of purpose. Her coppery hair was pulled back in its usual twist, but she'd accented the style with a red bandanna. It was tied with the knot at the top of her head like Rosie the Riveter's. Round cheeks glowed with good health as she pushed up the sleeves of her white long-sleeve thermal henley and then bent to cuff the hem of her denim overalls. She was in her early sixties and had more energy than I'd ever possessed.

"I think she means it," Harper whispered to me, a trace of horror hovering in her voice.

"Oh, I mean it," Ve stated firmly. "Think of the cavernous space I'd have in here if it were empty. I could turn the garage into a craft studio."

"You don't craft," Harper pointed out as she wrestled a tall box into the middle of the driveway.

The box was almost as big as she was. At just five feet, twenty-four-year-old Harper personified Shakespeare's quote of "though she may be but little, she is fierce." Her brown eyes glinted in the sunlight as she looked back at us. "Well, not in a *studio* kind of way."

Technically we were all Crafters, witches with a unique set of abilities. My family happened to be Wishcrafters, who could grant wishes, but there were dozens and dozens of other witchy varieties that lived and worked among oblivious mortals here in the Enchanted Village. This charming neighborhood of Salem, Massachusetts, was a tourist hot spot . . . and what I now considered home.

"Fine," Ve said, relenting to the truth of the matter. "How about a yoga studio?"

Shooting her arms out to the sides for balance, she placed the sole of her right foot on her left inner knee, attempting, I presumed, the tree pose. Her arms windmilled wildly as she swayed to and fro. I resisted the strong urge to shout "Timber!" as I grabbed hold of her to keep her from tipping over.

Flicking me a wry look, she said, "Maybe not yoga."

"Maybe not," I agreed.

"Well, I'll think of something." With a sweeping wave of her hand, she added, "But first, this all needs to go."

By *all*, she meant the decades of flotsam that had been stashed and stored in the massive garage. Floor-to-ceiling stacks of boxes, bags, and trunks. Christmas and Halloween decor. A tattered love seat and other assorted furniture, dust-covered bookshelves and side tables. Simply sorting through everything was going to take weeks, never mind pricing it all. "Maybe waiting till spring for a yard sale would be best," I suggested.

By then this particular flight of fancy of hers might pass.

I hoped.

"No, no," she countered as she strode over to a clothing rack stuffed with zipped dusty black garment bags. "An impromptu yard sale is just what I need to take—"

Abruptly, she bit off her words, and I swallowed over a sudden lump in my throat.

To take her mind off the fact that I was moving out.

I sent Harper a pleading look. She gave me a sympathetic nod and said, "You know what can occupy your time, Aunt Ve? Helping me figure out how to avoid having dinner with Marcus's parents tomorrow night. The Debrowskis don't like me as it is, and you know how I get when I'm nervous. I'm bound to spill or break something."

"They like you," I said, trying to reassure her.

"No, they don't," Harper returned, perfectly calm and absolutely serious.

I picked up a plastic bin. Its label said only BEDROOM. Sheets and blankets, I figured. "Of course they do."

Ve unzipped a garment bag. "No, Harper's right. They don't. They don't like any of us." She said this as though it was common knowledge. "I'm sure they're having a full-sized cow that Marcus fell for Harper in the first place."

Harper looked at me with a smug smile. "Told you so." She loved being right.

Still disbelieving, I stared at our aunt. "Why don't they like us?"

"That Penelope is a jealous prune." Ve wrinkled her face, mimicking the dried fruit. "She fancies herself a free spirit, and was always most annoyed that I could grant wishes while she had to practice law. Don't let her bother you," Ve advised Harper. "Just focus on that man of yours and all will be well."

Color rushed into Harper's cheeks. "He's not *mine*...."

Ve met my gaze and we both burst out laughing.

Harper, who until she met Marcus had compared marriage to a prison sentence, shot us an annoyed look.

She then picked up another box and carried it out to the driveway, stomping the whole way. She hated being wrong about anything. Especially about strong beliefs such as marriage and lifelong commitments.

Ve unzipped another garment bag and laughed as she pulled out the frilliest wedding gown I'd ever seen. "Well, lookie what we have here." She held it up to herself, nearly poking her eye with a wayward ruffle. "It's the dress I wore to my wedding to Godfrey."

Godfrey Baleaux had been the third of Ve's four husbands, the one she once referred to as a rat-toad bottom dweller. She didn't call him that anymore. Not often, anyway. He owned the Bewitching Boutique, and I considered him family. An uncle of sorts, though he liked to say he was my fairy godfather.

"Did Godfrey design that?" Harper asked. "Because if so, maybe you shouldn't let him be in charge of your wedding dress, Darcy."

I couldn't imagine the dress was one of Godfrey's designs. He preferred classic, timeless fashion. That gown was . . . neither. "Aren't you getting ahead of yourself? I'm not even engaged."

"Yet," Ve and Harper said in unison.

I couldn't help smiling. Police Chief Nick Sawyer and I had been dating for more than a year, and a few months ago we'd had The Talk. A proposal was just a matter of time, and thanks to a slip of the tongue by his teenage daughter, Mimi, I knew he already had the ring. The anticipation of what he had planned—and when—was killing me.

I grabbed another box and set it next to the others in the driveway, near a spot where my dog, Missy, lay stretched out in a puddle of sunshine, watching us with sleepy eyes.

She'd been extra sleepy lately, and I was starting to worry. I added making an appointment with the local vet to my to-do list. It probably wasn't necessary, but I didn't want to take any risks with her health.

Glancing at my watch, I noted that Nick was due here soon to help move these boxes to my new house, which had been recently renovated top to bottom, including its stacked-stone fireplace. I had high hopes that Nick would end up with me in front of that fireplace tonight. . . .

"No, no, this was all me, my design," Ve said, looking at the dress. "The fact that Godfrey still married me despite this atrocity rather proves how smitten he had been with me. Perhaps I shouldn't have divorced him." She *tsk*ed.

"I thought you two hated each other by the end of the first year," Harper pointed out.

"That's true," she said thoughtfully. "But I don't hate him *now*."

Aunt Ve had monogamy issues.

And loneliness issues.

With my moving out of her house, I had the feeling she was casting out a wide net to replace my daily presence in her life. "Don't forget about Andreus," I reminded her. "Isn't he coming back to the village this weekend? He'll have your days occupied in no time."

"And nights, too," Ve mused with a wiggle of her eyebrows.

Harper clapped a hand over her mouth and said through spread fingers, "I think I'm going to be sick."

"You and me both," I added, putting a hand on my queasy stomach.

"Oh, you two," Ve said with a laugh. "He's a good man." She paused. "Mostly good." Another pause. "He's a man."

Charmcrafter Andreus Woodshall was the director of the Roving Stones, a traveling rock-and-mineral show that visited the village several times a year. Despite the fact that he was the scariest man I'd ever met, he and Ve had hit it off the last time he'd been in town. Whether he was good or bad was one of those questions that had yet to be fully answered. From what I knew of him, it was a mixed bag.

Ve frowned. "But he'll be leaving again soon enough. He has only a week off before traveling to a show in Florida."

"Live in the moment, Aunt Ve," Harper said, sounding more cheerleader-ish than I'd ever imagined she could.

Lifting her chin, Ve smiled. "You're right, Harper. That's exactly what I should do." She moved aside a dusty bookcase and wiggled behind it. "And the first order of business is to get this garage cleaned out for that big yard sale tomorr— *Oh.* Oh dear. Oh my."

"What is it?" I asked, watching her face drain of color.

"What? Did you find the veil that went with that hideous wedding dress?" Harper asked, chuckling. "I can only imagine what *that* looks like."

"No. No veil." One of Ve's hands flew up to cover her mouth as she stared at something deep in the recesses of the garage. Over her shoulder, she said in an unnaturally high-pitched voice, "Darcy, dear, would you please give Nick a call?"

"He should be here in twenty minutes . . ."

"We need him now," she said, still using that odd falsetto.

"Why?" Harper strode over and leaned on the bookcase to catch a glimpse of whatever had caused Ve alarm.

Harper's voice rose an octave. "Is that a . . ."

"Yes, dear," Ve said. "It appears so."

"It's not fake?" my sister asked. "I mean, there are Halloween decorations all over this garage."

"I don't think so," Ve said. "You see, I recognize that hat. I'd know it anywhere."

Hat? Halloween? I marched over to see what was going on for myself. I shimmied against the shelf next to Harper. "I don't see . . ."

Ve pointed.

I gasped. In a once-hidden nook created by a tower of boxes lay a skeleton fully dressed in men's clothing. By the layer of undisturbed dust covering the remains, I guessed he'd been there quite a long time.

Harper glanced at me, her eyes full of excitement. She was exceedingly morbid. Then she said to Ve, "Who is it? You said you recognized the hat?"

"That," Ve said, wiggling back out from behind the shelf, "is Miles Babbage. My second husband. And hand to heart, if he wasn't already dead, I'd kill him myself."